I0548801

BAD DAY FOR THE APOCALYPSE
JASON OFFUTT

SEVERED PRESS
HOBART TASMANIA

BAD DAY FOR THE APOCALYPSE

Copyright © 2017 by Jason Offutt
Copyright © 2017 by Severed Press

WWW.SEVEREDPRESS.COM

All rights reserved. No part of this book may be
reproduced or transmitted in any form or by any
electronic or mechanical means, including
photocopying, recording or by any information and
retrieval system, without the written permission of
the publisher and author, except where permitted by law.
This novel is a work of fiction. Names,
characters, places and incidents are the product of
the author's imagination, or are used fictitiously.
Any resemblance to actual events, locales or persons,
living or dead, is purely coincidental.

ISBN: 978-1-925711-17-2

All rights reserved.

June 5: St. Joseph
CHAPTER 1

Raindrops pounded the restaurant windows in windblown sheets as Nikki Holleran cleared Table Six; the few cars in the parking lot, half of them owned by employees, occasionally invisible in the torrent. Three tables of customers dotted the dining area at Hooligans in St. Joseph, Missouri. It was Friday, 7:30 p.m. Prime dining time. Tonight, nothing. No crowd, no hum of conversation, no line of people at the door, no lucky ones holding pagers waiting for a table to open. Just a young couple, two locals drinking beer at a table next to the bar and high fiving each other over the ball game on TV, and a fat businessman eating a porterhouse in Nikki's section.

"This sucks."

Nikki looked up from a plate of half-eaten cheeseburger to find Tammy leaning against the back of the booth, the top of her uniform plunging low. Nikki hated the Hooligans waitress uniforms. She wore hers buttoned high, keeping herself in check, but the waist was much too snug for her figure to fit anything but awkwardly in the tight uniform. Tammy wore it expertly.

"The rain?"

"The rain, the two guys in the bar who call me Jugzilla every time I walk by, all the people who were smart enough to call in sick tonight. Everything just sucks." Tammy was 23, a fifth-year senior at nearby Missouri Western State Community College and hated everything through a seductive smile. Nikki's tips were good because she was a good waitress; Tammy's were better.

Nikki scooped the dirty silverware from the table and dropped them into a bus tub. The bus boys had called in sick tonight; all of them, which is understandable because bussing tables is the worst job at a restaurant. Americans, given the knowledge someone else will clean up after them, soil everything they touch.

"There weren't many people in my summer class today, either," Nikki said. "And half of them looked confused. Not hangover confused, it's like they didn't know why they were there. Something must be going around."

"Well I'm not catching it. I don't have time to be sick. I have my midterm next week," Tammy said, slowly standing straight. "Oh, those assholes are waving at me. I gotta go. If you hear a scream, it's one of them."

Nikki wiped the rest of the discarded curly fries and great spots of ketchup from the table into the bus tub with a damp rag, and worked her way back to the kitchen. She slid the tub on a wire rack next to Benny, the assistant manager at Hooligans, who worked the dishwasher tonight out of necessity.

"Tough night?" he asked, smiling as he pushed the tub into the stainless-steel steaming monster, and slammed the door. The regular dishwashers had called in sick as well; two of the wait staff, too. That left Benny to man everything, and he did what he needed to do. Nikki liked him. For an assistant manager, he was a nice enough guy. Friendly, fair, and newly married, so at least with Benny, every waitress's boobs were their own. Nikki returned his smile.

"Tough for all the wrong reasons," she said.

"We're just lucky the weather's shit. If we got slammed. Whew. We'd be in trouble."

"What do you think's going around?" she asked, grabbing an empty tub. "It's summer. It's not like it's sniffle season."

Benny shrugged. "I dunno," he said. "H1N1? Bird flu? Swine flu? Brown bottle flu? Some guy on MSNBC today claimed the UN let loose the zombie virus to curb the world's seven billion or so population." He paused and grinned again. "But you know how they are at MSNBC."

Nikki nodded even though she didn't know what he was talking about, but she did know if a wave of illness caught the attention of the talking heads on cable, there might be something to it.

"Did the news report talk about symptoms?"

Benny opened his mouth, but his words didn't have the time to come out.

"Benny," Tammy said, stomping into the strangely quiet kitchen, and slamming a black plastic drink tray hard on a prep station, the front of her black and red uniform soaked with beer. "One of those fucking rednecks at the bar grabbed me, and when I shoved him away he laughed and poured his beer on me. If I have to go back out there I'm going to kill both of them."

"Christ," Benny whispered, shaking his head. He didn't know what would be worse to deal with, drunken rednecks or a pissed off waitress. It didn't matter; he had to deal with them both. "All right," he said, gently grabbing her by the shoulders, although he knew deep down the people at corporate HR would have his ass for that. "They'll be gone in two seconds. Do you have any other tables?" She shook her head. "Okay, just calm down back here. I'll take care of this." He dropped his hands from her shoulders, cracked his neck, and walked out of the kitchen.

Nikki watched as Tammy's shaking hands fumbled with her purse that hung on the wall next to the time clock. "You okay?"

Tammy nodded as she pulled out a prescription bottle of pills. Nikki didn't have to ask; it was Ophiocordon. Seems like everyone took Ophiocordon nowadays. "Yeah. It's just jerks like that. There's no reason for them."

She wrenched open the childproof cap, dropped a white oval tablet into her hand, popped it into her mouth, and swallowed hard. Seconds slunk by before Tammy gasped, and her body tensed. One of the side effects of the newest anti-depressant Ophiocordon; it gave women an immediate orgasm, then tapered off to simple euphoria. Nikki heard it did something like that to men as well, just not as sudden, not like she cared. Out of all the side effects modern pharmaceuticals carried, like diarrhea and the occasional hallucination, an orgasm wasn't too shabby. Nikki sometimes wished she suffered from some kind of depression.

"If he's outside when I go home," Tammy said, shaking the sudden wave of ecstasy throughout her body, "he's dead."

"They all get what they deserve, Tammy. Just focus on that," Nikki said, gently patting Tammy's hand, and walking toward the dining area. "I still have one out there, but I think he's about done. Hopefully we'll close early, and get out of this nightmare."

"Can I get you anything else, sir?" Nikki asked the fat businessman, although given his nearly spot-free plate that once sported medium-rare porterhouse and baked potato, she would have felt a little guilt at helping him die slowly with dessert. The man shook his head. Something about his demeanor worried Nikki. Sweat beaded across his round face, his skin was waxy and white. *Good God,* she thought. *A heart attack would just top off this night.*

"I ... uh..." wheezed past his lips in great blasts, his breath pinching Nikki's face tight.

Christ. What's that smell? She coughed, the taste of vomit in her mouth.

"Are you okay?" she asked, her left wrist over her mouth.

"I'm ... I'm ..." he heaved. "Oh, God. I don't feel so good."

"I'll get the ..." *manager,* Nikki tried to say, but the blood stopped her. Tendrils of thick, crimson liquid shot from the man's nostrils. He coughed, the rancid, sweet smell of death brushed over Nikki, a clot of blood splattered across his plate.

"Benny," she screamed, backing away from the table. "Benny. Benny. 9-1-1. Oh, my God, 9-1-1. Benny, 9-1-1."

"What the hell?" came from behind her from one of Tammy's rednecks Benny hadn't been able to make leave. "What the … holy shit."

"Heh… heh… help me," the businessman hissed, grabbing for Nikki's uniform, blood now running from his nose like his face was a dam about to break. A red spot grew in his left eye and popped, sending another red river pouring down his cheek. Nikki screamed and stumbled away from the man's grasp.

"What the fuck?" Tammy's redneck whispered, backing away from the bleeding man who had fallen to the floor, and crawled toward Nikki.

"Do you have a phone?" Benny screamed at the redneck.

"What?"

"Do you have a God damned fucking phone?" he screamed again, grabbing and shaking the man's Toby Keith concert T-shirt.

The man nodded.

"Then call the cops," he hissed. "And if you ever harass my waitresses again, I will personally kick the shit out of you." Benny rushed to Nikki, pulling her away from the bleeding customer, and sat her in a booth. "You're going to be okay," he said, and turned to the redneck. "You got someone?" The man nodded. "Then tell them to send an ambulance here now. NOW."

"That was some fucked up shit," Tammy said, finishing a beer. "Did you see all the blood on the carpet? No way am I cleaning that up."

Nikki sat at the bar with Tammy, the lights low, the storm outside off somewhere to the east. Police filed through Hooligans, taking blood samples, food samples, and statements from the few people there. Nikki just wanted to go home. She saw a man bleed like he'd been hacked by Freddie Krueger, and drop over a booth table in a fat wet slap. Then he stood, pushing himself up from the table, and stumbled around, like he was dumb in every sense of the word. The EMTs put the man on a gurney, but his legs and arms moved like he was still walking. And he didn't make a sound, not even a moan. The EMT said the man wasn't dead, yet. No amount of beer with Tammy would change any of that.

"Did you even see it?" Nikki asked.

"No," Tammy said. "I got there for Benny saying 'if you ever harass my waitresses again, I will personally kick the shit out of you,' though. That's manager of the year stuff right there. I will nominate him."

Nikki took another drink. The beer was cold, sending alcohol dancing across the scene in her head, but it didn't change anything. The fat man, blood spewing from his nose, his mouth, his eyes, and his horizontal legs trying to walk on air, burned themselves into her memory.

"Did you see the blood on his face?" Nikki asked.

"Yeah," Tammy said, sliding out of her seat. "I'm going for another beer. Want one?"

"It was gushing," Nikki said, ignoring her. "Gushing."

Tammy walked behind the bar, slid open the cooler, grabbed a Bud Light and sat it in front of Nikki. "I had a customer the other night with a nosebleed," she said. "Nice guy, cute. Kinda dorky."

"And?"

Tammy shrugged. "I don't know. His friend was worried because he'd just taken an Ophiocordon. Something about it sending too much blood to his junk and not enough to his brain."

Nikki grabbed the beer and took a drink. "Were either of them worried about it?"

Tammy shrugged and opened another beer. "I don't know. They were pretty drunk, and I was showing these off pretty good," she said, pushing her arms under her breasts. "They tipped well."

"Did the man mention anything about his nosebleed?"

Tammy shook her head. "No. He just had a hell of a time stopping it. This might not sound attractive, but watching a drunk nerdy guy flirt while drinking beer through a straw because he has a paper napkin shoved up his nose is actually pretty cute."

A large body stood between them.

"Miss Holleran, Miss Dankenbring," a police officer said. Dan, Nikki remembered, his name was Dan. "I have your statements, and I'm sorry you young ladies had to see something like this. You can go home now. If you'd like, I can have an officer take you."

Nikki shook her head. "Thank you, Officer Dan, but I need to be alone right now. I can take Tammy home if she'd like."

Tammy shook her head. "I'm good. I just need sleep."

He nodded. "Understood. Just remember we're out there. I hope you're okay to drive." Nikki nodded and Officer Dan walked away.

The yellow glow from streetlights glistened off Hooligans wet parking lot as Nikki and Tammy walked across the asphalt, the storm long since gone.

"What do you think that was?" Tammy asked, stopping in the middle of the lot, fishing a cigarette out of her purse. The rush of the Ophiocordon must be wearing off, Nikki thought. "I mean, the fat guy. I saw him when he came in. Hell, I seated him. He looked fine. What do you think happened to him?"

Nikki shrugged. "I don't know. He just. He just started to sweat blood." Tears welled in her eyes. "It was awful," she said, stopping, words choked in her throat. "Just awful."

The yellow-orange flame of a cheap convenience store lighter erupted in the night as Tammy lit a Pall Mall and took a long, slow drag. "Not awful," she said, smoke rolling from her mouth. "Totally fucked up. We will never – never – see anything like that again. I guarantee it."

"I hope you're right," Nikki said, pulling keys from her purse and stepping toward her scooter. "And at least he's not dead." She paused to look at Tammy who stood in the full light of Hooligans parking lot. Things weren't right; they weren't right at all. They were very, very wrong.

"Shit, Tammy," Nikki said. "Your nose is bleeding."

June 6: Allenville, Missouri

CHAPTER 2

Goddamned Posey. The old man sat on his front porch with his fat old wife watching Craig mow the lawn, their stupid yip-yip dog Doofus barking the whole time. Craig knew Posey would let the little yapper loose on him if it were a Rottweiler; let him loose and laugh as it ripped Craig's face off. Dick. Craig pushed the red Craftsman mower across his crabgrass-choked backyard, over dandelions and burr patches. Posey's yard was immaculate. Deep green Kentucky bluegrass without a weed in it. No dandelions, no thistles, nothing. How the fuck does he do it? Voodoo most likely. Crazy old bastard. Craig wiped the sweat from his face with the sleeve of his powder blue Kansas City Royals T-shirt; the thunderstorm that passed last night about 40 miles south in St. Joseph left Craig's corner of northwest Missouri untouched.

"Your yard looks like shit, McAllister," Posey yelled across the yard. "Why don't you do the neighborhood a favor and eat a bullet? And do it outside. Your yard could use the fertilizer." Craig's hands pulled tighter on the mower's black metal handle and pushed harder as he fought to keep his eyes on the lawn. Goddamn him. Worst neighbor ever. Worst damned loser asshole neighbor ever. Craig didn't turn his head because he knew what he'd find; Posey and his fat assed wife asleep in their lawn chairs, their barking rat pissing on the potted plants. Voodoo. The man was getting inside Craig's head.

The Poseys had once tried to lull Craig into a false sense of safety. Fat Lilith Posey even brought Craig a casserole the day he moved to town. An egg casserole with mushrooms and sausage. Craig smiled and thanked her, even though he knew she was trying to poison him. He had no idea what was in that yellow slagheap, probably toadstools; he just fed the cheesy glop to the garbage disposal. "Hurry your fat ass up, McAllister," ran through Craig's head as he rounded the corner of the house and Posey's own home disappeared from view. The casserole was twelve years ago and that cocksucker hadn't shut up yet, except when Craig mowed on the north side of his little two-bedroom house. For some reason, it was quiet there. Craig thought he should sit out here in a lawn chair after he finished with the yard work and have a beer, or eight. Craig couldn't hear Posey very well after eight beers.

Craig moved to town after the accident. Some moron had dropped a board from the third floor of a construction job and it smashed into

Craig's hardhat. Rang his bell pretty good. Craig woke two weeks later in St. Joe Regional Hospital with a hell of a headache and a card from a lawyer who later told him he (they) were due a hell of a payday. Negligence, the lawyer said, even though they both knew it wasn't negligence, it was just an accident. A stupid accident and Craig happened to be in the wrong place. Didn't matter, the lawyer told Craig, "hire me and you'll never have to work another day in your life." The lawyer was right. The most work Craig has had to do since the accident is mow his yard in the summer and move snow from his driveway in the winter. His life was nice enough, but why did he have to move next door to Posey? It was that damned real estate agent, fat-assed Billy Bob Purdy. Craig knew he'd see him dead one day.

Craig quickly finished the small slip of shaded side yard. He'd finished the back yard and the Posey side of the house; he always got that one done first. Posey only badgered him a little as he mowed the back yard; the Posey side was a constant barrage. The only thing left was a small patch of yard in front of the house. He stood at the corner, the mower handle vibrated through his hands and up his arms, but Craig didn't notice. He was focused on Posey; to mow the front yard, Craig would be in full view of Posey's house, that old fart sitting out there, laughing at him. Why wouldn't he just die? Craig steadied himself and stepped into the sun. He chanced a glance at Posey's house. The old man and his wife – his murdering wife, with her poisoned toadstool and dog shit casseroles – pretended to be asleep. Doofus had sniffed its way into a corner of Craig's yard and squatted, looking squarely at Craig. That little fucker is taking a dump. In *my* yard, ran through Craig's head. I'm going to run your little ass over with this mower one of these days you little bastard. "You like that, McAllister?" came Posey's words. "A little present from the Poseys to you. Merry Goddamned Christmas, McAllister. Doofus has a lot more for you, McAllister. A lot more. We feed him well, better than you eat."

"I'm going to kill that dog, Posey, you old fuck," Craig mumbled under the roar of the mower. "Kill it dead."

"Over my dead body," Posey said loud in Craig's head, then laughed. "Over my dead body." Craig smiled. That's the best thing he'd heard all day.

He didn't know why Posey had it in for him. Craig moved into the house quietly, a moving company carrying in his scant belongings. It's not like they parked their truck on Posey's lawn. Craig's old Toyota pickup didn't leak oil in the street, he kept his yard clean and trimmed, and he was quiet. Posey couldn't see Craig at night, sitting in his darkened living room a few feet back from the window so the faint yellow glow from the streetlight didn't betray his presence, a beer on the table next to him, and binoculars pressed tightly against his face, glaring at Posey as the old man sat in his Archie Bunker easy chair, drinking beer and watching The Weather Channel. Posey was up to something, something dark; Craig just didn't know what. He was, however, going to find out.

He almost found out four summers ago, or was it five? It was at the Block Party. Every July 4, Mulberry Street, between Forest Street and Cunningham Drive, became a festering wall of people from all over the multi-block area who dragged their canvas lawn chairs and mini-gas grills, their beer coolers and, what's worse, their children; their loud, screaming children, over to Craig's street and mingled, waiting for the yearly fireworks show. Posey was their king, strutting up and down the street with a German beer stein like he was the Goddamned Kaiser. Craig sat on his porch every Block Party, smiling, and waving at the neighbors who strolled past his house, not knowing that in the right side pocket of Craig's cargo shorts rested a .38-caliber pistol. With the streets crawling with vermin, Craig couldn't take any chances. He didn't move from his porch; he didn't eat his neighbor's offered food; he didn't join them in conversation. But he did watch. If that fucking Purdy had told him on one night a year, evil walked this street, he would have bought another house, but he bought one on Mulberry Street.

Shortly before dark the year Craig knew Posey wanted him dead, about the time the fire-fighters on the high school football field across town were ready to light the first fireworks of the Independence Day show, Posey and that nosey Don Bing from down the street met on the sidewalk in front of Craig's house, and said a few words Craig couldn't hear, but they both turned and looked at him. Looked directly at him. As they stood there, plotting, Craig's hand instinctively crept into his pocket and slid around the smooth wooden handle of the .38. Would they come get him? Right there in front of all the drunks wandering the street? He gripped the handle tight. Why not? They were all in it together. Posey turned away from Craig, laughed, and slapped Bing on the shoulder, then walked back toward the spot on the street Lilith shared with their grandchildren, their noisy, noisy grandchildren and that shitty little dog. Craig's grip relaxed and he pulled his hand from his pocket, but at that moment, Craig knew he was marked. That's why he watched Posey closely while he mowed his lawn.

Craig turned off the Craftsman and wheeled it to the shed in the backyard, the sudden silence loud in his ears. The shed was close to the house, but the short walk exposed him to the Posey house. Posey never rested. Never. He might look asleep in his chair on the front porch, but he wasn't. Posey didn't sleep – he waited.

"What you going to do now, McAllister? Play with yourself?" Craig tried to hum Posey out of his head, but that rarely worked. He banged open the shed door and slid in the mower next to the snow blower he'd have to use soon enough in northwest Missouri. His eyes dragged across the chainsaw hanging off the back wall. Craig grinned. That would be fun to run across Doofus' backside, or maybe Posey's. "You're not man enough, McAllister," Posey's voice shouted. "Not man enough by a long shot." Craig slammed the door shut and locked it.

"Shut up, Posey," he mumbled. "Shut up, shut up, shut up."

The Poseys' home, a white bungalow with red shutters, fenced-in porch, and flower pots by the front door, seemed to Craig a looming monster as he stood at the shed. Posey moved. Oh, shit. He moved. The man was old, at least to Craig. He might have been sixty, seventy, one hundred. Hell, Craig didn't know. All Craig knew was old man Posey spent almost every afternoon sitting in that damned lawn chair, pretending to nap, but watching Craig every second. *I'm on to you, old man.* Posey stretched, gently shook Lilith's shoulder and said something to her. Something, Craig knew, about him. Posey noticed Craig standing by his shed, staring at them. How does it feel, Posey? How does it feel to know someone's watching you? Always watching you?

"Well hey, Craig," Dave Posey shouted from his front porch, Lilith rose slowly from the canvas chair, yawning all the way. "The lawn looks nice. Real nice. You need to come over for dinner some time." The old man smiled and waved as the couple walked inside the house, Doofus skipping quietly under their feet.

Asshole.

June 21: Paola, Kansas

CHAPTER 3

Silence hovered through the shop at Doug's Muffler and Brakes, broken only by AC/DC's "Hells Bells" playing much too softly on the radio in the empty front waiting area. Angus Young's guitar riffs drifted over the cold, dusty coffee maker, fuzzy black and white Magnavox TV, and two year's worth of *Car and Driver*. Doctor's offices aren't the real havens for old magazines no one reads; mechanic shops are. Doug Titus sat in his office, the smell of oil and grease as unnoticed to him as the scars on his knuckles, there from years of dinking his hands while twisting a wrench under automobiles.

"We gonna stay here all day, boss?" Terry asked, leaning on the doorframe of Doug's office. Terry Jenkins always leaned on something. Doug smiled at the thought of Terry's mom yelling at him to stand up straight. Doug figured his mechanic's mom used to yell at him a lot.

The Built Ford Tough clock on the wall read 4:20 p.m. through the sticker of Calvin pissing on a Chevy logo. Terry put the now-cliché sticker there about three years ago, and he still thought it was funny. Good old Terry. Terry had worked for Doug the past five years and was the same person he'd hired; hadn't matured a bit. Doug usually shut the shop down at 5 p.m., but there was no sense in staying open any longer. Not today. Heck, not yesterday either. The one appointment scheduled for today, the back brakes on Donny Rodenberg's F-150, canceled on him, the ring from the black AT&T office phone giving Doug a start in the silent shop. That call, that uncomfortable call.

"Doug," Donny had wheezed. "I can't bring the truck in today. Sorry, man. But I, I," he paused to cough. "I'm not going to make it." Then the line went dead. Terry thought the call was strange, really strange. But thinking about it, Donny didn't sound so good. And there was the cough, the wet, almost gurgly cough. Doug shook his head.

"I think we should shut down early. Thanks, Terry. I've just sat here staring at the walls." Doug smiled. "Besides, I think I've paid you enough for sitting on the toilet all day. That's pretty good work if you can get it."

Terry grinned. "Wanna go get a beer?"

Doug nodded. "Sure." He stood and reached for the office light switch. Even the Makita Power Tool model for June, Catalina, looked sad on the wall calendar as she leaned forward on the slick two-dimensional page, her cleavage and pouty dark red lips took command of the photograph instead of the air wrench she held like it was a different type of power tool. "Sorry nobody's been in to look at you today, Catalina," Doug said, kissing his right index finger and pressing it on her lips. "I'm here for you, though, baby." Then he shut off the lights, and sent the quiet building into darkness. Terry had already shut off the back shop lights and leaned in the doorway, silhouetted by the light of the bright summer sun. Yeah, Terry was ready for a beer, but Terry was always ready for a beer.

"You comin' slowpoke?" Terry shouted. His booming voice echoed through the empty shop, bringing home the fact something wasn't right; no, something was definitely wrong. Shouts never echoed in his shop; there were usually too many vehicles sitting on racks, and too many bodies and whirring tools to absorb the sound. But there were no cars, no whirring tools, and no one there. Terry was the only mechanic who didn't call in sick today. Yeah, something was wrong.

The Corner Bar squatted in a two-story brick building at the intersection of Centennial Avenue and First Street, a 1960s tavern that didn't get the notice it was the 21st century; a Schlitz sign featuring a man in a crew cut betrayed its age. The place was a dive, with sticky floors, bar shuffleboard, and really bad Karaoke on Friday nights, but Doug liked dives. You didn't have to change clothes for a dive, and the owner, Mike, didn't care when you dropped peanut shells on the floor. Hell, he expected it. The Corner Bar usually wasn't full on a Friday around 5 p.m., but with the Honda plant just down the street that's mid shift let out at 3:30 p.m., it was never quiet, not like this. Doug and Terry stepped through the heavy front door and into the dark, silent bar, the lack of cigarette smoke and cracking pool balls all too obvious. The only person in the bar was Mike, who smiled a forced smile when Doug and Terry walked in and sat at the bar.

"I almost shut down, boys," Mike said from behind his usually neatly trimmed white beard. Today the beard was shaggy; Mike looked tired. "If the guys from the plant didn't show up after their shift on a Friday, I figured nobody would."

Mike shouldn't be standing behind the bar. All Doug ever saw Mike do was bullshit with customers and call the cops if Lester Ropey got piss drunk and started another fight with the missus, although she could usually take pretty good care of herself. It should be Carrie behind the bar pulling taps, hot Carrie, Mike's secret weapon on a Friday after work, bringing in guys from all over Paola just to get a look at her tight shirt and Daisy Duke shorts.

"Well, we're here," Terry said with a grin. "How about a couple of Buds?"

Mike nodded. "You bet."

Doug wasn't a regular at the Corner Bar, but he was regular enough to see what was missing. Frank, the greeter from Wal-Mart, should be sitting at the bar feeding quarters into the Keno machine, Ben Gilroy and Delbert Benson from A-1 Movers should be arguing Chiefs football way too loudly in the corner, and Gary "Sissy" Conrad who worked at the flower shop down the street should be at the bar drinking a Captain Morgan and Coke, trying to chat up Carrie who wanted nothing to do with him. Gary hated it when the guys called him "Sissy," but hell, he worked in a flower shop. He was asking for it.

"Where's Carrie today, Mike?" Doug asked as Mike tilted a frosted mug under the Budweiser tap and pulled the handle, golden liquid rising from the bottom of the mug.

Mike shook his head. "Sick," he said. "She called in yesterday and didn't sound good at all. She didn't call in today, but the way she was yesterday; I figure she's still down."

"Did she cough?" Doug asked.

Mike nodded, setting one mug down and picking up the other. "Yep," he said. "And it sounded pretty productive."

"Productive?" Terry asked. "What the hell does that mean?"

"She was coughing something up," Doug said, turning back toward Mike. "Everybody but Terry called in sick down at the shop, too. So did the brake job for today. All the same, kinda gurgly. What do you think's going around, Mike?"

Mike sat two cardboard Kansas Speedway coasters in front of Doug and Terry, sprinkled them with salt, and put the mugs down atop them.

"Some kinda virus, I guess," he said. "I've been watching a lot of TV in here, and that's the word. Well, one of the words." He stopped and pointed toward the old Sony above the bar. "Not much else to do the past couple of days but watch TV."

"Could I get another beer, Mike?" Terry asked, holding out his empty mug, remnants of foam coated the bottom. He looked at Doug and shrugged. "It was a long afternoon. Sittin' on your ass all day takes a lot out of a guy." Mike took the glass and went back to the tap.

Doug took a long, slow drink. Carrie sick, the crew from Honda gone, not even Lester Ropey was here. What the hell? "What are the news guys saying?"

Mike sat the beer in front of Terry, who immediately picked it up and took a drink. "Something from Asia. Hell, they all come from Asia," Mike said. "That seems to be what a lot of the news guys are saying, but according to the reports, the scientists haven't found anything. None of them really seem to know what's making everybody sick. Fox News had some guy in a white lab coat claiming it's caused by radiation from that Japanese nuclear plant that went hot back in 2011. They said it could just be now infecting us. Somebody on MSNBC said it was that new antidepressant."

"Ophiocordon." Terry put his beer on the coaster, nodding. "The Piper."

"Piper?" Mike asked. He reached behind the bar and pulled up a white medicine bottle. "This stuff?"

Terry nodded. "Where'd you get that?"

"It's Carrie's."

Terry took a swig of beer. "Well, that's what they're calling it. Not the news guys, just people. Everybody's using it. The Piper. It's from that old Led Zeppelin song."

'Stairway to Heaven,' Doug knew. 'The Piper's calling you to join him.' Well, if it makes you feel half as good as it's supposed to, no wonder it's popular.

"You must have seen something about it," Mike said to Doug.

No, Doug hadn't. He rarely watched the news. It was too depressing.

"Got any peanuts, Mike?" Terry asked. "Oh, and another beer?" Terry was almost thirty, but never quite made it past twenty-one. He lived in a one-bedroom apartment with movie posters on the wall, and a life-sized cardboard cut-out of a beer model dressed for Oktoberfest he'd gotten from the liquor store down the street. Terry was a regular there, too. Mike slid a shiny tin bucket of peanuts in the shell toward Terry and went to pour another beer. The bucket of peanuts stopped in front of Terry like Mike had done it thousands of times. He had.

"That sounds BS to me," Doug said to Mike who lifted a fresh cold mug up to the tapper.

"What? This Piper?" Mike asked.

Doug shook his head. "No. Do you know how much shit a new drug has to go through before a doctor can prescribe it? This Ophi-cotton stuff is fine. I'm talking about that earthquake and tsunami. That happened so long ago."

Mike's face grew stern, his brow pinched; he put his knuckles on the bar and leaned closer to his only customers like someone else might hear.

"I thought so, too. I've been wondering the past few days. I haven't said to no one, mainly because there's been no one here to say it too, but you think it could be terrorists? I know Saddam had biological weapons, what's to say Al-Qaeda, and Hamas, and ISIS, and all those groups couldn't have them, too. I mean, they might be assholes, but they're smart assholes. They might be killing us with science. Probably something the CIA gave them to use against each other. You know that's where these groups got started, don't you? The CI fucking A."

"It's aliens," Terry said in almost a whisper. He paused and took a long pull off his beer glass, draining it.

"Aliens?" Mike asked, the surprise not hidden in his voice.

"Yeah," Terry said quietly, pushing his empty mug toward Mike. "Think about it. Something's making everybody sick, nobody seems to know what it is, and no terrorist group's taking claim for it – and you know damn well and good them camel-fuckers would be hackin' each other's heads off to take the credit for this. What else is left? Aliens."

"Well," Mike said, seriously. "What do you think they want?"

Terry looked from side to side, squinted and leaned closer to Mike. "Water."

"Water?" Mike asked, almost entranced.

"Come on, look around," Terry said. "What do we have no other planet in the solar system has?"

"I don't know? Cows? Air?"

"Water," Terry said. "Lots and lots of water. We need water to survive, why shouldn't they? They just come down, and make us all sick, then we can't stop them from sucking every fucking drop of it up into their space tankers and, whoosh, bye-bye water, bye-bye Earth."

Doug finished his beer and looked at Terry. Was his mechanic serious? "I think you've been watching the Syfy Channel too damned much," he said. "Next thing you'll be quoting 'Sharknado.'"

"Pfft," vibrated on Doug's lips, enough of an answer as he wanted to give his boss. "Well, what do *you* think it is?"

Doug slowly shook his head. He didn't know, all he knew was something bad was going down around him – maybe something biblically bad – and he wondered if it had hit the few people he even remotely cared about. Doug stood and dropped thirty dollars on the bar. "Mike, this should cover what we've had so far and maybe a couple more for Terry. I think I need to go home." He patted Terry's shoulder. "I'll see you Monday, right?"

Terry raised his mug and grinned. "You betcha, boss. You betcha."

June 25: St. Joseph, Missouri

CHAPTER 4

The gentle glow from Nikki's MacBook Pro bathed her face in blue. Soft clicks from her fingers on the keyboard filled the quiet bedroom, posters of Johnny Depp and SpongeBob SquarePants stared over her shoulder. Nikki hated summer college classes. Summers were for swimming, trips to Colorado, and maybe parties on some far-off farm road; not work at a chain restaurant when waitresses with the best rack got the best tips, afternoons sitting in lectures, and evenings in front of her computer writing a term paper on the Baroque Era. Summers were for fun. Fun. This wasn't the summer of fun. Fun didn't mean watching a man nearly choke to death on his own blood. She'd had fun before, and that, Mister, weren't it. At least with whatever was going around, the community college canceled all classes effective today. The beauty of the internet kept everything running smoothly, even her Western Civ assignment.

Nobody knew what to call the odd behavior blanketing the world. Well, at least anyone in charge. People on social networking sites, from Facebook and Twitter to conspiracy theory podcast message boards, were calling it the Zombie Virus. Whatever. There were no zombies, and the scientific community hadn't even pinpointed the cause as a virus. There were no reports of people attacking and eating anyone. Nobody was attacking anyone at all, only the illness. Sick or healthy, young or old, poor or wealthy would suddenly start bleeding from everywhere, eyes, nose, ears, pores, rectum, everywhere. Like the fat businessman at Hooligans who lumbered after Nikki, blood spewing from every point on his face, before he collapsed on a table. But then he got up, and didn't know where he was. Zombie? No, of course he wasn't a zombie. He was still alive when the EMTs took him away, but he wasn't all right either. Those were the calling cards, blood, collapse, then their mind was gone. What was it? A terrorist attack? A plague? A curse? The news faces on cable simply referred to the wandering, mindless people in the streets (and Nikki's restaurant section) as victims of "the Outbreak," although nobody seemed to know what kind of outbreak it was.

"Nikki," brushed across her consciousness. The voice was faint, so faint she didn't know if it was a voice, or something in her Baroque Era brain. "Nikki," it said again, just as faint. For once she didn't have her iPod buds plugged into her ears, nodding along to Katy Perry or Lady

Gaga; if she had, the sound of someone quietly calling her name would have died in the air. The only person in the house was Dad. Nikki hit "save," shut her laptop and dashed down the stairs.

Darkness hung heavy over the first story of the Holleran house. Gene Holleran would tell Nikki he extinguished the lights to save electricity, but Nikki knew otherwise. Ever since the Outbreak hit, people started going crazy. Looting, breaking and entering, raping, killing, like the world didn't have enough problems. Gene wouldn't tell her, but he kept the house dark to keep her safe. If the bad people, the crazy ones, thought the house was empty, they'd just keep on moving. No fun raping and pillaging if there's no one to rape and nothing to pillage. Ever since Nikki's mom died in 2000, losing Nikki was not going to happen on Gene Holleran's watch, not ever.

"Nikki," Gene wheezed as his daughter bounded down the steps and into the living room, kneeling beside his prone, shadowy figure. Nikki fumbled for the table lamp on Gene's nearby desk. She clicked it on and flooded a small patch of room in yellow haze. Gene lay on the rug next to the coffee table, his eyes trying to focus on something, anything. She looked in his face. No blood streamed from his nose, none leaked from the corners of his mouth. She ran her hands through his thick hair, just starting to gray, looking for trauma. Nothing.

"Are you okay, Dad?" she asked softly. "What happened?"

He swallowed slowly and took a breath, the effort in those simple actions caused Nikki's stomach to flutter.

"I," he started, then stopped, closing his eyes. Nikki choked back a scream. His chest raised and lowered; he was still alive. "I fell," he said a few long moments later. "I was walking across the room." He paused for a breath, the breathing labored. "And my head got light. I don't remember falling. I just opened my eyes and I was on the floor." He paused again and ran the tip of his tongue across his lips. "How's the term paper coming?"

Nikki shook her head in three short strokes. "That's not important, but this is," she said, cradling his face in her hands, a day's worth of stubble scratched her palms. Her dad had always had a heavy growth of whiskers. A quick burst of memory exploded in Nikki's head, of Dad rubbing his stubbly chin over her four-year-old tummy, and her uncontrolled giggles. "Dad. Can you understand me?"

Gene nodded slowly.

"Is it the Outbreak, Dad? Do you have the Outbreak?"

He frowned. "The Outbreak?"

"The sickness that's going around," Nikki said, trying to keep the nervousness growing inside her. "The one making people bleed and, and …"

"Go stupid," Gene finished. He shook his head slowly. "No. I haven't been outside in two weeks. If this was a disease or something, it would have shown itself before now."

Nikki stared into her father's eyes, the green irises losing their luster in the dim light. "Your nose is bleeding."

Gene smiled. "I must have caught my nose on the coffee table on the way down," he said. "I'm surprised it's still attached."

Nikki relaxed. Nosebleed caused by landing on the floor by way of a coffee table; that made sense. She grabbed hold of that information and held tight, but he'd fallen because of light-headedness. That wasn't good.

"Then what happened, Dad?"

He pointed toward the corner. "Would you get something for me?"

Nikki nodded. "Sure, Dad."

"That bottle of medicine in the desk," he said, then coughed, a trickle of blood rose in the corner of his mouth. "Third drawer down."

Nikki stood and covered the short distance in three quick steps, and pulled open the drawer. A yellow-gold medicine bottle with a pop-off cap (no children in this house to protect, no siree) sat on a thin sheaf of papers. Nikki paused as she grabbed the bottle. The papers were Gene's will.

"Your *will*?" Nikki's voice rose as the words pushed out of her mouth. "What's going on, Dad?"

He waved her closer. "Just give me a pill."

Nikki looked at the bottle in her hand. It was Ophiocordon.

"The Piper? Since when did you need the Piper?"

Gene's brows pinched. "The Piper?"

"That's what people are calling Ophiocordon," she said. "Because so many people are taking it. The Piper's something from an old rock song."

Gene's face grew soft, peaceful. "Led Zeppelin," he said, a smile teasing the corners of his mouth. "The song's 'Stairway to Heaven.' The lyrics are 'the Piper's calling you to join him.'"

"Yeah?"

Gene laughed. "I get that. Now, give me one."

Nikki popped off the cap and dropped a white oval capsule into the palm of her hand. Just one. She always tossed the right number of pills into her hand. Aspirin, antibiotics, diet pills. She always felt if regular people had super powers, this was hers. "Since when have you needed antidepressants?"

Gene's face grew soft, peaceful. "Since your mom left us. I had a harder time than you knew. But I had to stay strong; you needed that."

Tears forced their way to Nikki's eyes. Guilt rushed through her; she hadn't known. Seventeen years and she hadn't known. How could she not have seen what her father was trying to cope with? Gene grabbed her wrist, his grip painfully weak.

"Do not do that," he said, his voice soft; too soft. "You were so young. You needed to think about growing up. I couldn't let you know what I had to deal with. That wouldn't have been fair. Now give me that thing, that Piper. I need it to push through this."

Nikki slid the pill into her father's mouth. He dry swallowed and lay still, his eyes closed. Less than a minute crawled by, though it seemed like hours. A smile broke his face; the Piper's bliss had kicked in.

"Now," Nikki said, looking into her father's peaceful face. "What happened to you?"

His mouth opened slowly. "I think it's my ticker giving way." He tried to force his smile into something encouraging, but failed completely. That was the Piper's strength; it made you feel that good. "Your Papaw had a bum ticker, so did his dad. But at least I've got something doctors might actually be able to fix, at least for a while. I'll be fine, baby. I'll be fine."

"You'll be fine when I call an ambulance," Nikki said. She gently pulled her hands from her father's scratchy face and stepped toward the desk where he paid bills, and did his taxes every April – "I'm not going to send these in until the last minute. I'm going to make those IRS bastards wait for Gene Holleran's money." That's where he kept his phone. Not a cell phone, not a wireless phone, but a heavy black Western Electric 2500; a model about a year past having a rotary dial. She picked up the handle and dialed 9-1-1.

"I don't need an ambulance," Gene said weakly.

Beep-beep-beep.

"What Dad?"

Beep-beep-beep.

"I can make it to the van," Gene said, slowly propping himself on his elbows. "I don't need an ambulance. I can make it to the van."

Beep-beep-beep.

Holy shit, ran through Nikki's head as she dropped the handset back on the cradle. *Nine-one-one is busy.*

"You're right, Dad," she almost whispered. A few minutes ago, sitting in her room, staring at her computer, writing a term paper for a jerk-off summer class at a jerk-off community college, everything seemed normal. It seemed safe, even though she knew there was something outside her house that wanted to kill her. No, Nikki, no. Damn, damn, damn. Inside her house, with SpongeBob leaning over her shoulder suppressing his infectious, if not annoying, giggle, and her dad downstairs having a beer and watching TV, she felt things were going to be fine. Scientists, or the government, or Dr. McCoy from "Star Trek" – somebody would fix this Outbreak thing and the world would go back to the way it was. She now knew something was seriously fucked. Nine-one-one was supposed to be the savior. Got a fire? Call 9-1-1. Getting robbed? Call 9-1-1. Your father is lying on the floor dying from a heart attack, or the Outbreak, or Mexican banditos? Call 9-1-1. But 9-1-1 isn't coming today. Nine-one-one had something better to do. "Here," she said, grabbing his right elbow and shoulder. "Let me help you up." And she pulled.

The hospital sat just about a mile away and would only take a minute or two to drive there, but getting Gene Holleran to the family van Mom and Dad once used to take little Nikki to the water park, or miniature golfing, or to youth soccer, seemed to take hours. "You still with me, Dad?" Nikki asked, Gene's weight heavy against her. Gene wasn't a big man, but at 5'9", 185 pounds, it took a heavy toll on Nikki just to walk him step by step out the back door to the van.

"Yeah," he said, the word coming out in a forced hiss. "I'm here, baby. I'm here."

"Just a few more steps, Dad."

She leaned forward, unlocked the passenger-side door, helped him in and fastened his seat belt, then ran around the front and jumped into the driver's seat.

"Aren't you going to buckle up?" Gene asked softly.

"I've got something a bit more important to worry about here, Dad," she said, starting the Dodge and backing out of the driveway. "Just sit tight and save your strength."

She pulled onto Fontaine Avenue and turned left on Frederick; this usually busy street empty, traffic lights blinking yellow. A figure, a lone figure, stood in the eastbound lane of Frederick, just standing. Nikki reached down and fastened her seat belt. An Outbreaker. The man's legs moved slightly like he was sleepwalking, but he didn't go anywhere. His arms swayed as if caught in a slight breeze, his face blank. As Nikki drove past the man, she watched the Outbreaker's face; he never noticed the ton of steel pass within feet of him. Whatever this thing did, it made people lose their mind – all of it.

"Have I been a good father?" Gene asked seconds later in short, weak breaths.

"What?" Nikki gasped.

"Have I been a good father?" he said again. "It was hard after your mother died, but I tried the best I could. I wanted you to have everything."

Tears Nikki had held back burst from her eyes.

"Oh, Dad," she started, the words stuck in her throat.

"I wanted to make you strong, too, Nikki," he said, his voice trailing. "That's why I taught you to punch, and how to ride the motorcycle. I didn't want you to ever take crap from anybody." He stopped, his chest still.

"Dad," Nikki screamed, the van swerved.

"I'm here, dear, I'm here," he said, his chest rose and fell again. "But I, I didn't teach you something I think you're going to need."

"Dad. You've done everything. You've taught me everything. I love you."

Gene waved a finger as if to quiet her. "I love you, too, dear. But this is bad. This world." He motioned slightly with his arms. "It's gone. I've followed the news. I've followed it a lot. This Outbreak thing has killed millions of people, most of them here, but it's spread everywhere. No one heard of this shit two months ago, and now it's everywhere." A laugh broke through, splattering blood over Gene's shirt. "And they don't even know if it's an outbreak of anything."

"Dad," Nikki screamed as she turned onto the lane leading to St. Joseph Regional Hospital, hoping like all hell she would get there in time to save her father. Gene reached toward her and grabbed her arm, his grip weak as a child's. "I never taught you to shoot a gun," he said.

A gun? "A gun?" she barked. "Dad, I don't want to use a gun, not ever."

"There's one in my red toolbox in the garage. Second drawer, behind the ratchet set," Gene whispered. "Take it. And if someone comes to get you, shoot them. Shoot those bastards dead."

The van's tires squealed as Nikki stopped at the ER. "Dad, what are you talking about?"

He smiled at her. "I love you, baby girl. And there's nothing," he stopped. His breath coming slower. "There's nothing gonna hurt you."

A tendril of blood broke from Gene's left eye and he slumped further into the passenger seat of the van. This time Nikki screamed.

The glass doors of the emergency room slid open and Nikki ran through, but no one came to greet her. A chorus of steady beeps played in the background behind the heartbeat in her ears. Loaded body bags lay on gurneys pushed three deep against the walls; more lined the floor, all moving as if they were filled with windup toys.

"Hello?" she said, walking through the maze of undulating body bags, then screamed, "hello?" She pushed her way into the waiting area, a man still holding a coffee cup sat slumped on a flower-print chair, his face covered in blood. As Nikki stared at this bloody, bloody man, he stood and started to walk, the waiting room table in front of him stopped him, but his legs kept moving. Nikki pressed her hand to her mouth and ran to the door for the lobby. Emergency lights flooded the lobby, a grinning Garfield with suction cups stuck to the gift shop wall stared blankly at her, a card strapped to its stomach read, "Dr. Garfield Prescribes Lasagna."

"Hello?" she called down the hallway. "My father needs help."

Movement.

Nikki stopped, suddenly afraid. Her father was right, and she knew it. There were bad people in the world, and for some reason bad situations made bad people multiply. A shadow leaned from a doorway into the bright emergency lights revealing a man, a man of about thirty in a lab coat streaked with blood. He held a Tasmanian Devil coffee mug. "Can I help you, miss?" the man asked.

"Oh, thank God," Nikki spat, running toward him. The man stepped back, holding Taz in front of him to keep their distance. Nikki saw this and stopped. "It's my dad. He thought he had a heart attack, but now I don't know."

The man put his right hand out in front of him. "Calm down, miss, miss…"

"Holleran," she said.

"Miss Holleran. I am Dr. Davault. I am the only person here to help you so I cannot promise you anything. First, where's your father?"

Nikki motioned down the hall. "Back there, through the ER. There wasn't anybody there. Nobody. Just nobody. He still, he's still in the van."

"Okay," Dr. Davault said, stepping slowly closer. Nikki got a better look at him. The man was exhausted, black smudges circled his eyes, and a few days' growth of beard darkened his face. But it wasn't a bad face. It was a caring face. "We need to walk that way," he said, and motioned back toward the waiting room. The waiting room with the churning, bloody coffeeman. She turned and walked. "What are your father's symptoms?"

"Well, dizziness. He passed out. He said it was his heart," she began, then stopped, tears flowing again. Dr. Davault grabbed Nikki's shoulders, but she didn't resist, she welcomed the comfort. Dr. Davault was an authority figure. She no longer had to be in control.

"Miss Holleran, if I can help your father, I need to know everything. Please. What else is wrong with him?"

Nikki steadied herself under his grip and wiped her eyes. "When I stopped outside the ER, his nose started bleeding."

Dr. Davault dropped Nikki's shoulders and bolted toward the waiting room door. Nikki followed, the coffeeman looking mindlessly through blood-soaked eyes as they ran through the room, the ER doors making a "shwoosh" when they went outside. The doctor stopped at the van, and gently opened the door. His head dropped toward his chest and he turned to Nikki, his face looking more like fifty than thirty.

"I'm sorry, ma'am. Your father's already dead."

Nikki fell to the asphalt drive screaming.

June 28: Paola, Kansas
CHAPTER 5

Another day, another nothing. Doug sat at his desk at the muffler shop, staring at Catalina looking back at him from the Makita power tool calendar with barren, empty eyes. This might be the last time he saw Catalina. The model, whatever her real name was, most probably lay in her apartment somewhere, her body swollen, unrecognizable, dried blood crusted over her surgically-supple lips, or maybe she simply wandered in the street, her amazing gray eyes dead, unseeing. Doug doubted he'd ever flip the calendar to July because June 28 might be his last day at Doug's Muffler and Brakes, Paola, Kansas' finest muffler and brake shop. He came to the shop more out of habit than need; there hadn't been a customer for more than a week. Ever since the Outbreak came to town, nobody needed muffler and brake work. Either the Outbreak sure liked to take people out of the driving business, or he was one hell of a mechanic.

The Beatles' "Oh! Darling" gave way to the Rolling Stones "Gimme Shelter" on the local AOR station coming through the radio above Doug's desk. A few days ago, the local station said FEMA was setting up a shelter at the local amusement park, Worlds of Fun, but the station wasn't local anymore, it gave way to a national satellite feed days ago. Gimme shelter? Hell, yes. And while you're at it, gimme strength. Gimme a shotgun. Gimme a fucking phone call. Somebody, anybody. "Lord, I'm gonna fade away" suddenly snapped into static. Now the radio was gone. If the satellite feed died, what did that mean? Gimme, gimme answers. Doug didn't have answers, just more questions. If the radio was dead, the electricity would be soon. The Outbreak wouldn't be far behind either. The Outbreak was out there, looking for him. Doug was sure of that. He might not die directly from the Outbreak, but Doug was sure the Outbreak wanted everybody one way or the other.

"Terry," Doug said aloud, the sound of his voice hollow in the empty room. "I gotta get to Terry." Doug sent Terry home the day after they'd talked to Mike at the Corner Bar. No need for employees if there's no work. 'How the hell am I going to pay my bills, or buy booze?' Terry had said, more scared than angry. 'What am I going to do without a job?' Terry is (or maybe was) a good man. Not the best dog in the hunt, but a good man all the same. Doug smiled at Terry, although he felt no humor in his heart, and said, 'the post office isn't delivering, so there's no mail.

No mail, no bills. Your landlord is in the morgue, and the front door of the liquor store down the street is held open with a brick. I think you'll be okay.' Terry thought for a few seconds, smiled and nodded. 'Yeah, I will.' That's the last time Doug had seen Terry, and if the Outbreak still hadn't visited him; he may still be alive. Doug hoped so. He couldn't stay here, in Paola, any longer, and he didn't want to go alone. This town was dead. Doug knew it. He *felt* it. He had to get somewhere safe, somewhere untouched by the Outbreak. The last person he'd talked to had called the Outbreak victims zombies, but they didn't look like any zombie Doug had seen in the movies. They were dumb, all right, but they just stood there, pacing. Then they eventually fell over and stopped moving.

If Terry was still alive, he had to come, too. Doug stood from his office chair, stepped toward the door and stopped to the sound of Catalina making pouty noises in his head. He smiled and plucked the calendar off the wall. "I ain't goin' anywhere without you, baby," he said, folded the calendar and shoved it in his mechanic uniform's deep front pocket. The shop clock read straight-up noon as Doug pulled the rear door of the shop closed and locked it for no other reason than he had the key. He'd walked the ten blocks to work every day for the past few weeks, realizing he should have done that the past five years. He felt better, his breathing not so labored after a walk. And, the streets of Paola were pretty pleasant when people weren't around. But Doug had to fight his imagination from sending visions of bodies lying on blood-soaked carpets just behind the friendly front windows of the homes he walked past, some of them with big, colorful, plastic toys in the front yard. He fought the feeling because he knew he was probably right about the bodies, about the blood.

Terry lived in an apartment on the opposite side of downtown from the muffler shop. The streets, usually rumbling with midday traffic; people driving to Clem's Diner or running errands on their lunch hour, but Doug didn't bother looking for traffic as he stepped onto the dead street and walked toward Terry's apartment above the drug store. No need to look. The streets of Paola were quiet, he hadn't seen a vehicle more complicated than a bicycle for days since Squirrelly Bob pedaled past Doug like a mess of Bushwhackers were on his ass, the arms of a blow-up fuck doll tied around his neck, and a half-empty gallon of whiskey bouncing in the bike's front basket in a mound of medicine bottles, the basket bouncing the bottles out like popcorn. For years, Squirrelly Bob rode his bike all over town, stopping to pick up loose change some people dropped for him on purpose. He was harmless. Bat shit crazy, but harmless. Squirrelly Bob had trailed blood as he wheezed by Doug, and Doug knew Squirrelly Bob was probably now picking up coins in heaven. Doug bent and looked at one of the medicine bottles that had come to rest on the street. He turned it with a stick. If Squirrelly Bob had the Outbreak, he wasn't going to touch anything. Ophiocordon. A grin pulled at Doug's mouth. The Piper called Squirrelly Bob to join him. No wonder he looked so happy.

Crossing the street, Doug heard a telephone ring somewhere. For weeks Doug had heard an occasional telephone ring and had grown numb to it. The first few calls sent him running around like the character in an old "Twilight Zone" episode, the one where a guy is alone in a town with no people and goes a little nutty. Doug was that character for nearly a week before he gave up. But, unlike that character, he wasn't going crazy. At least not yet. If someone was going to call, they could sure as hell leave a message. Doug reached the other side of the street, and rounded the corner of Centennial in front of the Corner Bar; Mike slumped in a red mess over the bar's shuffleboard table. Doug had stopped by to check on Mike a couple of days after Terry's talk of aliens, and didn't like what he found. No one at 9-1-1 answered Doug's telephone call about Mike lying dead, and he left the cord of the bar's wall phone hanging, knowing that if he found Terry dead, too, he might be the only person left in town, or in the world, who would ever use that phone, or walk down any street, or breathe – then he saw the woman.

She stood in the street, her permed brown hair flat on one side like she'd slept on it wrong. The woman, about 30-something, and built like God felt particularly inspired the day she was conceived, stood looking away from him, but Doug knew that figure, that curvy, tight figure. Doug had fantasized about wrapping his arms around this woman's waist during all four years of high school and never got close enough to get to first base. Hell, he never got off the bench.

"Connie?" Doug said, then called louder. "Connie?" The woman slowly turned toward him. Yeah, it was Connie. Connie Dornberg Mickelson worked at the First National Bank of Miami County and only wore the name Mickelson out of habit. Her high school sweetheart Enis Mickelson left her years ago. Dipshit. As she stood in the street, her eyes staring blankly at Doug, terror suddenly swept across her face.

"Connie," Doug said again, holding his hands in front of him, walking toward her slowly. "It's me, Doug Titus from high school. I'm okay. No Outbreak here. I'm healthy as a moose." At least from ten or so yards away she looked like the Outbreak had passed her by, too. No blood on her face. No blood on her lavender blouse. But something was wrong. Her nametag was still pinned over her left breast. Doors to the bank had been locked for weeks. The drive-through, tellers blasting every transaction with disinfectant (no, you can keep the pen, please. We have lots), stayed open for a short time after. But the drive-through had been closed for a while now, too. Connie still wore her banker uniform; she hadn't changed her clothes for at least a week, most probably two. My God, Connie. What happened?

The stench of sweat and her period, either current or long gone, struck him as he stepped within five feet, the desire of getting anywhere near first base with the former prom queen and valedictorian ran screaming from Doug's pants. She didn't move, the look of terror frozen on her face.

"Connie," Doug said softly. "Where have you been?"

Her mouth, lips chapped and cracked, moved slowly like a fish's, no sound escaped. "Connie," Doug said again. "Things are pretty fucked up right now. I don't know why; I don't know how. I only know almost everybody's dead. But I'm not, you're not. I think a friend of mine is still alive. I know you're scared. So am I." Hearing that admission come from his own mouth stopped Doug's words. He hadn't verbalized that feeling; he hadn't even allowed himself to think it. Yes, he was scared. Hell, yes, he was scared. He'd be as crazy as Squirrelly Bob riding a bike with a blow-up sex doll trailing behind him if he wasn't scared. "What has happened to you?"

Connie slowly moved her hands to her face, covering it.

"I. I. I. I hiding," she said, like she hadn't spoken to another human being for weeks. Maybe she hadn't. "I hid. I locked myself in my house and hid in my basement, eating food out of cans and drinking out of the downstairs bathroom sink." Once she started speaking, the words poured from her mouth. She pulled her hands from her face and looked squarely at Doug, the terror still there. "Frank, the bank manager, the fucking bank manager, died in front of me. Then he got back up and started walking. Walking around his desk over and over and over. He didn't know his name anymore; he didn't know anything." Tears, long choked back, rolled down her face. "Then Carla puked blood all over a customer, and I couldn't take it. The TV reports about the Outbreak scared me. They scared the shit out of me. I ran to my car and went home."

"How long ago was that?" Doug asked.

Connie's eyes glazed for a moment, her focus wandering. "Last week, or maybe the week before," she said, sobs starting to stagger her words. "And I hid. I tried to hide from whatever is killing everybody. I sat in the basement with the lights off. Then somebody broke into my house."

Doug had survived the Outbreak, at least to this point. He wasn't afraid of the Outbreak anymore, at least not as much as the other people who survived it. He read "Lord of the Flies" in high school. He knew what happened when the rules of society broke down. People didn't have to follow them anymore. "What did you do?" he asked.

Her tears came even more heavily. She took a step toward Doug. "I had a gun," she said. "Daddy always said a girl has to know how to protect herself. He said that. He said it when I was thirteen, he said it when I graduated high school, and he said it when I married Enis. He bought me a gun." Connie paused, wiping tears with the sleeves of her blouse. "He bought me a gun and took me out target practicing every weekend until I was good."

"What did you do?" Doug asked again, flatly. "What did you do to the man who broke into your house?"

"I shot him," she said, looking into his eyes. "It was Donnie Ferguson. Math club Donnie Ferguson. He snuck down my steps, holding a beer from my refrigerator in his hand – my refrigerator – and said, 'Well, well, well. It's Connie I'm too good for you Dornberg.' Then he came close to me, too close, and unzipped his pants. Then I shot him with my pistol. I shot him in the face."

Good Christ Almighty. What has happened to us?

More tears sprang from Connie's eyes and she stepped toward Doug. "Can you help me?" she sobbed. Doug reached out to her and stopped. Connie's tears were red.

"You're bleeding, Connie," he said.

She put her hands to her face and wiped them over her eyes. When she pulled them off, her palms were slick with blood. Connie looked at Doug through a red mask. "Run," she whispered, flecks of blood splattering her lips. "Run."

Doug turned and ran. Away from his former fantasy, away from a woman who committed the murder of a high school classmate, away from death. About twenty yards down the street, Doug turned and looked at Connie, beautiful Connie, dying Connie. She stood in the street, the front of her lavender blouse streaked with blood, her feet shuffled, but she didn't go anywhere. Connie was one of them, the Outbreak people. Doug stifled a scream and ran again, ran like he hadn't since high school. Years away from the track team, and too many nights of Swanson microwave dinners and beer, brought Doug to a stop in the street, hands on knees, breath heaving. He looked up and stared at the shattered front window of Phillips Drug Store. An off-white newspaper end roll sign handwritten in Sharpie flapped against the broken glass: "The Outbreak is a lie. Ophiocordon is death. The Apocalypse is upon us." Doug staggered toward the window, air just starting to suck back into his lungs. Through the window, the interior of the drug store looked like a toy box, its contents strewn across the floor, posters and displays dangling from the walls. A homemade, blood-splattered sign still hung from the counter: "Phillips Drug is out of Ophiocordon. Will shoot on sight."

"Holy shit," Doug whispered. He turned and ran up the metal stairs on the west side of the building to Terry's apartment, a stitch pulling at his right side. Moments later, pounding brought Terry to his door in his underwear holding a Natty Light loosely in his right hand. "Oh, hey, man," he said slowly to Doug, grinning. "How's it goin'?"

Doug pushed past Terry and slammed the door shut behind him. "I just saw Connie Dornberg bleed to death from her face," he said before he grabbed the beer from Terry's hand and drained it. "We gotta get outta here, man. We gotta get outta this town. We gotta find someplace safe. Today. Now."

Terry nodded. "Cool," he said, the zombie first-person shooter game Left4Dead played in the background. "Can I finish my videogame first?"

July 1: Harrisonville, Missouri
CHAPTER 6

A branch snapped. Karl jumped from sleep and snatched the hunting rifle from the edge of his sleeping bag, lifted it to his shoulder and scanned the forest. The naked trees, trimmed in morning fog, betrayed nothing. Karl slipped out of his sleeping bag fully dressed and turned slowly to examine the woods. Still nothing. He tightened his grip on the gunstock. A rustle in the underbrush. Karl crouched to make himself smaller and aimed at the sound. Another rustle and a movement low to the ground pulled his attention to his left. Karl's lip twitched; something hunted him. He raised the gun sight to his eye and gently squeezed the cold trigger. Another rustle, then it rushed him. Golden fur tore through the forest and leapt at Karl. He fired and a big dog dropped in a heap next to his sleeping bag.

"Goddamnit," Karl spat, watching the now-wild dog's taut body bleed into the forest floor. This was a big fella. People were dying off and animals were already going wild. "Sorry, Fido." He stroked the dog's fur. "It was you or me." Karl stood and looked around. Somebody heard the shot. He knew that. And it was probably somebody he didn't want to meet. There were bad people out there; nasty people and Karl Derking didn't take shit from anybody. He pulled out the rifle's clip to count his remaining bullets – four. Only four. He rolled his sleeping bag into a tight bundle and strapped it onto the green backpack that held everything he had. The sleeping bag, the backpack, the rifle – all taken from looting. Them or me, Hoss. Them or me. Karl slung the backpack over his shoulders and walked north, Harrisonville lay a few miles away.

An hour later, Karl sat on a small hill, leaning against a gnarled oak tree, binoculars pressed against his face. The black and gray pavement of U.S. 71 cut the countryside into two parts, its four-lane surface webbed with cracks and dotted with an occasional dash of yellow paint. A small herd of white-tailed deer, about six, walked calmly across the highway, a doe stopped in the median to graze. A month and they'd forgotten about us, Karl realized. A buck walked past the one car on the highway, a Chevy Lumina, its hood up, its driver nowhere to be seen. Karl's pickup sat just like it fifteen miles south of that hill near Archie, Missouri, dead like it had the Outbreak, or whatever the hell was killing people. Karl thought the Outbreak scare was bullshit. Something was killing people, all right, but he didn't think it was some kind of virus.

U.S. 71 brushed against Harrisonville, population 10,190, although now it may well be zero. Two church steeples and a water tower peeked over the treetops of the town, a Wal-Mart and Price Chopper grocery store sat like big concrete blobs on the town's outskirts. That was his goal. He needed food, clothing, water, and ammunition, all at everyday low prices. Nothing moved in town, at least that Karl could see. Heck, he might even find a car to take; it's not stealing if you take something from a dead guy. He stood and began walking.

Deserted. Highway 7 that branched off from U.S. 71 was empty. Nothing. The coast isn't going to get any clearer, Derking. Panic gripped Karl as he stepped onto the highway and began ascending the off ramp, but nothing happened. Boot steps on the pavement he normally didn't notice, tapped an uncomfortable cadence through the morning air, but that was it. A hawk cried in the distance, but there were no motors, no shouts, and no car radios to break the silence. Karl was alone. He liked it like that. Karl had jumped in his pickup in Vinita, Oklahoma, and pointed himself toward Miami (pronounced Miam-uh for all you Yankees) two days ago, only to find the city gone. Gone gone. Whether by accident or by some madman with a match, he didn't know, but the city lay flat, the occasional chimney and hollowed husk of a brick storefront still stood. So, he kept driving, this time north, just because it seemed to make the most sense. If someone were alive, still fighting this biblical pox, terrorist attack, or whatever it was, he might find them in Kansas City. He was close, but he still hadn't made it.

Karl stopped and pulled the binoculars to his face. Four bodies lie in the Wal-Mart parking lot, a great, black turkey vulture stood on a woman's chest, ripping at the soft flesh of her face, but that was it, the only movement he could see. If anyone in this town were alive, they were somewhere inside a building, watching him. He suddenly felt exposed. The Wal-Mart building butted up to a line of trees that rose from a dip to the right of the off ramp; Karl could see the back door not a dozen yards from the trees. A body lay next to it. The Dumpster and a stack of boxes would help conceal his approach. Karl stepped off the pavement and back into the cover of brush.

He squatted behind Wal-Mart for 20 minutes before moving. The body by the door had been there for a while; he could smell that from the trees, but something else mingled with the odor of death, something thick, earthy. The back door had been propped open by a box. The poor guy was probably having a smoke when he died from the whatever, not like the smoking wouldn't have done it eventually. The only things moving within eyesight were flies fluttering around the corpse. He ran for the door, but the corpse had fallen too close for Karl to open it. Flies scattered as he reached toward the bloated body to drag it out of the way, but the gray skin held him back. Karl was used to death by now, watching blood shoot from the face of everyone he knew, only to watch them wander around mindlessly until they eventually fell, never to move again.

But what the hell was up with the man's skin? Karl sat his rifle on the pavement next to the corpse and leaned close. He gagged and almost vomited; fuzzy gray fungus grew all over this man's flesh. Fascinated, he leaned in closer. Holy shit, it was moving, growing as he watched. Karl stood and staggered back. That was the smell, the fungus. "Oh, my God," Karl whispered, the quiet city forgotten, the turkey vultures pecked at the parking lot corpses now in some other world. The corpse, the man in the blue Wal-Mart vest, the name "Kelly" on a red, white, and blue plastic nametag pinned to the front, moved. Not on his own, something moved him. Karl grabbed his rifle, slung it over his shoulder, and took two more steps back. *Is this normal?* he wondered. An unnatural lump began to rise between the open flaps of Kelly's vest.

"What the hell?"

He looked around for something, anything long enough to push this living dead guy away from the door so he could get inside. A branch. A branch about six feet long and as big around as a salami had fallen atop the Dumpster that sat next to the tree line. Karl moved away from the body and grabbed the branch, breaking off smaller limbs with furious snaps he should be alarmed with, but he didn't have time to worry about the noise. He had to get inside.

"Sorry, Kelly," Karl said softly, and pushed the trimmed branch into the side of the bloated, fungus-covered corpse. It didn't move. "Shit." Karl pushed harder; Kelly lay still, if not slightly jiggly. Karl shifted the branch to press beneath Kelly's ribs, and the body moved. Karl smiled and he shoved again, then the branch snapped near the tip, the jagged wood ripped Kelly's shirt and stabbed into his flabby gut.

"Jesus Christ."

The branch pulled open the shirt across Kelly's torso; gray fuzz covered his hairy gut. The lump, a knobby ball on a stem, sprang from the center of Kelly's chest. It grew from Kelly's sternum. Holy shit. The sharp end of the branch lurched forward under Karl's continued pressure, and split Kelly's skin. A small cloud of yellow spores shot into the air.

Karl dove back dropping the branch, the palms of his hands scraped the pavement as he landed on the weed-choked parking lot; the rifle that hung over his shoulder clanked behind him. "Holy shit," Karl hissed as the yellow cloud dissipated into the afternoon. Fungus. Fungus was eating this man. What? Karl shot to his feet, ignoring the throbbing pain in his hands. His eyes scanned the parking lot in front of the store, the corpses still under the talons of the great, black, greasy birds. Nothing else moved. His eyes shot back to Kelly. The cloud of spores was gone, but the stem and disco ball growing out of Kelly's chest moved, throbbed. Karl took a deep breath and ran for the door, leaping over Kelly's face and landing inside the back room.

Inside the store, the lights were still on, but nobody was home. Stacks of beige boxes loomed around Karl as he walked through the storeroom, looking over his shoulder toward the still open door, the stem and party ball still pointed toward the sky like the devil's erection. It was going to blow soon, Karl knew, and blow a larger cloud of yellow spores into the wind. What the hell was happening? Karl had never been claustrophobic, but good old Kelly had fixed that.

Near the employee exit sat a small bank of security cameras. Karl paused and watched them flip through their sequence. Nobody in books. Nobody in shoes. Nobody in cosmetics. Nobody in children's clothes, sporting goods, or automotive. Good. He pushed open the aluminum employee door and walked silently into the world of Wal-Mart and the fuck away from dead, fungusy Kelly. Shattered glass from the gun cabinet littered the floor of the sporting goods department. *Somebody else had your idea, Hoss. Just be glad they're gone.* He reached an arm through the shards of glass and felt for boxes of bullets. There were only four left of his caliber.

"Shit," he whispered. Karl shoved the boxes into his backpack, and pulled it back onto his shoulder. That wasn't enough. He took a .22-caliber rifle from the cabinet, and slung it over his shoulder as well. He knew the little gun wasn't powerful enough to take down much, but he couldn't be picky when that's all there was. He grabbed as many boxes of .22 cartridges he could stuff into his backpack and left sporting goods.

Karl stayed to the perimeter of the store, trying to keep out of the open, like in zombie movies. Zombies. Could fungus cause zombies? Karl paused for a second. *Had I read something about some fungus turning ants into zombies? Fox News? CNN.com? The Daily Show? Where the hell had I heard that?* He shook his head. Zombies were in bad movies. There's no such thing in real life. Besides, these things didn't act like zombies were supposed to. Not at all.

Glass crunched under Karl's feet as he walked through the pharmacy, empty white medicine bottles scattered across the floor with each step. People should have raided the pharmacy for painkillers, antibiotics, cholesterol medicine for an America that was still fat after the apocalypse, and birth control pills, but Karl knew those prescription medicines were an afterthought. A red letter on a white banner stretched across the shattered pharmacy window read, "Wal-Mart Has No Ophiocordon: Check Back Monday." *Monday came and went, my friend,* Karl thought. *No more Ohio-cum-on for you.*

The food aisles were near the front, but close. Karl walked through baby clothes, girls' clothing, then … Clink. Karl froze. Something hard and plastic had hit the store's tiled floor; he knew he wasn't alone. Another clink. Someone was in women's clothing. He crossed the aisle into the men's section and ducked behind a rack of men's shirts, half-off.

"La, la, la, I'm ready for love …" danced shakily through the air. Karl looked <u>around</u> a teal golf shirt that hung from his hiding place. A woman, maybe 21, stood in front of a mirror, her long auburn hair hung to the middle of her back. Karl's heart thundered in his chest. The woman stood not 20 feet away, she breathed, she walked, she sang. She didn't cough, she didn't bleed, she didn't die, she didn't sport a big ball of fungus on a stick out of her sternum. She was okay. Karl suddenly realized he held his breath.

The girl spun, looking at her reflection in each pane of the three-way mirror and Karl saw her face – she was plain, like teachers he'd had in high school, but in the empty land of the Outbreak, you couldn't be too choosy. Besides, she might be pretty if she tried. But what in the hell was she doing? The girl smiled at herself in the mirror, unzipped the peach sundress she wore and let it fall to a pile at her feet. Karl almost gasped. The girl stood naked, admiring herself in the mirror before she plucked another dress from a rack and held it in front of her. Good Christ, the world's come to an end and she's trying on clothes. She dropped the plastic hanger to the floor (clink) as she slipped into a hot pink mini. Karl stood slowly on wobbly legs.

"Hello," he said unevenly. "Don't be <u>afra</u> …" The girl spun to face Karl and screamed. "I'm not going to hurt you," Karl said.

She stood, clutching the front of the hot pink dress, her eyes wide, green; her freckled face, framed by flaming red hair, pinched with terror. Karl stepped from behind the clothes rack and gently laid both rifles on the floor.

"I don't know what you've been through," he said softly, and slowly stood again, his hands held open to her. "But if it's how I've spent the past month, I'd be scared, too." He took a step forward. She didn't move. "My name's Karl. What's yours?"

Karl thought for a moment she might run, but she didn't. She released the front of her dress and let her arms drop. *Hmm, front's not much better than the back, but still, not bad.* "Jenna," she said flatly. Karl pulled at the collar of his red flannel shirt. It had gotten hot in the store.

"Jenna," he said. "I'm happy to meet you. I haven't talked to another human being for weeks. I'm ..."

"Do you have the, the thing?" she asked, panic starting to rise in her voice. "The Outbreak. You don't have the Outbreak, do you?"

Karl shook his head; Kelly's gray, fuzzy body growing with fungus loomed before him. He shook his head again, trying to dislodge the lump wedging open the back door.

"No. I don't. I was around people when the Outbreak started and they died. I didn't. I don't think it wants me." He paused for a second, and looked at Jenna's freckled, frightened face. "Have you been living here?" he asked. Jenna nodded. "The people still around, some have gone kinda crazy. I see that some of them broke in here to take things," he said. "Don't mind me asking this, but how come you're alive?"

She looked down from Karl's gaze, and pulled on the dress she'd dropped. "I, I found a place they didn't look for. I stayed there until they were gone."

"I'm sorry," Karl said. "But they're not gone. They're out there. There aren't as many people as there used to be, but there are still some." He took a step forward. "I'm going to head north to Kansas City. There's supposed to be a shelter there, and it's supposed to be safe."

She looked at him, her eyes heavy with fear. "I don't want to go out there."

Karl forced a smile. "Look, Jenna, you can't stay here forever. Eventually the electricity will shut down. The water will shut off. The food will spoil. And more people will come. You don't have to say yes, but I wish you would. Would you come with me?"

Karl looked at her for a moment, drinking in the sadness from her face. He wondered about her family, her friends. He wondered if she'd watched them die. He held out his hand to her. Jenna slowly took it; her touch was warm, soft. Karl's arm quivered slightly as he held her graceful fingers.

"Great," he said. Karl picked up his rifles and walked toward the front of the store. "First, we've got to get you into a pair of jeans and some hiking boots." Jenna stopped.

"No," she said, and pulled her hand out of his.

Karl turned to look at her. "Why?"

"Because," she said, running the palms of her hands gently over the fabric covering her stomach. "This looks really good on me."

Are you fucking serious? "Fine," he said and turned. Jenna followed him like a puppy. "We need food that's light and won't spoil," he said, walking through the food aisles. He stuffed the remaining space of his backpack with <u>stick</u> after stick of beef jerky, and packages of dried fruit.

"I've killed some rabbits out in the woods, but it makes too much noise. I'm trying not to let anyone know where I am." Jenna nodded as he spoke, eating Cap'n Crunch out of the box.

"Can we take these?" she asked holding three cereal boxes.

"It's not very efficient," he said.

"But I like it."

Karl grinned again. He couldn't help it. "Okay, but you get to carry them, unless we can find a car or truck, then you can have as much Cap'n Crunch as you want."

She grabbed six boxes. "My car's in the parking lot."

"You have a car?" he spat, the words louder than he intended. A grin split his face. "Then, lady, we're in business."

Jenna giggled in front of Karl for the first time sending pangs of tension raking through his mind. *Man, that giggle's going to get on my nerves.*

July 4: Allenville, Missouri
CHAPTER 7

Son of a bitch. July 4. Craig was a patriotic man, as patriotic as they come, by God, but as he looked at the Jeff Foxworthy "You Might Be a Redneck if ..." tear-off calendar on his kitchen counter (today's was "... your bumper has more stickers than a NASCAR race"), he knew July 4 in this town meant the Block Party. The night when everyone sat in his yard, breathed his air, and plotted his death. Bastards. Craig wished all his neighbors were dead. Maybe they were. It had been pretty quiet the past week or so. Only Posey was around to bitch at him, shouting from across the yard. The old man had gotten clever though, bold. He and his fat wife sat on their front porch night after night in their canvas Kansas City Chiefs lawn chairs, staring at him when Craig knew Posey should have been inside the house watching The Weather Channel. Or maybe The Weather Channel routine was just a ruse to lull Craig into believing this psychotic mastermind was just an amiable old fart who gave a damn about the rainfall in Jacksonville.

"I'm not fooled by your shit, Posey," Craig said aloud. It was one thing to say something aloud in the yard because the insane old man had the voodoo about him, but inside the safety of Craig's house, he could say whatever he wanted. And he did. When he reached inside the refrigerator to grab his morning Budweiser, it wasn't there.

"I gotta go to the goddamned store," Craig spat. The closest beer was at the grocery store, and Craig hated going to the grocery store anytime but between 2 and 4 a.m. when Posey's TV was off and he felt safe. Any other time there were people at the store who wanted to talk with him. People who said things like, "Isn't it a beautiful day?" or, "Hey, McAllister. How's it goin'?" *Why, it's goin' fine. And no, it's not a beautiful day. The sun's so bright I can see your fuck-ugly face, asshole.* Between 2 and 4 a.m., the grocery store was different; filled with aisle after aisle of food, and that was it. No people but the occasional drunken college kid buying frozen pizzas, or the lone weirdo buying his groceries for the week. Craig knew that was usually him. He didn't care.

The bedroom window on the north side of Craig's house slid open and he slipped out, dropping onto the neatly trimmed grass. As he hit the ground, a smell brushed his nose. There was a fire somewhere; something was cooking. Craig hadn't always crawled in and out of the window of his own house. Just since he realized Posey was out there watching him, plotting, that Craig knew he had to be all secret agent when he came and went. The old man couldn't see this side of the house, and if he couldn't see it, he couldn't see Craig. If he couldn't see Craig, he couldn't fuck with his head. Craig pulled the window shut, unlocked his pickup and stepped in. The old Toyota fired up softly and Craig backed it slowly into the street, Posey's house crawled inch by inch into his view.

"I hope you're planning on running that rust bucket into a tree?" Posey hollered as Craig reached the end of his drive and backed into the street, the man sat still in his chair. Craig cranked the wheel then straightened it, popped the clutch into first gear and gunned it away from Posey's house. "And take off that damned seat belt," Posey screamed as Craig tore down the street. "I'd hate for you not to kiss the safety glass. If you hit it just right, it'll taste like brains." The street dipped halfway down the block and Posey was gone from Craig's head.

Old, deciduous trees hung over the streets of Allenville like the scene from a Bing Crosby movie. There might as well have been a parade, and a song as middle-America-1940s as this place was. *Where were the people?* Craig wondered. There were always some damned thirty or forty-year-old women trying to care what they looked like power walking up and down the streets, but not today. Where were the cars? Where were the kids playing in yards? It was a Saturday morning, for Christ's sake; Jeff Foxworthy told him so. Craig pulled his pickup onto Main Street, not bothering to do more than pause at the stop sign. Why bother? Nothing but birds moved in this town. *Hmm. There seemed to be a lot of them circling in the sky near the grocery store. And was that where the smoke came from? Wonder what's going on?* The sweet, barbecue smell grew stronger as he drove. Maybe the Block Party was going to be somewhere new this year.

Then he saw the bodies. The first one was at Sonic, splayed over the pavement like it was taking an uncomfortable nap. He pushed hard on the brake pedal, sending the Toyota into a squealing halt. The body was that of a carhop, maybe 18. Hell, they were all maybe 18. She lay on the pavement of the empty drive-in restaurant, her right hand still gripped the lip of a tray; the soda, burger and fries it once held spilled from her fall a day before, maybe two. Craig looked hard toward the girl, her skin was gray and fuzzy, and what was wrong with her chest? Did she have a tumor or something? Conjoined twin, maybe? What the fuck was between her boobs? *Posey.* The old man's killing everybody one at a time. Craig's chest grew tight as he stared at the dead girl. *Bastard's going to kill us all.* His eyes shot from the dead girl toward the surrounding stores. The few cars sat idle in the parking lot. No lights shone from inside the big, blocky Budget Barn store, or from the neon outside. No movement. Wait. Something moved near the edge of a Volkswagen Beetle. Craig put the truck into first gear and crept forward. Another body lay on the sidewalk between the Beetle and Trimmed Locks Salon and Spa, fuckin' Herbie probably smiling at the kill. Then Craig saw the movement – a turkey vulture tore at the face of a woman in a power business dress. A stalk with a knobby ball at the end rose from her chest. He punched the gas pedal, shifted into second gear, and tore down Main Street.

Craig had seen death before. Construction jobs begged accidents. So did drunken car wrecks. He'd never caused either, but he'd been around when they happened. Nothing short of war could have prepared him for the grocery store. He pulled the pickup into the store parking lot and stopped, his breath pulled away by the sheer volume of shit. A pile of human bodies, as tall as the darkened Burger King next to it, sat smoldering, the blackened human remains stacked like firewood. Two fire trucks and an ambulance sat quiet in a ring outside the dying human bonfire. Craig pulled a red handkerchief out of his back pocket and tied it across his nose and mouth, then slowly drove around the pile. There was no life here, only death. Three firemen and an EMT lay on the gray pavement in puddles of their own blood, stalks of something, what was that? Mushrooms? grew from their bodies. What was happening here? He pulled next to one of the fire trucks, stopped his Toyota and got out, gagging at the oddly sweet stench of burning bodies.

The fire, which had probably burned for days, was now a blackened, smoldering hell; seared, fleshless skulls grinned into the sky. The firemen had tended the fire (for Posey), Craig realized. But what killed them? What killed all these people? Staring at the mass of smoking remains, Craig resisted the urge to grab a pole off the fire truck and poke the pile. Something had happened in town, something bad, something maybe even biblical. Why hadn't it happened to him? He grabbed an ax off the truck, its steel head heavy in his hand. He still had to go grocery shopping and didn't know what to do if he met anybody. He slid the ax into the front seat next to him, drove the Toyota to the front door of the store, and got out.

Florescent lights bathed Craig with shadowless light when he stepped through the automatic doors and into the store. He stood just inside the store silently; his fingers gripped the ax handle tightly. Music didn't play from the store's speakers; the greeter wasn't there to welcome him. Craig saw no shoppers, no employees, just a mess. Boxes littered the floor, many ripped open, their contents of cookies and uncooked pasta scattered everywhere. *There must have been a fight here.*

People making a run on the grocery store. Damn. A cough. Craig's fingers tightened their grip on the ax handle at the sound of the cough. He wasn't alone. He walked toward the sound, careful not to step on something that might crunch. The canned meat aisle was mostly empty, a few cans of potted meat and chunk chicken still on the shelves. Canned vegetables and condiments were picked pretty clean, as well. The Mexican food section was also stripped bare. *Well, Beaners in town get hungry, too.* Craig stepped slowly into the wide produce and meat aisle, the refrigerated sections and rows and rows of fresh fruits and vegetables still stocked with meat and produce. Maybe the looters were thinking of the future, not the present. Then he saw the man. A man in a trench coat, his arms and pockets stuffed with packaged meat, stood, struggling to pick up a bag of bright, red apples in his already filled hands. The man saw Craig, the bag of apples dropped to the floor.

"Stay away from me," he screamed. "Stay the hell away from me. These are my pork chops, mine. You can't have my goddamned pork chops."

Craig stared at the man. "I don't want your pork chops, asshole," he said softly, resting the ax head on his shoulder. "I'm here for beer, and maybe a steak or two. If you don't fuck with me, I won't fuck with you. Understand? Comprehendo?" Pork Chop Man stared at him. Sweat ran down the man's face in the cool, air-conditioned interior of the store. After a few seconds, he nodded. "I do have a question, though," Craig continued. "What the fuck happened?"

He looked confused. "What do you mean?" he wheezed.

"This," Craig said, spreading his arms. Pork Chop Man flinched as the ax rose in Craig's hand. "All this. This mess, the people lying dead in the street with mushrooms growing out of their fucking chests. That pile of burned bodies in the parking lot. That's what I mean."

Pork Chop shrugged. "The Piper," he said. "The Piper came. The Piper's calling you to join him."

"What the hell are you talking about?"

"Don't you ever leave your house?" Pork Chop asked. "Don't you turn on the TV? The radio? Talk to people on the phone?"

Craig shook his head, resting the ax again on his shoulder. "Not if I can help it."

Pork Chop laughed, which quickly ended in a fit of coughing, packages of pork chops fell from the man's arms from the spasms.

"Not if you can help it," the man spat. "The world is dead. *Dead.* The Piper, Ophiocordon, a goddamned antidepressant, started killing the fuck out of people. Those assholes made a wonder drug out of a fungus that turns ants into fucking zombies, and it's eating us – *alive.*" Pork

Chop Man howled with laughter, a line of snot danced from his nose. "And no one can fix it. No one." He bent and picked up his dropped other white meat. "Enjoy your beer," Pork Chop said as he straightened and walked past Craig in an arc, keeping out of range of the ax, and scampered out the automatic door.

Dead? Everybody's dead? ran through Craig's head, and surprisingly didn't bother him. That meant maybe Posey and Lilith weren't playacting. Maybe they were dead, too, sprouting mushrooms like an old stump. The devil is dead. Craig smiled at that as he watched Pork Chop Man dump all that meat into the back seat of his car and drive away. But not everyone was dead. Craig wasn't dead, neither was Pork Chop Man. *Hmm,* Craig thought, *I wonder if old Pork Chop knew he had a nosebleed?*

July 6: Belton, Missouri
CHAPTER 8

Jenna stood on her toes to hold the deep, green curtains up to the living room picture window. She went flat on her feet, pulled the green curtains down, and stood back, looking at the burgundy curtains that already hung there. The house where they stayed – where the red curtains hung – was just a stroke of dumb luck. Karl had pulled Jenna's 2011 black Nissan Altima down the long country lane off U.S. 71 just south of Belton, Missouri, and stumbled upon this grand, two story house with a three-car garage and backyard in-ground pool. Better yet, the property was almost invisible from the highway.

"We gotta stop," Jenna had said a few miles south of Belton, then whined, "please."

"Why do we 'gotta stop'?" Karl mocked.

"Because I gotta pee," she said, pinching her knees together for effect. They'd been on the road from Harrisonville less than a half hour and she already had to stop.

Karl shrugged. "Sure," he said, taking his foot off the accelerator. "I can see a gravel road up ahead; you can pee there."

Jenna slapped Karl on the shoulder. "Ow," he barked.

"I need a bathroom. Eww," she said. "Find me a bathroom."

Our relationship will not end pretty if I have to put up with shit like this, Karl thought as he pulled off the highway onto the gravel road and brought the car to a stop, because Karl Derking didn't take shit from anybody

"I'm not going here," she said, sinking into the passenger seat and crossing her arms. "It's dirty. I'm not getting dirty."

Fuckenheimer. Karl put the car in gear and crawled, as slowly as he could manage, farther down the gravel road, looking for a good place to turn around. *Let her piss in her seat.* The car topped a rise and the house greeted them like a rich uncle.

"This clean enough for you, princess?" Karl said softly, his eyes taking in the big building. There was even a working fountain out front, with cherubs and everything. A fucking fountain.

That was five days ago. "Which do you like better, the green or the red?" Jenna asked. Karl looked up from a laptop that belonged to the couple that once lived in this house, and grunted. "I'll take that as the green," she said and dropped the green curtains on the floor. "Don't bother to get up. I can change the curtains all by myself," she said, and trudged into the dining room for a chair.

Five days ago, finding the house with Jenna was a dream with boners. Sure, Jenna wasn't a centerfold, but she wasn't ugly, and she's all he had. Karl scoured the house with Jenna in tow. Holding his rifle like a soldier, he looked in every room, every closet, under every bed. No one was there. Jenna eventually found a note on the refrigerator that read, "We're done. By the time someone reads this, we'll be in a better place. Please, take the house and anything you find in it. Use it to stay alive – The Peckinpas." Karl and Jenna were alone in something that was, to them, a mansion. After showering in separate bathrooms, Karl found steaks in the freezer, potatoes in a plastic bag in the pantry, and a bottle of merlot in the cabinet. An hour later, cleaned, scented, and shaved, they had their first warm dinner together.

"Not a bad meal, huh?" Karl asked. He'd watched her every bite, every chew. Karl had been away from people for so long, he took in her movement, her sound. Until now, he hadn't realized he'd been lonely. Jenna looked up from her plate and grunted; blood from the medium rare beef ran down her chin. Karl laughed for the first time in a very long time. She wiped her mouth on a linen napkin, stood, walked around the table and slid into a chair at the table next to him. She wrapped her arms around Karl; he shuddered at the closeness of her warm body.

"I'm scared," she said.

Karl put his arms around her, trying to hide the weakness that suddenly tugged his limbs.

"I've taken care of myself for the past month or so. I can take care of you, too. Don't worry. Don't be scared."

"Karl," she said, brushing her lips against his cleanly shaven cheek. "I want something."

"What?" came out in a whisper.

Jenna stood, the presumably dead Mrs. Peckinpa's robe slid to the floor.

"You," she said, pressing her naked body against him. "I want you."

"Jenna," he started before she pressed her warm lips, still bloody from the steak, onto his.

"Shhhh," she hissed as she pulled off his clothes and climbed on top of him.

Yep. Five days was a long time. Jenna bumped into Karl's shoulder as she dragged a heavy, wooden dining room chair into the living room. "You could be a gentleman and lay off that stupid computer and help me," she said, stopping at the couch where he sat and looked over his shoulder. "What's so freaking important, anyway? Spider solitaire?"

Karl looked up, frowning. "Have you ever taken Ophiocordon?" he asked, looking at Jenna through pinched eyes.

She rested her hands on her skinny hips and frowned. "No. What's that got to do with anything?"

Karl shook his head. "Probably nothing," he said, closing a window before Jenna saw it, the headline 'The Zombie Drug' vanishing from the screen. "Look, the Internet's still up. I don't know how long that's going to last. If I can just find somebody, anybody, there's a chance we'll all live through this."

Jenna crossed her arms over her chest. "The chances of that are jack and shit," she said. "We've both seen what this Outbreak thing has done to everybody, probably everybody except us. Trying to find somebody else is just as silly as you playing with that Porsche out in the garage. You're never going to do anything with that either." She paused. Karl glared at her. She never paused. She never fucking quit talking. "I think we're going to be here together for a very, very, very long time, so let's start being happy. Now are you going to help me hang these green curtains or what?"

The next morning, the Porsche was gone, and Karl along with it.

Jenna sat at the breakfast table in the kitchen, wondering if he'd just driven into town for something and didn't want to wake her. Over a bowl of cold Frosted Flakes, Tony the Bear on the cover of the box telling her they were G-R-R-R-E-A-T!, she pulled open the laptop Karl had worked on the night before and got online. Nothing had been updated. Fox News, Hulu, Cracked.com, Facebook. They were all showing dates from two weeks before. She checked her email account; not even spam. Then she noticed a Word file tucked beneath the Google Chrome browser labelled "Jenna." She clicked the file.

"Dear Jenna," the letter read. "I'd like to say I'm sorry for leaving, but I can't. I'm not sorry. You're fucking crazy. I hope there's someone alive out there, someone you can travel with, but it's not me. I advise you to travel. If we found the house, somebody else will find the house. Don't stay there. I haven't left you unprotected. I found a .38-caliber pistol and ammunition in the upstairs master bedroom closet. I put it in the middle of the bed. Please take it with you, and be safe. Karl Derking."

Hmm, Jenna thought. *I didn't know his name was Derking.* She closed the laptop, drank the milk and last few flakes of soggy cereal out of the bowl, and threw the bowl against the wall, shards of it scattered across the floor and table. Jenna giggled like Betty Rubble and got up. There was something important in the upstairs master bedroom and she was going to try it out. She'd found a bikini in the chest of drawers a few days ago and she wanted to go swimming.

"Stupid Karl," Jenna screamed into the cloudless sky as she lay on an inflatable raft floating in the concrete pool, the hot July sun shining down on her, a margarita in her hand. She laughed for a long time.

A few hours later, Jenna determined the Nissan handled better after she'd had a few margaritas. It was late afternoon by the time she got out of the pool, and dark before she ate dinner, packed food for the next few days, and took along a few nice things she found in the Peckinpa house (they had such good taste). The dark didn't really bother her tonight. Besides, it's not like she had to drive with her lights on. The bright, full moon shone on Jenna's part of North America, the long, straight stretch of U.S. 71 she pulled onto from the Peckinpa's gravel lane glowed blue in the moonlight. She gunned the Nissan and zipped toward Kansas City, the glow of the still working city lights filled the horizon. She hoped to see the Porsche wrapped around a tree, and Karl bruised and bleeding standing on the side of the highway, begging for a ride she wouldn't give; but she didn't see it. No Porsche, no Karl. Soon, an exit for a mall went by, then the zoo. She hoped some dying idiot, blood gushing from his face, didn't let the animals loose as his last act of compassion. As she pulled onto the onramp to Interstate 435, she smiled as she thought of a rhinoceros lumbering across the road, or a … a flash of movement. Jenna slammed on her brakes and pulled the wheel tightly to the left. The movement skittered and danced in front of the Nissan that hit it hard, the thud ran through Jenna's body. The car's driver-side air bag popped open, and pinned Jenna to her seat as the Nissan spun to a stop in the middle of the interstate.

She pushed against the air bag, trying to catch her breath that came in quick, heavy gasps. What the hell was that thing? It wasn't a rhinoceros; too small. It wasn't a person; wrong shape. As the air bag deflated, and Jenna sat panting, she saw lights. Headlights. And they pulled up behind her. Jenna pushed the slowly shrinking air bag to the side and fumbled for her purse. It had fallen to the floor. Her heart pounded in her chest, so loudly she thought she could hear it. Wallet, sunglasses, phone, gun. She grabbed the loaded .38 and swung toward the door, thrusting the nose of the pistol out the open window.

"Whoa there, little missy," a calm, genial voice said in the darkness. "We're all friends here. No need for that kinda hardware." The voice stopped for a second. Jenna heard a deep breath. "I'm going to turn on a flashlight, now, and show you who we are. Please don't think I'm just trying to give you a better target."

"You think that's a good idea, Doug?" a shaky voice said from the darkness. "I kinda like not getting shot."

The soft click of the flashlight switch was loud in the empty city night, a yellow light shined into the face of a man in a mechanic's shirt, the name Doug written across the right breast in red stitching. Jenna thought it was a kind face. "Okay," Doug said, holding up his other hand palm out. "I'm now going to show you Terry. Terry, are you ready?"

"I think I might throw up," Terry said in the night as the light washed over him. Jenna thought this face was kind, too, and kind of drunk. Probably so. He held a can of Natural Light. The world either had come to an end, or was seriously swirling down the shitter, and this Terry guy was still drinking Natural Light. Jenna grinned. Terry looked too frightened to be dangerous.

"My name's Jenna," she said, and pulled the .38 back inside the car.

"Pleased to meet you, Jenna," the man with the Doug shirt said, bringing the light back on himself. "We're up from Paola, Kansas. Nobody's left there. We're trying to find somewhere safe."

"Me, too," Jenna said through the open window.

"What happened?" Doug asked.

A beer can snapped open to Jenna's left. She could only assume Terry felt better.

"Well," she said. "I met this guy named Karl and we hung out for a couple of days, then he dumped me. I ..."

"No," Doug interrupted. "I mean what happened here. To your car?"

"Oh, uh, I hit something. Something big. Not like rhinoceros big, but big."

"Are you okay?"

"Yeah," Jenna said. "Just kinda pissed off."

Doug smiled. She liked his smile. It seemed natural, genuine, nice. Jenna put the pistol back in her purse and slung the strap over her shoulder. "I'm going to get out now," she said, and pushed open the door, a few aches in her body from the impact telling her she would be sore as hell in the morning. In the combination of flashlight and moonlight, Jenna could see Doug standing in the highway, as Terry leaned against their pickup drinking a beer. She didn't think these guys were dangerous, but then again she didn't think Karl was going to be a complete dick. At least they weren't like the others she'd seen wandering aimlessly with bloody faces, or the dead ones sprouting mushrooms. "I don't trust you yet."

"I don't blame you," Doug said, then turned to Terry. "Hey, go see what she hit. It might be a deer. Deer sounds good tonight."

Terry drained his Natty Light and tossed the can onto the highway before he reached into the bed of Doug's truck and pulled out an aluminum softball bat. "You got it boss," he said, and disappeared behind Jenna's car.

"What's he going to do?" Jenna asked.

"Finish what you started, for one thing," Doug said. "Get us supper for another."

Jenna slid her hand into her purse and fingered the butt of the gun. "What if it's not a deer?"

Doug smiled again. "What else do you think it's gonna be? A mountain lion?"

A scrambling in the brush next to Jenna's car brought Jenna and Doug around. "Boss," Terry shouted as he ran up the onramp embankment and slid across the crinkled hood of Jenna's Nissan. "It's not a deer, it's a mountain lion. A goddamned mountain lion. We need to go."

July 6: St. Joseph, Missouri
CHAPTER 9

Five days. Dad has been gone five days. Nikki walked around the house, picking up Gene Holleran's things and just holding them; his coffee mug, his old GameBoy (57 years old and he still loved his Tetris), his St. Joe Mustangs baseball cap. She brought the cap to her face and breathed in. It still smelled like Dad. A tear ran down her face; Dad was gone. Nikki had helped Dr. Davault zip him into a black body bag and carry him through the emergency room door of St. Joseph Regional Hospital. They stacked him with the rest. Was his body moving like the others? she wondered. Dr. Davault told her it would, but Gene Holleran wasn't alive anymore, his limbs just didn't know it. Something, whatever was killing the infected, kept them going for a while before they dropped. Their brains didn't know anything; they were dead, but something foreign inside the body kept it moving, trying to go somewhere. Dr. Davault had mentioned something about Ophiocordon and a Southeast Asian fungus, or had he? Nikki drove home crying that night, like she was now, tears streamed from both eyes as she breathed in her father's scent; sobs came in short, quick bursts. Dr. Davault didn't know what was going on, but he did know only the people who'd taken the new antidepressant had come down with the Outbreak. One thing he did reassure her of, he told her these walking dead were not zombies.

Nikki had done little in those five days, her term paper long forgotten. And why not? Her instructor at the community college stopped responding to her emails. Mr. McFee was probably lying across his desk in a bloody mess, his hand still grabbing his pecker. Nikki saw the way he looked at the skinny girls in class, like they were part of a harem. She figured the Outbreak came to him while he jerked off to some girl's spring break photo album on Facebook; maybe he was still moving, jerking off with a cold, dead, gray fungus-covered hand. Nikki was glad she never had to see that letch again. She laughed as she wiped the tears away with the front of her T-shirt. At least the Outbreak was good for something. Or was it an outbreak after all? News reports shifted from a virus to Judgment Day; it did look like the dead were rising from the grave, if only to wander the streets a few days then drop to the pavement, some kind of gray fungus quickly consumed their bodies. The news channels died about the time the discussion turned to the fungus. Nikki had seen the fungus herself, sprouting from bodies in the streets like mushrooms from hell. Conspiracy bloggers had started writing about some crazy shit. Ophiocordon, linking it to some fungus in Thailand that turned ants into zombies, then they just stopped posting. Nikki could only assume the bloggers were dead.

"I gotta stop doing this," she said, speaking aloud for the first time in days, the sudden noise filled the room. Tears started to well again, but she pushed them back. She needed something to do, a purpose. Nikki showered and changed into clean clothing. She knew what she needed to do, no, had to do – gather everything that was important to her, truly important, pack it in the Harley's trailer, and get the bike ready to leave. Dad was too afraid to keep the lights on at night, too afraid the survivors he called Leftovers would see, too afraid the Leftovers would be the bad people who always seem to survive a tragedy. He'd been afraid for her.

The Harley was Dad's pride. An Electra Glide like all the old gray-haired men drove, with built-in saddlebags and strong enough to pull the small trailer he'd bought to go with it. Gene had told Nikki for years he'd bought the trailer to take her camping, but they'd never gone. She knew why he really bought it. As soon as she graduated college, got a big girl job, and left the house, he was going to drive that thing all over North America. Gene had never seen the Rocky Mountains, and he wanted to camp by a glacier and chip chunks off the ancient ice for his gin and tonic. Nikki smiled as she stacked a box of photo albums atop a pile of winter clothes. She didn't consider the albums frivolous; they were her life. The pup tent was next, along with a small gas stove and stainless steel cooking gear, a machete, and Dad's box-o-stuff; Fix-A-Flat, tire punch kit, spare spark plug, oil, a can of gas, and other mechanical things Nikki hoped to figure out how to use if she needed them. The rest of the space in the trailer she left for food and water jugs, the Coleman cooler already packed, filled with a half-gallon of soon-to-be expired milk, butter, seven eggs, and a package of olive loaf.

She walked back into the kitchen from the attached garage and opened the cabinets, pulling out what was left of the non-perishable food in the house. There wasn't much. Two jars of peanut butter, and cans of beans, tomatoes, tuna, and pumpkin pie filling. *Did anyone ever use that?* She slid them all into a canvas bag, and included a few boxes of macaroni and cheese, stuffing, saltine crackers, and store brand Hamburger Helper, although she didn't know where she would get hamburger. She laughed out loud for the first time in days, her sudden outburst caused her to laugh more, remembering Cousin Eddie telling Clark Griswold in Dad's favorite movie, *National Lampoon's Vacation*, "I don't know why they call this stuff Hamburger Helper. It does just fine by itself." Yeah, Cousin Eddie, it'll have to. Nikki grabbed the handles and carried the bag to the garage, put it into the trailer, and shut the door tight. She was ready, although she didn't know where she was going. Hooligans, first, maybe, she thought. To see if anyone was there. Then north. Some high school friends attended school about an hour north in Allenville; she could try there. After that, she didn't know.

Nikki walked through the house for one last look. One last look at her bedroom, Johnny Depp, most probably dead somewhere in France, stared at her with his smoldering eyes; her father's bedroom, pictures of her long-dead mother still sitting exactly where she'd put them years ago. She walked down the stairs, tears began again, as she stepped into the living room and stood in front of her father's chair, his Mustangs hat sat on the armrest. She picked up the hat, adjusted it for her head, and slid it on. "Good-bye, Dad," she whispered. "I love you." Nikki turned toward the kitchen and the garage door, ready to leave all she'd ever known behind. A thud sounded on the front door. Nikki turned to see a gloved hand smash through the door window and feel blindly for the lock. Nikki screamed, the piercing noise echoed throughout the house. The hand found the handle and turned. The door slammed open, and more broken glass hit the floor.

A man stood in the doorway, a greasy man, food and beer stains soaked into his once white Megadeth T-shirt. "We-hell," the greasy man said. "Looky, looky what we have here. A little present for Danny Boy." He took a step into the house, Nikki's house, a place that was supposed to be safe. "Don't worry, porky," Greasyman said. "I won't hurt you too bad."

Nikki screamed again and ran. Living room gave way to dining room. "Oh-ho," Greasyman shouted behind her. "I like ones with a little spunk in them."

Nikki tipped the dining room chairs over behind her, to slow the Leftover down, and looked around her for something, anything to grab. 'There's one in my red toolbox in the garage. Second drawer, behind the ratchet set,' Gene Holleran whispered in her ear. She knew what he meant, just as she knew the voice wasn't really her father; it was just his memory. The gun, the pistol in the toolbox. 'Take it. And if someone comes to get you, shoot them. Shoot those bastards dead.' Nikki shot through the garage door, slammed it and locked it behind her. Greasyman crashed into it. It didn't budge. Nikki scrambled for the big red toolbox and pulled open the second drawer, just as the sound of glass breaking made her wince a second time.

"Hey, hey, little lady," Greasyman said from behind her, the door smashing open. "You're a slick little thing. I don't want to hurt you, baby. I just want to talk."

Nikki's right hand fell on the grip of the pistol. She grabbed it hard, pulled it out of the drawer and swung around, the barrel pointed at Greasyman's chest. She'd never fired a weapon before; her hand shook, so she grasped the gun with both hands. Greasyman stood about ten feet away. She doubted she'd miss at that range. From the look on his face, she knew he doubted it, too.

"Whoa, now," he said slowly. "I'm just up for a little fun and games, missy. No need to be waving that piece around."

Nikki pulled back the hammer with her thumb like she'd seen so many times on television, the click deafening in the small garage. "This is my house," she said, the words coming out quietly, but sharply. "You will turn around slowly, put your hands behind your back, and leave my house. I will be behind you every step. If you run, if you try anything funny, I will blow your fucking brains out."

"Now, honey," Greasyman said, holding his hands in front of him. "There's no ..."

"Fucking do it," she screamed.

Greasyman turned slowly and put his arms behind his back. "Now grab your right wrist with your left hand, and walk." She followed him on shaky legs through the kitchen, the dining room, and the living room, hoping like hell they didn't betray her and send her to the floor. Greasyman stepped onto the front porch and walked down the steps. "Get into your car and get the hell out of my neighborhood." Once down the steps, the man bolted toward his car, a brand-new Corvette Nikki was sure he'd driven right off the lot. Two people stood in the street, bobbing back and forth on their barely moving legs. A body lay on the sidewalk in front of Old Mr. Jennings' house next door, a gray, bulbous knob on a stalk rising from its chest. Thailand ants? Fungus?

Greasyman threw open the car door and jumped inside. "I'll be back, little missy," the greasy Leftover shouted through the open car window. "And you're goin' down. I ain't gonna be nice about it." Her finger squeezed the trigger out of reflex, but the gun didn't fire. She didn't have the strength. Greasyman fired up the engine of the stolen Corvette and tore down the street, his left hand flipped the bird through the open driver's side window as he swerved to clip a shambling man in jeans and a T-shirt, and disappeared around a corner.

Nikki dropped to her knees, the world swam around her, the acrid taste of vomit grew in her mouth. She swallowed.

"You don't have time for this, Holleran," she said softly. "You don't have time." Using the porch railing, Nikki pulled herself back to her feet. The house seemed dangerous to her as she hurried through the place she had grown up, it looked alien, filthy, harmful. Nikki hurried to the garage door and heaved it up, the chain creaking like it always had. "Gotta put some WD-40 on that," Dad had said every time he opened the door, but he never did. Nikki put the pistol back in the toolbox behind the ratchet set and slid the drawer shut; she didn't need the gun. Nikki knew she wouldn't shoot anyone. She couldn't, even though she knew the Piper had done more than <u>kill</u> almost everyone; the rest, the Leftovers, had all gone crazy.

July 6: Kansas City, Missouri
CHAPTER 10

Just from the few minutes he'd known Jenna, Doug could tell she was a sweet girl, and pretty. Probably pretty; it was kinda dark. He couldn't tell much more about her because Terry wouldn't shut the hell up. "That sucker was big," Terry said, giggling and opening another Natty Light, foam shot onto his shirt. "I mean, I've seen a mountain lion before, at the zoo, but damn." He took a long pull from his beer, and shook his head. "Whoo-wee. And it was movin', too. Thing wasn't dead."

"Terry," Doug said.

"It was twitchin' like it was tryin' to wake up."

"Terry."

"You should have seen the head on that thing."

"Terry," Doug barked, his voice loud in the pickup cab. "It's over. It's gone. And we have a guest."

Terry looked at Jenna who sat between the two men. "Geez, I'm sorry, ma'am," Terry said. "I just. It was. You know? Big."

Jenna smiled, her face looked like something from a Sears catalogue. Doug wondered what the rest of her looked like. "It's okay," she said. "I'm the one who hit it, remember?"

Terry laughed and took another drink of beer. "Hey," he said, his face growing serious as he pointed out the windshield. "Look at that." Nearby lights popped from between the thick growth of trees on the onramp. They glowed even brighter than the full glow of Kansas City that stretched across most of the horizon. It was something big, something close. "It's the ballpark," Terry said. "One of them. Kauffman and Arrowhead are just over that hill on I-70. Somebody left the lights on, man. Let's go see."

No. No. No. The plan all along had been to hit I-435 and go to the shelter at Worlds of Fun. If there were any survivors, what place would be better to find them than an amusement park? Terry knew the plan. Hell, he'd come up with it. On second thought, Doug realized, maybe the plan wasn't so good after all. What the hell? "All right, all right," Doug said, putting on his turn signal at the sign that read 'I-70 East: St. Louis' only out of habit. Turn signals were important.

"Shit yes," Terry hooted and reached to Jenna for a high five that never came. He pulled his hand down, slowly.

"We'll drive by the stadium," Doug said, turning off the pickup's headlights. "I'm not going to promise we'll stop."

"I want nachos," Jenna said. "Oh, and a hotdog."

"Hell, yes," Terry hooted, slapping the dash of Doug's pickup.

There weren't any fucking nachos and there weren't any fucking hotdogs. Doug knew that. There probably were things that looked like nachos and hotdogs, but by now they were covered in fur, like most of the bodies Doug had seen since they pulled out of Paola. "We're going to drive by," Doug reiterated. "And see why the lights are on."

Terry bounced in his seat. "Yeah, boys," he said, giggling.

Oh, shit. Terry's gone past his limit. "If it looks dangerous," Doug directed at Terry. "I'm not even turning in."

"But I wanna go in," Jenna said, quietly, her face somewhat sad in the glowing green dash light. "I've never been to a baseball stadium before, and now I may never get the chance."

Damn it.

Doug pointed the pickup up the off ramp and onto Blue Ridge Boulevard; the road curled around the Truman Sports Complex revealing the lights of Kauffman Stadium that bathed the still green baseball field in light. No one moved on the field, or in the stands, at least from what Doug could see. He knew this was wrong. This fully lighted Major League Baseball stadium in a city of mostly dead fuzzy people could only serve as one thing – a beacon.

"We gotta get outta here," he whispered. No one wanted to hear.

"I want a Coke," Jenna said, not trying to choke back her giggles. "And peanuts. I really, really want peanuts."

"And popcorn," Terry shouted. "Pop fucking corn."

Doug pulled to the side of the road and stopped the truck, Kauffman Stadium at their right looking like a prom date.

"Guys," he said, turning to face Jenna and Terry. "We're alone, right?" They nodded their heads. "The people who protect us, like cops, and the military, are probably all dead, right?" They nodded again. "And we know there are people out there, probably crazy as shit, who might fuck us, or kill us, or fuck us while they kill us, or kill us while they fuck us, right?"

"Yeah, man," Terry said. "It's all true, Doug. What's that have to do with me eating a hotdog?"

"And peanuts," Jenna chirped.

Doug shook his head and put the truck back into drive. "I'm going to regret this." The pickup rolled down the asphalt lane toward the stadium, past an abandoned commuter bus, the back half blackened by fire, and through a line of empty booths, the signs of "Parking: $20" rolled by, the lack of people in blue and white uniforms waving him toward the parking lot obvious. Doug stopped the truck in the middle of the road; the three stepped out, and walked toward the stadium.

"That guy was my dad's hero," Terry said as they walked beneath the bronze statue of three-time hitting champion George Brett, the only Kansas City Royal in the Major League Baseball Hall of Fame; like that meant anything now.

"I was little, but I saw him play," Doug said softly, not out of respect, but out of fear. The lights of the stadium were bright, but black patches of shadow loomed everywhere. They could be packed with monsters that looked like people. "It was in his last years, but he still played balls out." Doug paused for a moment. "Sorry, Jenna. I'm used to talking to Terry."

She giggled, the sound raked against Doug's nerves. Whoa, that laugh was painful.

"Let's go eat," she said, way too loudly for Doug, and dashed toward the gate.

"Jen…" Doug started to call, but knew it wouldn't do any good. He could already tell she was stubborn. He jogged after her, Terry behind him. Doug found her in front of a concession stand, the lights on, the TV above the spot where the lines would form showed a baseball game. The uniforms were archaic. Must be on a loop, Doug thought.

"Shit, yes," Terry hooted, and slid over the stainless-steel counter like he hadn't drunk eight beers in the past hour and a half. He leaned toward them and raised an eyebrow. "What can I get you?"

Jenna giggled again. *Damn, girl,* Doug thought. *We're going to have to watch Titanic or something to sadden you up a bit. That giggle's going to kill me.* "I want a hotdog, good sir," she said flatly, then giggled again. Terry pulled open the shiny metal lid to the hotdog tray and steam rolled out.

"Whoo-we," he said. "There be hotdogs here."

"I wouldn't eat those," Doug warned.

Terry grabbed a pair of plastic tongs; "Armour" stamped on the side, and pulled a hotdog-shaped, foil-wrapped lump from the tray. "Why not?" Terry asked. "It says July 6. It's written right on the foil in Sharpie."

"What's today," Jenna asked.

Doug looked at his wristwatch. "July 6."

Terry grinned and tossed Jenna a warm hotdog in a bun. She giggled as she caught it. Terry pulled mustard and ketchup from the refrigerator and put them on the counter, then took the last two hotdogs from the warming tray. "Want one?" he asked, looking at Doug.

No. No. No. We can't eat those, ran through Doug's head. Who's here? Whose hotdogs are these? Why the hell are they even here? WE CAN'T EAT THESE. But, damn, he could smell the one Jenna was gobbling at like a porn star, and couldn't help it anymore. This might be the last fresh hotdog on Earth. A grin slowly crawled across Doug's face. "Sure do, buddy." Terry didn't hear him; he was busy pouring Jenna a Coke, the soda foaming quite nicely. Doug reached onto the counter and grabbed the last hotdog himself. "Get me a beer while you're back there, Terry."

They walked around the corner from the concession stand, the stadium spread out before them. Rows of royal blue seats, enough to hold the butts of 40,000 screaming fans, sat empty; although after the Royals won the World Series in 1985 and the team forgot how to win, since then it had been more like 16,000 indifferent people eating expensive peanuts. Sure, they finally won the World Series again in 2015, but attendance might be a little down this year.

"This is pretty cool," Jenna said, taking a sip of Coke. "But this is going to get really boring, really fast."

"It might not," Doug said. He held up his right hand, and took a step forward. Images ran across the Jumbotron; a baseball game. The same old uniforms that were on the television at the concession stand. He looked across the field; the grass that should have been knee-high by now was neatly trimmed. "Somebody's here."

"Whatever, dude," Terry said, the grin on his face showing the number of beers he'd consumed.

"No," Doug hissed. "Somebody's here. The hotdogs, the lights, the mowed grass, the game on the Jumbotron. This shit ain't because of the baseball fairy."

"Oh, yeah," Jenna said. She stepped in front of Doug, and pointed toward home plate. "There he is."

Doug and Terry grew hush as they stepped even with Jenna; she stood with her right hand on her hip and drank Coke from a straw. Someone sat in the bottom row, right behind home plate, wearing a blue baseball cap. "Holy, shit," Terry whispered, turning away from the field. "What are we going to do?"

"Are you fucking kidding me," Doug said. He didn't ask. "You insisted on coming here. You ate this guy's hotdogs. Now you're worried about the situation? How do you think Jenna feels? Jenna? Jenna? Where'd she go?"

Terry looked around. "She's down there," he said, pointing toward the man in the blue hat. "She's walking toward him and, noooow, she's sitting with him."

Panic played with Doug's chest, poking it, pulling it, stretching it like Silly Putty. "What's he doing?" Doug asked. He'd just met Jenna an hour before, and to him she'd become his responsibility. What if...

"He's offering her popcorn," Terry said.

Doug grabbed Terry's shoulder with his free hand, and clutched his beer in the other. "And what's she doing?"

"Eating it," he said, shrugging off Doug's hand. "I'm going down there. I want popcorn, too."

Doug clutched the beer Terry poured him and marched down the concrete steps.

Jenna had already found the man's name was Johnny. When Doug reached the bottom of the row he folded his arms and nodded at the man. Thin, gray hair stuck out from the man's Kansas City Royals baseball cap, a powder blue jersey hung off him like he weighed nothing. "How long you been here?" Doug asked.

Johnny shrugged. "A month or so," he said, his voice soft, raspy. "It's easy to lose track of time when time doesn't mean anything."

Deep. "My name's Doug. You've already met Jenna and Terry." Doug took a slow drink of beer and wiped his mouth with the back of his hand. "Anybody else around here we should know about?"

Johnny shook his head and smiled. "Just me," he said. "Just me and my baseball."

"Yeah, there, Johnnyball," Terry said through a mouthful of popcorn. "What the hell are you doing here, anyway?"

The man smiled. "Johnnyball. I like that." He took a small handful of popcorn from the nearly empty box and popped one kernel into his mouth. "When the Outbreak hit, teams stopped playing baseball, networks showed an old game here and there – 'classic' games. But the networks went away, too." Johnnyball coughed, the sound came from deep inside his frail chest.

"So you came to the ballpark," Doug said. "You figured if anywhere had baseball, it would be here." Johnnyball nodded. "You were right." Doug paused, picking over his next words carefully. "Listen, Johnny ..."

"You don't look so good, Johnnyball," Terry said. "You dyin' or something?"

Damn it, Terry. Damn it, damn it, damn it. Tact, man, tact.

"Cancer," Johnny said, waving him off. "From years of smoking. I knew it was going to happen sooner or later. So I came here. My wife and family are gone; the Outbreak got them. I at least got them in the ground before they started sprouting mushrooms, and I wanted to die someplace happy."

Doug stole a look at Jenna expecting to see tears; there were none. She saw him look at her and smiled. "Hey, Johnnyball," she said. "You need anything?"

Johnny looked into the now empty popcorn box. "You could get me a refill," he said, and handed her the white and red striped box. She took it and scampered up the concrete steps; Doug fought to keep his eyes off her bouncing bottom. He failed. Doug turned to Johnny.

"Is there anybody else here?" he asked.

Johnnyball shook his head. "No, not since the people who burned the bus on the entryway came through. I heard them coming, heard the gunshots. I locked myself in one of the luxury boxes and watched them come down the stairs, and run out onto my field. One of them peed. Two of them fornicated," he said, spitting the words. "Fortunately, it was in the daytime so they didn't know I was here. They didn't stay long."

Doug nodded and looked deeply into Johnnyball's eyes, the whites yellowed and crisscrossed with veins, the blue iris washed pale. "Johnny, most of the people out here, the ones of us still alive are probably like those people who burned the bus," he said. "Do yourself a favor and turn off those lights."

He coughed again. "No," he said, wheezing. "I'm going to finish the '85 season before I die. I want to see the Royals win the World Series."

"Then I guess you're not coming with us?" Jenna asked, walking down the last few steps to her seat and plopping down beside Johnnyball.

"No," he said. "I'm only on game 39. It's May 24 and they just opened a three-game home stand against the White Sox. I've got a lot of season to go." He patted Jenna's knee and smiled. "I do appreciate you stopping by for a visit, but I have work to do."

"You sure?" Doug didn't know why he asked; a cancer-stricken old man would only hold them back.

"Yes," Johnnyball said, waving them off. "Help yourself to beer and nachos on the way out. I put the cheese on right before the 'National Anthem.' It should be ready by now. Shoo."

They walked back to the truck in silence, stopping at the concession stand long enough to fix nachos, pour beer, and grab a case of peanuts. There were plenty, and Johnnyball didn't look like he ate much. Terry leaned on the truck, his nachos gone before they left the stadium. He took a drink of beer and sighed. "Is there anything we can do for him?"

Doug shook his head. "Nothing other than this. He knows what he's doing."

"Is Johnnyball going to be all right?" Jenna asked, a glob of orange cheese on her cheek.

"Nope," Doug said, popping the last chip in his mouth. "Not at all."

July 7: Topeka, Kansas
CHAPTER 11

It was about 5 a.m. the third day after Darryl had met Maryanne when he realized he was no longer in control of his life. He stared at the snow playing through the fuzz and dust on the cheap motel television screen, a half-full bottle of Ten High wedged between his legs. Darryl almost felt tired, but he couldn't go to sleep. Not anymore. Not now, anyway. The ride wasn't over yet, nor were the amphetamines she kept him on. Darryl sat in bed, leaning against a fake headboard nailed to the thin motel wall, listening to the sound of running water trying to drown out the television hiss. Maryanne Davies was in the shower again. She had been in there an hour, at least. Darryl was sure the woman had a phobia about being dirty. She was always in the water, scrubbing. It must be the blood, he thought. That stuff was hell to wash off. Darryl wondered if the Piper had driven her mad, but he had to admit to himself that it wasn't sanity that caused him to stay with Maryanne the past two days. When Maryanne popped out of the shower, a towel wrapped around her, she just looked too damned good for Darryl to really care about anything. The water stopped. Darryl took another pull from the Ten High bottle and waited for her to stalk into the bedroom.

Darryl Cousins walked down a stretch of Interstate 70 that led to Kansas City when he met Maryanne, her dirty brown LeBaron the first car Darryl had seen since his own piece of shit had died outside Salina, Kansas. He'd pointed his car toward Kansas City, Missouri, from Goodland, Kansas, to escape, to run. The Outbreak, or whatever in the hell it was, had hit hard in Western Kansas, and everything, everyone Darryl had ever known was gone, dead. He didn't think about anyone much anymore, Darryl figured if he did, he might go off and join them. All he wanted to do was get to Kansas City, Missouri; Denver was closer, but that was out. The Air Force had dropped bombs on it. At least that's what somebody passing through Goodland said. The LeBaron had squalled to a stop beside Darryl. The driver side door swung open and a female voice said, "Hop in."

Darryl slid into the driver's seat, the upholstery still warm, but he didn't expect anything like Maryanne. She looked like a high fashion model with a blond ponytail dressed in skin-tight polyester. The pants were white and spotted with blood, her T-shirt dirty and sweat-stained, but nobody was too picky about clothes anymore. He didn't know it, but that was the last time he'd ever see her dirty.

"Can you drive?" She asked, her ponytail dancing as she spoke. Darryl nodded. The girl smiled with a mouth full of white teeth. "Good," she said, her voice close to a laugh. "Let's go."

He put the car's transmission in drive and started west. A highway sign, the white on green letters pocked by shotgun blasts, read *Kansas City 175 miles*.

"Are you going to Kansas City?" Darryl asked. Maryanne's face suddenly appeared in front of his, blocking his view of the road.

"No talk," she said, smiling. "Just drive." The girl ducked toward his lap and unzipped his denims. "If you see an open gas station," she said. "Stop." The girl grabbed him with delicate, sure fingers and gave him head as he drove. When Maryanne finished, she laid her head in his lap and slept. That's why Darryl was still with Maryanne. She did anything, and she did it a lot.

The sound of running water slowed to a drip and Maryanne came out of the bathroom moving like a cat, her long, smooth legs ready to pounce. She wore a towel, holding it in front of her like a bullfighter, and she danced for Darryl. But, Darryl figured she'd probably dance like that for anyone, he just happened to be one of the lucky few left alive. He wondered what she'd been like before everyone started to die, walk around, then die again. Probably still crazy

"Are you ready?" Maryanne said as she crawled across the rickety motel bed on her knees, the towel still draped over her. She smiled at Darryl, looking to him like a hungry lioness. Her eyes glared with a spark of excitement as she crept up to him and dropped her towel. He gripped the bottle of whiskey tighter as a warm flush rushed over him. Maryanne was beautiful, and she knew it. Her naked body was about as perfect as people could still get.

"Ready for what?" Darryl asked, glaring at the smooth, naked body that was kneeling so close to his own, his voice soft, low.

"To go see the killings," she said, a giggle capturing her attention. Maryanne's body moved with her laughter. That's all she'd talked about for the two days Darryl had known her. Well, that and sex. Since the day she picked him up and stopped at that gas station in Junction City, Maryanne scared the shit out of him.

"Hey, wake up," he'd said in the car, grabbing Maryanne's shoulder and shaking it gently.

Maryanne had sat up and yawned, rubbing her eyes with the backs of her hands like a child. Darryl watched her every move. Fluid, smooth. Maybe she'd been a dancer before the Outbreak, he thought, or a really expensive hooker. She looked at Darryl and smiled, her teeth seeming to glow in the dash light of the dusty car.

"Hiya, handsome," she said. "Why don't you get out and pump us some gas?"

A man stood in the doorway of the station as Darryl pumped premium unleaded into the tank. Darryl was surprised to see him, but anymore he was surprised to see anyone. Maryanne reached for something in the backseat, her butt stuck high in the air as she leaned into the open window. Darryl stared at it. Her ass was splattered with blood, too. He wondered what had happened to her.

"Whatcha got to pay for that?" the attendant asked. Darryl turned to him. The man, about six feet tall, was at least 50 pounds heavier than Darryl. He stepped out of the doorway and walked slowly to the car, a baseball bat, notched and scarred, in his thick, callused hands. "Don't take money no more. Shit ain't no good. I'm about out of gas, too. So it's gotta be somethin' I want."

"We've got something," Darryl heard Maryanne say. He hadn't seen her move, but she stood out of the passenger side of the car, and leaned against the LeBaron's roof. She looked at Darryl and winked before she stood straight and pulled up her shirt, her breasts bounced out of her bra. "This good enough for you?"

The man grinned as he stepped closer to the car, his clothes filthy; Darryl could smell the man's body odor as he stepped around to the front of the car. *No bath in a while, huh, Bubba?*

"You got something more than that, sugar?" he asked Maryanne. "'Cause he's pumping premium."

Maryanne pulled her shirt down and motioned for the man to step around to her side of the car. Darryl just stood and watched as Maryanne dropped back into the passenger's side and pulled a shotgun from behind the seat. The attendant's yellow, bloodshot eyes grew large as she brought the gun up and blew a red, ragged hole in his chest. He gurgled as blood swam into his ruined lungs, and he fell to the pavement.

Maryanne dropped the shotgun into the backseat and blew Darryl a kiss. "Gotta go shopping, honey," she said, walking toward the gas station office. "Could you wipe the bugs off the windshield while I'm gone?" Yeah, fucking crazy. She killed a guy and all she came back to the car with were candy bars.

They fucked before leaving the Super 8 motel in Topeka. Darryl didn't know where they were going other than Kansas City. Maryanne pulled on her bloodstained polyester pants and T-shirt she'd washed in the motel bathtub. Most of the blood had come out, some of the newer stuff anyway. She still fooled with her hair as he pulled out of the motel parking lot and headed back toward the highway. Kansas City was just an hour away. They drove in silence.

The skyline of Kansas City soon rose from what had once been prairie and cattle ground; but the city had grown since its Cowtown days, now a big spot of concrete on the western corner of Missouri. "Downtown," Maryanne said as Interstate 70 zipped through the cookie-cutter suburbs of Johnson County, Kansas, and into Missouri. "I want to see the fountains." Darryl took a drink out of the Ten High bottle as he drove onto an off-ramp and toward downtown Kansas City. He started to see shapes on the highway in the morning light, but he knew they weren't there. He hadn't slept since he met Maryanne, and the hallucinations were coming. Shadows danced across the highway. He wanted to sleep, but no longer thought he could. Maryanne snuggled close to him and kissed him on the ear.

"You're doing fine, baby," she whispered, holding the shotgun between her legs. "Just a little while longer."

Weeds, brown and thirsty, grew between the cracks of the downtown sidewalks. The LeBaron crawled around the husk of an overturned car burned black on Baltimore Avenue; paper blew in the streets. Darryl's family took a trip to Kansas City from Western Kansas when he was a boy; its downtown skyscrapers gleamed bright in the sunlight, and people hurried up and down the sidewalks. He remembered an old black man sitting at a Metro bus stop. The man smiled at Darryl as Darryl's father stopped at a traffic signal next to the bus stop, his teeth big and white. Darryl smiled back and waved. The man waved too, his bony elbows stuck out of the holes in his shirt. Darryl thought of the man as he drove through the deserted streets. *The Outbreak got him,* he thought. Or maybe the man was lucky. Maybe he'd already died.

"Slow down," Maryanne said, and slapped the dash with a palm, sending dust into the air. "Look at that." Darryl slowed the car. A sign, painted in red and white, hung over a Metro bus stop. "YOU LIVE OR YOU DIE," it read.

"My God," he whispered.

"Shut up," Maryanne screamed, the first traces of anger he'd heard in her voice, although she smiled like a hyena. "The killing's here. Can't you feel it? Can't you smell it? Don't you want it?" Maryanne bounced in the passenger seat, as excited as a teenager before a date. She stroked the barrels of the shotgun like she was jerking it off. Her face beamed. *What the hell am I doing?* Darryl wondered. He drank from the whiskey bottle and emptied it. But she was right, he could smell it. Death, sweet and pungent hung in the air, along with something. But what? What was the other smell?

"Drive," she said, slapping the dash again. "Just drive." The signs started coming by the dozens, hanging from abandoned Metro buses, mounted on buildings, spray-painted on the street. They saw the first body at 12th Street and Baltimore. The man was in his 20s, Darryl thought, just a few years younger than him. A thin wire, maybe an electrical cable, pulled tightly around his neck. His body, puffy, bloated, swung slightly in the wind as it hung from a lamppost. A rod stuck from his bare chest, the knot on the end burst open. Darryl had seen a few of these bodies on the highway after his car stopped working, and he started walking. He stood mouth agape as one of those knots grew like a blister under a dead woman's blouse and burst through the crease in the shirt, two buttons popped onto the pavement. Darryl didn't stick around to see any more; he ran until he thought his heart might burst. Darryl thought he might vomit. "There's another one," Maryanne screamed, pointing down the street. "Another bad citizen."

"And another," Darryl whispered. As far as he could see, gray, fuzzy bodies lined the road. They had been hanged from the lampposts. He could smell them now, raw, rancid, strangely sweet, but heady, like dirt. He took his foot off the LeBaron's brake pedal and touched the gas. The car moved down the street under the eaves of swinging bodies, things that looked like mushrooms grew from all the flesh he could see, all sporting one stalk, about two feet long, with what looked like a burst seed pod. He giggled as people appeared in the doorways of abandoned office buildings, and stared at them from insane eyes. Some of them had weapons. One man, gray-haired and grinning, gave Darryl the finger. "This is it," he said, the Ten High bottle slipped from between his legs and dropped onto the LeBaron's floor. "We're dead, baby."

He took the shotgun from the seat next to Maryanne, a moaning, bucking Maryanne, her hand down the front of her pants, masturbating. He laid the weapon across his lap.

Darryl punched the gas sending flies clinging to the swinging bodies buzzing off in waves. A crowd of people rushed from the shadows of the buildings and into the street behind them. Some fired shots that went wild. Some, Darryl saw in his mirror, shot each other. "Oh, yeah, baby," Maryanne screamed from the seat next to him. "Drive, drive, drive."

Darryl drove. By the time Maryanne had finished and fallen asleep, he'd pulled off Interstate 435 toward the amusement park Worlds of Fun, signs along the highway proclaimed "Survival Shelter." He sure as fuck hoped so. She was probably going to kill him one way or another.

July 7: Savannah, Missouri
CHAPTER 12

Tears dried on Nikki's cheeks as Gene Holleran's Harley-Davidson rumbled up Interstate 29. Everything she knew was gone. Sure, the buildings were there, and St. Joseph was just as friendly as it ever was with its darkened storefronts and danger at every corner, but everything important to her was gone, just gone. The Piper had taken most of it; her father, her friends, her civilization. The shit residue of people left behind took the rest. 'A little present for Danny Boy,' the Greasyman had said as he walked toward her, probably already sporting the beginnings of a hard on, as he stalked her in her house, her own house, a place she should have been safe.

'Don't worry, porky. I won't hurt you too bad.' *No, you won't, cocksucker. You won't hurt me at all.* Nikki pulled the bike toward an off ramp, an arrow on the billboard sporting "Jesse's Last Stand Convenience Store: 25-cent hotdogs" pointing to the west. The coward Bob Ford assassinated outlaw Jesse James in Nikki's town more than 110 years before she was born and people still used the name of that sociopath on everything, even convenience stores that sold Powerball tickets and quarter hotdogs. At least they used to. If she never heard the name Jesse James again, she'd be just fine.

The off ramp took her to Business U.S. 71 through the nearby town Savannah, home of the politically incorrect Savannah High School Savages, their American Indian mascot staring toward the sky as she drove by the high school. No one in the area thought twice about the name. Only people from places with too few things to occupy their time raised a fuss over the school mascot. If any were still alive they were busy running from the new breed of savages, none of whom were probably offended by the high school mascot. Savannah had been a fine enough town, a Subway, Dairy Queen, Pizza Shoppe restaurant; everything short of a Wal-Mart to keep it going. Now it was dead. Nothing moved in the streets, grass and weeds already grew between cracks in the asphalt. Nikki slowed the bike when a stoplight on Business U.S. 71 switched to yellow a block in front of her, her mind quickly calculated it would turn red before she reached it. A grin slowly crawled across her face as she gunned the bike and shot through the now-red light. There were no rules anymore, none but what you made yourself, and she didn't want to stop at a stupid red traffic light.

What did the rest of the world look like? she wondered, the drone of the Harley's motor somewhere in the back of her mind. Were the Chinese or the resurging Russians licking their chops at the thought of a desolate United States sitting across the water like a cheap buffet, ready for poor families to storm in and pick it clean? Or were they dead, too, lying in pools of their own blood, growing beards of gray fungus? Nikki wished she'd spent her time watching "16 and Pregnant" like Tammy and laid off Fox News and CNN, and she'd be more worried if Taylor and Nathan could ever patch it up for the sake of their baby, Aubri Rose, than knowing what was going on in the world. Being blind to life is easy. She gunned the bike and shot up Business U.S. 71, the Shop 'N Hop gas station was close to the highway on-ramp, and she had shopping to do.

A big Budweiser truck sat outside the Shop 'N Hop, a side door rolled up revealing box after box of Bud Light. The deliveryman lay face-first on the pavement, a lump on his back pushed against the gray material of his work shirt, six cases of beer spilled over the parking lot. Gene had come home one day after work grinning like a kid who'd just found a prize in the bottom of a cereal box, a couple of cases of beer in his arms. "These fell off a truck," he'd told Nikki's mom about three months before she died. "I flagged down the driver, but he told me if a can popped out of a six-pack ring, they couldn't sell it, so he gave this to me." Nikki's mom laughed and hugged her husband, not knowing a few months later a college student talking on a cell phone would drive her over in the street.

Nikki pulled into the convenience store parking lot and killed the Harley's motor; this northwest Missouri city that once housed 4,762 people dead quiet under the midday sun. A dog barked blocks away. Nikki hadn't heard a dog in a while; it didn't sound comforting. She slowly drew her leg over the seat of the Harley and stepped to the pavement on weak legs; weak not from the motorcycle, but from fear. What lay behind that plate-glass door of the convenience store that sat before her like the gates of hell? The Greasyman, his now full hard on fighting its way through his jeans, filled her mind. Was Savannah's Greasyman behind that door? Do I need to go in? *Yes, I do,* Nikki thought, answering herself. She needed more gas for the road, she needed more water than the milk jug she'd filled before leaving the house, and she needed tampons, or would soon enough.

A bell jingled when Nikki slowly pulled open the door, this absent background noise as loud as the Harley to Nikki in the small convenience store. She froze, waiting for the rush of a body toward her. It didn't come. She was alone. Nikki grabbed two cases of bottled water, a five-gallon gas can, and walked cautiously back to the parking lot. The bottled water slid easily into the trailer, and the pumps were still on. Sweat ran down Nikki's back, partly from the summer heat, partly from fear. Something was wrong here. She could feel it pressing against her like the heat from a fire. The can filled painfully slow with gasoline as she stood by the pumps, nervously scanning the city streets around her, the only noise in the still day the clicking of the gas pump, and the dog. The fucking dog had gotten closer. "Come on, come on," Nikki whispered under her breath. Two gallons, three gallons, four. Movement. The dog, a big brown mutt, sniffed its way around a small, pale yellow house. Nikki stood still, her breath came in shallow huffs. It crouched next to the porch and barked. A small brown ball scampered from under the steps and shot through the yard – a rabbit; the dog ran after it. "Shit," Nikki whispered, as gas gushed over the lip of the can and spilled onto the asphalt. She slid the gas handle back into its cradle with a click, screwed the lid on the can and set it in the trailer. Nikki couldn't see the dog anymore. She hoped it caught that sqwewy rabbit.

Nikki didn't notice the bell this time as she stepped back into the Shop 'N Hop, grabbed a basket and walked up each aisle, stuffing the basket with beef jerky, peanuts, pain relievers, coffee, chocolate, toilet paper, and cans of pork and beans, spaghetti, chili, beef stew, and chicken soup. She paused at the end of the aisle; something silver caught her eye. A can opener hung from a peg, the price tag read $2.45. Nikki smiled.

"Sorry guys," she said as she pulled the tool off the peg and dropped it in the basket. "That's a bit too steep. I'm going to have to shoplift." Nikki turned toward the door and froze, her breath stopped dead in her throat. A man, who was a banker by his nametag, loomed outside the door, his white shirt yellowed with sweat and spotted with blood, a red paisley tie hung loosely around his neck. He coughed, and red splattered the glass. Nikki's heart pounded against her chest; she screamed, the sound pierced the small room.

The Banker pushed open the door, his hand smeared blood across the glass. Nikki screamed again, the jingle of the bell hanging by a string off the door again driven to the background.

"Help me," he wheezed, as he tried to step forward, but stopped, holding the door to keep standing on shaky legs. "Help me."

"Stay back," Nikki screamed at the Banker, stepping back and hitting a display of Little Debbie's. Chocolate cream-filled cakes scattered across the floor behind her. The man's breath came heavy and hard, blood dribbled down his mouth, red spots appeared on his white shirt.

"I'm, uh, I'm dyin'," he said, gurgling.

He had the Outbreak, or whatever; that much was certain. Nikki wasn't afraid of the Outbreak anymore. She hadn't caught it from the fat businessman at Hooligans, she hadn't caught it from her own father, if it was something she could catch at all. She was beginning to buy the load from all the Internet bloggers. It was the antidepressant that infected people, like her dad.

"Stay away from me," she said, pointing at the Banker, her hand shaking. "You stay the hell away from me."

The man leaned against the door, pinning it open, and pushed a shaky hand into his pants pockets. He pulled out a pistol. Nikki took another step back, squishing a pack of Zingers beneath her sneakers. The man's eyes, rimmed red with blood, grew wide with surprise. He shook his head and coughed.

"No," he whispered. "I'm not. I'm. I'm. I'm not going to hurt you." He paused, breathing hard, his lungs sounded to Nikki like they were full of liquid. They probably were, Nikki knew, probably with blood. He held the gun in his open palm. "Kill me," he wheezed. "Please kill me."

"I…" Nikki started, and stood stock still as the Banker's legs collapsed beneath him and he dropped to the floor; the door slammed against his body that lay in the doorway, and held it open. Nikki stepped slowly toward the man, eyeing the gun next to him.

His eyes swam like a cheap doll's as he tried to focus. Nikki walked into his field of vision and he reached for her, she took a step back. "Ple… please kill me," he said. "We hid. We hid away. Away from the Outbreak. As long as we could." He paused to catch his breath. "But my wife, my daughter, she's in college. Dead. All dead. They moved for a while, but they, they didn't know me, they didn't know anything." He caught his breath again, this time it took longer, much longer. Tears of blood began to flow. "They're covered with something. Some kind of shit is growing on them. One of these ball things exploded and got all over me. I can. I can't live anymore." You won't, ran through Nikki's head as she stood, looking at the dying man, his left hand quivered dangerously close to the pistol. "Please."

She shook her head; tears ran from her eyes. "I can't," barely came out of her mouth. "I can't." Nikki gripped the handle of the basket and eyed the door pinned open by the Banker's body. She couldn't kill the Banker; she couldn't even kill the Greasyman. She knew she couldn't kill anybody. She walked slowly toward him, the Banker's entire body quivering now. Nikki stepped over the man, and walked through the open door.

"Puh. Puh. Please," came from beneath her. She lifted her leg over the dying man and set it flat on the pavement, exhaled, and ran to the

Harley. Nikki threw the basket into the trailer, slammed the door, and jumped onto the bike. She fired it up, covering the dying Banker's pleads with the motorcycle roar. Nikki slid her helmet over her brown, unkempt hair – something that didn't seem important anymore – and saw she wasn't alone. The dog, the big brown mutt, stood fifteen feet from her, its muzzle red from the rabbit bared toward her – its white teeth ominous.

"Fuck you, Fido," Nikki said between her teeth as she gunned the bike and went right at it, the beast scampered away from the motorcycle as it ran back toward the highway. She didn't look back, tears streamed down her face. Nikki knew what she'd see; the Banker getting his wish at the teeth of the feral dog.

Twenty miles later she realized she'd forgotten to grab Tampons.

July 7: Clarinda, Iowa
CHAPTER 13

Corn stood tall and green in the fields that spread across Nodaway Valley, running in long, straight lines, some with the highway, others away from it and up over the hills. Stacy Tracy thought the corn beautiful. Growing up in Philadelphia, the only cornfields he'd seen were 30,000 feet below him on flights to Des Moines on his way to visit family, or on late night infomercials about the twenty-disc DVD "Hee Haw" collection. Corn, to him, was something home-style restaurants served next to mashed potatoes. He knew enough, however, that these great, green, orderly fields that ran beside him would be a tangled jungle in a few years, corn playing host to weeds, grass, and trees that would soon retake the land. Stacy flew into Des Moines June 4, to spend the weekend with his family in Atlantic, Iowa, for Grammy's 80th birthday – then the Outbreak hit. Airplanes stopped running, soon after trains and buses, then people. Grammy lived to see her birthday before she died, dropping from her wheelchair onto her kitchen floor, her cake still at the grocery store, probably moldy or brittle as Styrofoam. Nobody in the family was alive to buy it; nobody except Stacy. He ran to the telephone in the living room and tried to call an ambulance, but no one answered. When Stacy turned back toward the kitchen, Grammy stood in the doorway, her always sharp eyes unseeing. She stood on legs she hadn't fully used in three years. She fell again, and didn't get back up. Stacy said a prayer over Grammy and buried her in the backyard next to the birdfeeder she loved to sit and watch on summer evenings. That was a month ago. The phone lines were down, the Internet was down, there was no way for him to get home except to drive. And who the hell wants to drive to Philadelphia? But he couldn't stay anymore – the food Grammy had squirreled away was nearly gone. He had to find more.

Stacy lashed a small trailer to the bumper of Grammy's 1996 Geo Metro with bailing wire and bungee cords, loaded it with empty gas cans he hoped to fill at the Sinclair station down the street, and water jugs he filled from the bathtub tap. He sat in the front seat, the small engine sending only a slight vibration through the cab, and slowly spun through the radio dial. Static, just static as he scanned FM. Stacy clicked the switch to AM and scanned again. In the 700s, a voice crackled through. "... shelter at Worlds of Fun. There is a survivor's shelter at the Worlds of Fun amusement park in Kansas City, Missouri. Food, beds, and water." More static, then it started again. "There is a survivor's shelter at the Worlds of Fun amusement park in Kansas City, Missouri..." Then it repeated, and repeated, and repeated. Automated, Stacy knew, but it was something. Kansas City, Missouri. Everyone back home was dead. They had to be; the people at his accounting office, Marcia with the great legs, the office manager Tim, and Denny – fucking Denny who ate out of everyone's lunch. The people in his life he knew were gone, too, like Tracie. He'd had three dates with Tracie, beautiful Tracie with bobbed, deep brown hair, green eyes flecked with gold, and a smile that did all but hypnotize him. They had a drink at the airport as he waited for his flight to Des Moines, his a domestic beer, hers an import, and Stacy teased her about being Tracie Tracy, married to Stacy Tracy. She'd laughed an honest laugh. Stacy didn't want her to be dead, but as he put the Geo in drive and drove toward the Sinclair station, then hopefully toward the Signal in Kansas City, he knew she probably was.

A white cat scampered across the city streets as Stacy made his way to the highway. No people though. He drove with the window down, hoping to hear something human. A car, music, a fight, anything. The Sinclair station where Stacy had bought beer on his first night in town loomed over him as he walked to the front door like something evil. Thoughts of men with knives, waiting for him between the aisles of Doritos and motor oil, ran through his head. His hand stopped when his fingers touched the metal door handle, still cool in the Iowa morning. He swallowed hard and pulled open the door. Someone – many someones – had cleared the Sinclair station of food and beer; a few stray water bottles and jugs of iced tea dotted the walk-in coolers, a package of cheese puffs sat on the floor. Someone had stepped on the bag of orange corn and grease, many times. Fine enough, Stacy hated cheese puffs. But at least the electricity was still on in town. He filled the gas cans and drove south.

An hour later there was only highway and corn, the occasional car or truck stopped on the highway, a decomposing body with tendrils of gray mold stretching over every piece of exposed skin slumped in the seat, the smell grabbing Stacy and holding onto him for miles. Nothing unnatural moved outside his windows as the car hummed south, nothing but birds and deer, their lithe, graceful bodies bounding away from the coming car, white tail up alerting danger. "Clarinda: 13 miles," a road sign read as he drove past Villisca, Iowa, home of the haunted Axe Murder House and not much else. When Poppy was alive, he and Grammy took twelve-year-old Stacy and his cousins to watch the minor league Clarinda A's play baseball, and they stopped by the Axe Murder House as a surprise on the way home, its Amityville Horror windows scaring the children too much for anyone to go inside. Stacy drove past the off ramp because there was no reason to see a haunted house. With the number of people the Outbreak had picked off, the whole fucking planet was probably haunted. But he slowed the Geo and turned off the highway to a Casey's convenience store. This was a small town; if the Outbreak hit Villisca like everywhere else, there probably weren't as many people to take all the food.

Fluorescent lights shone in the store as Stacy pulled open the door, a bell on a string alerting the empty building of his presence. Stacy froze. No movement. He was alone – except for the smell. As he walked cautiously through the store, boxes full of beef jerky and peanut packets sitting on the shelves alongside great bags of chips and popcorn, pizzas cooked probably a month ago sat on the still revolving glass-lined display, sat rotting. "Hello?" Stacy called. He was relieved when no one responded, grabbed a couple of trash bags from the back room, filled them with as much non-perishable food and water bottles he could, and hurried back to the car. He grabbed a twelve-pack of Budweiser just because.

A sea of trees in a valley hid Clarinda, Iowa, two water towers and the spire of the county courthouse the only indications of a town. "There is a survivor's shelter at the Worlds of Fun amusement park in Kansas City, Missouri. Food, beds, and water," crackled softly over the Geo's radio. Stacy left the radio on so he could at least hear a human voice, but kept it low and the car windows down. If some sound of living humans was out there, he wanted to hear it. "There is a survivor's shelter at the Worlds of Fun amusement park in Kansas City, Missouri. Food, beds, and water." The streets of Clarinda were clean, at least of trash, and abandoned vehicles. He slowly pulled the Geo to a stop in front of Clarinda's Single A baseball stadium, at least twenty cattle slowly ambling across the road. For the first time in a while, he smiled. Cattle. Cattle walking down a city street with no fences, no major predators, no worries. The moo shall inherit the earth. Stacy honked the Geo's muffled, high-pitched horn, sending a few head of cattle scampering off; most ignored the intrusion. "Hello?" Stacy yelled out the window, not at the cattle. "Is anyone there?" Silence. "Hello?" He drove away from the baseball stadium and toward downtown, calling out the car window every few blocks.

Trees decorated downtown Clarinda like it was the setting of a 1950s sitcom. Stacy pulled the Geo to a stop in the middle of the street in front of The Hunting and Sports Shop, a humming vending machine advertising live bait sat out front, although Stacy doubted how live the bait still was. "Hello?" he called into the afternoon, blue jays chattering at him from the tree boughs above him. Stacy turned off the Geo's engine and pocketed the keys.

"Hello?" he yelled again as he began walking around the square. "Is anyone there?" Fat red squirrels scampered across the sidewalk and into the tall, unmowed grass of the courthouse lawn in front of Stacy before bounding up tree trunks. No response. Stacy sat on a park bench, the growing heat of the young day breaking him into a slight sweat.

What the hell, man? ran through Stacy's head. Family's dead, friends dead, Tracie's dead, Atlantic's dead, and every fucking person in Clarinda's dead. Worlds of freaking Fun? Tears started to well in his eyes, loneliness clamping down on him like Vicegrips. What the fuck? Stacy started to wipe tears from his cheek with the back of his hand, but stopped dead still. Something moved. Stacy sat on the bench and watched. A head popped from the red brick corner of what was, until a month and a half ago, a restaurant, unlucky patrons probably right now rotting at their tables, more mushroom than man. Breath froze in Stacy's chest. It was a girl. She moved, tentative as a mouse as she came around the corner of the building and hid from Stacy's view behind a brown Ford F-150. This girl was the first person Stacy had seen since Grammy died. He had to talk with her.

She crept around the bed of the truck, not seeing Stacy on the park bench. Her focus was on the Geo, and why not? It was the stranger in town. As she crouched, studying this interloper, Stacy could see her full on. The girl was young, maybe thirteen or fourteen, her greasy brown hair hung around her dirty face like she'd been lost in the woods, and she had, woods of brick and concrete. This feral girl dropped to her hands and toes and crawled six feet from the back of the truck to the cover of a new Cadillac. The girl was skinny, Stacy saw, too skinny; the girl was alone in Clarinda. She had been fending for herself.

As the feral girl hid from his view behind the Caddy, Stacy glided from the bench and loped ten feet to the cover of a big maple tree on the courthouse lawn. He took a deep breath and peeked around the side of the tree. The feral girl hadn't seen him; her partial shadow unmoving on the pavement behind the car. She was just across the street. Stacy had run track once, long ago, and went to the gym a few times a week, trying to keep in shape. He had to talk with her and he thought if she ran, he could catch her. She was just a young girl, after all. He froze. She slunk around the back of the Cadillac, hiding herself from the Geo, but stepping slightly closer to where Stacy stood. She still didn't see him. Stacy swallowed, stepped out from behind the tree and spoke.

"Hi," he said.

The feral girl's face shot toward Stacy, the stark terror and pain on her face almost dragged tears out of him again.

"I'm not going to hurt you," he said, taking a step closer, his hands palms-up before him. "I'm here to help."

She remained for a second in a crouch, just a second, then bolted like a rabbit. "Shit," Stacy hissed and ran after her. The feral girl rounded the corner of the restaurant for a moment out of Stacy's sight. He dashed across the street, his tennis shoes slapping on concrete as he hit the sidewalk and followed her around the side of the restaurant. Another street spread out before him, her legs disappeared down the alley behind the restaurant. "Girl," he called after her. "I'm not going to hurt you. I have food. I want to help. Who else is here?" He swallowed and took a hard breath. "Who else is here?" Stark shadows hid in the corners of the alley, slowly disappearing under the growing morning sun. The girl ran before him, almost to the next street. "I want to help," he screamed. A stitch bit into his side when he popped onto the next street, the feral girl already three houses down a residential block. Stacy stopped, his hands on his knees and his breath coming in hard bursts; a month and a half away from the gym wearing hard upon him. The girl leaped over a garden fence and disappeared from his view.

"Damn it," he hissed and stood, the stitch biting deeper, then screamed, "Damn it. I'm here to help you."

Stacy stood in the street for ten minutes, then twenty. The feral girl didn't return. She was dirty, alone, and frightened. He wondered what had happened to her. "I'm going to Kansas City," he screamed into the late morning Iowa air. "There's a shelter there. A shelter with food and water and bathrooms. Won't you come with me?" A hawk cawed, momentarily breaking the silence. The girl was gone. He knew she wasn't coming back. Poor thing.

"I'm going to leave food and water on the street," Stacy yelled toward the garden fence where the feral girl had disappeared. "It's yours. I will stay here at my car for one hour. If you want to come with me, hopefully to safety, please come to my car. If not, the food's yours." And he walked back to the square. An hour later, Stacy Tracy drove south, a loaf of bread, six cans of tuna, a bag of Doritos, and two-quart water bottles sat in the street in front of the county courthouse. Dark clouds had crept onto the horizon as Stacy started the Geo and slowly drove south out of town. By nightfall, the food was gone.

July 7: Platte City, Missouri
CHAPTER 14

Rain rattled off the tin roof of the old barn like God was pissing marbles. The barn sat off a rural blacktop highway south of Platte City, Missouri, just close enough to hear if a vehicle drove by, just far enough away not to see it. Doug, Terry, and Jenna snuck into the barn about an hour and a half after they left Johnnyball sitting exposed in that big, lighted stadium that might have been visible from space for all they knew; Doug just hoped Johnnyball had enough sense to get inside, out of the rain. North of Interstate 70, they drove by the amusement park Worlds of Fun, big, homemade signs along the highway reading "Survivor Shelter."

"I fucking told you," Terry screamed out the truck window. Doug pulled the pickup off the highway and toward the entrance to the park, the skeletal frames of roller coasters and hulking buildings looking suspiciously abandoned in the cloud-filled night.

"This is pretty dark for a shelter," Jenna said as they went through the gates. Doug nodded his head, and Terry opened another beer. Cars dotted the vast lots of the amusement park; a random knotted mess of them clogged the park entrance. They avoided looking inside the vehicles afraid of what they'd find; furry gray masses that used to be human bodies.

"Wait here," Doug said as he stepped out of the pickup and grabbed a flashlight and baseball bat out of the truck bed. Terry and Jenna were happy to oblige. Doug came back five minutes later clutching a piece of notebook paper. "Nobody's here," he said, trying not to let the defeat creep out with his words. "The note says the few of them here all went to Omaha. Something about the military or something like that."

"Are we going?" Terry asked.

"What choice do we have?" Jenna more said than asked because she was right.

That was miles and miles away.

"Hey, there's a building over there," Terry had yelled at Doug as they pulled off the highway to wait out the downpour, a slight orange glow on the edge of the storm showing the A-frame building. "Looks like a barn, or something." Doug pulled down the dirt turning-to-mud driveway. It was a barn, a tin barn with the big sliding door open. The truck's headlights flooded the inside of the building – nothing moved.

"Oh, thank God," Jenna said. "I can't stay in this truck two more minutes. I can smell Terry's burps."

"I don't feel comfortable with this," Doug said softly.

Terry laughed a loud, drunken laugh. "Nothin' to be worried about, boss," he said. "Ain't nobody out here. Even if there were, they're going to be up at the Finish Line watchin' the rest of the fireworks." They'd stopped at the Finish Line convenience store on the side of the highway to look for food. Terry wanted to burn it down so he did, although Doug told him since they were trying to fly under the radar someone just might notice a burning convenience store – especially if the gasoline storage tanks blew. Which they did.

"I want to stretch, Doug," Jenna said. "Please, let's go in. I'm tired and want to lie down." Truth is, Doug was tired, too. After all that beer, Terry shouldn't be up much longer either, but Doug had seen Terry put away a shitload of beer before, then just walk away straight as a string.

"Okay," Doug said, slightly goosing the gas; the pickup crawled into the barn. The barn was a machine shop, really. Doug felt more at home than he had in nearly two weeks. He hopped out of the truck and slid the doors shut as Terry found the light switch. The lights in the shop still worked, but they only left the tungsten bulbs on long enough to make sure they were alone. Machines sprinkled the shop; a drill press, arc welder, air compressor, a wall of tools, a beer fridge Terry was already fishing around in, and a 1968 GTO, the hood up exposing the giant engine underneath, an engine that would never run again. Doug also saw a Makita power tools calendar. Catalina smiled at him like she knew him. Doug smiled back and flipped the calendar to Marissa. It was July after all.

"I get to sleep in the car," Jenna said as she stepped out of Doug's pickup.

Doug nodded. "I guess I can take the bed of the truck."

"I want to start a fire," Terry said, dropping a few chunks of wood he'd found in the corner into a pile on the barn's concrete floor. "I stole some bratwursts from the Finish Line. We could roast them."

Good lord. "Terry, you didn't steal anything," Doug said. "Taking things from dead people isn't stealing, and since the old guy behind the counter didn't have a head, I'd say he didn't care that you took his bratwursts."

Terry huffed, then chugged at his beer, then huffed again.

"Second," Doug continued. "We can't light a fire; somebody might see it."

Terry cracked open another beer and handed it to Jenna who took a long, slow sip.

"So, we could use some company," he said, blinking like a teenage girl who'd watched too many bubble-gum movies. "You're no fun. You never take me anywhere."

Doug grabbed a piece of wood off the floor of the shop and chucked it at Terry who ducked. The wood clattered on the concrete.

"Come on," Terry said, tossing a beer at Doug, who caught it in two hands. "Why don't we want company?"

Doug frowned.

"Because we can't trust anybody," Jenna said.

Doug nodded. "She's right. If anybody's alive after that Outbreak thing (*or the Ophiocordon thing,* Doug thought, *The Outbreak is a lie. Ophiocordon is death. The Apocalypse is upon us*), we have to be careful. You saw the guy without the head at the Finish Line. And before that, do you remember when we saw the chicks," he said, then paused and nodded at Jenna. "Sorry about that." She waved him off. "Somebody hanged them at that church over by Olathe, W-H-O-R-E spray painted on their bellies like they were at a football game cheering on the Whores."

"Yeah, so?"

"You actually saw that?" Jenna asked in a small voice.

"Yes, we did."

She looked at the two men silently for a few moments. "Then why did you pick me up?"

Doug shrugged. "Because you needed help," he said, then turned toward Terry, staring at his buddy for as long as he thought sitting and staring at Terry might make him think what he had to say was important. Jenna crawled onto the trunk of the GTO and sat there sipping her beer. "There were a lot of dead people in what I just told you," Doug said. "I don't want us to be like them."

Terry nodded. "I won't light a fire tonight, Doug," he said. "But I don't like cold bratwursts."

Doug wrapped a dusty tarpaulin he'd dragged from the floor of the shop and curled into the fetal position in the bed of his pickup. He'd had a shitty couple of weeks and it didn't seem to be getting any better. Before the Outbreak, he'd have bent over the GTO's engine, and probably kissed it. Today it meant nothing to him. He folded more of the tarp around him, although it wasn't at all cold, and quickly fell to sleep.

Doug woke to a rumbling stomach. The smell of roasting meat – or, more accurately, roasting meat-like food product – crawled over his olfactory nerves like it wanted to fuck them. The smell of cooking bratwurst was the best sensory input he'd experienced for weeks. Goddammit, Terry.

"Hey, you're up," Terry said, grinning like he'd found a really neat prize in a box of cereal. He and Jenna sat on old plastic milk crates eating blackened bratwurst and drinking Diet Coke they'd found in the beer fridge. "Want breakfast?"

"Terry," Doug hissed. "I said no fires. Fires make smoke, they …"

Terry waved a bratwurst in the air under Doug's face. "I promised I wouldn't light a fire last night. Sure you don't want one?"

Doug grabbed the scorched sausage from Terry's hand and bit into it. Good, God. Ambrosia, manna, Christmas morning with a bike under the tree, all ran through Doug's head as the salt and nitrates hit his system like meth. Doug stood as he chewed the bratwurst, then punched Terry in the arm. He didn't feel any better, but at least Jenna giggled. "What time is it?" he asked, soft, warm light drifting through the cracks between the big, sliding doors.

"About eight o'clock," Jenna said. "I need a shower."

Doug stretched his shoulders as he walked toward the barn door. After all the driving and sleeping in the bed of his pickup, he felt like he'd had the shit kicked out of him. But it could be worse. As the Outbreak had finally gone from a monologue joke on The Tonight Show, to a brief news story, to a nationwide panic, to a worldwide panic, to people putting a bullet in their neighbor for a canned ham, he knew the alternative would be a lot worse.

"I'll take a look outside," he said, a yawn stretched his face. Barn dust sprinkled the yellow morning light as Doug walked to the doors, scratched the back of his head, and pushed one side of the creaking rolling doors open enough for him to get a good look. "Rain's stopped," he said. "And everything's quiet. Jenna, honey, we aren't going to find a shower here, but I promise I will find you one. And clean clothes, and someplace safe to stay."

It wasn't Platte City. Platte City, Missouri, squatted under a great orange water tower, a truck stop area with what might have been a QuikTrip, McDonald's, and Taco Bell sat in a blackened heap of rubble. Someone had pulled a Terry and blew the gas tanks.

"Whoa," Terry said, a giggle dancing at the edge of his words. "That's messed up." Doug pulled the pickup down side roads to maneuver around the blast site, much like everywhere else they'd been, people were invisible. A number of cars crowded the parking lot of a Subway, the lights still on, although Doug knew it wouldn't be long before the utility man shut everything down. But nothing moved. Bodies in fuzzy lumps scattered the pavement. Doug shuddered when he realized he was getting used to seeing them.

"Hey, there's a park," Jenna shouted suddenly, pointing a finger out Terry's window. "Let's go finish off our brats."

"Jenna, I think ..." Doug started.

"Hey," she said softly, resting a warm hand on his forearm. "It's the end of the world as we know it, and I feel fine." She giggled. "Wherever we're going, we might be going there to die. Let's just have a meal first. Oh, and beer."

"Shit yes," Terry said, then stopped, his eyes fixed on something they'd passed by.

"What is it?" Jenna asked, the pickup pulling to a stop on the gravel drive near the park's first set of benches.

"I just saw a video store with a going out of business sign. I thought they were all already out of business," he said, opening the cab door, his tennis shoe-clad feet dropping swiftly onto the rocks. "Roast me up one of those weenies. As long as the juice is on, I'm going to catch me some movies." He hooted and Doug and Jenna watched as Terry jogged up a short hill and out of sight.

"Where'd you get him?" Jenna asked, Doug walking beside her carrying a red and white Coleman cooler filled with German sausages, Diet Cokes, Bud Lights, and a jar of pickled eggs. Terry had found most of that in the shop's beer fridge along with a half-gallon milk carton full of ice in the freezer. Doug bent and gathered sticks for a fire.

A smile tugged at his mouth. "Terry? Aw, he's a friend of mine from back home in Paola. He used to work for me at my muffler and brake shop."

"So, you're a mechanic?"

Doug nodded. "Yeah. I can fix enough to keep us going." He paused. "You?"

Jenna slid onto the top of a park bench, and pulled the cooler up with her. She took a beer from the red Coleman and offered it to Doug. He waved her off. Jenna popped the top and took a long drink. She studied Doug for a few moments before talking again, softly. "I've never really done anything," she said. "I'm spoiled. My parents are ... well, were, loaded. I body-shotted my way through college, and came out with a liberal arts degree. What the hell was I going to do with that? So, I mooched off my parents until everybody died." A tear ran down her right cheek. "I haven't done anything." Doug started to reach for her, but stopped himself.

"It's okay," Jenna said. "I think I need a hug." Doug stepped close to Jenna and wrapped his arms around her, drawing her soft, but firm body gently onto his, the smell of her hair flooded his nostrils like a drug. She pressed back, squeezing into him, and ...

"Hey," Terry yelled from atop the hill. "Look at what I found."

Doug's eyes painfully swung from Jenna's gentle, freckled face, her caring smile, and green eyes, to Terry holding an armload of movies and leading a skinny guy of about thirty carrying a DVD player. "What the hell?"

"Who's that?" Jenna whispered, her breath soft and warm.

"I don't know," Doug said. He stepped out of the embrace, and turned toward the two men. "But I don't like it." He motioned toward Terry. "Get over here."

Terry skipped down the hill into the park, the man behind him walked slowly, surely, mechanically. "What's up, boss?"

Doug rested a hand on Terry's shoulder. "Who the hell is that?"

"That's Arnold," Terry said.

"Arnold?"

Terry nodded.

"Where did you meet Arnold?"

"In the video store. He was standing there watching 'The Terminator' on one of the TVs hanging from the ceiling, and I just walked up and stood next to him," Terry said, giggling. "And guess what? He didn't move. It's like he didn't even notice me. Then I said, 'Hey, buddy. You got a dead cat in there, or what?' And he said, 'Fuck you, asshole.' Ain't that the best shit ever?"

No. It's not. "What are you talking about?"

"The dead cat/asshole thing, it's ... well, just listen to him talk," Terry said, turning to Arnold. "Conan. What is best in life?"

"To crush your enemies," Arnold said, his words heavy with a fake Austrian accent, "see them driven before you, and to hear the lamentation of their women."

Terry turned to Doug, grinning like a monkey.

"What the hell is he talking about?" Doug asked.

"I have no idea, but everything he says is all from Arnold Schwarzenegger movies," Terry barked, a laugh coming from deep inside. "Can we keep him?"

July 8: Kansas City, Missouri
CHAPTER 15

The amusement park sat as dead and silent as a corpse. Not that Karl expected to see the wooden Timber Wolf roller coaster shaking across its 4,260-feet of track, but the radio said there was a survival shelter at Worlds of Fun; hand-painted signs on Interstate 435 led him there. Karl had been to the amusement park as a child, all he survived was the Tilt-A-Whirl; the Timber Wolf made him puke. He pulled the Porsche into the parking lot near the main gate and stepped out, a .44-caliber pistol strapped to his waist. He'd left Jenna the .38 he'd found in the upstairs closet of the Peckinpa's home. He hadn't thought of Jenna since he climbed into the charcoal Porsche and crept down the hidden gravel lane back toward the highway. That skinny, auburn-haired girl with her ninth season of "Friends" bitchiness was better off left behind. Even if she'd been hotter than a Victoria's Secret model wrapped in bacon, another week of her and Karl might have shot her himself.

Some amusement park ride he didn't recognize from his two decades ago visit loomed over him as he wound around the choked mess of cars, trucks, and motor homes filled with moldy bodies at the head of the parking lot. He walked through the ticket booth, pimple-faced high schoolers long gone from their posts. Nothing moved in the park.

"Hello?" he yelled into the bright, summer, Kansas City, Missouri, sky. Nothing. No caws from birds, no barks from dogs, no screams of people from a horror movie, and no laughter from humans in an amusement park. Karl wandered from the park's Americana section with shops, car rides, and arcades, to the Scandinavian section with Norse names like Viking Voyager, and Finnish Fling. The designers of Worlds of Fun wanted this concrete and steel maze to represent all the continents, sprinkling Europe next to Africa, which butted up to Snoopyland. Karl never was sure where Snoopyland was on an actual globe, but as a boy he loved it. "Hello?" he called again. An arrow and the words "Survival Shelter" spray-painted in red on the asphalt that covered the park led Karl toward a concert hall his parents had dragged him into for a 1950s musical revival simply because it had air conditioning, and summer in Missouri was goddamned hot. Karl ran toward the building and threw open the doors.

The smell pushed him back outside. Karl dropped to the pavement; vomit streamed from his mouth like his body had turned on a hose.

Death. Worlds of Fun was death. Karl wiped a tendril of vomit from his lips and fought to catch his breath. The bodies, all the bodies. "Fuck this," he hissed and spat onto the hot pavement. Karl knew he had to look again, to make sure no one was alive in there. He slowly pulled open the metal door and stepped inside.

"Hello?" he screamed into the building, his voice echoed throughout the hall. Makeshift beds scattered the stage where some wannabe actor had portrayed Elvis all those years ago. Blankets and clothing spread across many of the red velvet-covered seats that stretched into the darkness. The smell of death and soil was heavy here; the smell dragged Karl back to Wal-Mart in Harrisonville, bodies scattered the stage in bloody lumps, their moldy chests ripped open by some sort of growth, like they were impaled on corn stalks, just like Kelly. The rows of stalks pointed toward the ceiling some kind of demon harvest. The bulbous knob on the stalks had all burst, scattering yellow clouds of spores over the interior of the auditorium. Someone had spray-painted "Gone to Omaha" across the back curtain. Shit. "Hello?" Karl screamed again. He froze; something moved.

Karl took a step forward on shaking legs. A body lay in a festering gray lump across the theater seats, the threads of the fungus consuming it laced into the red fabric of the cushions. The two-foot tall stalk, its pod swollen tight, bobbed on the end. It stopped as Karl stepped close, then turned toward him, the bulbous knot leaned forward, pointing at him. Karl staggered back outside, the door slamming shut behind him as he heard the pod pop. Good God, it knew I was here. It attacked me. That fucking thing attacked me. This is no shelter; it's a damned science experiment. Karl bent, hands on knees and vomited again; what was left of the Dr Pepper and Ding Dongs in his stomach splashed across the asphalt and splattered onto his shoes. Oh, God. He tried to catch his breath, then he heard something he thought he'd never hear again. A car horn blared in the direction of the parking lot.

"Holy shit," he whispered, the taste of vomit in his mouth. "Holy shit." He bolted upright, the sudden movement made his head swim. "Hey," he tried to yell. "Hey. I'm here. I'm here." Karl took a deep breath and stepped his pace to a fast walk, nausea slowing him. The horn honked again. This time Karl heard a voice, too.

"Hey, assholes," a woman's voice shouted. "Anyone here? This is a goddamned shelter, isn't it?"

Karl lurched out of Scandinavia back into Americana, the front gate twenty feet away. The woman honked again. "Don't leave," Karl whispered, then shouted. "Don't leave." He saw the woman before she saw him. Holy shit, she was hot, but there was something else about her.

This woman looked hard; she could hurt people. He stopped and stood behind a long dry lemonade stand, pulled the .44 from the holster, shoved it down the front of his pants and untucked his shirt to cover the bulge. As a man stepped out of the woman's car, a 1990-something Chrysler LeBaron, and talked to her, Karl released the buckle on his gun belt and let it drop to the pavement. No chances. No chances at all. Karl couldn't hear what the man said, but the hard woman smiled, pulled him toward her and kissed him deeply. Karl relaxed and stepped away from the stand, painfully aware of the powerful handgun wedged next to his testicles. "Hello," he yelled toward them. The woman's head shot toward him and she waved him over. "What's your name?"

"Maryanne," the woman cooed, looking at Karl in long glances like he was on an IMAX screen. Karl glanced at the man, his face unnaturally pale in the summer sun. "Where's the goddamned shelter?"

"Gone," he said, looking back at Maryanne, her bright blue eyes blazing in the late afternoon sun. "Nothing but dead bodies here. The survivors have gone to Omaha. At least that's what they spray-painted on the wall back there."

Maryanne grinned. "Omaha? Who the fuck wants to go to Omaha?" The man forced a laugh. Karl could tell he was scared. "You ran into anybody?" Maryanne asked. "Anybody alive?"

Karl started to mention Jenna, but didn't. Not worth mentioning at this point. He shook his head. "No. Not for a month or more. You?"

"Yeah," the man spoke for the first time. Karl would later find his name was Darryl, not that it mattered. "Saw some old guy at Kauffman Stadium sitting in the rain watching a baseball game on the Jumbotron."

"Is he here?" Karl asked, looking around, suddenly more uncomfortable by someone he couldn't see lurking around this heart attack of cars. "Is he supposed to meet you here?"

"No," Darryl said slowly. "He's nowhere."

"Well, where ..."

Maryanne whipped a rifle from the back seat and drew a bead on Karl's face. He stepped back, his breath frozen in his chest, the heavy weight of the pistol that sat on his junk seemed miles away. Maryanne said, "Click, boom," then grinned, and lowered the barrel of the gun toward the pavement. "Shot him," she said. "Put him out of his fucking misery. He was obviously crazy. He was sitting in the fucking rain watching a thirty-year-old baseball game. He's better off where he is. Lying in a pool of nachos." She laughed, the sound pierced Karl's heart. It wasn't Jenna's giggle, Jenna's annoying giggle. There was feeling in that giggle. This was a soulless cackle. Maryanne motioned toward the car. "We're going to Omaha. You coming?"

Karl stole a glance at Darryl; a bead of sweat ran down the side of the man's face. He was scared, Karl knew. Damned scared. He felt he should be, too. Darryl nodded at him nervously. At that moment, Karl knew if he said no, he'd have a bullet in his back before he could make it to cover.

"Sure," he said slowly, forcing a smile. "We're all going the same direction. It'll be safer if we're together." He motioned back into the park hoping that maybe, maybe she'd let him get to the Porsche, then he'd be free of this woman. This crazy, crazy woman. A vision of him reaching into his pants, coming out with the .44 and blowing this woman's head off flashed through Karl's mind, but it died there. Something told him she knew he was thinking that. She still held the rifle and could take him out before he got the pistol past his pubes. "I'll just go get my car. It's in the back parking lot."

"No," Maryanne said, all humor, if there was any, gone from her voice. "There's plenty of room in here. If there's anything in your car you need, every day in America is Black Friday without the crowds. You'll be okay. Now, let's move. I'm getting jittery." Darryl stepped toward the driver's side door, but Maryanne stuck her hand in the middle of his chest. "Not now, baby," she said. "The Cowboy's going to drive." Then she turned to Karl. "Let's see what you got, big man." She tossed him the keys.

Maryanne fell asleep in the backseat of the LeBaron about five minutes down the interstate, cuddling her rifle like a lover. Karl stole a glance at Darryl. The man was a wreck. Crescent moons of darkness cupped the underside of his eyes; his hair long and unkempt, days of just-graying stubble covered his chin. And the man was thin; too thin.

"I got a Snickers bar in my shirt pocket," Karl said, his voice in the front seat of the convertible caused Darryl to jump. Karl tried to smile, but thought it might look like a grimace. "I'll give it to you if you're hungry?" Silently, Darryl put up the palm of his right hand and shook his head. Maryanne snored from the back seat.

"What's her deal?" Karl said in a whisper, leaning close to Darryl. "Why'd she pull that gun on me?" Darryl sat silently, staring ahead.

"Hey," Karl said slightly louder. "I got questions."

Darryl shook his head, reached into his front pocket and pulled out an ink pen, then grabbed a Taco Bell napkin from the floor of the LeBaron and wrote in blue block letters: "She knew you were there. Shut up. She will kill us both." Darryl's hands shook as he held the note where Karl could see it, but was hidden from Maryanne's eyes, her bright blue all-seeing eyes. His head twitched. Karl didn't know what this guy had gone through, but he didn't want to know. He just wanted out, but he might not have a choice. Darryl crumpled the napkin, stuck his arm out the side of the car and dropped it onto the interstate, watching in the side mirror as it fluttered onto the shoulder, and away from Maryanne's watch.

They drove forty-five minutes in tense silence until the lights of St. Joseph, Missouri, covered the darkening horizon.

"Let's pull over here," Maryanne said from the backseat, startling Karl and Darryl. "Let's find a motel room and some whiskey. I need to get fucked up." Karl pulled the LeBaron up to a convenience store and started to hop out, to walk calmly into the front of this building, smiling all the way as he ran the fuck out the back. Maryanne's cold voice stopped his thoughts. "No. Not you, Cowboy," she cooed, draping an arm around his shoulder. "Go, Darryl. Get me something good. And popcorn. Bring me some popcorn, something for dinner, get some Bic razors, and a 'People' magazine." Darryl slowly released the door latch, stepped from the car and slunk into the store.

"You pump gas," she told Karl. "Pump it good."

The next two hours burned itself into Karl's mind. By the time he finished filling the LeBaron, Darryl came back to the car with a half-gallon of Jack Daniels, a pint of Jim Beam, and a fifth of Evan Williams, four big bags of Barrel-O-Fun white cheddar cheese popcorn, a frozen box of microwaveable White Castle Hamburgers, and a stack of shitty gossip magazines. Maryanne hooted as he dumped the armful of booty into the backseat and they drove to the nearest motel. With anywhere to choose, Maryanne told Karl to pull into a Motel 6; she wanted doors on the outside.

"Let's eat and get drunk," this blond maniac screamed, laughing like teenagers do at Will Ferrell movies. They got out of the car, the usually humming traffic on Interstate 29 below them, gone. A deer walked slowly across the road, nibbling at grass in the median, as they grabbed the booty and busted into a room. Karl didn't remember much about the night. Maryanne took a shower and shaved herself bare. Karl thought about running then. He pulled the .44 out of his pants and looked up to see Darryl holding Maryanne's rifle level with his head.

"Put that away," Darryl said quietly, but forcefully, any fear that had been in the man was gone. "Now's not the time. Put it in the drawer next to the Bible. She won't find it there. Wait until she's asleep. Then we can do business." Staring at the barrel of the gun, Karl slid open the top drawer of the desk and sat the pistol on top of the Holy Bible, hoping like hell he wouldn't need to smite anyone before he could get it back.

A microwave oven in the room she chose, 126, "right next to the ice machine," made the hamburgers somewhat palatable, and the popcorn was still crunchy, but it was the whiskey that raked terror across Karl, his gun across the room, and a madwoman next to him. The drunker Maryanne got, the louder she got.

"Where you from, Cowboy?" she said to Karl, a half bottle of Evan Williams between her smooth legs, the pink Bic razors not leaving a scratch on them. Maryanne sat on the bed naked, munching popcorn. Jenna had looked like that girl in high school nobody noticed, but might look hot if she took off her glasses and let her hair down; Maryanne looked like a Playboy bunny. Jenna just annoyed him, but she hadn't threatened to kill him. It wasn't the last time he wondered if he'd made a mistake leaving her.

"I'm from Vinita, Oklahoma," he said, trying not to sound nervous. He didn't tell her he'd been a car dealer; nobody likes a car dealer. "I almost went to Dallas, but I decided to go north. Lucky me, huh?"

Maryanne grinned at him through a mouth full of straight, white teeth, eyeing him with the cold eyes of a predator.

"You bet your sweet ass," she said, spreading her legs and moving the bottle of Evan Williams, grinning as Karl's eyes moved to look at her. "You want some of that? Well, you have to earn it." She took a pull from the bottle and sat it on the motel's bedside table. "Strip down, boys." When Karl looked, Darryl was already naked, his jeans spread across the TV. Holy shit, his cock is huge, ran through Karl's head. He knew why Maryanne kept him around.

"Lay on the bed," she ordered Karl who thought about throwing a punch to the side of her head, and getting out of this madness, but something stopped him. The looming idea of death at the hands of this maniac, and the desire to see what the fuck else was going to happen. Maryanne hopped on top of his legs, grinning. "If you can show you're a good boy like Darryl, you can do things to me, Cowboy." They drank whiskey until he finally passed out.

Karl's eyes painfully crawled open at sunrise; Maryanne's naked, nearly perfect body sprawled over his legs. In the meagre light that filtered through the motel curtains, he saw something that chilled his soul. The pants Darryl had draped across the TV were gone, the drawer with his pistol lay open, and the motel door sat ajar. Karl looked around, only with his eyes for fear of waking Maryanne, but he could see Darryl had bolted with his gun. That lucky bastard was gone and Karl was alone with this psychotic bitch. Fuckenheimer.

July 8: Allenville, Missouri
CHAPTER 16

Sweat rolled down Craig's face as he pushed the red Craftsman lawnmower across the yard, the steady hum of the motor filling the air for blocks. The sweat formed a dark stain on his shirt and his breath came in hard, deep bursts, but the exercise felt good; it was nice to get out of the house; besides, he didn't want his lawn to look like the Posey's next door. Disgraceful. Just disgraceful. The mower hit a hidden rut and the front tires stuck, shoving the handlebar into Craig's stomach. He stopped, smiled and wiped his face with a sleeve, the sweat left the sleeve dark and damp. Yes, it felt good. So would a bath, but the town's water stopped running; the faucet didn't even hiss anymore. Nope, no pressure at all. A few dark clouds sat on what little of the horizon was visible through the trees that shaded the neighborhood. It might rain tonight, Craig thought. I'll set out the wading pool and have a bath tomorrow.

The quickly receding patch of uncut grass drew Craig and his mower closer to the Posey's yard. Stupid Poseys and their stupid dog. The last time Doofus crapped in Craig's yard he told Old Man Posey he was going to shoot it in the head. That had been months ago. Craig smiled when he thought of that ridiculous yapping ankle-biter hit by a car and lying in a lump in the street outside Posey's house a few days later.

Two more passes and Craig could reach and touch the Posey's lawn. This side of his yard was slightly sloped, giving the Poseys his runoff when it rained. One more pass and the yard would be finished. As he pushed the Craftsman up the small incline, the Posey's grass waved in the slight breeze, and brushed against his arm. The Posey's own lawnmower was in that grass somewhere, buried with a concrete bird bath and what was once a tomato garden under what was now more prairie than yard.

Craig pulled the mower even with the Posey's porch and killed the engine, the loud afternoon suddenly quiet as a cemetery. "Look at that lawn, Posey," Craig yelled to figures still sitting in chairs on the Posey porch, fungus stalks reaching toward the sky like boners. "Best lookin' lawn in town. You should probably do something about your piece of shit lawn. It's knockin' down my property values." No reply. Fucking Posey didn't say too much anymore, but he did sometimes, even though he and his fat wife still sat on the porch. They hadn't moved for weeks.

The white of Mr. and Mrs. Poseys' skulls showed through parts of their face birds had pecked through. The rest of them sagged in their rotting clothes that were quickly melting in the moist Northwest Missouri weather; the smell of death long since gone, the gray, creeping fungus that consumed them all but spent. Craig was happy the Poseys had the courtesy to die outside the house, watching the body of their dog that had crawled across the street and collapsed; he didn't have any surprises when he broke through the back door to see what food they had left. Old people kept a lot of canned food and marshmallows. Craig also rifled through their medicine cabinet. Tylenol, Alka Seltzer, blood pressure pills, cholesterol pills, arthritis pills, Ophiocordon. *Sucks getting old,* Craig thought, and dropped the Tylenol, Alka Seltzer, and antidepressants into the black plastic garbage bag he used to carry the food. Ophiocordon? Craig had read somewhere this shit gave you one hell of a rush. He grinned to think of old man Posey and fat Lilith getting their hornies off with some antidepressant pills. What the hell? Might be worth trying.

The sun began to sink in the mid-afternoon sky. It beat Craig's back as he dragged the quiet mower into the shed behind his house and walked to the porch to have a warm beer. That's one of the few things that bothered him about all the deaths – the lack of electricity. He didn't need a clock anymore, but he missed reruns on TV, air conditioning, his computer, and mostly, cold beer. He didn't mind the room temperature bottled water he'd horded by the case in his garage and basement, but room temperature beer kind of took the fun out of drinking it.

"Hey, Posey," Craig yelled across the yard. "Wanna beer? I just got it from the gas station yesterday; I already drank all yours." A faint 'fuck you, McAllister,' drifted across the lawn. 'Tonight I'm going to eat your soul.' Craig's head snapped toward Posey's house; the Poseys sat motionless as they'd been for weeks, slowly rotting into their lawn chairs. *Goddamned Posey,* he thought. *I'm glad he's dead.* Craig chugged the Budweiser, threw the empty can toward Posey's yard and went into the house to grab another. He kept his beer in the basement, but in the summer heat, the basement didn't keep it much cooler.

Boxes of canned and dried food, crates of bottled water, cases of beer and soda filled the rooms of Craig's house. He'd packed away everything he could take from the grocery stores before the smell of rotting meat and produce prevented him from going in. The few convenience stores in town didn't smell so bad, but he could only eat so many Doritos. Guns and ammunition he'd taken from houses and the sporting goods store were scattered across the living room. In the early days, Craig never walked outside his house unarmed, but now he didn't care. No one was left in this small town except Old Man Posey, and he was just talk.

The stairs creaked slightly as Craig left the basement and stepped into the kitchen; the stove, refrigerator and microwave sat quietly, buried by boxes of food. They were useless for anything now anyway. The last meal Craig had cooked before the electricity went out was ramen noodles. He still regretted that.

But as the basement door slid shut with a click, Craig heard another noise, a quiet hum that slowly grew louder. "Christ," he hissed. "A car." The last car engine he'd heard pull through was a man shouting verses from the Book of Revelation from the open driver's side window. Craig had watched the crazy man with a Charles Manson face pass as he hid in the shadow of the courthouse on the town square. That car didn't stop; it kept going north into Iowa. This time he might not be that lucky. Craig grabbed a hunting rifle and threw himself out the door.

Grass and weeds grew from cracks in the asphalt. Soon enough, Craig thought, the streets would be mostly vegetation. He sprinted across his newly cut lawn. It would be a signal, Craig realized, a beacon telling whoever was behind the wheel of the car someone in town was alive, someone they could steal from. The noise faded into a steady drone as the vehicle drove slowly on Main Street, a long, faint "hello" occasionally broke through the day. The driver was a man, or at least the voice was a man's; the car or truck could be filled with any number of people. Are there any good people left after the end of the world? Craig wondered as he ran up the street. "Run, McAllister, run," Posey's voice called after him. Craig rarely wished someone else in town was alive, the bastards, but as the weeks crawled by, he wanted to know if Old Man Posey's rotting corpse was talking to him, or if he was just crazy.

Mulberry Street gave way to First Street. Craig ran down sidewalks, avoiding the gray pavement. If the car rounded a corner, he could drop to the concrete, the overgrown yards and the small swath of grass next to the street would give him some kind of hiding place that the open street wouldn't. Craig turned onto First Street and went toward Main. The car would be headed through the center of town before branching onto the side streets, looking for people who were still alive – looking for him. As he ran, a vision screamed through his head. Craig lay on his front porch, head split open, an unearthly living mold bursting from his chest, dead eyes staring at the Poseys on their porch, the corpses laughing, laughing at him while faceless men, women and androgynous things walked in and out of his house, taking his food, his water, his beer, his guns. White knuckles gripped the wooden stock of the rifle as Craig approached Main

Street. The car traveled slowly and was a few blocks away by the sound of the shouts.

Crouching and looking toward the hum of the oncoming engine, Craig saw nothing and broke onto the street, slipped into the safety of the overgrown grass, weeds and bushes on the courthouse lawn; the spot he'd hidden from the Revelation Man as he drove through town. "Hide, little girl. Hide," Old Man Posey called to him. Craig looked for the voice, expecting to see Posey sitting in his lawn chair on the courthouse yard, the stiff, dry corpse of Doofus lying at his feet. No one was there.

Across the street, the sporting goods store where Craig got the rifle he held, the restaurant where he'd cooked a steak before the electricity left town, the pharmacy, Purdy's Hometown Real Estate, the T-shirt shop, were all dark, lonely, dead. Craig put the rifle to his shoulder and waited.

Minutes later a decades-old Geo Metro crept into view. Nothing to eat a lot of gas, something for traveling on next to nothing. The man is smart, Craig realized. Gas is hard to get without electricity. The Geo pulled to a stop in front of the courthouse and the driver stepped out; a slight man, bearded, his I Heart Philly T-shirt filthy and splattered with grease. "Hello?" the man yelled. "Is anyone there?" The breeze blew through the tall grass hiding Craig, the courthouse lawn looking like a great, green lake. "Is anybody there?" the man called again.

"Well, answer him, McAllister," Posey whispered into his ear. Craig flinched; he could feel someone behind him.

"Shut the fuck up, old man," Craig hissed and threw an elbow that hit nothing.

"Hello?" the slight man called as he walked a circle around the little car. "If anyone's there, I'm traveling to Kansas City. I heard a station come in on my radio. Someone's alive in Kansas City. Please, come with me. I have water, and enough food for a few days."

Liar, ran through Craig's head. You don't have food. You want *my* food. Craig steadied himself and pointed the rifle at the man's chest. "Yeah, your food," Posey said. "He wants your food, your water, your beer, and he hasn't seen a woman in months. He wants your ass."

Craig shook his head. "This is my town, Posey, you motherfucker," he hissed. "You're dead. This is my town. My town. Go to Hell where you belong."

"So you two can be alone?" the voice taunted.

"No," Craig screamed and squeezed the trigger. A thunder crack split the quiet square and the slight, bearded man dropped dead in the street. As dead as the Posey's dog.

"Well, you screwed the pooch now, McAllister," Posey said, laughing. "That was your ticket out of Deadsville. What are you going to do now?"

Craig pulled the bolt on his rifle, loading another shell into the chamber, swung toward Posey's voice and fired into a patch of high, waving, prairie grass. Posey wasn't there. He was never there. Fuckin' Posey.

Craig pulled his legs through the high grass and weeds and stepped onto the street. The young bearded man lay in a heap, a pool of red that gathered on the gray asphalt beneath his black hair. Craig stumbled to him and dropped to his knees; the man didn't move.

"Touch his pecker," Posey whispered.

Craig screamed and shot into the air. He reloaded the rifle and shot around him, shattering windows in J.J.'s Bar and Grill, Stoner Pharmacy, and the blackened bronze statue face of Col. Alexander Duncan of the Confederate Army that had stood in front of the county courthouse for 120 years.

"Goddamn you, Posey," he screamed.

Craig stood in the Square, his voice echoed in his head seconds after it had vanished on the slight breeze. Then the world was silent. *What did I do?*

Craig sat his rifle gently against the side of the Geo and walked across the street to Mac's Hardware. He emerged with a shovel and buried the man on the courthouse lawn on the spot where Posey had whispered in his ear, the spot where he'd pulled the trigger. Craig left the shovel sticking out of the fresh earth as a marker for the man's grave; the man he knew Posey killed. Craig walked to the Geo, slid into the driver's seat and drove it home. The man had said he had water and food; Craig could always use more.

That night, Craig McAllister threw Doofus onto the Posey's porch and set their house on fire.

July 11: Exeter, Missouri
CHAPTER 17

The glow from the Kum and Go shone like a lighthouse in the waning dusk. It caught Nikki Holleran by surprise as she topped a rise on this stretch of hilly, rural highway. That light shouldn't be there. Nikki pulled her Harley-Davidson to a stop on the highway and killed the engine. She pushed the kickstand down, stepped off the bike and stared at the convenience store that sat atop the next hill. Despite her trailer with boxes of macaroni and cheese, and cans of beans, her stomach rumbled at the thought of food that wasn't good for the next two years. The sight of a convenience store in this region of hills and farm fields north of St. Joseph was a somewhat welcome, but unexpected sight. Especially the lights. The electric grid still had juice, so the Kum and Go meant food and a microwave, cold soda, and working gas pumps, but it also meant one of the other Leftovers may still be using it. *I'm either lucky or fucked,* she thought. But no sound of machinery or human activity drifted along the slight breeze that whistled in the growing darkness. A coyote yipped somewhere to her right; another joined it, then another. Close, but she wasn't too worried about coyotes, they had things to hunt other than her. Nikki pulled a pair of Bushnell binoculars from one of the bike's saddlebags and started walking.

Grass grew high on the highway shoulder. In just a few years, plants and weathering would break the world's highway systems into so much rubble; grass and saplings would take it completely over short years after that. Nikki knew she would eventually have to find something with four-wheel drive to get anywhere, if she lived that long.

About a hundred yards from the Kum and Go – Ejaculate and Evacuate, her friends had called it at Missouri Western State Community College – Nikki stepped off the road and hid in the tree line, a remnant of days gone by when farmers planted rows of trees to keep the wind from pounding their crops, farmers who died a hundred years before people started turning into mushrooms. Leaning her right shoulder on a big oak to steady herself, Nikki pulled the Bushnells to her eyes and scanned the store. Two pickups, a Ford F-150 and a Dodge Ram, average vehicles for this part of the country, rested on the store's big gravel lot. A flat tire caused the bed of the Ford to dip to the right. Near the back of the lot, sitting outside the aura of yellow light, a White Freightliner with a sleeper cab sat quietly, a rotor blade for one of the big windmills that apparently still helped supply electricity for this part of the grid loaded on its flat-bed trailer. Nikki eyed the sleeper cab almost with hunger. It had been three days since she'd slept in a bed, and she already missed it. Past the Missouri Lottery and Budweiser neons in the front window, the store seemed still, quiet, but that didn't mean anything. A Leftover might still be ... something moved. Nikki tensed at the suddenness of it, then it was gone. *Where'd you go?* Her breath came in short pants as panic began to creep over her. If another Leftover had claimed the store, she'd have to run, praying he didn't have a faster ride than hers. She couldn't risk meeting an unfriendly. *Please, oh please, don't let it be.* A head peeked over a rack of Doritos – a deer. Nikki almost laughed. A young doe wandered the small aisles of the Kum and Go. On a second pass of the windows, she noticed one had shattered; the deer must have leapt through it. Nikki smiled.

"I'll get you out, Bambi," she whispered. "Just gotta open the front door."

Popcorn and potato chips dotted with deer droppings scattered the floor of the Kum and Go. Nikki propped open the glass front door and tossed rocks into the store from the broken window until the doe found its way out. Someone else would have shot the deer and eaten well, Nikki realized, but she wasn't a hunter, she was a waitress, and Hooligans hadn't prepared her for the end of the world. Nikki filled the pockets of her cargo pants with packages of peanuts, beef jerky, and candy bars as she made her way to the back of the store. The snacks were for later, when she had nothing else. Today was for something hot.

A rush of cold air danced across her arm as she slowly pulled open one of the cooler doors.

"Thank God," she moaned. The refrigeration still worked, but the burritos had expired more than a week ago. Nikki's stomach growled again and she unwrapped a burrito and put it in the microwave oven. Fuck it. Microwaves fix a lot of problems. It tasted fine, so she ate a second one.

Tossing the wrappers into the trashcan out of habit, she knew it was time to move. Any Leftovers who saw the lights of the Kum and Go, the only lights on for miles, it would draw them in to do what she was doing. In less desperate times, people would call it looting. She called it surviving. Nikki packed three Styrofoam coolers from the store into the small trailer attached to her motorcycle. In went bacon, lunchmeat, eggs, milk, and cheese from the convenience store coolers, and enough ice to keep them cold for a few days. Three cases of bottled water and a 12-pack of Diet Coke sat beside them, along with six red five-gallon cans of gasoline and all the batteries, flashlights, coffee, bread, and all the hunting gear Nikki could find. She didn't think she'd ever be able to bring herself to hunt, she didn't even have a gun, but it would keep her warm when the seasons changed.

Munching from a bag of Fritos, she walked back into the store. There was one more task. The acrid stench of rotting urine struck her face as she opened the door to the women's restroom. Someone had forgotten to flush – Nikki was glad she'd eaten first. She used the toilet, the first time she'd used an indoor toilet in a week, then washed her short-cropped hair in the sink; the hot water felt better than she'd ever remembered. But she knew she had to hurry, to get back into hiding. She was exposed in the Kum and Go. A few minutes ago, her pants were down and Dad always said never get caught with your pants down. It took her a few minutes to find the switches for the lights, but she needed to find them. Had to find them. The lights were a welcome sign, and nobody was welcome. With a click of the breaker box's master switch, the electricity of the Kum and Go went dead.

Outside, the slight breeze fighting her still-wet hair, was quiet. She could see for miles atop this hill. No lights, no cars, no human life. Above her a satellite moved in a steady line across the sky, sending information to people who were no longer alive to receive it. She yawned and stretched her tired muscles – muscles tired of riding, tired of sleeping on the ground, tired of moving. The roar of the motorcycle's engine exploded in the night as Nikki started it on the short trip around the parking lot. She winced at the sound; anyone within miles would have heard her fire up her ride. She pulled her father's motorcycle and its little trailer to the back of the lot and parked in front of a grove of trees and behind the Freightliner. The bed that sat in the truck's cab waited for her. Killing the engine amplified the dead silence of the country night. No other engines had come to life. Nikki hoped that meant no other people were around to hear it, but she knew that was just hope.

The Freightliner cab loomed ominously over her as she got off the bike and grabbed the handrail to pull herself up to the door. Visions of the driver ran through her head, dead on the thin mattress in the sleeper section of the cab, blood crusting his face, his chest burst open, and mushrooms growing throughout the cab like it was the Thailand jungle. *Was he still there?* Nikki wondered. *Dead, rotting, waiting for me?* Or, she realized, the door may simply be locked. Nikki looked into the driver's window, flicked on a flashlight and looked inside. The cab, the bed, were empty. She exhaled deeply and tried the door – it was unlocked. *Okay, Holleran, when's the luck going to run out?* she thought. The door, unused for weeks, moaned softly as she pulled it open and slid into the driver's seat. The light from her flashlight dashed throughout the cab; a pistol sat between the seats.

"That luck's not going to run out anytime soon," she said softly. Then Nikki locked the doors, crawled into the sleeper bed and fell quickly to sleep, cradling the newfound weapon next to her like it was a teddy bear. And for the first time since death took her family, her friends, and her world, she slept soundly.

Nikki woke later than her now normal "up with the sun." She turned on the convenience store electricity long enough to microwave two cheeseburgers, filled a plastic bag with salt, pepper, mustard and ketchup packets, and Double Bubble, and headed north. The first green highway sign on the road read:

Council Bluffs – 122 miles

Clarinda – 60 miles

Exeter – 5 miles

She sat on her Harley at the foot of the road sign, chewing gum, her right foot on the pavement helping balance the bike.

"Next stop, Exeter," Nikki said, more to hear a human voice than for any real need. Nikki hadn't heard another voice since she'd left the Banker to the hungry teeth of the dog in Savannah. She pulled the Freightliner driver's pistol from a pocket in her cargo pants and did something that hadn't occurred to her before; check to see if it was loaded. Five bullets. Five bullets for a chain junk-on-the-walls restaurant waitress who'd never fired a gun. Not even enough bullets to practice. *I'm either lucky,* she thought, *or fucked.*

Nikki spat the spent wad of Double Bubble onto the highway and took off slowly, the farm fields on either side of the road, corn and soybeans growing full and green. The fungus didn't hit the plants, just people. Birds seemed unaffected, as did deer and pastures full of cattle. She smiled. I guess cows didn't need antidepressants. Nikki once thought of releasing the cattle from their multi-acre cages, but the thought of topping a hill and finding a 1,600-pound beast in the road terrified her. Sixteen miles later, it was something else.

The sign, "Exeter: Population 2,859," lay on the ground, the wooded posts that once held it up blackened and burned. Nikki turned the Harley from the highway onto the Main Street of Exeter, the ground of the town black, all the buildings levelled by fire – some of the debris still trailed white smoke into the sky. Mass electricity overload? Arson? Act of God? Nikki drove slowly through the streets of town, the occasional black, smoking tree stood next to a foundation, or a crumbled chimney.

"What the hell?" she whispered. The entire town – a town that once held almost 3,000 people – was gone. It was just gone. Except the church.

Nikki knew she should just punch the accelerator, and leave a streak on the ash-covered pavement as she sped out of this dead town. Staying would be a mistake. Still, there was the church, untouched, its steeple jutted toward Heaven like a giant thumbs up. The only structure that survived the unforgiving wall of hungry death, eating everything it touched, was a holy place. A haven? A sanctuary? A morgue? She put the bike in gear and slowly pulled through the ash-covered streets of what was once a town. The church, a tall brick building as most Midwest churches are, regardless of denomination – fire and brimstone Southern Baptist, or mellow, grape juice Methodist – stood near the town square. That much of the town was still identifiable. Most of the upper floors of downtown businesses, wooden frames betraying the weakness of their red brick fronts, had collapsed, but she could still make out the courthouse. These places were dead. The church might still be alive. Somebody might still be alive.

Smoke from smoldering debris drifted past her in brief puffs. The fire had raged through town recently, eaten everything it could eat and now took its last breath. But why hadn't it eaten the church? Nikki hoped for a miracle. She stopped her Harley in the street in front of steps that lead to the big, wide wooden doors.

"Why didn't you burn?" Nikki whispered. She stepped off the now-silent bike and ascended the concrete steps.

The big, wooden front doors opened with a long, low creak, the ominous sound nearly explosive in the darkened narthex, the gray interior of the church punctuated with yellows, reds, greens and blues from sunlight that streamed through the stained glass. The angels on the glass looked sad. She stepped slowly toward the sanctuary, the great, lofty ceiling and dark wooden pews that had probably been a third full on most Sundays stretched before her. "Hello?" Nikki said, her voice cracking. She coughed and tried again, louder. "Hello?" Her voice echoed uncomfortably in the darkness. The sound that came back was even more so.

"My child," a deep, gravelly voice said from the area of the altar. "You've come. You've come for salvation."

A movement. Nikki stood in the back of the sanctuary as a black mass rose from a chair beneath a huge wooden crucifix. Nikki gasped. The pistol sat heavily in the right pocket of her cargo shorts. Her brain screamed at her to take it and blow the fucking brains out of whatever was coming at her. As the mass grew closer, walking into the light from the stained-glass windows, it became, as it always was, a Preacherman, his black robes enveloping him. The Preacherman, unshaven for weeks smiled an honest smile and spread his arms.

"I'm so happy to see you, my child," he said, his voice smooth, comforting.

Fear and tension rushed from Nikki, and she was able to breathe again. Although she hadn't stepped into a church since her mother died, a man of God stood before her, and that meant comfort.

"Hello, Father," she said, her voice in a whisper. "I'm happy to see you."

The Preacherman's smile grew larger. "As I am to see you," he said. "The Day of the Lord has come. As with Noah, our Father has cleansed the world of the unclean, the impure. We are saved, my child. We are pure. Rejoice." The Preacherman motioned for Nikki to sit on the deep red cushions that lined the oak pews, and she sat, the thought of grabbing the pistol in her pocket and blasting his brains out gone. Nikki sat on the pew, the Preacherman slid slowly next to her. "Where are you from?" he asked.

From? From? The shock of this town, this man, of her dead father squirming in his plastic body bag, flooded her mind. She found it hard to grasp the answer. "St. Joe," she finally said in a whisper. "I'm from St. Joseph."

"Do you have anyone with you?" he asked. "Or are you alone, like so many of the Pure are?" Nikki could only nod. The Preacherman smiled an understanding smile and nodded with her. "Exeter was gone, empty," he continued. "Despite my faith in the Lord, this town was full of unrepentant sinners. Satan and the pharmaceutical devils who brought upon our world the Piper, the Ophiocordon, the fungus drug, took them all, then the Beast took the town by fire. This town is cleansed by fire." The Preacherman's voice rose to a preaching cadence, his hot, putrid breath pushed against her face like a sewage leak. She gagged. "Their sin cleansed by fire." Then his voice grew quiet. "Forgive me, child. This event, this Biblical event has weighed heavily on me as well." He smiled again. "Would you take communion with me?"

Sweat began to run down Nikki's back. Something was wrong. Something was wrong with this man. But she couldn't answer him. The Preacherman stood and walked to a table before the alter. *Had he been waiting for me?* she wondered.

"Come," he said gently. "Come and share in the blood and body of Christ." Nikki didn't know why she stepped slowly toward this man. She wanted to run, to jump on her motorcycle and scream out of this blackened town. But she couldn't. This man was a preacher, a man of God, and he wanted to care for her. She walked to the table and knelt.

The Preacherman picked a small communion wafer from a tray and put it on her tongue. "And he took bread, and gave thanks, and broke it, and gave unto them, saying, 'This is my body which is given for you. Do this in remembrance of me.'" Then put a simple clay cup to her lips, the smell of cheap merlot, not grape juice, swam through her nostrils. "Likewise also the cup after supper, saying, 'This cup is the new covenant in my blood, which is shed for you,'" the Preacherman droned as Nikki drank, a sudden flush of warmth and a wave of dizziness spread over her. "How do you feel, my child?" the Preacherman asked, his voice suddenly loveless, dark. "Do you feel repentant? Do you feel saved?"

Wow. That wine's hitting me awfully fast, she thought. The room grew darker, and the Preacherman smiled, the flicker of candlelight dancing in his eyes. It wasn't a bad smile, but it wasn't a good smile either. Nikki had seen that smile before on Patrick Bostich. Patrick Bostich always smiled like that; he probably smiled like that the night in seventh grade when he killed his family in their sleep. Nikki never saw Patrick after that, except on the front page of the St. Joseph News-Press when he was sentenced to life in prison. It was a crazy smile.

"I'll be okay," she whispered as the room spun into blackness and she dropped unconscious on the floor.

Nikki slowly awoke to hundreds of lighted candles filling the sanctuary, her panic dulled by whatever the Preacherman had used to drug her. What the hell happened? She scanned her immediate surroundings, not moving her head. Nikki lay naked on a table underneath the huge wooden cross, her hands bound by ropes, but her legs were free. Something moved to her right – the Preacherman. She suppressed a gasp as he walked slowly, purposefully toward her. Nikki slid her eyelids closed, leaving slits to watch this bastard who'd kidnapped her. Yellow candlelight flickered across the Preacherman as he ascended the carpeted steps to the altar, his robes loosely swung from his shoulders, the black cloth open down the front, scabbed-over crosses decorated his chest and thighs.

The Preacherman raised his arms toward the ceiling and bellowed, "The Day of the Lord is at hand." Whatever peaceful sanity his voice had greeted her with was gone. "You have given me, my Lord, this pure soul, to save this Earth with goodness, and righteousness. As Noah sought to rid this world of the wicked, so does this child. Thank you, my Lord." The Preacherman stepped to the table, and flashed a serrated kitchen knife, probably used to carve ham for holiday church dinners. "But first, let me carve unto her your holy mark, so sinners will know to bow before her." When the hot, sweaty fingers of his left hand twisted around her ankle, and the knife rose in his right, Nikki jerked back her left leg and thrust it forward, and crushed her heel into the Preacherman's face. The crunch of his breaking nose filled the sanctuary. The Preacherman lurched back screaming, blood spewed from his ruined nose. His left foot stepped off the altar and he tumbled backward, knocking dozens of candles onto the sanctuary carpet.

"Fuck you," Nikki tried to scream as she struggled off the table, but it only wheezed from her dry lips. "Asshole," she whispered and found her wrists bound by a rope he'd strung under the table. The Preacherman grunted as he tried to stand, flames from candles grew across the floor around him. Nikki flipped the table with a crash and pulled the rope over its upturned legs.

"Jou 'ezabelle," he spat through the blood from his crushed nose. "Jou vill burn."

Nikki grabbed a lit candelabra standing next to her and tossed it at the Preacherman. "You will first," she said, moving on rubber legs. Flames that grew in the sanctuary lit the room with an eerie, dancing glow. Her clothes lay in a pile on a pew. She limped toward them, the drug still swimming in her head.

"Jou 'itch," the Preacherman screamed.

Nikki collapsed over the pew as she reached toward her clothing, her head slapped against the red cushion. As she pushed herself up with weak arms, the dark form of the Preacherman loomed over her.

"'itch," he bellowed.

Numb fingers wrapped around the pistol in her shorts pocket. She pulled it out and fired wildly. The Preacherman screamed.

"Fuck you," Nikki wheezed, the pistol dropped from her fingers and landed onto the carpet with a soft thud. She didn't bend to retrieve it. "Fuck you." She stumbled up the aisle, the Preacherman wailed in pain behind her. The light of growing fire flickered through the sanctuary as Nikki nearly fell into the narthex. Standing at the door to the outside, to freedom, Nikki grabbed a flagpole bearing the white Christian flag emblazoned with a red cross, and stepped into the night. She jammed the flagpole through the door handles, cutting off this exit from that crazy bastard.

"Burn," she whispered, then hobbled to her Harley and drove away from the church, away from the first person she'd trusted since her father died.

July 10: St. Joseph, Missouri
CHAPTER 18

Arnold sat in the cab of Doug's pickup like an uninvited party guest. Jenna squeezed close to Doug, freeing less than an inch between her and Arnold. Terry sat in the passenger seat, his right arm resting on the open window, a beer between his legs like he didn't care a stranger who spoke like Arnold Schwarzenegger was wedged between Doug and Jenna staring straight ahead like, well, like a robot. The four rode in silence north from Platte City, the destroyed gas stations long behind them, only an occasional dead car sat on the side of the road. Doug expected to see more vehicles as they approached St. Joseph, a town of about 75,000. Did no one try to flee? Or did people just die too quickly to try and escape? As a large, green road sign grew closer on the east side of the highway, Terry bounced in his seat.

"Big town ahead. Let's live it up," Terry hooted and tossed his empty beer can out the window.

"The sign said 'St. Joseph,'" Doug said. "What kind of living it up are we going to do in St. Joseph?"

Terry thought for a minute. "I don't know," he said, cracking open a warm beer.

"Do you even know anything about St. Joseph?"

Terry nodded. "Sure," he said. "Pony Express."

"Anything else?"

"Uh, no."

"How about Jesse James?" Doug said, seriously considering taking one of Terry's beers, even though it was only 10 in the morning. *It's the Apocalypse, you wake early, you start drinking early.*

"The guy from 'Monster Garage?'" Terry said. "Didn't he cheat on that Sandra Bullock?"

Doug shook his head. "No, you moron, not the guy from 'Monster Garage.' Jesse Woodson James, the fucking outlaw. He was murdered here. Jesus H., Terry, you wouldn't know if the president had come from St. Joe."

"I'm not into politics," Arnold said, staring at the road before them. "I'm into survival."

Jenna looked at Arnold as she reached across him and took the beer from Terry; he didn't flinch, his expression blank. "Eminem's from St. Joseph," she said, turning away from this strange little man.

"No shit?" Terry said, popping the tab of another beer and taking a quick drink before anyone else wanted it. "You think he's there?"

Doug laughed. "Why the fuck would Eminem still live in St. Joe?"

"Maybe his mother lives there," Jenna said. "Well, probably not anymore."

Terry laughed.

"Your levity is good," Arnold said. "It relieves tension and the fear of death."

Nothing roamed the streets of St. Joseph when Doug pulled his pickup off the interstate and onto Highway 6 that cut through the business district. Cars that hadn't moved for weeks stared at them from parking lots and the middle of the street as Doug pulled slowly through town. Black traffic lights sat dead while they drove through town, and the Dunkin' Donuts, well, wouldn't you know it? It was closed. A homemade banner hung across the Highway 6, "The Piper is death: Ophiocordon is killing you." Blackening gray blobs dotted the streets and sidewalks, great knob-topped stems grew from what were once human beings. *Did an antidepressant do this?* Doug wondered. *And if it did, how will we ever know?* Doug drove with the windows down, hoping to hear some sound of human life. There was nothing. "Well, it looks like the electricity's gone," he said, scanning the storefronts. "It had to crap out sometime."

"Damn," Terry spat. "And we got all those Schwarzenegger movies. How are me and Arnold going to watch them now?"

Doug sighed and turned the truck off the main street into the parking lot of a building that had apparently been under construction when the Outbreak hit. He pulled to a stop next to a small trailer office and slid the transmission into park. "Come and give me a hand, Terry," he said. "I don't think the guys at Lobo and Sons Construction need that generator anymore. You boys can watch your movies."

"I am humbled," Arnold said, as Doug and Terry stepped from the cab of the truck. "I am honored and I am moved beyond words."

Jenna scooted as far away from Arnold as she could until the boys loaded the gas-powered generator into the truck bed. Doug slammed the tailgate home and wiped his forehead with his shirtsleeve.

"Damn thing's heavy," he said to Terry, breaking into a forced smile. "Kinda like that Penny girl you dated in high school." Terry leaned on the side of the truck, his forearms hung over the bed. He didn't smile. Doug frowned. "I was just kidding about Penny."

Terry nodded. "I know, man," he said, leaning closer to his friend. "Now, I don't really want them to hear," he whispered. "But what do you figure we're doing here?"

"Here?" Doug asked. "We're getting you a damned generator so we can cook and have lights and let you watch TV. What do you think we're doing?"

Terry lifted a finger over his mouth. "Not here," he said softly, dropping his hand back over the bed. "I mean here like, well, anywhere. Where are we going, man? Omaha? What if it's like Kansas City? Everybody's dead. Should we find some place to live? Or are we going to just keep driving until all this shit catches up to us? Or maybe something worse."

Doug stepped closer and leaned closer to Terry. "Worse? We might be the last fucking people alive on Earth. What is out there that's worse than that?"

"Other people, man. There's a nice, sweet, pretty girl in the cab of that truck. We ain't going to do nothing bad by her, but if we're alive, there are other people out there who will," Terry spat. "And Arnold. Well, I don't know what the fuck's going on with him, but at least we'll take care of him."

Terry's eyes burned in a way Doug had never seen. He shook his head. "I don't know," he said. "I've just been running. From something, not to something. I couldn't stay in Paola. Too many memories. I knew too many faces on too many dead bodies. Do you think we should settle down? Find a place and hide?"

Terry nodded. "Yeah. Yeah I do," he said. "Someplace out in the country, but close enough we can come into town for beer."

Doug smiled and nodded. "Okay, Terry. That makes sense. Let's give it a shot. There's a lot of small towns north of here, we'll head there tomorrow. Tonight, we'll party."

A grin grew across Terry's face. "Shit yes," he said, then walked back to the cab, opened the passenger side door and slid back into his seat. Doug dropped into the driver's side seat next to Jenna.

Jenna looked at Doug. "We heard everything you said."

Terry cracked open a beer. "Damn."

"I agree with hiding. I also agree with partying. And him," she said, motioning toward Arnold. "I have no idea what the heck he thinks." She held out her right hand. "Now beer me."

They decided on a hotel, the biggest one they could find. A Ramada Inn with a restaurant and indoor water park. Doug drove through town, down Belt Highway, Fredrick Street, and through the south part of town that probably looked desolate even before the Outbreak. After driving through the city for hours they knew St. Joe was as dead as Platte City. Near the Ramada they raided a grocery store for as much canned food as they could carry out, and enough beer to keep Terry happy for at least a while, the stench of the rotting meat and produce kept Jenna in the parking lot. After about twenty minutes, the three men walked out of the store each pushing grocery carts loaded with food, and they drove toward the Ramada. They didn't make it.

"Hey," Jenna yelled a few blocks from the hotel. "A mall. There's a shopping mall here." She turned toward Doug, a smile pulling her face tight. "Back in that garage you promised me clean clothes and a safe place to stay." She started bouncing in the seat. "You promised. And the clothes are in there. And guess what?" she paused for a moment to giggle. "Everything's on sale." She burst into laughter. Doug took his eyes off her enough to steer the truck into the mall parking lot and park it right in front of Dillard's.

It was stupid, Doug knew. A vast, dark building full of who knows what. If the human race had been decimated by an alien invasion or real zombies instead of something like a disease or a gypsy curse, Doug wouldn't have said "no," he would have said, "hell no." Stay small, stay safe. But this wasn't an alien attack. There were no monsters except those they imagined. As far as he knew, most of the people on the planet were just dead. He hadn't heard any news report about this happening in Europe, Russia, China or anyplace else, but he didn't see troops planting flags he didn't recognize. Whatever started turning people into mushrooms, if it were the Piper, there used to be a lot of depressed people in the world. "Okay," he said. "I keep my promises. I just hope this doesn't get us killed." As Jenna grinned at him, her eyes melting into his, he knew he really didn't care. Doug pulled the baseball bat from behind his seat, Terry grabbed a beer, Arnold cocked a pretend pistol, and Jenna pulled the strap of her purse over her shoulder for some reason Doug couldn't imagine. Maybe it was her time of the month. Terry was the first to the door. He pulled the glass entryway wide.

"It ain't locked," Terry said. "Welcome shoppers to, uh, some fucking mall in St. Joe. Enjoy your shopping experience." They all went inside.

Before the Outbreak, malls had been dying across America to the point it looked like the end of the world had already hit. Not this mall. As they walked through the concourse, skylights bathing the walkway in warm, yellow light, every storefront sported a sign, and every store was full of merchandise. The group kept near the front, under the skylights and the occasional window, steering clear of the corners black with shadows.

"Hey, Arnold," Terry said, lightly hitting the thin man on the arm. "Look over there." He pointed. "GameStop. Let's get an Xbox and some video games and shoot us some zombies." And they were gone, half-jogging toward the video game store. Doug watched them go out of sight. His chest grew tight; it didn't feel right to be separated.

Doug jumped at the sudden warm touch of Jenna's fingertips on his forearm. "Are you coming with me?" she asked softly. Doug turned, her deep green eyes grabbed his every thought. At that moment, nothing else mattered; not the moldy bodies in the street, not the crazy people in the world, not the boys in the GameStop, nothing. Doug nodded and followed her into a clothing store. The vastness of the store, the deep shadows along the walls and behind the racks of clothes immediately made him nervous.

"We can't stay here long," he said, wondering if Jenna could hear the wavering in his voice.

"Relax," she said, brushing the palm of her hand gently down his chest. "I'll just try on a few things. It won't take a minute." Softly singing something Doug couldn't make out, Jenna raked her hand across racks of dresses, and finally plucked one off. "Turn around," she said, grinning. "Don't peek."

Doug's hand squeezed down hard on the neck of the aluminum bat as he turned to face the front of the store. Hair rose on the nape of his neck, and his heartbeat made the front of his shirt jump as he waited for Jenna to change, but, he wondered, was this feeling the mall, or Jenna naked behind him?

"What do you think of this?" Jenna asked. Doug turned to find her in a form-fitting blue dress, cut low enough he could see the lower curve of her small breasts.

"It's, uh. It's nice," Doug stammered, feeling a flush rush over him. "It's nice for, you know, a date or something."

"A date?" Jenna said, playfully crossing her arms under her breasts, pushing them close to popping out of the tiny dress. "Did you say a date?"

Doug nodded. He hadn't felt this uncomfortable since high school. A bead of sweat ran down the small of his back. "Yes, I did. And we should take the dress. But right now, we need clothes like jeans, or cargo pants. You know, something tough with lots of pockets."

Jenna smiled and grabbed a few pairs of jeans from a shelf and some shirts with sleeves and collars. "I know. But I'll keep the dress for later. Maybe we can ..." A scream echoed through the empty mall. Terry.

"Doug, Doug," Terry yelled from down the mall court. The scream was followed by a thud.

"Damn it," he hissed and started to run toward the door. "Terry," Doug called back.

Jenna grabbed his arm. "Don't leave me," she whispered.

"Never," Doug said, wrapping his hand into hers.

The angry barks of dogs rang down the mall court as Doug and Jenna shot from the entrance to Dillard's, Terry's grunts came closer in the darkness. Arnold was first, Terry followed closely behind, a box under his arm. Arnold paused and looked at Doug and Jenna. "Come with me if you want to live," he said, and pushed them toward the exit, and they followed this strange little man through the shopping mall.

Furious barks rang through the empty, shopperless mall walkways, getting closer with every flapping step the four made toward the exit.

"Guard dogs," Terry hissed, the morning, noon, and nights of beer dragging him down. "Hungry. Hungry guard dogs."

Doug turned his head as he ran, holding Jenna's hand so tightly their knuckles were white. The dogs, Dobermans, foam flying from their lips, appeared briefly in sunlight before the shadows quickly reclaimed them, their skin pulled tight over their ribs. He knew these dogs were going to kill them and eat them. "Run," he wheezed. "Get outta here."

Sunlight streamed through the big glass doors as they moved too slowly to reach them in time. Something hit the tiled mall floor with a slap; Doug turned his head to see Jenna's clothing lying behind them. Jenna wrenched her hand from his.

"What are you doing?" Doug shouted as Jenna's hands started fumbling in her purse. "There's no time."

Jenna pushed him away and stopped. "Get them out of here," she screamed and stopped, turning to face the flying bodies of claws and teeth. Doug stumbled and fell to the floor; the first dog ran over Jenna's clothing pile like it wasn't there.

"Come on," Terry called from what seemed to be miles away.

Jenna pulled her hand from the purse, the bag fell to the floor. Doug watched, incapable of moving. Jenna stood still in the form-fitting blue dress, levelled the Peckinpa's .38-caliber pistol in a policeman's stance and fired, the pop of a bullet discharge echoed through the long hall. The lead dog yelped and jerked backward like its owner pulled hard on an invisible leash. Another pop dropped the second dog. Jenna stood next to Doug like a really pissed off prom princess. She turned and knelt beside him, so close her hair brushed his face.

"Are you okay?" she asked. Doug nodded slowly. Jenna smiled. "We should probably go."

July 10: U.S. 71 in Rural Missouri

CHAPTER 19

When the highway sign on Interstate 29 read "U.S. 71, Seven Miles," Darryl nearly giggled, but didn't; Maryanne might hear him. The hot July wind whipped through the Mustang as he drove north on U.S. 71, Maryanne somewhere out there in this great, wide, dead world – but Maryanne wasn't in Darryl's new ride, sucking his dick, or sleeping in the passenger seat with a rifle pointed at his face. That bitch. That crazy, crazy bitch. But she could hear him anyway, Darryl knew she could. He felt it. St. Joe was still in his rear-view mirror. He might still be in the city limits, the limits of what was left of the city. St. Joseph itself was still there, but the people were gone. Even Maryanne. He'd made sure of that.

As he lay in that bed in St. Joe's Motel 6, Maryanne passed out from liquor, the Cowboy next to her in a heap, Darryl knew he would probably die when the sun came up. Now that this fucking psycho had some new toy to play with, he was as dead as the guy at the gas station in Junction City, Kansas. He knew Maryanne shot the big, sweaty man in the chest because if she'd blown his head off he wouldn't have had time to suffer. She watched the man bleed and wheeze until he finally shook and didn't move again. Darryl thought blankly of her smile, her cold, cold smile.

Maryanne's soft, blond hair rested on Darryl's shoulder, her right arm and leg draped over the Cowboy. Darryl knew if he didn't move now, he might never move again. Darryl slipped out of bed, ready to mumble some excuse about taking a whiz, but Maryanne didn't move, her breathing steady. Yeah, enough Evan Williams will do that to you. The man she called the Cowboy moaned softly in his sleep, freezing Darryl, but neither of them moved. Moonlight shone through the window, lighting the room, every contour of Maryanne's gorgeous body visible through the thin sheet. He peeled his pants gently off a chair, thankful he no longer had keys or change in his pocket to betray him, picked his tennis shoes from the floor, and took a step toward the door, wide open to let in some kind of breeze. It didn't. He stopped and smiled a nervous smile. The Cowboy had shown him something, a present. A present for him. A .44-caliber pistol sat in a hotel drawer behind the Gideon Bible. He knew if Maryanne ever caught up with him, he would need it.

Darryl stepped softly to the dresser and slowly pulled the metal handle on the cheap pressed-wood furniture, keeping his eyes on the maniacs in the bed. The slight scrape of the sliding drawer sounded like a scream in Darryl's head, but neither of them moved. He slid his shaking hand into the drawer, a feeling of strength rushed over him as his fingers curved around the cool handle of this machine made to kill. He pulled it from the drawer, the moonlight shone off its silver barrel, and wondered if he should just kill her. Kill her now. Put the gun against the back of her head and, boom, no more fear, no more torture, no more days wired on amphetamines fucking until Darryl's cock was a raw, throbbing lump. He stepped toward the bed and stopped. *But what if I miss?* Doubt crept through the dark parts of his brain. He knew what she'd do if he missed his chance to kill her.

Darryl turned and crept out of the motel room as quietly as a thief, and never looked back.

Once he cleared the second-floor walkway and hit the steps, he ran, wincing when his bare feet met a rock on the pavement. He didn't stop. He couldn't stop. He was gone from her and he had to keep going. But where? Ducking behind abandoned cars, he made his way to a UPS truck that sat on the entrance to a bridge over I-29. He stopped. Nothing moved from the dark room of the Motel 6, Maryanne's room, the only room with the door hanging wide. Darryl slipped on his jeans and tennis shoes as he caught his breath. No shouting, no shooting. They must still be asleep. Darryl grinned. He was free. He'd only known Maryanne for a couple of days, but she'd beaten him, broken him. Darryl now knew real fear.

A new Chevy Impala rested a few yards from the UPS truck; the moon silhouetted the owner slumped over the steering wheel, alien lumps covered his body. He wanted to run, to hop in the Impala and go. But she'd hear him. Oh, yes, Maryanne would hear him, she would follow him, and she would catch him. Then Maryanne would cut off his dick and roast it over an open fire, smiling as she ate it while he lay next to her bleeding his life into the dirt. No, he had to make sure she was gone. He couldn't have her chasing him. She was going to Omaha, that much he knew. He just had to make sure she went.

From Darryl's view atop the interstate overpass, the skyline of St. Joseph looked like American consumerism had thrown up. A Red Lobster gave way to a Dunkin Donuts, which gave way to convenience stores, a Starbucks, Lone Star Steakhouse, a shopping mall, Budget Barn grocery store, an old Motor Coach Inn, and dozens more businesses, dark and deserted. The Motor Coach sat directly across the highway from Motel 6. Darryl grinned; his heart beat quickly in his chest. His right front pocket held a Ziploc bag of amphetamines. He knew if he could get to the Motor Coach and break into a room that faced Maryanne's, he could wait them out. He squatted for a few seconds, watching the quiet, open doorway then broke into a sprint over the bridge.

Every room on the second floor was locked. Darryl squatted behind a cleaning cart, the remains of the cleaning lady lay where she fell, most of her exposed flesh sunk, buried under the dying, blackening mold, two stalks protruding from her abdomen hung limp, their pods open, spent.

"Shit," he hissed, but not too loudly. As the young sun washed the horizon with pink, Darryl realized he might be fucked. "I know you don't care, there, Maria, or Bonita, or whatever in the hell your name was. Crazy bitch can't do anything more to you. She's going to fucking *eat* me." The morning grew light quickly. Darryl knew he had to move now or be stuck behind the cleaning cart with towels covered with gray mold in the humid Missouri summer. Then his eyes fell on Maria's belt. Keys. This motel was so old it still used keys. He leaned toward her, and pulled the keyring from Maria's belt, the revulsion of death beaten from him the day he met Maryanne. Two minutes later he sat in the dark motel room's stagnant air, already sweltering in the mid-July morning. He popped a White Cross and swallowed it without water, turned a crank to open the window, and stared at the second floor of Motel 6 through a slit in the curtain. He could wait on them forever.

Nothing stirred until probably noon. Darryl sat in the motel room; sweat beaded on his stubbly upper lip, as he watched the sun draw through the morning sky. A squirrel ran along the railing outside his window, a brief thought slamming through Darryl's wired brain like a tennis shoe in a dryer. Hunger had crawled into Darryl, and that squirrel on the railing, nibbling on something it held in its clever little hands, Darryl knew he could catch it. He knew if he crept outside he could snatch that squirrel off that railing; then he'd eat it, eat it raw. He tensed to move, to follow the call and jump out of the door to chase that goddamned squirrel, that goddamned tasty squirrel. Then there was a gunshot.

Darryl screamed, or thought he screamed. The squirrel froze. The little bastard was only about five feet outside his window and Darryl didn't know if it froze from the gunshot, or from his scream. Did Maryanne hear him? Yes, the devil goddess heard everything.

Something moved at the Motel 6. A shoe flew from the blackened doorway of the motel room and tumbled over the railing into the parking lot. The Cowboy followed it out, slamming into the metal railing. The scalp-tightening amphetamines made Darryl giggle – the Cowboy didn't have pants. Then Maryanne appeared in the doorway, her perfect, firm form naked in the sun, a rifle at her shoulder. I would so do that, ran through Darryl's head, an erection pushing tight inside his jeans. I would. He giggled again, because he knew he had. "Get in here, asshole," Darryl heard from Maryanne's shrill mouth, or maybe it was from her thoughts. As the White Crosses did their magic, Darryl thought he might be able to read her mind. The Cowboy slunk inside the motel room, and Maryanne followed. A few minutes later, screams punched through the dead still silence. It wasn't pain, or fear. Maryanne always screamed like that when she took it from behind.

Hunger gnawed at Darryl. He thought of leaving the window to find something in the room, or search the cleaning cart for melted, moldy mints, but he didn't move. He sat in the motel room chair, and stared through the slight part in the curtain at the room across the highway. An hour later, or was it two, the Cowboy walked from the motel doorway, a bag of food and booze in his arms, Maryanne close behind him, her rifle pointed at his back. Darryl stared at them. Stared as the Cowboy retrieved his shoe. Stared as they got into Maryanne's LeBaron. Stared as they pulled onto the onramp. He watched until the brown car disappeared up the northbound lane. Darryl smiled. She was gone. The bitch, the devil, was gone. He stood and stumbled on legs that had gone numb hours ago, fell onto the bed and watched as blackness overtook him. He never realized he'd pissed himself.

Darryl didn't know when he woke. It could have been an hour later, or a week. The sun stood high in the sky when he pulled back the curtains an inch. Maria still lay in a rotting pile outside his window, the squirrel (had there been a squirrel?) long gone. The door to the motel room across the highway still hung open, but the brown LeBaron was gone. Gone. Darryl had seen Maryanne and the Cowboy drive away. He was sure of it. "Fucking A," he whispered, pushed the Cowboy's .44 into the back of his loose jeans and stepped out of the room on wobbly legs.

That was hours ago. Darryl slunk down the steps of the motel's outer walkway and into the semi-crowded parking lot, staying low and behind cars, working his way to the convenience store at the edge of the motel's parking lot. People had already raided the store, but packages of pork rinds and potato chips, and cans of chili and Progresso soup with pull-off lids still dotted the shelves. Darryl sat on the floor in the convenience store and ate chili until he was full. He packed the rest into plastic bags, grabbed a 30-pack of warm beer, and walked outside, the amphetamines out of his system, his head clearer than before he met Maryanne.

"Hey, mother fuckers. This is my town," he wanted to yell into the now darkening St. Joseph sky, but didn't. Even though he'd watched the

LeBaron drive out of sight, Maryanne and the Cowboy might still be out there, waiting for him. He threw back his shoulders, bearing the weight of his groceries evenly in both hands, and walked toward the gas pumps. A decomposed body covered in black goo lay on the pavement, a dry rusty stain spread from beneath him. Next to the guy was a Mustang; probably a 2010 from what Darryl could figure. Not that it mattered. He wasn't going to pick up chicks in St. Joe tonight anyway. The keys to the car sat inches from the owner's fingertips, a dark blue US Bank debit card shown through the black layer that had once been thriving, gray fungus. The man was on his way to pay for gas when the Piper got him. How long ago? Two weeks? A month? "Thanks for the gas," Darryl said as he picked the keys off the asphalt, loaded his groceries in the passenger seat and started the engine. He popped a beer and took a drink. It was time to go.

Darryl drove north. He didn't know why. Omaha was north, and Maryanne was going to Omaha. Darryl turned off Interstate 29 and onto U.S. 71. Interstate 29 went to Omaha. Maryanne would be on Interstate 29. U.S. 71 went to … Well, Darryl didn't know where the fuck U.S. 71 went, but it probably didn't go to Omaha. The long gray strip of U.S. 71 snaked its way over the hills of Northwest Missouri, past dark farmhouses, and fields filled with corn and soybeans no one would ever harvest. As the Mustang shot up the rural highway Darryl shoved the first CD he pulled from the sun visor into the stereo. Bon Scott's shrill voice poured "Highway to Hell" through the open cab.

"Yes," Darryl whispered so Maryanne didn't hear him. She could. He knew she could. And if she could hear him, she could find him. If she could find him she could–

A taillight.

Darryl shoved both feet onto the brake pedal, his open beer dropped to the floor, foam quickly soaked into the carpet. The Mustang screeched to a stop in the middle of the highway. A vehicle somewhere in front of Darryl topped a hill and disappeared, its white and red lights vanished from sight. Maryanne. Maryanne. Maryanne. Maryanne and her soulless smile. Maryanne and her cold, frozen eyes. Maryanne and her hungry pussy. Maryanne and her gun. Darryl pulled his car onto a gravel road and behind a lonely tin barn, gently shifted the gear into park, and killed the engine. Maryanne was close to him, close enough to feel gnawing at the base of his brain. Darryl crawled into the fetal position and screamed for hours.

July 10: Barton, Missouri
CHAPTER 20

The woman's clothes didn't fit well. Nikki stood before the full-length bedroom mirror and smiled grimly at the sky-blue sun blouse festooned with daisies, and baggy jeans held tightly onto her waist by a long brown belt. The owner of the gardening clothes had about thirty pounds on Nikki, or at least she did. The owner and her husband sat out back in lawn chairs, looking over their once precious garden, gunshots taking their lives before the now blackened mold could. By the rate of decomposition, they must have been out there for weeks, watching from pecked-out eye sockets as weeds overtook their green beans, sweet corn, and pepper plants. Nikki walked from the master bedroom and into the mudroom on her way into the back yard. She propped a wide-brimmed straw hat on her head, shoved a pair of worn leather gloves into her back pocket, and grabbed a basket. If she was going to bury these poor people in their own garden, she was sure as shit going to pick any food that was ready.

Nikki stopped in Barton by accident. As she shot up U.S. 71, away from Exeter, away from the crazy Preacherman with his crazy smile and crushed nose, probably burning to death in the hell of his own church, a light flashed in her rear-view mirror. Headlights. Headlights were somewhere over a hill behind her. Hot night air pushed against her naked skin, her clothes now ash miles behind her, she knew danger followed. As she drove, the remnants of the Preacherman's drugs worked their way out of her system, she felt more vulnerable than the day the Greasyman stormed into her house, a day that now seemed like months ago. She flicked off the Harley's headlights and turned onto a paved rural highway, a sign reading "Barton: 2 miles" lost in the darkness. Nikki cranked the accelerator and shot away into the night, praying like hell a deer didn't walk in front of her bike onto the highway that was barely visible under the light of the waning moon.

Barton caught Nikki by surprise. The flash of a green highway sign flipped past – "Barton: Pop. 245 – freezing her breath in her chest. Then the town jumped into her vision, a dark jumble of long-empty storefronts, and a few dozen houses grew suddenly from the blank fields around her. Nikki released the accelerator and slowly braked to a stop in front of a weather-worn "Welcome to Barton" sign in a small, weed-filled city park, the "t" missing. Welcome to Bar-on. As she sat on the Harley, bearing the weight on her left leg, the bike sounded frighteningly loud in the darkness. She shut off the engine.

Silence rang in her ears, the kind of silence people must have heard before cars, before trains, before civilization. It was the kind of silence she knew probably now covered the world. A coyote yipped somewhere in the night, miles off, but the yip carried forever. As Nikki stood in the street straddling the bike, more detail of the town grew out of the darkness, the vehicle back on the highway behind her briefly forgotten. The town may have actually boomed sometime, possibly during the First World War. A bank, a few grimacing stone faces stared from intricate brickwork, and a small string of two-story brick businesses – all probably long empty – ran along the main street, foreboding darkness stared at her from empty windows. As fear grew through her, Nikki felt her nipples grow hard despite the heat of the Midwest summer night. She fired up the Harley, the engine alerting her presence to anyone who might be left in this tiny town, and moved slowly down the main street.

Past the storefronts, yards thick with trees masked the dark, blank homes of the town; Nikki imagined corpses covered in that strange gray mold lying on the floors of some homes; crazed, scraggly bearded madmen stared at her from the windows of others. At the end of the street her heart began to pound and she stopped the bike. Electric light poured from the front windows of the last house.

Nikki dropped a basketful of red bell peppers into a strainer in the spotless kitchen sink. There were plenty more in the garden. She figured she'd freeze as many as she could. There were large Ziploc bags in the pantry and lots of room in the huge refrigerator, the freezer taking up half the unit. It would be a shame to waste all these fresh vegetables. She turned from the sink and took a cold bottle of Aquafina from the refrigerator; with the few spoiled leftovers fed down the garbage disposal, the rancid smell had dissipated quickly, which was good. Nikki planned on making a hell of a dinner and there would be leftovers. The harvest, she realized, might spill into tomorrow. Apart from the two rows of red peppers, four rows of sweet corn, and six rows of green beans, Nikki found carrots, onions, tomatoes, celery, strawberries, and some root she didn't recognize, but this was enough food to last her for months. *Actually, some of the tomatoes could probably use a few more days to ripen,* she thought. The Marstens have sat out there for a while now; a couple more days couldn't hurt.

Solar panels lining the roof relaxed Nikki as she stopped the bike next to the mailbox, its door wide open and crammed with mail and the local shopper newspaper. There's a reason the lights are on, she realized; as long as there's a sun, they're always going to be on. The yellow glow streaming from the wide-open plate glass window dimmed once it reached the street, but was enough to illuminate "Jack and Jan Marsten" on the side of the mailbox. It didn't look like the Marstens were home. She sat on the big bike and stared at the house, the large flat screen TV black, the couches vacant. But where were Jack and Jan? Away to visit relatives when the Outbreak hit? Were they in body bags at the St. Joseph hospital, stacked like warehouse boxes along with her father? Then panic again gripped her. Were they still in the house, alive, waiting for someone to find them; waiting for her like the Preacherman? She slid off the bike and pulled a ball-peen hammer from the saddlebag where her father stored his "road tools," and walked toward the house in dark silence, wondering if Dad would have ever pictured his little girl carrying one of his tools with the thought of crushing someone's skull.

Nothing moved in the living room. Nikki walked as close as she could to the periphery of the light streaming from the large front window, holding the rubber grip of the hammer handle in her white knuckled fist. She moved slowly around the house, looking into windows like a peeping tom. All the shades were open wide. A computer sat in sleep mode in an office, a screensaver rolled through pictures of grandkids that would never pose for another picture. Jeans and a sun shirt were laid out on the tightly made bed in the master bedroom, waiting for someone who would never put them on. Nikki rounded the corner of the house, the master bedroom giving way to a darkened guest bedroom; enough light poured through from the open hall door to show the bed, vanity, and a large framed photo of an elderly couple she assumed were Jack and Jan holding hands on a white sand beach.

The crack of a nearby branch swung Nikki's head to her left, her fingers tightened on a grip that had started to relax. A doe stood at the edge of a tree row that ran along the back of the yard. It looked at Nikki briefly, then walked into the yard, this naked woman holding a hammer apparently not a threat. Nikki slowly followed the deer to the back of the house. A light popped on, and flooded the back yard as the deer crossed the lawn. The deer froze, its white tail twitched slightly. The light, Nikki prayed was controlled by a motion sensor, covered the yard. A garden hose snaked from the side of the house toward a large, weedy garden passing two lawn chairs parked next to a wheelbarrow filled with empty beer cans. People sat slumped in the chairs, the backs of their heads opened wide by the exit end of a shotgun blast. The deer, comfortable with the new light, walked slowly toward the garden, past the lawn chairs, and started chewing on a stalk of sweet corn.

Nikki, holding the hammer like a club, stepped away from the house and slowly moved toward the garden.

"Jack? Jan?" she said softly. The deer looked briefly at Nikki, and resumed eating. She released a heavy breath. She'd seen dead people get up and walk before, she didn't know if she had the nerves for that tonight.

"I'm not going to hurt you; I'm just looking for someplace to sleep tonight, okay?" As she stepped closer, the sweet smell of rotting flesh touched her nose. A month ago, Nikki knew she would have broken down crying in the yard. Now she was just relieved the Marstens wouldn't mind her sleeping in their bed. Nikki turned from the couple staring out of dead faces at a deer eating from their garden and walked to the house. The sliding glass door was unlocked. She pulled it open and walked into the coolness of air conditioning, locked all the doors, crawled into the Marstens' bed, and fell quickly to sleep.

The rest of the garden, except for a few dozen tomatoes, took well into the afternoon. "Thanks, Jack. Thanks, Jan," Nikki said to the dead couple, her newfound clothing wet with sweat. "I'll take care of you tomorrow." She hefted the basket of vegetables into her arms, walked past the Marstens and into the house. Despite the dead owners in the back yard, Nikki was ready to move into this house permanently. It had electricity, new appliances, water that most probably came from a well, and was close enough to larger cities she could run to for supplies, but far enough away to hide. As she took a shower, the steaming hot water caressed her body. She anticipated the cold blast of air conditioning that would hit her as soon as she stepped out of the shower and onto the bedroom floor. A smile grew on her lips; she felt good, relaxed. As she ran a wash cloth over her shoulders, she thought after she picked the remainder of the tomatoes and buried the Marstens, she would explore this out of the way, tiny town. But not today.

She stepped out of the shower; a different Nikki Holleran stared at her from the long bathroom mirror. She'd lost a few pounds since the Outbreak hit. As she turned back and forth, hands on hips, her stomach looked flatter than it had since junior high school, just before she filled out her last puberty growth spurt, and became Thickie Nikki. She also needed to shave. But her face had changed the most. It was a grim, joyless Nikki that looked back at her. She wondered if she'd ever be happy again.

Dinner was baked red peppers stuffed with hamburger Nikki had found in the freezer, and browned in a pan, sautéed with chopped onions, and celery. After she put away dinner and cleaned the kitchen as spotless as Jan had left it, Nikki ate strawberries in the living room, a glass of chilled Chardonnay on the end table beside her. Tonight, she knew, she could relax. Relax and be human. As she flipped through the shows the Marstens had DVRed, she grinned. Jan was a fan of "Project Runway." Nikki wanted something mindless to watch. Something to help her hide from the Marstens, the Preacherman, the Outbreak, the Piper, the spreading gray fungus, her dead father, and her sad, hard face. When the sound of a truck engine touched her ears, she threw herself down on the soft couch and cried.

July 11: Barton, Missouri
CHAPTER 21

Nikki lay on the Marstens' floral print couch, the sound of a truck engine grew closer, her tears soaked into the cushions. Why? Why here? Why now? The engine suddenly died in the late Missouri afternoon. Nikki's body tensed under Jan Marsten's lavender bathrobe. The truck wasn't gone; it stopped. Someone was here in this village, her haven, and everyone was a threat. She sat up and turned off the plasma-screen TV with a click on the remote control, and drained her glass of Chardonnay, the cool white wine sweet in her mouth.

Voices. Nikki slid off the couch and crawled to the great front window she'd left naked, the burgundy curtain pulled to the side. Dumb, dumb, dumb, Nikki, raced through her head as she looked around the house to see if there was anything to betray her presence. Doors were locked, TV off, kitchen cleaned. Light still poured from the summer evening sky. It was early; there was still at least two hours of good daylight left, so electric lights, even if the Marstens had something on a timer, weren't a problem – yet.

Three people stood around a red Ford F-150 at the spot Nikki first stopped in town, by the small, weed-choked park, a ramshackle sign welcoming visitors to "Bar-on." Two men leaned against the bed of the truck, one holding a beer, the other in a gray uniform, the kind with a nametag sewn over the left breast. The third man, a thin figure, stood motionless as a statue, or a robot. They all seemed to be staring silently at the house, at Nikki. Her stomach churned, fear stirring the dinner and Chardonnay into something volatile. *Why? Why this house?* she wondered. Then she saw her Harley next to the mailbox – right in the street. *They must know,* she thought. Despite the cool air of the living room, a trickle of sweat ran slowly down the center of Nikki's back. What are they doing?

A fourth head appeared. A thin woman in her 20s, with long auburn hair, stood from the front of the truck and called out something to the men. They pulled their heads from the Marstens' house and started talking as she walked from the front of the pickup, adjusting her cargo shorts. Nikki exhaled. She was peeing and they simply turned their heads. She watched as the Mechanic, the Redneck, the Robot, and the Librarian stood talking. Eventually they started pointing at buildings. Someone said something that made them all laugh – all but the Robot.

The Mechanic reached into the bed of the truck and pulled out an aluminum baseball bat, the Redneck grabbed a six-pack of beer, took a can and handed another to the Librarian, and they walked toward the town's only café.

"What the hell are you saying?" Nikki hissed. The four strangers stepped on the café porch, the Mechanic tugged at the door handle. The door didn't budge. He shook it, then stood back and kicked the door with a booted foot. It still didn't move. Nikki reached up, slowly unlatched the Marstens' front window, and slid it open an inch, the hot July air collided with the manmade coolness of the house.

"How's the windows?" the Mechanic hollered at the Redneck, who walked down the front of the small restaurant, tugging at the windows.

"This one's not locked," the Redneck said. He pushed it open, then shook his head. "I can't get through it, though." He looked at the Robot who never left his side. "But you can. Get in there."

The Robot shook his head. "This hero stuff has its limits."

"Come on, Arnold," the Mechanic said, walking toward them. "Me and Terry will give you a boost." The Robot grabbed the windowsill, and the Mechanic and the Redneck picked him up, and eased him through the window.

"Don't forget to let us in," the Redneck yelled through the window. "And watch out for raccoons and shit."

"Raccoons?" the Librarian asked.

The Redneck put his index finger over his mouth. Nikki could see he was trying not to laugh. The Librarian shook her head, said something to the Mechanic too softly for Nikki to hear and they walked to the front door. The Robot appeared moments later, eating potato chips from a bag and they walked into the café.

Who the hell are these people? Nikki wondered. And which of these do not belong? They went together as well as the Scooby gang would in real life. If the world hadn't ended, the Librarian wouldn't be riding with the Mechanic and the Redneck. But she is now, and laughing. And the Robot? He wasn't dressed like any of them, and he sure didn't act like anyone Nikki had seen outside nerds in junior high school. They didn't look dangerous. They looked …

A scream. Nikki winced as a shriek rang from the café. The Librarian shot out the door followed close behind by the Mechanic and the Redneck, the Redneck not spilling a drop from his open can of beer. The Robot calmly, mechanically, stepped onto the porch and pulled the door shut behind him.

"What the hell was that?" the Librarian screamed.

The Redneck, leaning against the truck breathing heavily, raised his beer hand and extended his index finger. "That was a fucking raccoon," he wheezed.

"How did you know?" she spat.

The Redneck shook his head. "How the hell would I know there was a raccoon in there eating Chips Ahoy! out of the goddamned bag? I was just trying to rile Arnold."

"Put that cookie down, now," Arnold said. Nikki picked up the trace of an accent. Was that German?

The Librarian started laughing, then they all started laughing. The Redneck drained his beer, tossed the empty can into the bed of the truck, and opened another. He held up what was left of the six-pack.

"Anyone?" he asked. The Librarian nodded and he tossed one to her.

"Let's keep going," the Mechanic said. "We're looking for a place to sleep. We need to find someplace safe …"

"And raccoon-free," the Librarian interrupted.

"…and raccoon-free by dark. There's got to be plenty of food and water left in this town. And hopefully at least one of these houses doesn't have a moldy body in it."

"Yeah," the Librarian said, a shiver running through her. "Those stalk things freaking creep me out."

The strangers walked across the street and approached one of the houses Nikki drove by in the night, the tall, straight trees in the front yard had masked the houses in shadows; they didn't look so ominous in daylight. The Mechanic turned the front doorknob and pushed the door open with the end of the bat. The door was unlocked and swung easily open. The strangers stepped in and disappeared from Nikki's view.

"They're going to find me," she whispered. "They're going to go from house to house and they're going to find me." Nikki stuck her hands in the pockets of Jan's bathrobe and balled them in fists to stop them shaking. Visions ran through her head. Rape, murder, the Preacherman cackling through his crushed, bloody nose as he slid his knife across her stomach, branding her to whatever he thought Christ was, flames bringing his church down around him. Gun. "Shit," she hissed. Her pistol lay on the floor of the ruined church. She was unarmed, helpless. The front of the robe moved with the thundering of her heart. "No."

"Oh, God," came from outside. Nikki looked back out the window, the strangers spilled from the front door of the house. The Librarian dropped to her knees and vomited in the tall grass. The Mechanic leaned against the side of the house, the baseball bat held loosely in his right hand.

"Why'd you open the freezer, Jenna?" the Redneck asked, kneeling in the grass. "That had to be a whole side of beef."

"I wonder how long the power's been out?" the Mechanic asked.

The Redneck shook his head. "Long enough to kill my appetite forever."

The Mechanic walked to the Librarian and held out his hand. "You okay?" he asked. She nodded. "Then we gotta go. We're running out of daylight." She nodded again, grabbed his hand and let him help her to her feet.

Sunlight burned through the Marstens' front window from low in the sky when the strangers stepped from the tall brick house next door. The Librarian and the Mechanic sat on the wooden porch swing, the Redneck sat on the brick railing and cracked his last beer, the Robot stood watch on the steps.

"I like this one," the Librarian said. "It's got boxes and cans of food and powdered milk and bottled water and four bedrooms..."

"And more beer," the Redneck interrupted.

"...and more beer."

"Thanks for not opening the refrigerator," the Mechanic said to her. "I don't think I could take that smell again today." He looked at the group. "Okay, we got the food. Anybody know how to cook?"

"I can warm up Pop-Tarts," the Librarian said. "And I pour a mean bowl of Cap'n Crunch."

The Redneck nodded. "Yeah, me, too."

"Well, I can grill, but I don't think I can grill canned chicken chunks," the Mechanic said. "How about..." The Robot raised his hand, stopping the Mechanic. "Arnold? You can cook?" The Robot nodded.

"Hell, you're full of surprises, Governator," the Redneck said.

For the first time in hours, Nikki relaxed. The strangers were close, too close, but they weren't coming any closer. She just had to stay quiet and they would go away tomorrow. She slipped from her place on the floor to a spot out of sight from the neighboring porch. A few more strawberries, another glass of wine, and a good night's sleep, and they might be gone, away from what she now considered her home, despite the real owners decomposing in the back yard. Nikki hoped the strangers eventually found a place as perfect as this – in another town.

Nikki stepped toward the kitchen, listening to the laughter from the porch next door. She tried to remember the last time she laughed. Was it at Hooligans, before the night the fat businessman died? Or did Dad say something? Maybe the strangers weren't ... she started to wonder, then shook the thought from her head. Nikki couldn't let herself trust anyone. Too much had happened to her. She thought about shutting the window, but enjoyed the laughter, the sound of conversation. She caught herself before she turned on the kitchen light, and smiled briefly. She couldn't give herself away. Not now. She'd escaped.

Cool air suddenly blew across her face as the air conditioning kicked on to battle the summer heat. Nikki froze. She could hear the compressor working, humming. "Hey," came through the crack in the open window. Nikki rushed to her spying spot at the front window and looked outside. The strangers jumped off the porch and ran toward the house – her house, toward the siren's call of electricity.

"Fuck."

July 11: Kingsville, Missouri
CHAPTER 22

Great green swaths of corn and soybeans covered the hills between gravel and paved roads north of St. Joseph; these crops would soon grow brown and rot where they stood. Karl's nervous eyes glanced at the dash of the LeBaron, the gas gauge needle dipped toward E.

"We need to leave, now," Maryanne screamed the morning they woke in St. Joseph to find Darryl had skipped town. Any sliver of composure gone from her, replaced by intense rage. Karl knew they needed to gas up the car before heading north, but he wasn't going to open his mouth. Not then – not in her insanity. They got in the car and drove, heedless of speed, heedless of anything. "After all I did for that weasel-eyed piece of shit," she said over and over, sometimes accompanied by, "I'm going to eat his nuts first, then his heart." Seven miles north of the city, Maryanne directed Karl to turn off the interstate and its regular abandoned convenience stores and onto a seemingly empty rural U.S. highway for reasons Karl didn't know and didn't want to know. About fifteen miles later, and a few belts of Evan Williams, Maryanne relaxed.

"We need gas," Karl said, necessity taking over where bravery failed.

"Are you shitting me?" Maryanne bellowed.

"No," he said. "The warning light just came on."

"Fuck," she spat. "Why didn't you say something when we were in St. Joe?"

Karl winced. "Because I thought you'd kill me."

Maryanne's silence in the passenger seat brought gooseflesh over his arms. Karl glanced over at her, and found her smiling. "You're right, I would have," she cooed, her voice suddenly too soft, too smooth, too happy. "But you're a good boy. Now slow down, here comes a road sign." Karl pulled the car slowly toward the green sign, battered by redneck target practice. It read "Kingsville: 2 miles"; the arrow pointed west. Maryanne's smile quickly faded. "Pull over at the crossroads." She motioned toward a gravel spot at the intersection between U.S. 71 and Route B. Karl put the LeBaron in Park, never looking back at her.

"Why did we stop?"

Maryanne unlatched her door and stepped out, gravel crunched under her feet. "Get out," she commanded. Maryanne walked around the front of the car carrying her ever-present rifle. Karl wondered if he would have floored it if he were still in the driver's seat. He knew he had to, sooner rather than later. This woman was insane, and she would eventually kill him, he knew that as surely as he knew that's why Darryl left – he knew he was first on her list.

"Move away from the door," she said as a parent might tell a child. Karl took two steps back into the weeds that now choked the ditches. No Missouri Department of Transportation tractors around to keep them clean anymore. No sir. After a few years, MoDOT might have its hands full. Maryanne slid behind the steering wheel and shut the door.

"Are you just going to leave me here?" he asked.

"Don't get your panties in a wad," she said, a grin tugged at the corner of her graceful mouth. "I'm going into town to get gas. You wait here and keep your eyes open. If somebody comes by, stop them. You'll know what to do, Cowboy." Maryanne's grin faded as she handed the rifle toward him. "Just don't get any ideas Momma won't like."

Karl reached for the rifle and saw his hand shake. He knew she saw it, too. Her blue eyes fixed on his, and they were dead, cold. *Can I do it?* he wondered as thoughts raced through his brain, thoughts of raising the rifle to her beautiful face and blowing her brains out the back of that blond head. His shaking hand tightened around the rifle barrel and she relaxed her grip on it. The rifle was his. He held the stock with his left hand, and wrapped his right index finger slowly around the trigger. Sweat started to bead on his lip. Maryanne grinned and pulled a .38-caliber police special from underneath the LeBaron's front seat and cocked it. "You know if you missed, I'd shoot your dick off first, then work my way up."

She laughed at Karl's slacked jaw, put the car in Drive and pulled onto Route B, the morning wind pulling her blond hair behind her like a bride's train. "Shit," Karl whispered as she quickly pulled well out of his range. He sat in the gravel.

The LeBaron ate those two miles quickly. Maryanne slowed as she pulled into town, although it wasn't much of a town. These tiny, piss ant villages dotted Missouri like pimples on a teenager's back. Two streets paralleled either side of Main Street, and maybe a dozen more ran perpendicular. She didn't plan to find out. An old Dairy-Freez, probably abandoned for years looking at the paint, sat at the entrance to town next to a NAPA auto parts store. Dusty, weathered houses followed, leading up to a business district of four buildings. Maryanne pulled up to the pump in the lot of the town's only gas station – not a convenience store, a gas station – and got out. A hot July breeze caressed her as she stretched. *Fucking Karl,* she thought. *He was going to kill me. That chicken shit was going to shoot me in the face.* These thoughts came to Maryanne often, but she didn't know where they came from. She just knew things, she always had. Now, in this dead, silent world, she knew things clear as a fresh glass of water. Nothing to interrupt the signal anymore, boy-o. That's why she wanted Darryl, no, had to have Darryl. That bastard had slipped out without her knowing anything. She couldn't have that.

Maryanne walked to the middle of the street and surveyed the town. Karl could wait out there on the highway, in the sun, with no water. *Asshole wanted to kill me.* Maryanne grinned. Yeah, he could wait as long as she wanted him to.

Main Street of Kingsville wasn't much to look at. A hair dresser, "Karla's Korner Klips," the Rooster Café with a homemade sign "Closed due to Illness" scotch taped inside the front glass, and a small mom and pop grocery store – Carlyle's Grocery, Best Prices in Town!" – made up the south side. City Hall, a city cop car out front, and the municipal park sat on the north. She tried the front door of Carlyle's; it was locked.

"Damn, Carlyle, I just need a candy bar and some pads. Let me in. You know I'm good for it," she said, then laughed. A red brick sat on the sidewalk next to the door; Carlyle probably used it to prop the door open on hot days like today. She wrapped her fingers around the brick, the weight felt good in her hand, and she tossed it through the glass door. The shatter sounded unnaturally loud in the dead air.

A smell wafted out, a sweet, rotting smell. It may have been old lunchmeat, or even Carlyle himself still minding the store despite being inconveniently dead, but she wasn't there for much; just in and out.

"Like I said, Carlyle old buddy," Maryanne yelled as she reached through the hole in the glass, unlocked the door and stepped in, "just a candy bar and some pads." Carlyle stared at her from an old office chair behind the counter, the once-gray blackened mold that covered his body now dry and dusty, the stalk that had sprouted from his chest after his limbs finally stopped moving limp and dangling like a flaccid penis. The bulb empty, its contents now dead in this hot, dry store. "Here we go," she said, holding up the box of generic maxi-pads. For some reason, she shouted. "Just something for my happy place. It's going to start feeling sad any day now." She pulled a couple of Snickers out of an open box and stuffed them in her front pocket, hoping they weren't too melted. She fished a five-dollar bill from her back pocket and left it on the counter next to a medicine bottle. She picked it up, Ophiocordon. Hmm, old guy liked to get his jollies off. "And you have a nice day, yourself," she said. Maryanne dropped the Ophicordon bottle onto the dirty floor, and walked from the store into the street.

The police car intrigued her. The LeBaron had served her well, but a cruiser had an engine the LeBaron couldn't keep up with. She might need that. Maryanne stepped toward City Hall when she suddenly knew something was wrong. She just knew it. Something bad. She wasn't alone in Kingsville, Missouri.

The grunt swung her around in the street. A half-dozen pigs, sows and one boar that had to run close to 450 fucking pounds, stood by the LeBaron, snorting. Some goddamned farmer, coughing up blood, or wandering around like some kind of brain-dead fungus bomb, had let them out. Probably died while doing it, falling into the muck and lying there still as a pile of chewed bones. A hog would eat anything – even the hand that feeds it. Even Kenny. Kenny worked on her daddy's farm outside Castle Ridge, Colorado. Maryanne didn't know why she liked Kenny, but she did. She was twelve; he was twenty and didn't like her around while he worked. Maryanne just stared and stared and stared at his big, farm boy arms, and his square chin. "Shoo," he'd tell her. "I can't work with you gawking at me. Go play Barbies or something." But she wouldn't leave; she was the boss's daughter – she didn't have to. Until 'The Day', then she never wanted to go back out to the farm again.

Maryanne leaned on the wooden fence; white flakes of paint showed her grandpa had taken more pride in his farm than Daddy. Kenny climbed the fence across the lot before he noticed her. Maryanne had tried to dress grown up, to show Kenny she was a woman, not a little girl who still played with dolls (even though she did), but she might have gotten the makeup wrong, and her mother's clothes didn't fit right. Not yet, anyway.

"Go home, Annie," he said, grinning. "And wash your face. Wash it good." Tears welled in young Maryanne's eyes as she watched Kenny step over the fence, grinning – then she screamed. Kenny was going to die; she knew it. His gray eyes stared at her as he threw his leg over the fence, his grin mocking. Maryanne's anger, her embarrassment, turned to terror. His boot landed on a shoat, he lost his balance, and fell headlong into the muck. The tiny pig squealed and its sow, a huge Poland China, thundered over Kenny in an instant. Maryanne sometimes still heard his screams in her head, the screams that lasted only until the hog ripped open his throat, and his life bled into the mud. Her father reached the hog lot too late, and dragged her away wailing into the house. She didn't see the sow eat Kenny, but she knew it did.

"Shit," Maryanne hissed as one of the hogs looked up at her and snorted. The others turned and glared at her. For the first time in years, she was afraid. She was no longer the predator – she was the prey. The .38 sat on the front seat of the LeBaron where her happy little ass should be, screaming out of this bum-fuck pig town. She glanced at Carlyle's, with its shattered door and knew she'd find no shelter there. She looked nervously to her left at City Hall. The door was cracked, a black-shoed foot held it open. "Fucking great," she whispered, but not softly enough. The boar grunted and started running for her, the others followed.

Maryanne ran for City Hall, clicks of the pigs' cloven hooves on the pavement louder and louder with her every footfall. Her breath came hard. Kenny. Kenny. Gonna die like Kenny. Screams of the man she thought of when she explored her young body at night pounded at her ears, mixing with the grunts and squeals of the deadly hogs.

"Fuck you, pigs," she wheezed at first, then yelled. "Fuck you." Maryanne reached the steps of City Hall, the drove not ten feet behind her. She threw open the door and dove inside, the smell of death and human feces nearly made her vomit.

She scrambled to her feet and grabbed the doorknob as the first pig slammed into it, nearly throwing her to the ground. Grunts and snorts filled the room as she held onto the handle, some pigs threw their weight onto the door, others stuck their wet, pink, undulating snouts into the crack.

"Go away," Maryanne screamed. The figure below her was a cop; she could see a corner of his badge through the gray fuzz that covered his flesh and clothes. The stalk stood tall and rigid, not like Carlyle's; the bulb swollen and full. This boy was fresh. Given the size of the town, she was sure he used to drive the police cruiser parked outside, probably the only one unless the mayor liked to borrow it for joyrides that ended with blowjobs from teenagers. People who ran for any public office were fucked up. Dried blood lay in a two-foot radius around the cop's head; Humanity: three (so far), the Outbreak: seven billion. Another hog threw its weight into the door, nearly sending Maryanne flying.

"Fuck off," she yelled, pulling on the door handle. Another snout nosed its way into the crack; Maryanne raised a foot and kicked it hard. The pig backed away squealing in pain. "Take that shit." She kicked the cop's leg, eased off pressure on the door, and pulled, the leg light from decomposition and stiff as a branch, craned awkwardly up through the crack and Maryanne slammed the door shut and fell to the floor crying because in her head Kenny was crying, too.

Then, from somewhere inside the building, someone said "hello?"

July 11: Barton, Missouri
CHAPTER 23

The Mechanic and the Librarian came at a slight jog, the Redneck close behind, protecting his beer from spilling. Something in Nikki's head couldn't blame him; nobody was making more beer these days. Gold wouldn't buy you anything, but a case of beer might be worth a week's worth of macaroni and cheese to the right person. The Robot walked slowly, mechanically behind them. A knot grew in Nikki's stomach for the second time tonight. They were here. People. And they were going to find her. There was nowhere to go this time; they were closer to her bike than she was, and she didn't have a gun to even the odds. Her spying from beneath the window on the Marstens' living room floor didn't give her a reason to think these people dangerous, but the Preacherman hadn't seemed a threat until he drugged her, and the Greasyman probably smiled like a gentleman at Girl Scouts who sold cookies to him, not knowing he crawled back into his house with Thin Mints, poured the cookies onto his kitchen table and stared at those prepubescent stick legs and sashaying green skirts walking through his neighborhood as he masturbated into the empty box.

"Hey, it's solar powered," the Redneck shouted. "Hot damn. A refrigerator. A shower. A fucking TV." He looked at the Robot and slapped him on the shoulder, making the mannequin man wince. "Terminator, T2, T3, Salvation, Genisys. Hell yes."

"I now know why you cry," the Robot said.

The Mechanic hit the stoop first; the Librarian grabbed his arm as he reached toward the handle of the front door. "If the power is still on here, someone might be home," she said.

"Knock?" the Mechanic asked.

"Yes, knock," she said. "The rest of the world may be dead, but that doesn't mean we shouldn't have manners."

Nikki stood still, leaning her back against the door to prop up her shaking knees. The Mechanic's knock popped three times directly behind her head. Breath poured into her lungs like syrup.

"Hello?" the Mechanic called from less than a foot behind her head. "Anybody there?" He paused, Nikki seeing him in her mind turning toward the Librarian, the Redneck and Robot walking up slowly behind them. "See," he said softer. "Lights are on, but nobody's home."

Nikki took a deep breath, faced the door, grabbed the handle in her left hand, keeping her right hand hidden, and yanked the door open. The strangers stood still, their faces aghast.

"What do you want?" Nikki asked slowly, trying to keep the shaking from her voice. She nodded toward her right hand hidden behind the door jam. "I have a gun." Each stranger took at least one step back, except the Robot who stood behind the others like a prop in a movie.

"Hey, man," the Redneck said. "We're cool."

"Shut up, Terry," the Librarian spat. "We scared her. Don't come off looking like a redneck from Kansas."

"I *am* a redneck from Kansas," he said softly, stopped, then took a drink of beer.

Doug raised his hands, palms up. "Hello, ma'am," he said, smiling as honestly as he could muster. "I don't think you know how happy we are to see you. We've been traveling for a while, just a few miles at a time. Almost everybody's dead." He paused and the smile dissolved. "I know you've seen that, too, and I'm sorry for your loss."

Jenna elbowed Doug in the shoulder and he stopped talking. "Hi," she said. "My name's Jenna. Men, as you know, are tactless and dumb." She stopped and motioned toward Doug and Terry. "These guys picked me up after I wrecked my car. Total gentlemen. That guy," she motioned to Arnold. "We found him in Platte City. I don't know what his story is. Asshole won't talk like a normal person." Jenna stopped and looked at Nikki, her eyes starting to grow moist for a reason that only pissed her off. "If you want, we'll walk back over to that house for the night and we won't bother you again. We're just glad someone else is alive."

Nikki frowned. Yeah, she was, too. "Where are you headed?" she asked. The Mechanic rested his right leg on the first step and leaned on his knee.

"Omaha," he said. "There was a survivor's shelter in Kansas City, but it had signs saying everyone went to Omaha."

The strangers stood outside the Marstens' house, Jenna looking at Nikki, while the men stared at their shoes. A cow lowed somewhere in the distance. Nikki knew these people weren't the Preacherman, they weren't the Greasyman, and they weren't the Banker blocking the convenience store doorway, wheezing through blood-choked lungs, begging her to kill him. Nope, not even close.

"Hi," she said, moving her hidden right hand toward Jenna and tried to shake it, but Jenna grabbed her and hugged her tight.

Jenna suddenly released her and stepped back. "Sorry," she said. "I'm just excited."

Nikki smiled a happy smile for the first time in more than a month. "My name's Nikki. Please come in. It's hot out there."

It took less than an hour for Terry to fill the refrigerator with the beer from the truck and hook up the Xbox. He and Arnold sat on the floor of the Marstens' house, using digital shotguns to explode the heads of zombies that walked through a fully furnished world with few humans – much like their own world, without the zombies. There were real monsters out there; they all knew it. Monsters that looked just like them, monsters that walked and talked, and did horrible things.

"This is amazing," Doug said through a mouthful of leftovers, his fork full of stuffed bell pepper. "We've been eating old bratwurst and boxes of hamburger helper without the hamburger."

Nikki waved him off. "If that's all you've eaten, that could be dirt for all you know."

Doug looked up from his plate, his face stone. "No ma'am," he said. "I'm serious. This is delicious."

Ma'am. Nikki grinned and thanked him. He'd called her "ma'am." The Mechanic, Doug, had only about ten years on her, but whatever little town he came from they sure taught manners.

"Are you from here?" Jenna asked. "Barton?"

Nikki shook her head. "I'm from St. Joe. When my dad died ..." She hadn't thought about Gene Holleran for days. Tears flooded her eyes. Jenna reached across the dining room table and patted her forearm. This stranger's warm, soft hand brought comfort. Maybe, Nikki thought, she needed these people. "...I left St. Joe. The town is mostly dead. There's nothing there for me now. I just got lucky and stumbled on this place."

"You know what happened to the people who owned it?" Terry asked. Nikki didn't know how this redneck from Kansas did it, but he didn't slur a word through all the beer she'd watched him down.

"Yeah." Nikki pointed toward the back yard, the moon painting the night gray. "They're out there in lawn chairs. Dead. I've only been here for two days. I haven't had time to bury them yet."

"We'll help with that," Doug said.

Nikki nodded. "Thank you." A deer, a buck this time, walked across the backyard setting off the security lights. The Marstens sat in their black and gold canvass chairs as they had for at least a month, watching a garden they'd never tend again. The deer froze for a moment, then wandered into the garden, nosing around for anything Nikki hadn't picked. "What about you guys?"

Paola, the Peckinpa house (Jenna leaving out any mention of Karl), Johnnyball, Worlds of Fun, Platte City, the St. Joe shopping mall, and the people each had lost.

"I guess we still don't know anything about each other," Jenna said, pausing and looking at each person around the table. Then she frowned at Arnold. "Especially this guy. What's your deal?"

Arnold sat stiffly in the wooden dining room chair and looked Jenna in the eye. He turned his head slowly toward Nikki. "Where's your bathroom?"

Nikki pointed toward the hallway. "Second door on the right." Arnold stood and took a step toward the hall.

"Dude," Terry shouted, grinning like a kid. "That is NOT from a movie."

Arnold turned and looked at Terry, his face blank. "I'll be back," he said, and walked into the hallway.

"You sure he's not dangerous?" Nikki asked.

Jenna nodded. "I'm pretty sure. The whole Arnold Schwarzenegger thing is probably just a psychological defense mechanism. He's trying to cope with whatever personal losses he's had to deal with. That, coupled with the fact that the world he knew is gone has driven him to temporarily adopt a different persona. Classic psych stuff. Just don't make a big deal out of it; it'll fix itself."

The table was silent for a moment. "Where'd that come from?" Doug asked.

Jenna shrugged. "I was a psychology major at a liberal arts college. Things like that will come up from time to time. Get used to it."

Plates clanked in the kitchen as Doug and Terry washed the dishes. The Marstens had a dishwasher, but nobody suggested using it. People needed time to get used to one another. Nikki and Jenna sat on the floral print couch, each held a glass of chilled Chardonnay, watching "16 and Pregnant," featuring people they knew were no longer sixteen, or pregnant, or alive.

"It's nice here," Jenna said, the girl on the screen yelling at her baby daddy for not having a job.

Nikki nodded. "Yeah. I got lucky."

"How long are you going to stay?"

She shrugged. "Haven't thought about it. There's enough food for a few months, more if I scrounge the other houses. Even more if I go back to Savannah or St. Joe. I could probably make it through to next spring."

"Then?"

Nikki frowned and took a drink of wine. "I don't know." She paused. "How about you?"

Jenna drained her glass and poured another. "I'm sticking with the boys. We talked about finding a place like this, a place to just ride out the apocalypse, but I don't know if we could handle it for long. I think we should go to Omaha."

A shatter of china and a "shit" rang out from the kitchen. Nikki and Jenna laughed toward each other like it was a personal joke. Then Nikki's face grew hard. "I don't want to be alone," she whispered.

"Hey," Terry yelled from the kitchen, walking into the living room, drying his hands on a red dishtowel. "Dishes are done."

For the next hour, the five sat in the living room and talked; Arnold on the floor, Nikki and Jenna on the couch, Terry and Doug in chairs.

Doug yawned. "It's getting late," he said, draining the glass of wine Jenna had handed him. Doug was never a wine guy, except for the cheap stuff with a screw-on lid he drank in high school. He only drank wine when he took communion at St. Mary's Catholic Church, and that had grown seldom. Beer was it for him. "What are the sleeping arrangements?"

Nikki froze, Jenna felt it. "Hey," Jenna said. "We can go to the other house, if you want?"

Nikki shook her head. "No, that's okay. There are three bedrooms. I get the master bedroom. The rest of you can figure it out on your own."

"Dibs on the couch," Terry said, then smiled, facing Arnold. "If they're taking the bedrooms, and I'm taking the couch, I guess you'll have to sleep outside in the wind, buddy."

"Crom laughs at your four winds."

Nikki stood and waved them off. "Nobody has to sleep outside. I think this is a pull-out couch."

Terry, still grinning like a clown, walked into the kitchen. "If I'm sleeping in the same bed as Arnold, I'm going to look for some sleeping bags out in the garage. No offense, buddy." The kitchen still smelled like supper as Terry walked past the table where they'd eaten. He grabbed the handle of the door next to the refrigerator, he unlocked it and pushed it open. The blackness of the room was complete, like he'd stepped into a box. Terry reached across the wall next to him, his hand slid over drywall until he found a switch, and flipped it, light flooded the room. Loaded gun racks lined the walls.

"Uh. Hey, guys," Terry said slowly. "You should really see this."

July 11: Kingsville, Missouri
CHAPTER 24

The voice caught Maryanne somewhat by surprise, but not entirely. She'd felt she wasn't alone in Kingsville, she just assumed it was the pigs, those 400-pound, man-eating porkers still snorting from the porch, one occasionally slamming its huge body against the door. Maryanne knew this crazy fucking world hadn't turned into "Animal Farm," or one of those porkers would have opened the door, killed her, and eaten her with onions and a nice béarnaise. She smiled at the insanity of that picture, of the whole fucking world. Then there was the voice. It came from inside the building, but it sounded muffled and far away. The voice could wait; she wasn't kneeling over the voice, she *was* kneeling over a dead cop, and the cop had been dead for a while.

He'd been young, maybe 21 if he lied well. A dusting of moustache (the molestache, what all the cool pervs are wearing) graced his upper lip and was covered in a fine gray mold. Goddamnit. Did that thing move? Maryanne stared at the stalk, one of those creepy fungus stalks that grew out of everybody when they died. She swore it moved, like it was looking at her. Maryanne scooted away from the alien-looking tree sticking out of the kid-cop's chest to the floor. His black leather belt lay next to him, the gray mold not yet making it across the floor; he must have been carrying it when he fell. Lucky her; cops had more shit on their belt than Batman. *Not bad,* she thought, standing and buckling the belt around her waist. She had to hitch it in the first hole, and it still hung loose, resting at an angle off her hips like she was Lara Croft: Tomb Raider. The belt held pepper spray, handcuffs (might come in handy, Hubba hubba), utility knife, .9mm pistol, ammo, and, most importantly, a big set of janitor keys, one of which would fit nicely into the ignition of the cruiser that would hopefully start.

"Hello?" the voice called again, more urgently. "Is someone here? Please help me."

Maryanne stepped away from Barney Fife, Jr., and scanned the first floor of City Hall. Bo-ring. A computer with a dead black screen sat in the city clerk's office, surrounded by pictures of grandkids, and greeting cards with that crabby old lady that made Hallmark a shitload of money just bitching about being a crabby old lady. Fuck you, Hallmark. Unless you have a Welcome to the End of the World line of cards, your products have probably worn out their usefulness. Maryanne tugged on a door handle across the hall from the clerk's office, expecting a closet with brooms and mops, but instead of cleaning supplies, a rack of black handled weapons greeted her. "Fucking A," she whispered. "Christmas just came early." She grabbed a shotgun off the rack, and went off to find the voice.

"Where are you?" she called, holding the shotgun stock pressed to her hip as she walked slowly through the rest of City Hall. "Can't hear you, baby. Speak up."

"In the basement," the voice yelled, excited, eager, desperate, or probably all of the above. "God, I'm so happy to hear you."

You might not think that for long, Maryanne thought, a grin tugged her lips. She ran her free hand up the barrel of the shotgun. No, not long at all.

"Happy to hear yours too, baby," she shouted and walked toward a door opposite the clerk's office, next on her grand tour of Kingsville City Hall. Stairs lead into a dark, foul-smelling pit. She put her right foot on the first creaky step. "You down here, hun?"

A rustle. Maryanne pointed the shotgun at chest level and kept walking down.

"Yes, yes, yes," the voice shouted. "Please help me."

Maryanne reached for the light switch at the bottom of the stairs in the dim basement, a concrete floor greeted her shoes when she left the last step. Her hand found the nipple of a switch and she flipped it; nothing happened but a click. Electricity was gone, probably was everywhere on the planet.

"You look like a fucking angel," the voice called through the gray light.

As Maryanne's eyes adjusted to the basement; one small window cast the only light into this dungeon; she saw one lonely jail cell, and boxes of papers stacked almost to the ceiling. Nice filing system, Kingsville. A man stood at the door to the cell, a good-looking man even with the weeks' worth of beard and the smell of body odor. She stepped closer to the cell, but not too close. A simple bed, toilet, and sink. Typical. Empty boxes and cans of food scattered across the floor. If the water still ran he was okay in that department, but looks like the groceries ran out a while ago.

"You hungry?" Maryanne asked. He nodded his head.

"Dooker thought he was dyin'," the man said. "So he brought me a shitload of food and stuffed it through the bars. Said the whole world was dyin'. Then he disappeared. I don't know when that was, but the food's been gone for two, three days." He paused, looking at Maryanne with hurt, confused eyes. "If the world was really dyin', don't you think Dooker'd let me out? I mean; it'd be only decent."

This guy wasn't an idiot, she could see that, but he wasn't a fucking Ph.D. either. "Dooker the cop?" she asked. The man nodded again. She shifted her weight to her right leg, and let the shotgun droop for effect. She didn't know this guy, and what she felt she wasn't sure of. He seemed nice enough, but nice guys don't get locked in jail and left to die. "What are you in for?" she asked.

He looked down and answered, "assault."

So, he's ashamed of it, too. Maybe not so bad after all. "Who'd you hit?"

The prisoner looked back into Maryanne's eyes. "Dooker."

Maryanne smiled. "You don't have to worry about Dooker anymore. He was right, he was dying. Whatever's killing everybody, it got him; it got most of the people. He was right about that too, the world died. Well, not the world, just most of the people." She paused and looked at his face and wondered what this guy was doing before the fungus took over. She couldn't think of it as a disease anymore, not with that fucking branch moving toward her. Was this guy fixing cars in the local shop, or driving a tractor? Five years ago? Maybe homecoming king, or the high school quarterback.

"You hungry?" He nodded furiously and Maryanne grabbed the candy bars in her pocket and held them in front of her. "You going to be a good boy?" He just kept nodding, eyeing those Snickers bars like they were prime rib. She stepped closer and he gently took them from her hand.

"Thanks, ma'am," he said as he unwrapped the first bar and bit it in half. "I was starving."

Well, you're going to need your strength, buckaroo. I ride my posse hard. She cocked the gun, the ratchet of the shotgun deafening in the small space. "Step up to the bars."

He stopped chewing; the melted chocolate on his lips made him look a bit too much like a kid caught stealing his little sister's Halloween candy, but that disappeared quickly enough. "What?"

"Listen, bucko, in case you haven't noticed, you're locked in a jail cell, I'm outside the cell with the key, and I'm holding a gun," she said, leaning the barrel of the shotgun toward the cell. "Now, if you want to get out, step up to the bars."

"But, the gun ..."

Maryanne frowned. "Now."

The prisoner held the half-eaten candy bar between his teeth, and stepped up to the bars. Maryanne levelled the barrel at his chest.

He tried to step back, but almost tripped over his feet. "What the fuck?"

"This is the true or false part of our exam today," she said, and shoved the end of the barrel closer to the prisoner. "I don't know you. I don't know if I can trust you. Good old 10-gauge here does. I just grabbed this thing upstairs. Don't know if it's loaded. So, if you're a good man, if I can trust you, this fucker ain't loaded. That would be true." She paused to let him take this all in. "If it is loaded and I paint the cell walls with your guts, Mr. 10-Gauge says false."

Tears started to well in the man's eyes. "Please," he said in a whisper. "Don't."

"Sorry. You must not have read the test instructions." The prisoner lurched back as she pulled the trigger; he tripped over empty food boxes and spilled onto the floor. The shotgun simply clicked. Maryanne grinned; she thought the gun probably wasn't loaded, but she didn't really know. Neither did he.

"What the fuck was that about?" he screamed.

"Like I said, it was a test, baby," Maryanne said as she tried keys in the lock of the cell. She found the one that fit, and the door swung open. "Looks like you got an A."

July 11: Rural Northwest Missouri
CHAPTER 25

The sun sat high when Darryl woke, his clothes soaked with sweat. He didn't know how long he'd been out. Overnight? A day? Two? Aching muscles met him as he started to rise, his eyes slits in the mid-July sun. The front seat of the Mustang, he figured, was probably not the most comfortable bed. Darryl opened his eyes fully and froze – he wasn't alone. A cow stared at Darryl through the open driver's side window of the Mustang, chewing grass, globs of drool fell on the leather seats. Darryl smiled.

Hey, Bossie," he said, the unexpected sound making the cow's jaws pause for a moment, but only a moment. The unexpected movement sent the cow off in a slight trot. Darryl pulled himself into the driver's seat and stretched. Bossie snorted and sashayed toward a wide, open field of green, maybe on her way to the pond for a drink on this hot day. Darryl smiled as the big black cow moved slowly away from him, the tail on its shit-stained ass swinging back and forth. The day on a Missouri farm. Darryl thought he might walk around the barn and look for gear, then go out to the pond with Bossie and see if he could catch some fish. Fishing would be peaceful; fish would be good. Fish–

Then Maryanne, a shadow at first, crawled into his mind, flitted around the corners like a bat, came to rest in the deep, dark spots like a dragon, waiting for its time to bring hell to Middle Earth. His stomach clenched and he wheezed for breath. That bitch was out there, that demon bitch, and she was looking for him. She would find him. She would torture him, and she would kill him. The first few days with Maryanne almost seemed like a good dream from another lifetime, although he knew it wasn't. It was just a blur of days and nights after she picked him up walking on I-70, 175 miles west of Kansas City. He gladly took the ride; 175 miles is a hell of a long way to walk. The booze, the sex. It was almost like the world hadn't come to an end and he'd won the blowjob lottery. Then she killed the man in Junction City, and the devil woman emerged. She never left.

Darryl took several deep breaths, in through the nose, out through the mouth like they teach pregnant women, and slammed three warm beers before slight tendrils of relaxation began to slowly feel their way through him. She was out there, somewhere, he knew. But she was not on this road. He was sure of it. Maryanne planned to go to Omaha (and do what? Fuck corn?), and this road was the long way around. But there were the taillights, the taillights from last night, or the night before. He still didn't know. Even if those lights had been Maryanne's – two glowing red eyes of a demon, staring back at Darryl in the night, although in his mind they were a bit too close together. Or were they? – she might be gone. Darryl cracked open another beer, foam sprayed the dash. But he also knew she was a wizard. She knew things before they happened, some things. She could find things, too. Things that didn't want to be found, like him.

"Things are going to be okay," Darryl said to himself, his voice sounded strange to his ears. Weak. Defeated. He unlatched the door and stepped onto the soft dirt drive that led into the barn, Bossie too far away to care. The thought crossed his mind of pulling the car into the barn, shutting the door and living there until he ran out of the beer, bottled water, and canned food he'd taken from the B-Mart convenience store in St. Joe (B-Smart, B-Thifty, B-Happy at B-Mart). But sitting still, he knew, was the worst thing he could do. He had to keep moving. Moving targets were harder to hit. Darryl stepped up to a patch of weeds, pulled out his penis and watered the thistles, knowing it was time to go, to shoot up this rural highway as fast as he could and find people. He felt he'd be safe at the Omaha shelter; even if Crazybitch made it to the Cornhusker State, as any feeb knew, there was safety in numbers. After a breakfast, a late afternoon breakfast of Spam, and saltines, Darryl slid into the Mustang, pulled it onto the highway, and drove north.

The road rolled with the hills and valleys. Darryl cruised with the windows down; wind gently pulled his hair. He'd turned AC/DC off during his breakdown, and left the stereo silent. He realized he was already on the highway to hell, and wanted to hear the demons approaching if he could. A few vehicles, mostly pickups with stickers of Calvin pissing on Chevy emblems, sat on the side of the road with flat tires, or bullet holes, or the remains of fungus-covered bodies slumped over the steering wheel. Darryl kept driving. He rolled by a Kum and Go convenience store, a tractor trailer carrying the rotor blade for a windmill farm sat near the back of the lot. The Kum and Go was as dead as everything in St. Joseph, Kansas City, Denver, and the rest of the world.

Darryl registered the green road sign that told him the town of Exeter was five miles up the road, but he didn't think much about small towns anymore. They were all empty, small town fast food joints like Pirates Cove, the Bearcat Den, and Bobcat Burgers showing their school spirit by closing forever. Darryl slowed as he pulled into Exeter because it was different than all the other small towns; it was gone. Smoke rose from a few spots, flames even danced from a once large church, the brick spire still giving the heavens the finger. The remainder of the church had burned like the rest of the town. The fire that wiped Exeter from the planet didn't even register with Darryl as a concern – shit happened in Deadsville – but the ash did bother him. Two different tracks ran up the highway the town once lived around, a three-wheeled track, maybe an ATV, or a motorcycle with a trailer, and a car. Darryl put the Mustang into Park and stepped onto the road, ash poofed under his tennis shoes. He touched the car track; he wasn't like the Crazybitch, he didn't just know things for no goddamned reason, but he knew this tire track was hers. He *knew* it. Darryl slid back into the driver's seat, ashy shoes leaving prints on the mat, and kept driving, the miles beginning to grow angry.

Tanya Smithmeyer. The last person Darryl had seen before people started dying and coming back to life as a mushroom farm, was Tanya Smithmeyer. Darryl walked into the Goatshead Inn, a British pub knockoff in Goodland, Kansas that was as much British as anything else in Kansas, and saw Tanya sitting at a table talking with some other teachers from high school, the few of them who were left in town. Darryl taught English at Goodland High for the past three years, and had tried to score with Tanya since, but rumor had it she was seeing the football coach Brad MacAtee. Brad who banged her in the equipment locker, and his office, and probably in the ass, or so he heard. She came to school one day with a black eye, and Goodland's finest came and took MacAtee away for a little while. Tanya didn't talk to men much anymore. The teachers, Bob in the science department and Kylie in home ec, waved him over and he gladly went, squeezing in between Bob and Tanya.

"What do you think's going on, Darryl?" Bob asked.

Darryl picked up the pitcher on the table and poured beer, probably Bud Light the Beer of the Midwest, into a plastic cup, then topped off the other teachers. "Don't know," he said. "I'd say that's your department Bob."

Bob sucked the foam off the top of his beer and shook his head. "Nobody knows, or nobody's fessing up," he said. "Probably a virus nobody outside the government's ever heard of. Got loose and nobody's immune to it."

"Do you think we'll get it?" Kylie said, fear and beer dragging a quiver through her voice.

Bob nodded. "The papers and TV say it's highly communicable. Best we can do is stay away from people who have it. Now that school's closed, it should be easy."

"I read it had something to do with the Piper," Darryl said.

"Ophiocordon?" Kylie asked, reaching toward the floor. She came up with her purse and pulled out a golden-orange plastic medicine bottle. The look on her face was stark terror. "What's wrong with it?"

"Have you taken any?" Bob asked.

Kylie shook her head. "No. With all the people dying, my doctor thought it best I have these just in case I needed, you know, a pick-me-up."

Darryl gently took the bottle from her hands and turned it in his fingers. *Ophiocordon: Take one pill twice a day, more if needed. Not more than four in a twenty-four hour period.* "Well, don't," he said, setting the bottle on the table in front of Kylie. "The article said the feeling of euphoria ..."

"Orgasms," Tanya interrupted, her voice dry, emotionless.

"... comes from the Ophiocordy-something fungus in the rainforest in Thailand, or Cambodia, or someplace like that. Its spores infect ants and makes them do things they don't normally do, but are things the fungus needs to survive."

Bob laughed. "It turns the ants into zombies?" he said.

Darryl nodded. "Then when the fungus gets what it needs, it kills the ants, and uses their bodies to sprout, something. I can't remember the term."

"Hyphae," Bob said. Everyone at the table stopped and looked at him. He shrugged. "Hey, I do teach science, remember. It's what you find on everything in the fridge in the teacher's lounge. The hyphae strands make up the mycelium, which is the fuzzy part of the fungus. It grows over everything, and releases spores to make more fungus. Given the right climate, we'd all be knee-deep in it."

Kylie pushed the pill bottle away from her. "And they used that to make Ophiocordon? A fungus that eats people? I just thought my friend at the hospital was trying to scare me when she said a dead girl sprouted a mushroom from her chest."

Bob laughed again. "This all sounds like complete bullshit. Ant fungus? What next?"

Tanya slammed an empty plastic beer cup onto the scratched table. "We're all going to die," she said flatly.

Bob reached in front of Darryl and pulled Tanya's cup away. "Looks like somebody had plenty." After two more hours, they all had.

Tanya asked Darryl to take her home, then made him pull over on a deserted bridge and screwed him until the cops came. Then she just stepped out of the car, naked as hell, climbed over the railing, and jumped into the water. Tanya never came back up. Darryl didn't go in after her. He would have on some other night, but whenever he thought of Tanya, her naked figure straddling the steel beams of the old bridge, smiling as she flung herself over the side, he knew deep down she was right. Even Tanya wasn't as fucking crazy as Maryanne.

Dusk would start to play in the sky soon, and Darryl knew he would have to find a place to sleep, or drive all night. He could. He'd slept longer than he'd slept in a week, and still had a baggie of Crazybitch's amphetamines in his front pocket, but he didn't want to use them; he hated the thought of being alone when his heart exploded. Darryl pushed his foot into the Mustang's accelerator and the car slid over the northwest Missouri road like it was on rails. Cows, some black like Bossie, some red, grazed in a pasture that sat amongst the long even rows of crops that followed the highway, the pure white clouds dotted the clear sky looked like God had hung wallpaper in the baby's room. The day seemed still, quiet, almost peaceful. The Cowboy caught him by surprise.

The Mustang topped a hill, the gray ribbon stretched and disappeared over and over in the hilly distance, and Darryl saw the man. He pulled his foot off the accelerator, the car's engine arguing as the speed began to fall from 75 mph to nearly 65 before he saw the man clearly, standing on a gravel patch at the intersection of the highway and Route B, holding a rifle in both hands – Maryanne's rifle. It was the Cowboy. A weight immediately pressed into Darryl's chest, his breathing came hard and shallow. Darryl's eyes met the Cowboy's as he cruised past, the man held the rifle flat, non-threatening, and he knew the Cowboy would never shoot him. But the Cowboy's face was solemn, soulless, dying, a face Darryl knew from mirrors. The Crazybitch had broken him. She was here, somewhere. But where? Where the fuck was she? Darryl gunned the accelerator and glanced into the rear-view mirror – the Cowboy turned to watch him go, to watch the only thing he'd ever see of freedom. Poor bastard. The Mustang streaked down the hill, over the next one, and the Cowboy disappeared in the distance.

"Holy shit, holy shit, holy shit," Darryl mumbled as he pushed the car's speedometer into the 90s, the vehicle briefly left the road at the crest of hills. Sweat began to bleed into Darryl's wind-dried shirt at the armpits and chest; tears welled in his eyes. She was here. Crazybitch was fucking here. Darryl knew she followed him; this time she just overshot the mark. What about tomorrow? Would she find him sleeping? Taking a dump? Praying she was dead? He ran the back of his left hand across the tears on his face, and started his pregnant breathing again, in through the nose, out through the mouth. Come on. Come on. Come on. She wasn't there, on the road. She wasn't with the Cowboy. She'd left this guy – with the hidden .44 that now sat in Darryl's front seat – on the road to keep watch. Watch for him. Crazybitch was miles away doing who the hell knows.

"I still have time," Darryl whispered, and pushed the car even harder. "I still have time."

As dusk began to wash the horizon pink, a road sign warned of an intersection. Darryl slowed the car to a roll by the time he reached the turn onto the rural highway. He didn't want to hit the corner hard and leave rubber on the road; that would just be stupid. Crazybitch didn't need help to find him. Darryl still felt Maryanne deep in his brain, the dragon perched, waiting to bring hell. Darryl pointed the nose of the Mustang east, eased the car faster than the posted 55, and drove, tears still pushing toward his eyes. Goddamn Maryanne, Goddamn...

Darryl rounded a curve in the road, thick trees hugged the ditches, and slammed his feet into the brake pedal. A deer stood in the road, frozen. "Shit," hissed between Darryl's lips as he jerked the car's steering wheel, sending it into a sideways skid. His bladder released, soaking his jeans, and he screamed as the green farm world in the car windows spun like he was drunk, then turned on its side. The Mustang crashed into an empty gulley, landing on its roof. Darryl's head slammed against the windshield and everything went black.

July 11: Kingsville, Missouri
CHAPTER 26

Maryanne leaned against the open cell door as the prisoner stood and dusted off his pants. "That was a dick move, you know that?" he yelled. "Did you really not know if the gun was loaded?" Maryanne shook her head slowly. "Shit, man. Shit." Yeah, not a Ph.D. by a long shot, but that was a good thing. The dumber he was the easier he would fall in line.

"What's your name, baby?" she asked.

The man stepped past Maryanne who thought of blocking his way with the gun, but decided not to push it. Freedom, sort of. "Trent."

Maryanne laughed. "Not anymore," she said. "It's Beavis. Your name's Beavis. Now, let's go upstairs. You can piss on Dooker while I find ammo for this baby. We got pigs to stick."

"Pigs?"

"Don't worry your pretty head, just get upstairs." Trent walked up the stairs in front of her, Maryanne cocked her head from side to side with each flex of his butt cheeks. "Must be jelly," she yelled even though he was three feet before her. "'Cause jam don't shake like that."

A huge Poland China sow, its hooves on the front windowsill, stared into City Hall as Maryanne and Trent emerged from the basement. It grunted, and squeals filled the afternoon. "Those are the pigs to stick."

"Jesus."

Maryanne laughed. "He drove demons into them, Beavis. Maybe these are some of the same fuckers." She pointed toward Dooker. Was that knob thing growing out of his chest bigger now? She just wished he wasn't lying right in front of the door. "Don't get too close to him. I don't know what that thing is on his chest, but I don't like it."

"Dear God," Beavis whispered. "What is that thing?"

"What's wrong?" Maryanne said from the armory. "Pissing your pants make you deaf? I said I didn't know. Just don't touch it."

She found boxes of shells, loaded and cocked the shotgun, stuffed two ammo belts with shells, and draped them over her shoulders. Fucking A. "Let's do this." She stepped out of the armory broom closet, walked past Trent standing over Dooker eyeing the stalk, and stepped to the front window. The sow stared at her. It was hungry, angry. Maryanne knew it; she could feel it. It felt hate, hate for her. How smart were pigs? Plenty smart. Too smart. A feeling rushed over Maryanne, and not a good feeling. Something bad was about to happen. Something really bad.

"Come here, Beavis," she snapped and grabbed Trent's arm, pulling him toward the door, the great swollen bulb craned on its stalk to follow him. It was going to blow. She knew it, and when it did, they were screwed. Maryanne pointed the shotgun toward the window and the hog's face and smiled as she blew its brains out the back of its thick skull. Squeals split the air outside the shattered window; pigs ran back and forth along the wooden porch.

"Showtime, Beavis," Maryanne said, and handed him the .9mm from her belt. "Remember, just the pigs. You might miss me, but I won't miss you." She heard a stretching sound, like someone was pulling a filled balloon, but she knew Beavis couldn't hear it; the sound was just in her head. Maryanne threw open the door and fired at the closest pig. It dropped down the steps in sickening squishy thuds. She pulled Trent onto the porch and slammed the door, just as a pop filled her head, and a thump hit the door. A small cloud of yellow wafted from the window Maryanne had shot out, a slight breeze blew it away from them. The bulb had exploded. It wanted them. Somehow that fucking thing wanted them. *Tough shit,* Maryanne thought, and cocked the shotgun.

A sow, close to 400 pounds, charged Maryanne. She raised the weapon and began to squeeze the trigger when a shot, silent compared to the 10-gauge, went off behind her. A red spot sprang from the center of the pig's forehead and it dropped onto the porch, now slick and red with blood. Pigs ran around the great porch that surrounded the building, ran away from the noise, the death.

"Nice shot, Beavis," Maryanne said. "Thanks."

"Just do the same for me."

Maryanne nodded and handed him the heavy keyring. "Find the key to the Chevy out there," she said and fired at a pig starting up the stairs. The blast struck its shoulder, and drove it to the ground. The hog groaned and tried to stand, its three working legs thrashed in circles. Maryanne raised the gun and shot again. The pig stopped moving. Grunts and squeals came closer as the pigs running around the porch neared them. Trent shoved the .9mm into the front of his jeans, and fumbled with the keys. The first pig rounded the corner of the building and Maryanne fired directly in its face.

"Let's go," she screamed, and they ran down the steps. Trent flipped through keys with shaky hands. The pigs, their hooves rattling on the wooden porch, thundered after them, heaving their heavy bodies over the slaughtered the survivors would later feast on.

Trent reached the Kingsville city police cruiser first. The door handle moved when he pulled it, and the door flew open; he threw himself in and slammed the door. Maryanne jumped and slid across the hood like the hero in a 1970s cop show, landing on her feet at the passenger side door. It was locked.

"Let me in, Beavis," she screamed. The boar, all 450 pounds of him, pounded down the steps and ran toward the car, toward Maryanne; three sows followed him. "Let me *in*." Trent grinned at her, casually leaned toward the door, and unlocked it. Maryanne heaved it open and dove into the car. The boar slammed into the door, banging it shut. Maryanne, breathing heavily, sat up and slowly pulled the seatbelt over her waist. "That was funny, Beavis," she said gently. "Real funny. Think about that if I ever give you head. Your wad might not be the only thing I spit out." She gently pulled shotgun shells from the bandoleers draped across her shoulders and fed them into the gun.

Trent pulled the police cruiser onto Route B, the cruiser Dooker used to drive around to bust all the dicks that gave him shit in high school, and to flirt with the girls who still wouldn't talk to him. Maryanne directed him to the highway.

"Where are we going?" he asked.

"We're not alone," she said. "There's a lookout on the blacktop, hopefully with news I want to hear." She motioned him to stop at the LeBaron, which he did. She hopped out of the cruiser and picked her .38 out of the seat, a box of RU486 out of the glove box, and their remaining groceries and booze from the trunk. She'd driven the LeBaron from Colorado and it took her safely through the mountains, and around the smoking ruin that was Denver, but the cop car was fast, and powerful enough she was sure it could ram through a fucking wall if she needed it to.

"Want some?" she asked after capping the Evan Williams and taking a long swallow.

Trent shook his head. "Not on two Snickers bars."

Fair enough. Two miles later they stopped at the intersection. Maryanne told him to get out of the car and they both stepped out onto a gravel patch. The Cowboy was gone. Shit. Maryanne liked the Cowboy. He was spunky, sure with his driving, and in good enough shape he could fuck as long as she needed him to. It'd be a shame if she had to put a bullet in his back.

"Hey, Cowboy," Maryanne yelled into the hot July afternoon, the clear Midwestern sky blue as a Kansas City Royals jersey. "I hope for your own personal safety you're still here somewhere, picking up trash for the Adopt-A-Highway people, or picking up aluminum cans to help the homeless. If you pulled a Darryl, baby, well ..." She fired Mr. 10-Gauge into the sky, sending Trent ducking behind the squad car. "I just don't know what I might do."

"Don't shoot, goddamnit," Karl's voice called from nearby. A square concrete culvert ran under the highway about twenty yards to the south of the intersection. A few seconds later Karl's head popped over the crest of the deep ditch. Maryanne stepped toward the ditch and met Karl walking up the embankment, buttoning his jeans and zipping his fly, the rifle cupped under his right armpit. "I was taking a dump. Shit, Maryanne, I'm still here." He stopped when he saw Trent, and gripped the rifle with both hands. "Who's this?"

Maryanne grinned and Karl wondered if at some point she'd hold a gun on them and make them fight just for the hell of it. "This is Beavis, baby. He was locked in the city jail, poor thing. Would have died, too." She looked at Trent with her cold, dead eyes, his knees suddenly weak. "And you're going to remember that too, aren't you? That I saved your life. If I hadn't stopped by, you would have starved to death."

Trent slowly nodded, and Maryanne smiled a smile he didn't like. No, not at all. She turned to Karl, the smile gone. "You see anybody?" she asked.

Karl tried to erase all emotion from his face, but he immediately knew he failed horribly. He didn't want to tell her what happened, who he saw drive by in a red Ford Mustang, but this devil woman would know. Oh, yes, she would know.

"Yeah," he said slowly. "Darryl. About a half hour ago."

Maryanne's smile returned; it was the small, tight smile of a hunter about to pull the trigger.

"Let's eat," she said right to Karl's 'what the fuck?' face. "I know that foul little bitch. He'll stop in the next town and look around for supplies, maybe survivors he can help." She looked at Trent. "Open the trunk, baby." He did and they sat in the middle of a once busy highway that connected Kansas City, Missouri, and St. Joseph to towns in southern and central Iowa, and dined the dinner of Post Outbreak Royalty: Spam, saltines, and sour mash. As Trent cracked open the tin of Spam and cut slices of the jellied meat with a plastic knife, Maryanne felt something wrong. She felt Darryl. Spam and saltines was something Darryl would eat; something Darryl did eat. He had it for breakfast.

"What's your story?" Karl asked Trent between bites of Spam and crackers, a couple of belts of whiskey eased his fear of that evil, evil bitch sitting nearby.

Trent shrugged. "Graduated from high school a few years ago. Went to college for a couple semesters up in Allenville," he said, nodding north. "Ran out of money and came home. Been working on the family farm since. I planned to go back to school, but I guess school's closed."

Maryanne tossed the empty Spam can onto the road. It rattled in the quiet afternoon, a silence that had only been broken by the caw from an occasional crow; the noise loud enough to be startling. "Beavis' been in jail since people started keeling over," she spat. "He don't know shit about what the world's been through."

Or what the hell you are, Karl thought. Maryanne snapped her head toward him, her glare boring into him like a drill. At that moment Karl was glad he'd taken a dump, or he would have right then, the moment he realized this woman could read his mind. Holy shit.

Maryanne stood, wiping crumbs from her once white pants. "Time to go, boys," she said and tossed Dooker's keys to Trent. He caught them in one hand. "You drive, Beavis. Cowboy, you ride shotgun. Put your weapons in the back seat fellas. I'm going to take a nap while you look for that skinny assed, big dick son of a bitch."

Then they got in the cruiser and went to kill Darryl.

July 11: Allenville, Missouri
CHAPTER 27

Sweat ran down Craig's face as he made his way up the dusty steps that zigged and zagged the ten-foot-square courthouse clock tower, the tall staircase scattered with boxes and cans of food, cases of beer and Dr Pepper, and stacks of books and magazines. Craig held a box of bottled water tightly as he took step, after step. If he tripped and didn't have a good handle, the flat box of twenty-four plastic bottles would bounce three stories down into the darkness. He'd already dropped one; it wasn't going to happen again. A few steps later, Craig's head broke the plane of the trapdoor to what he called the Observation Deck; he heaved the box onto the floor and pulled himself up. More supplies sat against the wall, a sleeping bag and pillow stretched across the floor. Craig reached into his shirt, pulled out a rolled 8x11 piece of paper and tacked it to the bare wooden wall. Farrah Fawcett in a red swimsuit smiled at him. This was now home.

The room had been dirty and bare when Craig forced his way into the courthouse, broken the lock to the tower door, trudged up step after step, and flapped open the trapdoor to the room at the top of the tallest structure in town. Hot, stale air seemed to suck breath from his lungs as he looked across the wooden floor littered with dead flies. That could be cleaned, he knew. The view is what he needed. Craig unlocked and pushed open the window, ancient weights hanging off pulleys groaned inside the walls as Craig slowly forced the dirty window open. He could see everything.

Streets ran in even east-west/north-south blocks; Main Street cut beneath Craig's courthouse perch and merged with U.S. 71 highway that ran around the town. Farms dotted the fields that rolled on forever, the monolithic white windmills from a wind farm near Stanberry, Missouri, that and the paved highways the only scars on a horizon that could be from 1880, for all Craig knew. He leaned out of the window and scanned the tall grass of the courthouse lawn below, the shovel handle he'd used to mark the shallow grave of the man Posey made him kill still visible in the tall grass. Fucking Posey.

Posey made him come to the courthouse. Craig sat on the front porch of his house, drinking beer, eating potato chips, and grinning as he watched Posey's house burn, and collapse into the foundation. Then he tossed empty beer can after empty beer can toward the smoldering pile of debris and never reached it. It didn't matter, because Craig had finally defeated that asshole. That taunting, mocking asshole. Then the dreams started.

"McAllister," drifted through Craig's bedroom the night the Posey house stopped spewing its filthy smoke into the pure night sky. "McAllister, wake up you pussy." Craig remembered his eyes sliding open to a dark room, the waxing half moon cast a dull gray glow through his bedroom, although he still didn't know if he were awake, or dreaming. More and more days seemed like that.

"What do you want, you fuck?" Craig, or was it Dream Craig, spat into the night.

Posey spoke as clearly as if he stood next to Craig's bed, although Craig knew no one was there. But it's hard to tell if you're asleep. "They're coming for you, McAllister. They're coming for you, and they're going to fuck you up the ass. But you'd like that, wouldn't you?"

Goddamn Posey. "Somebody's coming? Who's coming? Who's coming, you bitch?"

"Someone who will eat your soul," Posey said. Craig felt Posey's breath now as the dead old man whispered into his ear. "The Devil Woman."

Craig sat up straight in bed, screaming.

That was four days ago, or five. Craig had a hard time keeping track of things anymore. He'd thrown the Jeff Foxworthy calendar into the fire because he was drunk, so not even Jeff could tell him it was Thursday. "You might be a redneck if you find a new recliner for your living room because the garbage truck comes on Thursday." But Posey wouldn't leave him alone. The Outbreak had taken the bastard and his fat wife, a truck had taken his shitty-assed dog, and Craig had taken his house, burnt that fucker to the ground. *So, why aren't you in hell, Posey?*

"You gotta get ready, McAllister," Posey whispered to Craig the next day as Craig sat on the porch drinking warm beer and playing Super Mario Brothers on an old GameBoy Advance. Craig had every package of AA batteries in town, so Mario and his tall Guido brother Luigi could bounce off turtles forever. That which does not kill you makes you smaller, eh, Mario?

"You're dead, Posey," Craig said. "You and your fat wife. I'm not listening to you anymore."

"Don't be a fucking idiot," the voice said, softer this time, farther away. "People are coming. People who make you look like a goddamned prom queen. Get someplace safe, get someplace high."

Craig shoved the palms of his hands over his ears. "Go away, Posey. Go away, Posey, "GO AWAY, POSEY," he screamed. "YOU'RE DEAD. GO A-WAY."

Moments of silence later, Craig pulled his hands away from his ears and was greeted by crickets. Just crickets. He lay back onto his bed and slept. The next morning Craig broke into the courthouse clock tower.

July 11: Barton, Missouri
CHAPTER 28

A Hummer H3 sat in the garage like an alien spacecraft; the black, rectangular hulk seemed to absorb most of the electric light from the windowless room. But it was the walls that stole everyone's attention. Racks of Winchester SX3 shotguns, M-4 carbine rifles, and several M27 light machine guns lined the back wall over boxes and boxes of ammunition. Crates marked MRE, and gas cans were stacked along one wall, boxes of non-perishable food, camping gear, cases of beer and bottled water lined the other. Terry stepped into the garage to make room for the others pressing behind him. Jenna squeezed her way in first, Nikki and Doug followed, his eyes locking on a wall map above a box of crates. Doug stepped up to it as the others fanned through the garage and marveled at the booty. Four states stared back at Doug from the well-worn map; Missouri, Kansas, Iowa, and Nebraska, a gold thumbtack stuck into the spot where Doug now stood. Other thumbtacks, black, blue, and red, scattered across the four-state area. A line of evenly spaced blue tacks led from the gold tack in Barton, north through Clarinda and Atlantic, Iowa, to Interstate 80, and west through Council Bluffs, Iowa, to Omaha, Nebraska, before jagging away into the northwestern part of the state. Red tacks surrounded Des Moines, Iowa, Topeka, Kansas, and St. Louis, like moats, or castle walls, or zones of death. A line of black tacks ran down the far west part of Nebraska and the border between Kansas and Colorado. Marks in Sharpie ran up highways and rural routes, some scratched out, others peppered with exclamation points.

"What does this mean?" Doug whispered to himself, running his finger up the line of blue thumbtacks that lead to a blank spot north of Alliance, Nebraska, and ended at another gold thumbtack.

Terry patted the H3's right quarter panel. "Looks like these people were ready for what happened," he said.

"Except the part about not dying," Nikki said softly.

Arnold stepped into the garage and stood before the wall of guns. "The 12-gauge auto-loader. The .45 long slide, with laser sighting. Phased plasma rifle in the 40-watt range."

"Hey," Terry said, matching Arnold's 'Terminator' reference quote for quote. "Just what you see, pal."

Jenna touched Doug's forearm, a smile pulled at his mouth from the welcomed tingle. "What do you think they were doing?" she asked.

Doug shook his head. "I don't know. Probably just survival types, stocking up for the end of the world. People did it for the Hale-Bopp comet that was supposed to be pulling a planet behind it, they did it at Y2K, and they did it in 2012 for the end of the Mayan calendar. Doesn't mean anything; the world never came to an end, until now. They just weren't going to let anybody touch their stuff, that's all. But this map means something." He turned to Nikki. "These guys have a computer?"

She nodded. "It's in the spare bedroom on the left."

"I'm going to find out a little more about our hosts," Doug said, as he walked up the two steps to the kitchen, and disappeared.

Terry grabbed a case of beer and followed. "Well, come on, guys," he said. "Let's put this to good use."

Three beers into the night, Nikki realized she was smiling. When Terry hooked up the Xbox, he found a Wii installed to the flat screen, the game "Dance Dance Revolution" already loaded.

"Probably for their grandkids," Nikki said, remembering the computer screensaver of smiling young faces that were most probably lying in a rusty, crusted stain, skin picked from their skulls by a hungry growing fungus. "I can't imagine the Marstens boogying to 'Just Dance'." Nikki paused. She didn't know the Marstens apart from their wardrobe, their décor, and their corpses. But, then again, she did. She felt she knew them more intimately than anyone else on the planet. "Hey, turn it on."

Terry grinned like an idiot. "No way," he said. "We're dancin'?"

Jenna stood up, laughing. "Uh-uh. I don't dance, Terry. It's not happening."

"Come on."

"Nope. I'm going to check on Doug." Jenna stood and walked down the hall.

"That leaves you," Terry said to Nikki. "You up for '99 Red Balloons'?"

Nikki looked up at Terry, standing in the middle of the living room. He held out a calloused hand; this man had obviously worked for a living. He seemed nice enough, and was cute in a Larry the Cable Guy kind of way. "It's been a while," she said. "But I'm up for it."

Terry took her hand with surprising gentleness and pulled her onto her feet. "Hell yes."

Doug sat in a darkened room, the HP monitor bathed his face in soft white. Jenna walked in, and rested a hand on his shoulder. She felt the muscles under her hand quiver. "Found anything?" she asked. Doug turned to find her silhouetted in the doorway. He smiled.

"Yeah," he said, and stood. "Come here and see this." Jenna slid into the desk chair. Doug loomed over her shoulder, and moved the mouse. His scent drifted across her nose. Just months ago, this smell of sweat, beer, and cedar smoke may have caused her to wretch, but now it warmed her, excited her. "Check this out." He clicked on a file marked "Itinerary." A Word document popped onto the screen.

Date	Time	To-Dos
June 2	Noon	Drive to KC. Say good-bye to Jimmy, Karla and the kids.
June 21	8 a.m.	Shut off utilities. Change mailing address to PO box in Alliance.
	10 a.m.	Load Hummer with food, guns, camping gear. Don't forget photo albums.
	Noon	Lunch at the café. Tell Ben to come by and get tomatoes tomorrow.
	3 p.m.	Close out bank accounts in Allenville. Get three months of prescriptions.
	6 p.m.	Go to cookout at Johnstons. BYOB. Take German potato salad.
June 22	5 a.m.	Head to Tanelorn.

The last entry was June 22. Nineteen days ago. The Marstens were still here; they never made it to Tanelorn.

"What's Tanelorn?" Jenna asked. She turned and looked at Doug. He stood behind her, staring intently at the screen. "That's a strange word. Do you know?"

"Yeah," he said. "Tanelorn is a city in Michael Moorcock's Eternal Champion series where the heroes go when they die, retire, get fed up with saving everyone. Erekosë, Elric, Hawkmoon ..." His voice trailed off, and he looked at Jenna who looked back at him, smirking. "What?" he asked.

"That's fantasy, right? You read fantasy?"

Doug stood straight. "I read a lot of fantasy and science fiction in high school, yeah," he said. "I still do, sometimes. I also watch a lot of 'Star Trek.' But it's coming in handy, isn't it?"

"Don't get so defensive, nerd boy," Jenna said, turning back toward the computer. "What else did you find?"

He leaned back over her shoulder, his stubbly cheek grazed hers. "This is the good stuff." He minimized the Itinerary file and double-clicked a folder on the desktop marked "Tanelorn." The folder held document files named, "Essentials," "Food," "Medical," "Armory," "Movie Collection," and a JPEG called "Home Defense."

"These guys have a summer home," Doug said. "In the middle of nowhere, it's a half-day's drive away, it's stocked with everything we need, and it's armed to the teeth."

Jenna sat silent, scanning the "Medical" file. "You know they were even prepared to deliver a baby? What were they, like, 80, or something?" She turned the desk chair and faced Doug, the soft light of the computer rendered him gray in the dark room. "What are you thinking?"

Doug stepped back, leaned on the doorframe, and ran a hand through his brown hair, longer than it had been in a long time. "I think we should go to Omaha and try to find people," he said. "There has to be something there, or at least someone. I can't believe civilization is just gone."

"Isn't it?" she said. "From what we saw in Kansas City, civilization is gone." Jenna grasped Doug's hands, her soft warmth calming. "Why are you so sure about Omaha?"

"I'm not sure, but the shelter at Worlds of Fun pointed us there. If that doesn't work out, we should go to Tanelorn. This place is great, but Tanelorn is a fucking fort, pardon my French. It has its own water, its own electricity, and they stocked it with enough survivalist food for the next twenty-five years. We can wait out whatever else is coming."

Jenna nodded. "But we could do that here."

"Yeah, but we found 'here'. 'Here' is open, exposed. If anyone's driving by now, that big front window in the living room is a beacon in the night. There are no paved roads to Tanelorn, and when you get there, chances are you'll be electrocuted."

"What?"

Doug smirked. "You didn't open the file marked 'Home Defense,' did you?" Jenna shook her head. "There's a perimeter fence, twelve-feet tall and topped with razor wire. A flick of the switch and it goes hot."

Jenna nodded, she didn't know what else to do. "You're probably right, but I'm not going to tell everyone that. I'm going to print all this, and we're going to talk about it tomorrow. You, me, Terry, Nikki, and Arnold. We're going to spread everything out and make a decision as a group. We can't do it tonight."

"Why?" Doug asked.

Jenna smiled. "Because I think I'm ready to rule Terry at 'Dance, Dance Revolution.'"

Doug and Jenna walked into the living room to Nikki and Arnold doing the robot to 'Gonna Make You Sweat'. Jenna giggled. "Go Arnold. Terminate that song."

He paused and looked at her. "I cannot comply."

"Me neither. No more dancing," Nikki said, and dropped onto the couch. "Not tonight. Terry, would you get me another beer?"

Terry grinned and bowed like a stage actor. "Yes, m'lady." As he stood and turned toward the kitchen, something big hit the front window in a wet thud. Everyone turned. A man, his face and hand streaked in red, pressed against the glass, the skin that showed through the blood was painfully white in the tungsten lights. Nikki screamed. The man's eyes drooped shut and his face slid in a bloody streak down the glass and out of sight.

July 12: Rural Missouri
CHAPTER 29

The big white RV sat diagonally across the two northbound lanes of U.S. 71 south of Allenville. The Kingsville Police cruiser was partially on the gravel shoulder at the top of a hill about a mile away from the roadblock. Maryanne leaned against the back door of the car and took a swig of Evan Williams from the bottle. It was getting low. Trent stood in front of the car taking a leak; Karl stood on his own in the middle of the road, a pair of Bushnell binoculars, Dooker's binoculars, pressed to his face.

"Anybody there, Cowboy?" Maryanne asked.

Karl didn't answer; he didn't move. A moment later, he pulled the binoculars down to his chest and turned toward Maryanne, the beauty of this mad woman always surprised him. He cocked his head at her expression, a smile like she knew what he was thinking.

"Not that I can see," he said. "Nothing's moving down there, but that Winnebago didn't get in that spot by itself. There's a deep culvert on the right side of the highway, another drop off to the left, and southbound lanes are stuffed with cars." He paused for a few seconds and pressed the Bushnell's back to his eyes. "Somebody put it there as a roadblock."

"Why?" Trent asked. He zipped his pants, and walked back toward the driver's side door.

"Don't know, Beavis," Maryanne said. "But if someone's down there, they know we're up here. I'm sure they heard our car for miles. We have to get past that roadblock, so we might as well go down there and say 'hi.'"

Trent turned to face her. "And why do we have to do that? If somebody blocked the road, they don't plan to make good out of it. We can just go back to Kingsville, you can drop me off, and let me be. I can live a long time on the farm. I don't think I can if we go down there."

Maryanne stuck a finger in Trent's sternum, the spot she'd pointed the shotgun back in the Kingsville City Jail, and dug it in. Trent didn't squirm; he didn't even feel it because he'd never seen a look like Maryanne's on a human face. It was alien, soulless, reptile.

"Darryl's in a town about six miles on the other side of that RV," she said slowly, calmly, joylessly. "Or he's going to be soon. And I'm going to be there, too, whether you like it or not."

Sweat started to bead on Trent's upper lip. "What's so God awful important about this Darryl?"

Maryanne smiled and Trent felt the skin on his scrotum tighten. "Because he got away." She motioned to Karl. "You'd better drive from here on out, Cowboy. Beavis' gotta earn back my trust. Let's move." Karl nodded to Trent and he moved away from the door. Maryanne directed Trent to sit bitch, and she slid into shotgun. Karl eased the cruiser into drive, and slowly crawled down the hill.

A turn of the key and the world became silent. Maryanne, Karl, and Trent stepped from the cruiser and onto the cracked, gray asphalt of the rural highway ten yards away from the RV, the word HAVEN written across the side in red spray-paint. The shotgun and rifle sat on the front seat of the police car because Maryanne said so. She wanted them to look all friendly-like.

When they clicked the car doors shut, people came seemingly from nowhere. Four from the west side of the RV, a half-dozen from the east. They weren't starving stragglers. These men were well fed, their clothing clean for the most part. All were armed with shotguns and hunting rifles. One jerk off had a samurai sword on his belt. Asshole. Maryanne felt a shiver next to her, although she wasn't touching anyone. Beavis and the Cowboy were terrified. A grim smile crossed her lips. Pussies.

"We-hell," a greasy man in a deeply stained death metal T-shirt said, as he stepped from the side of the RV, cradling a deer rifle. "Looky, looky what we have here. A little present." He beat on the side of the RV once, twice, three times. "Hey, boss. Come look. We got company."

Maryanne, Karl, and Trent raised their hands, and the door to the RV slammed open. A big man, at least 6'2", maybe 225, stepped out, smiling through a skinny blond moustache. "Thanks, Danny. You know how much I love visitors," the man said. Weapons around them cocked as he stepped closer. "Hi, folks. Welcome to Haven."

Haven? Maryanne's smile never left her face. She put her weight on her right leg, and a hand on her hip. "Well, that sure is friendly," she said, her voice velvet. "Now, if you'd move this hunk of shit out of the road, my boys and I have business to attend to north of here."

"Ha," the big man bellowed, his laugh deep and more friendly than his face. "Oh, I'm sorry, little lady. Afraid I'm not going to do that. We have a good thing here, and wouldn't you know it, y'all are now part of our good thing."

Maryanne shifted to her other leg. "And what kind of 'thing' are we talking about? Because it's not good if you're keeping me from my business."

The big man spread his arms wide. "We're a traveling community," he said. "A great big happy family, and you're our new brothers and sister." He turned to Karl, and Trent. "You fellas are going to work hard for us here at the Haven. Movin' dead cars, changin' tires, liftin' boxes. Then there's …"

"We ain't doin' shit for you," Trent spat. The big man turned on him, and sent a box-like fist into Trent's midsection. He collapsed into a sobbing ball on the highway. The men hovering around the periphery stepped closer, but the big man raised a palm and they stopped.

"Anything else?" he asked, and kicked Trent in the ribs before he turned back toward Maryanne, smiling. "You, young lady," he said, leaning in close to Maryanne, hot rancid breath washed across her face. "I think I have a special job for you."

Maryanne smiled back. Karl hated that smile; she looked like a hunter, like a shark. He was just glad she didn't direct it at him. "What's your name, big man?" she asked softly, seductively. The man's smile grew bigger.

"Leonardo," he said.

"Like the painter?" she asked.

He shook his head. "No, the Ninja Turtle." He never took his eyes off hers while he barked. "Donatello, make sure these new gentlemen know their place in their new home." Only one man stepped forward as Leonardo slipped a tightly muscled arm around Maryanne's waist and lifted her up toward his face. They may have seen Maryanne reach behind her and pull a .38 from her belt at the small of her back, or maybe not. But everyone saw her swing the pistol around, press it against Leonardo's temple and pull the trigger, a shower of blood and skull fragments spewed out the side of his ruined head. The report commanded the night. Leonardo's arm loosened and Maryanne landed on her feet. The big man's body fell in a wet thud on the highway.

Maryanne looked around at the group of men, Leonardo's blood splattered across her face. "Looks like I'm your new boss," she said. "Anybody want to fuck?" Nobody moved. She pointed the pistol at a nearby abandoned car and fired, the rear window shattered. "Are you sure?" A man stepped forward on shaking legs. "What's your name, bubba?"

"Donatello," he said.

Maryanne frowned. "No, what's your *name*?"

"Darrian."

"Uh, Donatello's good." She waved her pistol toward the remaining men. "Where's Michelangelo and Raphael?" No one moved. Maryanne fired into the sky. "Where are they?"

"Here," a voice said. A young, thin man ran around the side of the RV to find a .38 pointed toward his face. He stopped and raised his arms. "Mike's right behind me. Leo..." He stopped; Leo lay in a heap on the highway, his exploded head in the middle of a pool of blood. "Uh, Leo had us watch out about a mile up the road." Mike ran up behind Raphael and stopped.

"What happened to Leonardo?"

"I'm Leonardo now," she said. Maryanne turned, and addressed the twelve men that surrounded them. "Anybody else here we should know about?" She pulled back the .38's hammer. "Anybody?"

"Yeah," the Greasyman said, his voice close to tears. "Got a truckload of slaves 'round back. 'Bout thirty of them."

"Slaves?"

"It, uh..." Raphael began.

She turned to face him.

"It was Leo's idea," Mike finished. "He said it was necessary. We'd need them sooner or later. To move stuff out of the way, to find food, to build shit ..."

"For blowjobs?"

"That was Leo's deal," Donatello said. "Not ours."

Maryanne nodded. "Good. Now get your asses in the van and strip down. I got plans for you." She turned to the Greasyman. "As for you, let the slaves loose. All of them. This guy..." She pointed to Karl. "This guy is in charge when I'm getting recreation in the vehicle with the Ninja Turtles. Tell those poor people they got five minutes to disappear or you're using them for target practice."

"But," the Greasyman started. Maryanne held up her hand, stopping him.

"They'll just slow us down." She turned away from the Greasyman and smiled at Karl. "I'll save you for later, Cowboy," she said, gently cupping his balls through his jeans. "If you're good."

He watched her bounce up the two steps into the RV, hoping like hell those three turtles would kill her before she came back out. He never wanted to be good again.

July 11: Barton, Missouri
CHAPTER 30

The bloody streak on the front glass gleamed in the light of the living room like fresh paint. The group stood in silence, the drone of Dance Dance Revolution now something far away.

"What the fuck was that?" Nikki whispered.

"A person," Terry said, setting his beer on a nearby end table before it fell from his shaky hand.

"I know it was a person," Nikki snapped, then looked at Terry, the expression on his face like she'd slapped him. "Sorry. I'm scared."

Doug stepped to the window, grabbed the drawstring and pulled the curtains shut. "Jenna," he said. "You still comfortable with that pistol in your purse?" She nodded. He turned toward Terry. "Go into the garage and grab a shotgun." Terry took a step toward the kitchen; Doug stopped him. "Don't forget to load it." Terry nodded and disappeared around the corner.

"What's the plan, then?" Jenna asked.

Doug raised his hand to silence her. "Let's wait for Terry," he said. Terry rounded the corner into the living room with a gun, sliding shells into the chamber. "Terry, Jenna, you guys go out the back door and sneak around each side of the house. Arnold … just stay out of everyone's way."

Jenna frowned. "What are you going to do?"

"I'm giving you two minutes to work your way around to the corners, then I'm going out the front door."

"Are you sure that's safe?" Nikki asked.

Doug smiled. "What is?"

Jenna rushed up to Doug, pulled his face down to hers and pressed her soft, warm lips against his, ignoring the stubble from days without shaving. Doug grew flush, his knees weak. He gently pulled back. "Wow," he whispered. "Jenna, honey, I'm going to be okay." He smiled and brushed his fingertips gently across her cheek. "But I think I want you to get worried about me a lot."

She forced a smile. "Just be careful," she said.

He nodded. "Just go, before I lose my nerve. Oh," he said, stopping them. "Don't shoot me."

Jenna pulled the .38 from her purse she'd slung over the back of a kitchen chair and grinned tightly. Doug had wondered why she carried that damned thing around with her everywhere when nothing in it mattered anymore, but after she killed the starving dogs in St. Joseph, he knew. I guess you never really know when you need to shoot something. Terry pulled on the sliding glass door to the back porch, cursed when he realized it was locked, then pulled again, the big glass door glided on silent rollers.

"Good luck," Nikki said softly.

Doug nodded and stepped to the front door on shaky legs. It wasn't Jenna's kiss anymore; it was visions of a shotgun blast at close range spreading his brains over the Marstens' floral print couch. The death, the strange fungus had made him give up fear, until now, until Jenna. He didn't want to die.

"If I open this door and get shot," he whispered to Nikki. "You and Arnold run to the garage and shoot anybody that tries to get in."

"But ..."

"And," he said over her. "It would probably be smart to throw a couple of guns and some food in the Hummer and drive like hell out of here. It's facing the garage door, so you don't even have to open it to tip anybody off what you're going to do. Just gun it and go."

Nikki nodded and stepped toward the kitchen. Arnold followed.

Doug exhaled slowly. Showtime. He reached for the handle, gently unlocked it and threw open the door; Nikki shrieked at the bang from the handle slamming into the wall. No shot. No rustle. No movement. Just a moan. To Doug's right, lay a lump; he bent toward it wishing like hell he'd thought to look for a flashlight.

"Anybody out here?" he yelled. "If you are, it'd be on the nice side if you'd just shoot me now and quit dickin' around. I've got stuff to do tonight."

Coyotes yipped in the distance, a cow lowed nearby, cicadas filled the chorus. Yep, another beautiful night in God's country. "Terry, Jenna," he said. "I think he's alone. Come and help me get him inside. And it'd be best to put something down, like towels or garbage bags; I think this is going to be messy."

Inside the house, Doug saw he was right. A gash crossed the man's temple, leaving a ragged flap hanging over his left eye; the right thigh of his jeans was soaked with blood. Doug sat on the end of the garbage bag-covered couch, wondering what all these people looking at him expected him to do.

"Is he alive?" Jenna asked.

The man's chest didn't move much, but it did move in slow shallow breaths. Doug nodded. "Yeah, but I don't know for how long. Anybody know anything about medicine?"

Nikki raised her hand. "I took a First Aid class in college. But it didn't cover anything like this."

Doug stood and pressed his hand lightly on her shoulder. "Then just do your best," he said. "My medical knowledge has to do with castrating pigs. I don't think that's going to come in handy right now."

"How'd he find us?" Terry asked, his face ashen.

"The light was on. If we were all asleep, we'd have found him tomorrow, bled out in the street."

Jenna stood next to Doug and wrapped her fingers around his. "What do you think happened to him?"

"Car wreck, I suppose. Looks like his head hit the safety glass and lost pretty good, and something on the steering column could have snapped and gouged his leg."

Nikki let out a loud moan. "What if there's someone else in the car?"

Jenna squeezed Doug's hand tighter.

Aw, hell. Doug nodded and pointed his free hand at Terry. "We have to go check," he said. "We have to make sure he's alone. Terry?"

"What?"

"Grab your shotgun," Doug said, then nodded toward Nikki. "Do you know where these Marstens kept their flashlights?"

She shook her head. "No, but everybody keeps them in about the same place; bedside table, under the sink, in the junk drawer. I'll go look."

"Uh, hey, Doug," Terry sputtered. "What are you saying, man?"

"We're going out there."

"Yeah, that's what I thought. Look, last time you didn't give me enough time to think about it. I, uh, I don't want to go out there at night. No tellin' what's waiting around for us."

Nikki brought two flashlights from the kitchen, big heavy Maglites. Doug flicked both on, the beams shone brightly. In the Marsten house, he wasn't surprised. He handed a flashlight to Terry. "The woods ain't crawling with monsters. If there is anything out there, it's somebody hurt worse than Herman Munster over there. Now, are you coming with me?"

Terry shook his head.

"Tough shit, you're coming." Doug pulled his hand out of Jenna's tight grasp and cupped it around the gentle curve of her face. "It's my turn," he said, and kissed her deeply.

Doug's Maglite cut harsh swaths through the night as he and Terry walked down Main Street of Barton; Terry held a shotgun with both hands, Doug rested his aluminum bat over one shoulder. It didn't take a Middle Earth ranger to track Herman Munster far. Bloody footprints showed few true steps and mostly shuffled feet down the center of the street.

"How far you figure?" Terry asked, his hush voice sounding unnaturally loud in the night.

"How the hell should I know?" Doug said. "We couldn't hear the crash over your damned dancing game. It could be just down the street, or miles away."

"Well, I don't think it's that far."

Doug shrugged. "Probably not. I don't think that poor bastard would have made it more than a mile."

The bloody footsteps grew stronger the farther they walked. "Herman Munster was banged up pretty good. I didn't think he'd have gone this far," Terry said, then whistled. "Hey, Doug, point your flashlight over by those trees."

The bright beam moved from the pavement near their feet to a streak of black about twenty feet away that suddenly turned from the road into a deep ditch. Doug lowered the light; the footprints came from there.

"Bingo," Terry said.

The car, a pretty red Mustang, lay on its side, the safety glass of the front windshield lay on the grass next to the car at the bottom of the ditch. Doug nodded to Terry, and they went down. Terry's foot slipped, maybe on Herman Munster's blood, and he almost skidded down the slope.

"That was a heck of a deal for him to crawl up that embankment," Terry said, wheezing when he reached the bottom. "That's damned steep."

"But he did it," Doug said, kneeling in front of the car, scanning the interior with the light. "Looks like Herman was alone, and..." He touched the car hood. "And this accident happened a while ago. Long enough the car's gone cold."

"He got knocked in the head. He don't know where he is. Probably don't know who he is."

Doug reached into the car, pulled out a beer, and handed it to Terry. "Thanks for coming with me, buddy."

"Don't worry about ..." Terry popped the tab on the beer can, foam shot across his face. "Aw, fucking great."

When Doug and Terry walked into the house, Herman's pants lay in a bloody pile on one of the black plastic trash bags that now covered the couch and the living room rug. Nikki tied a tourniquet around the man's thigh to stop the bleeding and taped gauze across his head like a turban.

"I got the bleeding to stop," she said. "That's the good news. The bad news is I don't know anything about head injuries. This guy might go to sleep and never wake up."

"Has he said anything?" Doug asked.

Jenna put her arm around his waist and pulled him tight. "Yeah," she said. "Crazy stuff."

"Like what?"

Arnold suddenly shot up from the Marsten's La-Z-Boy. "Oh, you think you're bad, huh? You're a fucking choirboy compared to me. A CHOIR BOY."

"What the hell's that?" Doug spat.

"It's from 'End of Days,'" Terry said. "Not some of the Governor's best work."

"No, I mean ..."

"Arnold's right," Nikki said. "He talked about somebody reading his mind, fucking his brains out, and killing some guy at a gas station. Then there was something about a cowboy."

"Yes," Jenna said. "And apparently, Nikki is a Tanya Smithmeyer, my name's Bossie, and the Devil Woman is coming to kill us all. It's been fun."

What the fuck? "Did he respond to anything?"

Nikki shook her head. "No, but he did cry when he told us this devil woman killed some old guy at a ball park. He kept saying the guy just wanted to watch the ballgame."

Doug felt like someone had punched him. Johnnyball? Was he talking about Johnnyball? Visions ran through Doug's head of the white-haired old man sitting at Kauffman Stadium watching the Kansas City Royals' 1985 World Series season while cancer ate away his insides. Doug, Terry, and Jenna ate the man's nachos and popcorn, and drank his beer. Then they just left him because he wanted to watch the Royals win the World Series again before he died.

"You think he was talking about Johnnyball?" Jenna asked. "Or just talking crazy?"

Doug looked into her deep, green eyes. He knew he could get lost in those eyes, and wanted to. He wanted to soon, but not here. "I don't know. Sounds like it, but what the hell are the chances?"

Herman Munster suddenly jerked, his arms thrashed like he fought with something. Doug knelt next to the couch, his knee soaking with Herman's cold, spent blood that pooled on a trash bag, and grabbed the man, trying to hold him still.

"There are probably some bungee cords or something in the garage to tie this guy down," he shouted. "Get something."

They used duct tape. Herman Munster lay on the couch in his silver bonds, relaxed now, his breath coming slowly, but steadily. The girls and Terry had gone to bed in the three bedrooms; Arnold curled up on the love seat, snoring. They had decided to watch Herman in shifts; Doug took the first one. He sat back in the brown La-Z-Boy and flipped through the seemingly endless list of programs on the Marstens DVR, and turned on "Top Gear." Five minutes later, sleep pulled him under. He never heard Herman Munster stir.

"Devil woman want me," Herman mumbled to no one. "Devil woman get me. Waiting. Waiting. She's got a big gun and a pretty flower. She's going to take us all."

July 15: Allenville, Missouri
CHAPTER 31

The afternoon sun soaked warmth into Craig's face. He loved summer, especially this summer. Grass in the yards that surrounded his house on Mulberry Street grew tall, disgraceful. They would go to seed in a month or so, but Craig didn't care. The lawn he battled that old fucker Posey over (hey, bitch. My yard looks like a goddamned golf course. Yours looks like the hair on my ass – with thistles), was now filled with dandelions. Proper lawn maintenance didn't matter anymore; the crazy bitch did. Craig sat in a canvas lawn chair on the sidewalk; his back to what was once Posey's house, now a black pile in its own foundation. He cracked open another warm Budweiser, took a sip, and smiled. He'd been this happy before, he supposed; maybe as a kid who didn't know how shitty the world was. But once high school rolled over him like a madman in a short bus, the words, "You can achieve anything. You can be president," blew out of his head like he'd been shot. That had all changed now, Craig might as well be president, or at least the mayor; he was the only person in town still alive. The neighbors were dead. No street party anymore, no forty-year-old fat women shuffling down his sidewalk in jogging clothes walking dogs that shit in his yard, no kids throwing footballs. Dead. Everyone was dead, even Pork Chop Man. If it weren't for Posey hanging on, Craig's world would be his favorite "Twilight Zone" episode. He'd be alone, forever.

He wanted that bad.

"I'm never leaving you, shithead," Posey said from across the lawn, the worthless old man calling from the concrete steps of his ruined house. Craig didn't move. He knew Posey wasn't there. He couldn't be there. Posey was dead, along with his fat wife. The fungus took them, and for good measure Craig set their corpses on fire. But the thought burned in Craig's head, if he turned around, toward Posey's house, that crazy old man would be sitting on the porch in his KC Royals ball cap, grinning through a fleshless face, and giving him the finger.

"Fuck you, Posey." Craig shoved his fist into the air. "Your shit's stale. I'm done with you." He drained his beer, crushed the can in his hand and dropped it, the can hitting the concrete with a clank.

The box on the porch, the last box he would carry the four blocks to the courthouse, held the last part of his life he never wanted to remember. A photo album, an old work shirt, his father's name stitched onto the left breast, his mother's wedding veil, a lock of blond hair in an Alligator sandwich bag, the yellowed twist tie keeping the hair prisoner forever. He knew the contents of the box, every picture, every stain on the shirt, and he never wanted to open it again.

"You're soft, McAllister," Posey called from across the yard.

Shut up, Posey. Shut up, Posey. Shut up, Posey.

"You gonna start crying now?"

Craig finished his beer and threw it into the street. This was it. He picked up the box, tucked it under his arm and walked up the sidewalk and away from his house on Mulberry Street, the house he'd lived in since moving to Allenville. Good-bye house, good-bye Posey. Craig had work to do; the Devil Woman was coming.

A slight breeze rippled through the prairie-like grass in neighboring yards as Craig made his way up Forest Street and took a right on George to Cunningham. Blank windows stared at him from silent homes. He'd have to break into those homes at some point, when the stores ran out of food. By then the fungus would have eaten people to the point they would be no more than bizarre decorations on the floor. After winter, the fungus would be gone, too. But the death didn't bother Craig; it was the smell. Hard to eat tuna out of the can with a rotting corpse across the table from you. A hawk cried from somewhere overhead. Now the people were gone, all those pesky noisy people, the silence was brilliant. That hawk could have been a mile away for all he knew, but it sounded like it was right overhead. A black cloud of sparrows suddenly spun from somewhere in the south shopping district, just a few blocks from the square. What the hell caused that? Two more steps and he knew – a car engine.

Craig froze. The corner of Cunningham and First Street lay half a block ahead, then two more blocks to the county courthouse, his new home, and more importantly his guns. The growl of the engine grew closer. This wasn't the hum of some little Japanese or Korean POS, this was the grumbling of a big American engine. Shit. He dropped his box of childhood memories into a weedy lawn and took off in as much of a sprint as he could muster. The stitch in his side came quickly, and jabbed at his innards.

"Too many cans of beer and not enough walks, McAllister," Posey said in his ear. "You're fat and lazy."

Craig swatted wildly around his head like he was attacked by bees and hit Main Street, almost losing his balance when he jumped off the curb. The grumbling grew closer, and Craig knew he wouldn't make it to the courthouse. He ducked into an alley that separated a row of houses from the businesses that lined Main Street and dropped into the shadow of a Dumpster, his breaths came fast. Oh shit, oh shit, oh shit.

"Try the door, McAllister," Posey said. Craig could almost feel the old man standing next to him. "They might just drive down this alley, then where would you be? At the corner of Shit Street and Butt Fuck Boulevard."

Craig craned his neck to his right, as far away from the sound, and the feeling of Posey as he could. A metal door with a simple knob was moored in a brick wall about ten feet away. He pushed himself up onto weak legs and walked like the Frankenstein monster to the door, wrapped his hand around the knob and pulled. It was locked.

"Damn it."

"Just break off the door knob, dickless," Posey taunted. "It's a simple knob. Won't be a thing to a big pussy like you."

"I... I..." Craig stuttered.

"Jesus, McAllister, do I have to do everything for you." Posey was close to him now, too close. Craig could feel his breath on his ear. "Break it."

Craig looked around the alley. A chunk of concrete about the size of a human skull sat amongst the weeds that grew on the edge of what used to be somebody's lawn. He grabbed the concrete in two hands and crossed the alley, the sound of the big engine coming closer. Posey was right, goddamn him. That car, carrying who? the Devil woman? was coming up Butt Fuck Boulevard. Craig raised the lump of fused sand and gravel over his head and brought it down hard on the cheap metal knob. The knob bent downward. He raised the concrete again, sweat rolling down his skin began to soak his underwear. He slammed the heavy mass onto the knob again. The knob dropped onto the gravel of the alley. The car turned onto First Street. Craig dropped the concrete, threw open the door and jumped inside the building, pulling the door shut behind him.

He collapsed on a carpeted floor and lay still, wheezing like a smoker. *Who the fuck is in my town?* He wondered. *My town.*

"Devil woman," Posey whispered in his ear, the wet tip of the dead man's tongue ran over his lobe. Craig pinched his eyes tight. No, goddamnit. No. No. No. He swung a fist that would have caught Posey in the face, but it connected with nothing. He opened his eyes.

The light of midday shone evenly through the big window that joined this room with the rest of the ground floor. Craig pushed up to his hands and knees, his breath still trying to escape him. This was an office, an expensive office. A large, clean, albeit dusty mahogany desk dominated the room. The room, the desk, belonged to Billy Bob Purdy. Craig could tell by all the pictures, and Purdy's name carved into every award that cocksucker had ever won. Top seller plaques lined the wood-paneled walls, along with fishing trophies, a stuffed fox, wild turkey, deer head, and a bobcat. Purdy owned Purdy's Hometown Real Estate, Purdy's Insurance, and Purdy's Funeral Home. Locals at the coffee shop said he got you coming and going and every fucking way in between. Craig grabbed the corner of the big desk and pulled himself to his feet.

He'd bought his house from Billy Bob Purdy, that fat bastard in an ill-fitting Sears suit. He hated the man the moment he met him.

"I tell you what, Carlton," Purdy had said, never getting his name right. Not once that whole goddamned afternoon. "I've got a beauty of a house. It's just about four blocks off the square, two bedrooms, right in your price range, and your neighbors are gregarious types." Gregarious coming out 'gree-garus'. "The Poseys are nice, nice, nice. Mrs. Posey will bring you over a casserole the day you move in. I guaran-damn-tee it. You'll love having them as neighbors."

Fuck you, Purdy.

Craig turned away from the desk and screamed. A huge, dark, bipedal form loomed in the corner of Purdy's office, arms stretched to strike. Craig lurched back, grabbing the desk to keep his rubbery legs under him; then his mind understood what he saw. A bear. A fucking stuffed grizzly bear with a brass plaque at the base that read, "Billy Bob Purdy, 1999, British Columbia." Goddamned Purdy shot a bear. Not enough to take a picture and put it on the wall, he had to put a bullet in the beautiful beast's heart. But the laugh's on him. In ten years bears, and elk, and fucking Sasquatch will be roaming all over this continent. Maybe even sitting in Purdy's chair smoking a cigar. Resting from the trophy base to the hip of the bear leaned a rifle with a scope. Craig stepped forward, cautiously eyeing the bear like it might animate and swallow his head. The car might still be out there, stalking the streets; he needed that rifle.

Craig moved slowly toward the bear, the great paws of the beast the size of his face. "Good boy," he whispered. "Gentle Ben. Gentle Ben." He snatched the rifle from the bear and quickly backed toward Purdy's desk. The rifle was heavy and cold in his grasp. This was a real weapon, he realized, not the popgun he had in his new penthouse apartment at the tower that jutted from the crotch of Allenville like a giant penis. Craig pulled back the bolt. A bullet sat in the chamber. He kicked out the clip – it was loaded. Craig grinned. With as many people in this county who hated that goddamned Purdy, he wasn't surprised the fat bastard would keep a loaded gun in his office. Craig slapped the clip back in and lifted the rifle to his shoulder. It felt good. *I can pick off fleas with this thing,* he thought. *Devil woman better not have any fleas.*

Craig hung the rifle off his shoulder and walked through the Kingdom of Purdy to the front of the real estate office, keeping low, away from the great front window. The day seemed quiet; nothing moved on the street. He slowly pulled open the front door that would spill him onto the square. A bell on a string jingled over his head. He froze, expecting what? A SWAT team to crash through the windows? No one heard the bell. He slipped out the door and ran across the street to the courthouse.

July 15: Allenville, Missouri
CHAPTER 32

A pile of burned bodies sat at the entrance to the Budget Barn grocery store parking lot next to a Burger King. "Charbroiled," Maryanne said, the sound of her smile painful in Karl's ears. The drive to Allenville had been a convoy, one after another of the half-dozen cars in the Ninja Turtle fleet peeling off to wait along the road to Allenville for the red Mustang, or any vehicle coming up the highway with Darryl. Darryl was coming. Somehow, some way, she knew it, and that frightened Karl like he'd never been frightened before. Maryanne instructed the drivers to follow any Traitormobile at a safe distance, shutting the door to any escape. The only car that remained with the RV was the Kingsville Police cruiser, carrying Trent and that greasy bastard in the Megadeth shirt. It followed the RV because Maryanne wanted Trent to stay close. Karl hated how excited Maryanne got when she talked about killing Darryl, that poor, poor bastard. When the sign "Allenville: 6 miles" grew in the great RV windshield, she took a shot of whiskey and hooted.

"Put this boat on the far side of the Budget Barn lot, north of the Burger King, across from the Taco Bell," Maryanne told Mike as the RV pulled into town, greeted by a concrete smattering of square cookie cutter stores a few blocks away from the old downtown, the tower from the courthouse loomed in the distance. Karl watched Maryanne's gaze as Mike pulled into the parking lot, around the fire truck and ambulance that sat on the perimeter of the long-cold funeral pyre, and toward Taco Bell. Her eyes never left the red brick courthouse tower that dominated the skyline of one- and two-story houses, and a thick canopy of trees. Karl almost asked what was so damned important about the courthouse, but didn't want her to look at him anymore.

Mike backed up the RV and tried to park a couple of times before it satisfied Maryanne. She wanted the word "Haven" Leo had spray-painted on the RV to face north, so Mike did it. If driving meant she wouldn't shoot him in the head like Leonardo, he was going to drive any way Crazybitch wanted.

"That's good," she told him, patting his shoulder, her touch soft and hard at the same time. "Now get out, boys. You have more work to do."

Trent and Greasyman stood outside the Kingsville Police Department cruiser talking when Maryanne threw open the door to the

RV. The Greasyman in his stained T-shirt laughed when Trent jumped. The rest, Donatello, Raphael, and a few of the other feral beasts that followed Leo were back on the highway, waiting for that goddamned Darryl. Karl and Mike followed her out of the RV; Karl watched her eyes that kept jumping back to the red clock tower.

Maryanne nodded toward Karl. "Beavis. Toss the keys to the Cowboy." She turned toward Karl and pushed herself close to him, her breasts pressed against his chest. "I need you to do something for Momma," she said softly, running a finger across the line of his stubbled chin. "Take Mike and drive around town. There's something here, something important, and I want it." She looked into his eyes, and as much as he did not want to, Karl couldn't help but look back. They weren't a shark's, they weren't a devil's, they weren't crazy. Maryanne looked like someone people fell in love with in movies. "It's big and it's beige. Will you get it for me?" Karl didn't want to, but he nodded. This woman, he knew, was some kind of sorcerer.

"Keys," he said to Trent, who tossed Dooker's janitor-sized ring of keys, only one of which fit anything within twenty miles of them. Karl caught the keyring and nodded to Mike. "Come on." He didn't look back at Maryanne as he opened the door to the police cruiser and sat behind the wheel. He couldn't look at her because he knew what he'd see; shark's eyes, and he didn't want to see that. He knew he couldn't see that and retain any of the little sanity he had left.

Maryanne snapped her fingers at Trent and the Greasyman as Karl pulled the cruiser out of the parking lot and drove down Main Street. Trent snapped to attention. *Damn, the Greasyman, this ain't right.*

"Hey, boys," she said. "Get over to the Budget Barn and find something nice to eat. Maybe a box of Ragu pizza; something I can cook in the RV oven. Maybe grab a can of mushrooms, and black olives, and a bag of pepperoni. Oh, and a bottle of champagne. I feel like celebrating." And because she snapped, they went.

Karl and Mike drove with the windows down, the yellow and green smell of summer gently flowed through the cab of the police car.

"What's her deal?" Mike asked, his voice loud, too loud. Karl put up the palm of his right hand and shook his head. "Hey," Mike said slightly louder. "I'm talking to you."

Karl shook his head, reached onto the dusty dash and grabbed an ink pen, then pulled a Sonic napkin from between the seats of the police car and wrote in big, blue letters, "She knows what we're thinking." Karl's hand shook as he held the note where Mike could see it. Mike nodded and Karl wadded the napkin into a ball, stuffed it into his mouth, and swallowed.

Mike shook his head. "Whatever, dude."

Main Street spilled onto the Allenville city square, the courthouse in the center, the lawn surrounding it starting to grow over the granite monuments honoring local men who died in wars back to 1861. Karl noticed a shovel handle sticking out of the tall grass and thought that odd. A few taverns dotted the storefronts, along with restaurants, and businesses with the name Purdy. Purdy Funeral Home, Purdy Insurance, Purdy Real Estate.

"He must have been a bastard," Mike said, and looked over at Karl. "Hey, man. You gonna talk?"

He nodded. "In a minute."

The square gave way to a short string of businesses, the public library, and a long municipal park, the empty swings swayed slightly in the easy breeze. From the moment Karl met the Devil Bitch, a door seemed to slam shut, trapping him in a room where Maryanne stood watch with all-seeing eyes. Past the park, that feeling simply vanished. Karl smiled for a moment, then terror dragged the smile away; she was still too close.

"You think I'm shitting you, Mike, but I'm not," Karl said. "That crazy-assed woman, I don't know how she does it, but she knows ... things. Just things. Shit that's going to happen, shit people are thinking. Hell, sometimes she knows it before I think it."

Mike laughed. "Man, that's just your imagin..."

"Fuck you," Karl spat. "You haven't seen her bad side yet. That woman is evil."

How evil? Try Hitler evil. John Wayne Gacy evil. The evil that woke Karl up in the dead of night, shaking, only to find that blond, crazy evil sleeping next to him.

"Okay, so why haven't you left her? I mean, this is a big country, lots of places to hide."

Karl shook his head. "Darryl. This Darryl she keeps on about. He left her; he got away somehow. He snuck out in the middle of the night, with my gun, and she woke up in a rage because he left and she didn't know it. Somehow he got under her radar and vanished. I think that scared her. Now that's all she thinks about, finding him and killing him very, very slowly. I don't want any part of being the next Darryl."

"Then why haven't you killed her?"

"How do you kill someone who knows you're going to do it?"

The next eight blocks went by in silence; the park gave way to squat, white houses, the paint peeling on most. Karl's foot eased off the accelerator as they drove by a two-story colonial that must have been grand at the turn of the 20th century, but now the gray porch sagged, and mortar crumbled between the bricks of the foundation. A body, mostly skeleton, lay sprawled on the steps in a DC hoodie, the flesh gone under a coating of black ooze. Karl started to think they were the lucky ones.

The brown street sign came out of nowhere. Karl pulled the police car around a bend on Main Street sheltered by trees, and a sign reading "National Guard Armory" loomed into view. It pointed to 16th Street to the west. He felt he'd been slapped.

"You think that's it?" Mike asked. "What Crazybitch was talking about? An armory? A fucking armory?"

Holy shit. Maryanne wasn't playing around. This was serious. Karl was sure Maryanne had never been to Allenville, Missouri. Hell, Darryl said he'd met her running from Colorado. How could she know an armory was here in this town Darryl was heading to, unless she just did?

"I'm sure of it." Karl's voice not more than a whisper. "Hey, Mike. What do you think we'll find there?"

Mike shrugged. "Normally at a small-town armory, probably some M-4 carbines, and some Beretta 9mm side weapons, but little-to-no live ammo. Even then everything'd be locked up tight." A grin slowly broke his face. "But this is the end of the world, baby. I can bet we'll find some M-60 grenade launchers, and M-249 SAWs just lying around." He paused. Karl glanced over for just a second, but was sure Mike licked his upper lip. "I hope there's a Bradley fighting vehicle. Those fuckers are fun to play with." He turned to Karl. "Ever see a building just fall down?" Karl shook his head slowly. "It's better than pokin' a piñata and watching the candy fall out."

"You were in the military," Karl said, but knew he didn't have to ask. The answer he felt coming already made too much sense.

"Army. Infantry."

"How about the other Ninja Turtles? Were they in the military?"

Mike shook his head. "No. Don worked security at a mall somewhere. I think Raph ran a meth lab."

"So, psycho bitch tells you to drive the RV. Tells you to go with me to find something she knows is here. That something might just be the armory, which might be armed to the teeth. And you're the only person in this entire fucking group who knows how to use what we might find there?"

Mike shook his head; his smile not so big anymore. "That's just coincidence."

"She didn't ask if you'd been in the military, did she?"

"No." Mike's words came slowly. "She didn't."

"But everything I said is right, isn't it?"

Mike pointed ahead. "The armory's right there."

The long, low brick building with a shallow green tin roof stood in the middle of a field under the watch of a new white water tower, "Go, Bearcats!" painted in green around the reservoir. Someone had been ready for something. A military ambulance rested in the new black asphalt armory parking lot, the back doors open, what remained of a body on a gurney behind it, half the shit Alice in Wonderland ate growing from it. Six beige Humvees also sat in the armory parking lot, the soldiers stationed next to them lay on the ground in dark gray lumps. A stack of decimated moldy remains in civilian clothing was about twenty yards outside the perimeter of the vehicles. The military must not have known what to do with so many.

"Shit," Mike hissed.

"This is what she wanted," Karl said, pulling Kingsville's only police car to a stop in front of the ambulance. "There's something big here, isn't there, Mike?"

Mike nodded. "You see that fucker over there?" He pointed to a tall chain-link fence, signs bolted to it reading '138th Infantry,' and 'No POV Authorized.' Karl nodded; it looked like a tank. "That's an M2 Bradley. It's equipped with heavy incendiary round machine guns and an MK-19 weapons system." Mike's voice shook with excitement. "That's a big damn gun, right there."

"What is the MK-19, in English?"

"It's basically an automatic belt-fed grenade launcher," Mike said, grinning again. "It can fuck some shit up." Karl didn't like Mike's grin; not at all.

July 15: Allenville, Missouri

CHAPTER 33

Doug wiped his forehead with a kitchen towel and stuck it into his back pocket like it was a grease rag back at the shop. He figured he'd probably gone through a thousand of those square, red rags since he started working on cars, but he wasn't fixing cars today. Didn't need to. The Marstens kept their vehicle in perfect shape. He slammed the H3's hood shut and hopped into the driver's seat. The engine turned over immediately. His old truck would get them to Allenville, and Omaha with no problem, but the H3 would get them to hell, and maybe even back. He hoped they wouldn't need it that far; Tanelorn would be fine. Doug turned the key, killing the huge engine and rendering the afternoon silent.

"Hummer okay?" Terry asked as Doug dropped out of the H3 and walked around the vehicle, the garage door open, throwing light over a survivalist's boner.

"Yeah. If we can keep it in gas, we could drive it to Hawaii." Doug peeled a morning beer off a case of Budweiser, the crack of the tab filled the garage. "What do you think we can put in it?"

Terry sat on a case of MREs and slapped the side. "These. All those tuna cans and bags of dried beans are great, but these babies are full meals, with dessert, a tiny bottle of Tabasco, a book of matches that might just light underwater, and they have a longer shelf life than Twinkies. We could eat on these forever." He took a Budweiser from the same case and popped it open, ignoring the spray of foam on his shirt. "And water. We need to load the Hummer with lots and lots of water."

"What about ..." Doug started.

"Guns?" Terry interrupted. "That's a no brainer. Guns and ammo."

"I meant beer."

Terry smiled. "That's what the pickup's for. We're not going in just one truck."

Doug started to laugh, then saw Nikki standing in the doorway that joined the garage and the kitchen. She didn't look like she wanted to hear laughter. "We've got to do something about Herman Munster," she said solemnly.

"Is he talking?" Doug asked. "The Devil Woman again?"

Nikki ran a hand through her thick, black hair and exhaled loudly. "Yeah. That's all he's been talking about. Crazy shit. Apparently, this woman can read minds and suck a dick like nobody's business."

Terry laughed. Doug mouthed "no" toward him.

"But that's not the problem. It's his leg." Nikki took the beer from Terry's hand and drank. "I've done all I can, but his wound's infected. There's a pink line running from under the bandage up toward his crotch. If we let this go much longer, he's going to die." She gave the beer back to Terry, walked past him and grabbed a beer of her own. "I don't know this guy, and I don't want to know this guy, but I also don't want to be the one responsible when his fever spikes at 105, he shits his pants, and dies."

Doug sat on a box next to Terry.

"We going to town?" Terry asked.

Doug looked at Nikki, her face too pale, too tired. "Yeah." He stood and stepped toward her. He hadn't realized how young Nikki was until now. Twenty-one, twenty-two maybe. The Piper had crept in and fucked up her life, now he was going to do it, too. Doug grabbed her shoulders gently and looked into her soft brown eyes.

"I know you found something special here, and you can stay, if you want. But we have to go. I don't want to let that man die any more than you do. We might get the medicine he needs and pull back into the driveway tonight, all smiles and Herman's fever broken, and sit out the rest of the apocalypse in Barton getting drunk and playing Scrabble. Then again, we might not. When we leave, we have to pack like we're not coming back."

Tears welled in Nikki's eyes. "I don't want to be alone," she whispered, not for the first time. "I'm coming with you."

They loaded Doug's pickup last, Doug and Terry carried a mattress from one of the spare bedrooms and bungeed it to the bed of the truck. They carried Herman Munster out next, the man's fever rendered his face bright pink.

"No, no, no," he said, sobbing as Doug and Terry laid him on the mattress, his face wet with tears and snot. Nikki wiped Herman Munster's face with a towel and crawled into the bed of the truck with him.

Terry started to say something, but Nikki shook her head. "You can't leave this man back here. In his state, if he tried to stand he'd fall onto the highway. Somebody's got to stay back here and take care of him. I don't think it's too far to Allenville, anyway."

The look of concern on Terry's face drew a smile on Nikki's. "You just hold onto something tight, okay?" he said. She nodded and Terry climbed behind the wheel of Doug's pickup, Arnold sat next to him.

Doug pulled the H3 out of the garage, stopped and punched the button on the garage door opener, the door closing slowly behind them, shut off the only comfort they'd had since the end of the world came.

"I have a feeling we're not coming back," he said to Jenna. She patted his hand and nodded slowly.

"It's for the best," she said. "We were running out of toilet paper."

Doug grinned and shook his head. She kept surprising him; he liked that.

The occasional car on the roadside didn't remind Doug most people were gone; it was something subtler; something a person not used to rural highways wouldn't notice. But he did. No road-kill. Usually a deer, or at least a possum or raccoon would lie in a bloody lump along a rural highway like U.S. 71, flies swarming over the corpse like it was a family reunion. He looked in the rear-view mirror; Terry drove slower than usual, probably because Nikki was in the back of the truck. He'd seen the way Terry looked at Nikki, like an awkward teenager too scared to talk to the cute girl who sat next to him in history class. He thought he'd seen it when she looked at him, too, but he wasn't sure. Guys are pretty stupid about things like that.

"We're getting close," Jenna said, pointing at a road sign – 'Allenville: 6 miles.'

Something was wrong in the Hummer, Doug just couldn't tell what. A tension, like before a football game was all Doug could compare it to. Jenna felt it, too; he could tell by the way she sat, and the fact that's the first thing she'd said since they pulled off the rural blacktop from Barton and onto the highway.

"You okay?"

Jenna's smile was fake. "Yeah, I'm fine."

Bullshit.

Five minutes later Doug pulled the Hummer to a slow stop just outside the city limits; the university town spread out before him, signs for Applebee's, Holiday Inn Express, and Taco Bell lined the way down Main Street, the tower from what looked like the courthouse gave him the finger. He got out and walked back to the pickup. Jenna opened her door and followed him.

"What's up, bossman?" Terry asked, leaning out the open window.

"Just making sure we have a game plan," Doug said. "You armed?" Terry lifted a M27 machine gun, Arnold a Winchester shotgun. Doug nodded. "Good. Can't be too careful." He tried a grin and wasn't sure he achieved one. "Now this is a strafing run. Go in, find a pharmacy, get antibiotics and get out. Right?"

Terry nodded.

Arnold turned his head mechanically toward Doug. "We're cool, we're badasses, blah, blah, blah."

Terry forced a laugh and slapped Arnold lightly on the chest.

"Did you put any of that beer on ice before we left?" Doug asked.

Terry shoved a thumb behind him. "Back there." Doug nodded and stepped to the back of the pickup.

Jenna took his place in the window. "Is he acting weird, or is it just me?"

"Just nerves, babe," Terry said. "Just nerves."

The back of the truck dipped under Doug's weight as he stepped on the bumper and pulled himself into the bed that was crowded with a mattress, cases of beer, and a bright red Coleman cooler. Doug reached into the cooler and grabbed a beer chilled with the Marsten's ice. He shut the white lid and sat down.

"Hey," Nikki said, sitting next to the bungeed mattress.

Doug nodded. "Hey." Herman Munster groaned. "He all right?"

Nikki shook her head. "No. Not at all."

"We plan to fix that in a few minutes." He paused for a moment and cracked open the beer, the can cold in his hand. "Are you all right?"

Her lips pursed and she looked at him hard. A 22-year-old girl shouldn't have a look like that, he thought. This world has done bad things to everybody.

"No, I'm not," she said. "And how about you? Do you feel it?"

"Feel what?"

"The air. It's like the air's heavier than it should be, thicker. Herman Munster's been mumbling about it in his sleep, about this Devil woman. About Hell." She motioned to the cooler; Doug stood, pulled out a cold Budweiser and handed it to her. "Aren't you worried, too?" she asked.

"Not a bit," Doug said, reaching behind him. He pulled a .9mm pistol from his belt and handed it to her before hopping out of the back of the truck. His boots scraped on dirt as they hit the pavement. He looked back up at her, the gun rested uncomfortably in her hand. "Not a bit."

As they pulled into Allenville, the town looked like a zombie movie without the zombies. There had been walking dead in Allenville, but by the black greasy spots that dotted the landscape, those had dropped and been consumed by the devil mushrooms long ago. Grass grew through cracks in parking lots, dark businesses looked ominous. A fire truck sat next to a Burger King in the parking lot of a Budget Barn grocery store;

a pile of burned human remains before it a black lump on the gray asphalt. An RV rested in a corner of the lot across from a Taco Bell.

"There's a pharmacy," Jenna said, the marquee under a nondescript oval Carter's Pharmacy sign read 'Father's Day cards 1/2 off.' Doug pulled the H3 to a stop in front of the red brick building. Terry pulled in next to him. "Are you sure we're doing the right thing?" Jenna asked as Doug reached for the door handle. He pulled his hand back.

"It's either this or what?" he asked softly, turning toward Jenna. "Let that poor guy die? Everybody's scared shitless. Hell, I'm nervous, too. But at what? Bullshit from the head of a guy with a raging fever." He pulled a shotgun out of the back seat. "Are you with me?" Jenna nodded and they stepped out of the Hummer.

"It don't feel right," Terry said when Doug walked up to him leaning against the F-150. "It's like when you walk into a room after somebody had a fight."

Doug laughed, although he knew it wasn't the right thing to do. Not now, not at all. "I don't mean to take your feelings lightly, but you guys are just letting your imagination run crazy." He stretched his arms and shouted into the Allenville sky. "Hey, boogieman. Come get us." The caw from a nearby crow answered him. Doug lowered his arms and nodded his head toward the pharmacy. "Nobody's here. Let's go inside and get some medicine for Herman Munster before we have to scrape him out the back of my truck and leave him for the crows."

"Negative," Arnold said softly. "I cannot jeopardize my mission."

Terry turned to him. "What is your mission?"

"To ensure the survival of John Connor."

Terry motioned to Herman Munster moaning in the back of the F-150. "How do you know he's not John Connor?"

Arnold let out a long, slow sigh, snatched Terry's beer from his hand and drained it. "I think I'm finally ready to be back amongst the world of the living," he said, and tossed the empty can out the window.

"What the…" Terry started.

"This is my time," Arnold said, stepping out of the truck. Everyone stared at him. "My name actually is Arnold. Arnold Pickrell, PharmD. I think this is why I'm here. Before the pharmacology geniuses distilled the Piper from the Ophiocordyceps unilateralis fungus in Southeast Asia and doomed everyone taking it to become mindless toadstool food, I was a pharmacist. We can talk Terminator later." He cocked his shotgun. "I don't like this town. Let's make it quick."

July 15: Allenville, Missouri

CHAPTER 34

Craig sat in the clock tower and watched his world change through the scope of Billy Bob Purdy's hunting rifle. Two trucks, one black, one red, drove north on U.S. 71, and turned onto Main Street. Craig had watched them coming up the highway, topping hill after hill, whispering for them to keep on driving, but they turned on Business 71, and headed closer to him, ever closer. The trucks pulled to a stop in front of Carter's Pharmacy and people stepped out, three men and a woman from the cabs, another woman climbed from the bed of the red truck. A man lay still on a mattress in the truck bed, his leg bandaged. The five stood in front of the red truck, talking. *Arguing?* Craig wondered. *What's wrong with that guy?*

"He's dying," Posey said. Craig felt the old man next to him again; a shudder ran through him.

"I don't have time for you Posey."

The group filed into the pharmacy. "You just going to leave him there in the sun?" Craig whispered. He levelled the rifle on the man, his bandaged head an easy target in the powerful scope. Craig knew he could end the poor guy's suffering with one squeeze of his finger, just a small voluntary muscle movement and no more pain.

"Don't do it, McAllister," Posey hissed. "You'll fuck everything up."

"Goddamnit Posey." Craig swung around and faced the voice, but nothing was there. No old man Posey in his Royals cap, no moldering corpse, nothing. "Leave me the fuck alone. You're dead." Craig started to turn back toward the pharmacy when something moving along South Main caught his eye. He hoisted the rifle and trained the scope to a spot near the city park. "Holy shit," he whispered. "That's a tank."

***

Darryl. A flush of warmth pushed through Maryanne as she peeked through the curtain of the RV's side window. A knot of people milled in front of an old red F-150. Darryl didn't stand among them, but he was there. She felt it in her loins. She had him. She could almost feel her skin pressing against his, but his was hot. Something was wrong with her baby. Was he sick? Momma could make him feel all better. Maryanne pulled her .38 off the RV's kitchen table where it sat amongst empty beer cans and paper plates of half-chewed pizza, and tucked it in the back of her tight white pants. She had a present for Darryl, and she wanted to save it for last. She opened the thin RV door and stepped into the afternoon.

The big front pharmacy window bled plenty of daylight into the building; bottles of drugs scattered everywhere. Before all the citizens of the town of Allenville fell to a killer in the guise of medicine, its citizens had a run on drugs.

"What are we looking for, Arnold?" Terry asked, poking through the few large medicine bottles that still lined the shelves.

"Don't worry about that," Arnold said. "You guys grab plenty of bandages, Benadryl, Acetaminophen, antacids, rubbers, Tampons, just anything you had in your medicine cabinet back home. I'll take care of Herman Munster."

Terry giggled at "rubbers" and Doug slapped him on the shoulder. "Dumbass."

They fanned through the pharmacy, filling green plastic baskets with over-the-counter medicine. Nikki grabbed deodorant, Jenna some chocolate, Doug, Bic razors and shaving cream. Arnold plucked a big white plastic jar off the floor, walked to Doug and dropped it in his basket.

"That's amoxicillin, an antibiotic. I'm going to give Herman two of these immediately with plenty of water." Arnold held up two yellow capsules between his index finger and thumb. "Then he needs three or four of these a day until his leg clears up."

Doug nodded. "He's going to be okay?"

"Yeah. He's going to be fine." Arnold looked sternly at Doug, furrows lined his forehead. "I'm just worried about what he's going to be like when he's healthy. You have a pretty good record with stragglers, even me, and I was going through a pretty bad time in my head. Can't say I'd do the same for you if you started spouting Rambo movies. Thank you. But this guy? I don't like the way he feels."

The tank kept south on Main Street; Craig knew where it was heading. He looked out the south window and leaned his elbow on the old wooden windowsill to keep the rifle steady, and rested his right eye against the scope. The people from the truck were still inside the store, but somebody outside moved. The side door of an RV parked next to Taco Bell popped open, the word "Haven" painted across the side of the long, beige Winnebago. *Hmm,* he wondered. *When did that get there?* A woman stepped out.

"The Devil woman," Posey whispered.

The blond woman in tight white pants descended the two steps slowly, tied her long hair into a ponytail, and walked around the big vehicle toward the red truck. Something about her walk, maybe the way she swung her hips, or the way she threw back her shoulders, or the way
…

"She sprouted those horns?"

"Shut the fuck up, Posey."

Craig didn't like her. There was something wrong about that woman, something bad. Something wicked. She stopped next to the pickup. She talked to someone, the man on the mattress. The helpless man. The sick man. She rested a hand behind her on the handle of a pistol tucked into her pants. Craig trained the rifle on that woman, right between those thrown-back shoulder blades.

"Devil woman."

His finger tensed on the trigger of Billy Bob Purdy's grizzly bear rifle and waited. Nope, Craig didn't like her. He didn't like her at all.

Darryl's world was blue, a big blue nothing. *The ocean? No, I've never been to the ocean. I'm from Kansas, how could I be at the ocean?* But the ocean was blue, right? And big, the ocean was big. Darryl's blue was big, and it swam. The blue nothingness rippled in his vision like waves. His mouth was dry, too dry, and he hurt. His head, his leg, his soul. If only he had water. But here was the ocean. Why couldn't he find water? A face suddenly loomed over his. Was this a mermaid?

"Hi, Darryl," the mermaid said. *How did she know my name?* He thought he said something, he tried to say something, but didn't know if it came out. "Aw, you're hurt, baby," the mermaid said. Was she here to help? He tried to sit, but that slight movement sent the great blue ocean spinning. But it wasn't the ocean. Three red walls imprisoned him, three short red walls, and the blue, the blue was the sky, maybe. The mermaid leaned on one of the walls, smiling. *Am I in a pickup?* Darryl lay back down, his eyes swam.

"You ran out on me, Darryl." The mermaid no longer smiled. *No, no. Don't look at me like that.* Her eyes had grown black; the iris and whites drowned in a pool of ink. Shark's eyes. The mermaid had shark's eyes. "Nobody runs out on me." *What is she talking about? I never met a mermaid before.* He tried to speak again, but he couldn't form the words. "You're going to hurt, Darryl. You're going to hurt like you've never hurt before." Pain shot through his leg as he thrashed, trying to move away from this mermaid, this evil, evil mermaid. She reached out a fist and jabbed it into the bandage on Darryl's leg. This time he knew he made noise.

Suddenly the mermaid held a gun. Why did a mermaid need a gun? Darryl felt he should be crying, but didn't feel tears. "I think we're about to get some company, Darryl baby. I wish you could watch." Then the mermaid smiled again, and Darryl screamed.

Karl followed the Bradley in the cruiser; the big thing's speed surprised him. *What the hell does Maryanne want with this beast?* he wondered. What was she going to do to that poor damned Darryl? Mike drove the Bradley through the square, swerving to strike a Geo Metro, the rusty little car careened off it like a pinball, spitting shards of metal and glass from its crushed frame. Karl glanced up at the clock tower and wondered what spooked Maryanne. He liked to see her spooked; maybe this demon wasn't invincible. That thought almost sent him around the square and out of town. He could outrun the Bradley, he could outrun … then he felt it. He felt Maryanne's gaze, and his bowels threatened to let loose. No, he had to see this thing play through. She wouldn't let him go.

The door to the RV hung open when Mike and Karl neared the Budget Barn parking lot. Maryanne was out, standing next to a red Ford F-150, waving. Not to him, but to Mike. The Crazybitch swung her arms in over-animated movements toward a building. Taco Bell? No, as the yards clicked away a pharmacy came into view. She pointed at the pharmacy, then pulled her hands to her chest and fanned them out, fingers radiated in what only could mean an explosion. Karl knew Mike understood all too well.

A scream, a weak scream, a man's scream called from outside. "Something's going on," Arnold said as he hurried to the front of the store. "There's a strange woman out there talking to Herman Munster."

Nikki turned to Doug. "He's been talking about some kind of a devil woman the past four days. Do you think …?"

Then they heard it. They all heard it. A rumbling sound coming closer. Arnold stood just inside the front glass, his small frame even smaller as the Bradley Fighting Vehicle pulled up to the store. A man popped out of the hatch and trained a mounted weapon on Carter's Pharmacy.

"Run," Arnold screamed. "Run toward the back. Run outside. RUN."

The mermaid didn't make any sense. Darryl lay in the truck, exhaustion trying to drag his eyes shut, and she kept talking. But he couldn't hear her. A big boat, tan, or beige, or pink, floated up behind her and he couldn't hear anything anymore. Just explosions. Clouds of dust grew over Darryl as the mermaid still talked, chunks of things, brick maybe, flew into the back of the truck. Yes, he was sure now he lay in the bed of a red pickup. What was a boat doing here? And what was the mermaid saying? She was beautiful, that mermaid. She looked like an angel. A mermaid angel. A mermangel. Darryl wasn't sure, but he might have smiled. *Wasn't I just crying?* A flower, a big, beautiful red flower suddenly bloomed in the center of the mermangel's chest. Darryl thought he liked that chest. Should a mermangel have nipples? Her head snapped back, and she dropped, taking the beautiful red flower out of Darryl's sight.

Something loud smashed into the pharmacy and the building shook. Then another. Then another. Doug grabbed Jenna's arm and ran as explosions rocked the building, the Bradley's MK-19 pounded grenade after grenade into the storefront. He hit the emergency exit bar on the brown metal back door and the door sprang open. The force sent Doug across a short expanse of gravel and onto a patch of grass, his feet left him as he spilled down sharp grassy slope, bottles and packages flew from the shopping basket. Jenna went down with him, followed by Nikki. Terry dug his boots into the gravel and slowed himself enough to turn his head and watch as Arnold nearly cleared the door when the walls gave through. The small man disappeared under the bricks, dust, and roof of Carter's Pharmacy.

July 15: Allenville, Missouri
CHAPTER 35

Craig was almost disappointed the Devil woman didn't put up more of a fight. One shot and she was gone. Just a slight squeeze of the trigger, and she collapsed, her devil body dropped to the pavement as Craig watched through the rifle's scope. A grin flirted with Craig's lips, but his work wasn't done. The scope he pressed tightly to his face might leave a mark around his eye when the day was out, but by then he'd know what he knows now; what he had done was righteous. The tank, well, not quite a tank, whatever in the hell that thing was, shot round after round into the pharmacy. Why was it doing that? Four of the people who'd walked into Carter's ran out the back and down the hill behind the building. Hmm, Craig was sure there'd been five. The building shook under the gunfire and collapsed in a dusty heap.

"They're coming for you next, bitch," Posey whispered. Craig shook his head, trying to shake out Posey, but he knew Posey was still there. He was now certain Posey would always be there.

Craig pulled the rifle bolt back and slammed another shell into the chamber. "Not if I can help it."

The scene was something out of a movie Karl had watched once, maybe Stallone had been in it. He stood in the open door of the Kingsville Police cruiser, light pops from the MK-19 buried under the force of the blows as grenades pummeled the brick building. Something may have cracked when the walls collapsed and the roof came down, but Karl couldn't hear it over the explosions. Dust belched from the building as it fell and Mike stopped firing. Karl hoped nobody'd been in the building, but he knew they were. Why else would Crazybitch want it down?

Then he saw her, lying on the pavement next to a red pickup in a puddle of blood. Her blood. Karl looked up at Mike who looked back, grinning like a crazed man. Mike gave a thumbs up that Karl didn't return. He cautiously stepped toward Maryanne, her silky hair matted in red. Was she dead? Was this a trick? Would this be like the movies? Karl could see her rising on unsure legs, her eyes milked over, and her undead voice demanding brains. But Maryanne didn't move. She'd never move again. Karl smiled; he was free. Ding-dong the fucking witch is dead. He knew right then he'd go to Omaha and try to find people, good people, sane people. Enough of this Ninja Turtle shit; he just wanted things to be normal again.

"Hey, Cowboy," Mike called from the Bradley. "What happened to Crazybitch?"

Karl bent and rolled Maryanne onto her back, a ragged hole had exploded on her chest. "Shot." He stood and looked in the bed of the truck, a familiar figure laid on a mattress strapped to the bed of the truck. "Darryl?" he said. "What the hell happened to you?" Did Darryl do it? Did he do Maryanne? The man moaned, his eyes seemed to float in his head. No, he couldn't have. Darryl was hurt, sick, fevered, that much was obvious. Darryl couldn't even talk. Something moved in the corner of his eye and he turned; Trent and the Greasyman walked slowly from around the side of the RV. Hiding? Were they fucking hiding until the dirty work was done?

"Hey ..." Karl started before a rifle crack broke the suddenly quiet day and the side of Karl's head exploded, blood rained over Darryl as he lay moaning. Karl's body slumped and fell on top of Maryanne. One last hump for old time's sake.

"Shit," Mike hissed. Trent and Greasyman dropped on the pavement. Another shot rang out. A buzz like a lead bee screamed by Mike's head, ricocheting off the Bradley's armor. "Shit," he said again. He turned and looked behind him as another crack split the air and hit the metal hatch behind him. The clock tower. There was a sniper in the damned clock tower. Mike motioned to Trent and Greasyman to follow him in the police car before he ducked inside the Bradley and turned the armored vehicle back toward the square.

"What the hell was that?" Nikki screamed. Nikki, Jenna, Doug and Terry stood at the bottom of the short, grassy hill, their shopping marked a path where they slid down. Doug raised an index finger to his mouth. The explosions stopped when the pharmacy fell; he didn't know what was up there.

"Shh," he hissed. Then a rifle shot cracked, and another, and another. Gravel and bricks shattered by grenades crunched under the treads of the rumbling tank. Was it leaving? A car engine started in the parking lot; sounded to Doug like it was turning around. They listened as the sounds quickly receded and were soon gone.

"I don't know what happened," Doug said, cradling Jenna under one arm. Tears ran from Terry's eyes, but he stood tall. Nikki just looked angry. "I'm going back up. I'll sneak that way and come up behind the Taco Bell. When I signal," Doug said, raising his arm and spinning his finger. "It's safe to come up. Grab whatever you can when you do." He kissed Jenna softy on the head and let her go. She bent, snatched the white jar of amoxicillin, and placed it in his hand.

"Thanks," Doug said, and crawled up the embankment.

"They're coming for you, McAllister. I told you they were going to come for you."

Shut up.

"What are you going to do, bitch?"

Craig knew they were coming. He could see them well enough; the tank followed by the police car. What were they going to do? Storm the courthouse? Craig wiped a short sleeve across his face. Damn it was hot up here. He didn't care about the police car. He could take that out. It was that tank. Unless people crawled out of that thing, he'd run out of bullets and not leave a scratch on it.

"Run."

Craig shook his head. "What?"

"Run," Posey spat. "Flip up that trap door, climb down all those steps and run. Run and hide."

"Where the hell would I go?"

Posey laughed, the soulless cackle of the dead man raked up and down Craig's flesh. "You're too goddamn stupid for me to play with anymore," Posey said. "Have a nice death, McAllister. I'll see you in hell."

And he was gone. Craig felt it. The old bastard was gone. "Posey?" he said softly. What the hell? "Posey. *POSEY.*"

Then the first grenade struck.

Doug signaled when he reached the top of the hill. Whoever destroyed the pharmacy had gone.

"Who are they?" Nikki asked, pointing toward the pickup, the bodies of Maryanne and Karl sprawled on the ground next to the F-150.

"Don't know," he said. "Don't care. Let's just get the hell out of here." He tossed her the bottle of amoxicillin and they ran to the trucks.

"Where we headed, bossman?" Terry asked.

"Home?" Doug said. Jenna looked at him, her green eyes plaintive. She shook her head. "What's the matter?"

"That," she said, pointing south.

"Oh, shit," Terry hissed. Vehicles moved north on U.S. 71; the first one turned onto Main Street. "I think Omaha might be better."

Goddamnit. "Omaha," Doug shouted and hopped into the H3. "Terry. Side streets." He nodded.

Nikki stepped on the tailgate, but Terry grabbed her arm. "No way, lady. We gotta move fast. I'll take care of Herman Munster. You drive."

She pushed his hand away, his big, calloused hand. "No way. You can probably drive better than me. I can handle it." She hopped into the back, grabbed the Marstens' black Winchester shotgun and smiled. "I promise to hold on tight."

"You got it, sister." The old F-150 sprang to life and followed the black H3 two fast blocks up Main Street, and west onto Mulberry. Nikki shifted uncomfortably in the back. "Hold on, baby," Terry said to no one but himself.

They drove with the widows down, explosions shattered the air. "Are we going to make it, Doug?" Jenna said, her voice barely audible in the battle that raged just a few blocks away. Doug nodded. *I hope so. I hope so.*

A right on First from Mulberry took them back north. A short glimpse showed the Bradley sitting in the street two blocks away firing round after round of grenades into the second story of the old brick courthouse. The clock tower, at least three stories tall itself, swayed like a drunk, teetered left, then collapsed, the brick edifice crashed to the ground, the impact sent the trucks skidding across the street. A police cruiser suddenly shot from a side street cutting off the Ford from the Hummer, a dust cloud from the courthouse billowed behind it.

"Damn it," Terry grunted, twisting the wheel. The F-150 hit a shallow ditch and popped into a yard, he left the seat, and his head hit the roof of the cab. Herman Munster moaned as his body jerked. Nikki gripped the mattress tight, hoping like hell the bungees held. The cruiser slid to a stop, the faces in the front seat white, terrified. One face froze Nikki's eyes. She knew that face. The Greasyman. The bastard from St. Joe, the man who came into her house, HER HOUSE, and threatened to rape her. She cocked the shotgun with one hand and waited for Terry to careen back onto the street before she let go of the bungee cords and took aim.

"Fuck you," she screamed and pulled the trigger, the blast sent her flat on the mattress, Herman Munster screamed at the body landing on his infected leg. Nikki leaned up to take another shot, but didn't. The car hadn't moved; the front safety glass had imploded.

"You bastard," she screamed as Terry straightened the truck on Mulberry and chased the H3 north.

A gun cracked and a bullet whizzed near Nikki. She turned as a yellow Mustang closed behind them. A car from the highway. "Shit," she spat and cocked the shotgun.

"Whazzit?" Herman Munster moaned. Nikki ignored him and got on her knees, the driver of the Mustang reached outside the window, a pistol in a gloved hand, and fired. It went wide again. Nikki aimed low and shot, the front driver's side tire exploded, and sent the Mustang into a skid, the pickup behind it smashed into its side.

"What the hell?" Terry screamed from the cab.

In the H3, Jenna screamed a different scream.

Doug snapped his head toward her. "What's wrong?"

"Cars," she said. "The ones pulling into town. Nikki just blew one up."

Shit. "You gotta drive," Doug shouted, the panic in his voice unmistakable. Jenna had never heard his voice sound like that. "Slip over me and take the wheel."

"Nope," Jenna said. She slid open the sun roof and grabbed an M27 light machine gun from the back seat and pulled back the bolt. "I got this. You just get us out of here." She stood in the seat, her upper torso stuck out of the sunroof as she held the machinegun. Doug slowed and let Terry pull next to him in the Ford.

Nikki cocked the shotgun as two more cars swerved to either side of the wreck and closed fast. She fired right between the headlights of the lead car, an old Grand Am, steam spewed from the ruined radiator. The second shot hit the driver's side windshield, the Grand Am swerved and hopped into a yard, smashing into a tall, thick oak that didn't budge. The impact pitched the driver through the ruined windshield, his limbs flailed as he disappeared into the yard's tall grass. The wheels of the fourth car, a Chevy Berretta, squealed as the driver locked the brakes, wild shots from Jenna's M27 danced around the hood of the car. For a moment Jenna and Nikki locked eyes, Nikki smiled, then Jenna nodded and dropped back into the H3 cab.

"You okay out there, babe?" Terry shouted out the window. Nikki gave a thumbs up in the rear-view mirror, then saw Terry's face. Oh, my God. Blood leaked from a cut on his scalp, cutting two rivers down his face. Nikki leaned over the driver's side of the truck and screamed into the wind.

"Terry, are you okay? You're bleeding."

He pulled a red handkerchief from somewhere in the seat and wiped it across his forehead, soaking the cloth. "Ain't got time to bleed," he shouted out the window. "That was for Arnold."

Four blocks later, Doug turned west on a side street alongside a park and back onto Main. A sign welcoming them back to U.S. 71 north read, "Burlington Junction – 10 miles; Clarinda – 30 miles; Interstate 80 – 120 miles."

"You know how to get there?" Jenna asked.

Doug nodded. "I just know that I-80 goes through Omaha, so we're headed for that." Jenna rested a hand on his leg. Her hand felt comfortable there. He relaxed and drove away from Allenville as fast as he could.

July 15: Exira, Iowa
CHAPTER 36

Green grew in the fields and roadsides of southern Iowa like unkempt hair. The H3 and F-150 shot up U.S. 71 through Clarinda, nearby Villisca, and into the great wilds of corn and soybeans, seed company signs barely visible through the tall roadside weeds. The great line of gray asphalt wound over hills and through shallow valleys, glaciers carved out of the Iowa bedrock millennia ago. An old white Primitive Baptist Church lay on the west side of the highway north of Villisca, its yard mowed low. Terry tapped one honk to Doug, but Doug kept driving. Eighty miles north of Allenville, north of the shooting, north of where Arnold lay crushed by the roof of a dead pharmacy, the left blinker of the H3 clicked on and off, and Doug pulled into a heavily treed roadside park, a small faded sign read "The Plow in the Oak Park." Terry followed him off the highway.

Doug killed the H3 engine and stepped onto the dusty park lane. "Everybody okay?" Terry stepped out of the pickup cab, his face crusted with blood. "Hell, Terry. What happened to you?"

"Didn't have my seatbelt on when I made a detour through somebody's yard. I'm all right."

"I still need to look at it," Nikki said. She hopped out of the truck bed and stood beside him.

Jenna walked around the F-150; the man they'd found glaring at them through the blood streaked glass at the Marstens' home, the man they'd sacrificed Arnold to save, lay still, his face ashen.

"Herman Munster doesn't look so good," she said, and pulled open the cooler, a plastic on plastic creak barely noticed in the still afternoon air. Beer cans floated in water mixed with a few ice cubes from the Marstens' freezer. She grabbed four cans and handed them out.

Nikki took a Budweiser from Jenna, the cold can felt good in her hand. "I pulled open two of those capsules and mixed them with a little water somewhere around Clarinda. I think Herman got most of it down, but Jenna's right. He doesn't look well at all. I need to change his dressing, and we have to get him out of the sun. This drive hasn't been good to him."

"How long you think?" Terry asked, leaning against the Ford, sipping his own beer.

"A couple of day's solid rest in a real bed with plenty of fluid and antibiotics should help a lot," she said.

Doug nodded. "I agree. And after today, I think we could all use a couple of days of nothing."

Terry moved the truck under the shade of an ancient oak tree to keep the July sun from baking Herman Munster's skin, then the four sat at a wooden picnic table at the shelter house, and slowly ate MREs.

"You know, these aren't half bad," Jenna said, shoving a plastic forkful of cold macaroni and cheese into her mouth. "I could live on these for a while."

"Where *are* we going to live, Doug?" Terry asked. "Omaha still the plan?"

Doug nodded. "If that's okay with the rest of you. We can at least try. If nothing's there, I printed out maps to Tanelorn. The Marstens' pictures looked real nice." He leaned over and dumped his empty MRE containers into a rusty 55-gallon can, "Plow In The Oak Park" painted on the side. Sure, he knew the world was over, but they didn't have to trash the place. "I saw a sign for I-80 a few miles back. It's about twenty miles up the road. There's bound to be motels where the highways cross. We could stay there until Herman Munster's more up for it."

"I could use a dip in the pool," Jenna said, sitting next to Doug. She peeled open an Army-issued chocolate bar. "Cold or not."

"And a shower," Nikki said. "Maybe the water still works." She stood and dumped her trash into the bin on top of Doug's. "But let me change Herman's dressing first." She looked at Jenna. "It's going to hurt him; I might need help holding him down." Jenna got up to help her.

Doug looked around the empty table. Terry was gone. He walked around a once worn path lined with decorative stones, weeds now threatening to cover it. Terry stood looking at a tree.

"You gotta see this, man," he said, pointing to half a plow blade sticking from the living tree. Doug walked around the oak, an ancient hitch protruded from the other side. "The plow in the oak," Terry read from a sign mounted next to the tree. "During the Civil War farmer Frank Leffingwell ploughed a field when he saw Union troops marching nearby, leaned his plow against a young oak tree, and went off to join the war. He never returned. This mighty oak grew around the plow, forever a symbol of nature's power, and ability to conquer what man has made." Terry paused for a moment, the buzz of a few nearby flies filled the silence. Nature's power showed everywhere, and Terry finally understood it was greater than them. "Who's going to write down everything we did so people don't forget?" he asked.

Doug slapped his shoulder. "I don't know, buddy. I don't know."

The Super Wal-Mart at the entrance to Atlantic, Iowa, no longer offered groceries, clothes, oil changes, and flowers. Fire had left a great, black stain on the parking lot where the store used to be, a few cars still dotted the asphalt waiting for drivers who would never come. Maybe a month ago Doug would have been tempted to drive through town, honking his horn looking for survivors, but not anymore. Not after Allenville. There were bad people out there, and they needed to stay out there.

"Hey," Jenna said as they drove by a red billboard on U.S. 71. "Atlantic is the Coca-Cola capital of Iowa. Ooh, and Coca-Cola Day's is next week. Want to stop by the Chamber of Commerce for some fliers?"

Doug smiled. He liked this girl. Before the world went into the shitter, the most a girl like this would have said to him was, "my brakes are squeaky," in the safe confines of his shop. But this is after-shitter; the eligible bachelor pool was cut pretty slim. He braved a look into the rear-view mirror, not bad for a guy who desperately needed a shower and shave. But, then again, she did too. Everyone did.

"Maybe next year's vacation, dear. I've got my heart set on Nebraska. I hear they have corn there."

Jenna laughed, the joy, even after what they'd been through was unmistakable. Her laugh didn't hurt his head anymore. Yeah, he liked this girl a lot.

Four miles later they pulled into the parking lot of a Hampton Inn; only one car sat in the gravel lot. "The sign says 'pool'," Jenna said. "The only thing that will keep me out of that is a dead body floating in it." Terry followed Doug as he drove behind the building, the rear of the motel, a line of trees and the motel itself sheltered the trucks from the highway. Jenna looked as they drove by the pool. No bodies.

Silence ruled the afternoon. Doug wondered if he'd ever get used to all the silence. The gray fungus didn't just take people; it took cars, trucks, airplanes, televisions, radios, telephones, and crowds. He pulled a shotgun from the back seat of the H3.

"Terry and I will go in, make sure everything's all right." Terry nodded and grabbed his own shotgun from the front seat of the F-150. "We'll signal when it's okay to come in."

The click of a machine gun bolt pulled everyone's eyes to Jenna. "Bad idea," she said. "You are not leaving Nikki and me out here alone with Herman. You ..." She pointed at Terry, "and me are going in there." She pointed at Doug. "You are going to stay out here with her and unpack." Jenna walked toward the back entrance to the lobby and slowly opened the door. Terry followed her in.

"She didn't give you a chance to say, 'no,' did she?" Nikki said to Doug, a smile teasing her lips.

No, she didn't.

The air stank from two months of closed windows and doors, the cadaver of a cleaning lady sprawled across the lobby couch didn't help. The fungus had killed her, too, but it was gone now, a matted black crust flaked over her bones. Jenna and Terry checked every room, doors easily swung open; the electric locks useless when the power went off. Each lock was equipped with an AA battery backup in case of a power outage, but not a two-month power outage. Every bed made, every coffee tray stocked, every pillow sported a piece of chocolate that had melted during the heat of each summer day, and hardened during the cool of each night.

"Looks like everything's all right," Jenna said.

Terry frowned. "Like hell it is. Cable's out."

Jenna laughed. That, she realized, was good. She might have to spend the rest of her life with these people. It was comforting to know she liked them.

"Anything?" Doug asked as Jenna and Terry walked toward the truck, carrying their guns less as weapons, more as luggage.

"Cable's out," Jenna said, and winked at Terry.

"And there's a body in the lobby," Terry said. "But just one. And the good news is, there's plenty of clean towels."

They took turns carrying enough water, food and beer into the motel to last a couple of days. Nikki and Jenna picked out two rooms on the ground floor with double beds connected by a suite door. Herman Munster came last. Terry and Doug slowly pulled the mattress to the end of the tailgate and tipped it toward the ground, and caught Herman by the shoulders as he slid. Supporting him with Herman's arms over their shoulders, and their arms around his waist, they walked him into the motel.

"Everything okay?" Nikki asked, holding the lobby door open; Jenna already stood beside the pool, stripped down to her underwear.

"Are you kidding?" Terry said. "I feel like I'm in 'Weekend at Bernies.'"

Herman Munster moaned as they stepped into the lobby, his lids opened to reveal unfocused eyes. His head lurched to the side, and he stared at the corpse of the cleaning lady.

"Bonita," he whispered. "Maria Bonita."

"What the hell does that mean?" Terry asked.

"I don't know," Doug said. "Let's just get him into bed. This guy creeps me the hell out."

They walked down the hall; 101, 102, 103. Room 104 stood open. Doug and Terry dragged Herman Munster across the darkened room, the shades still drawn, and laid him on the bed. Herman moaned.

"Sorry dude," Terry offered, then wrapped his fingers around the plastic rings on two six-packs of beer, and looked at Doug. "Pool?"

Doug froze. Music. He heard music. From the look on Terry's face, he heard it, too.

"Holy shit," Doug hissed. "I thought you said this place was empty."

Terry leaned to the window and pulled back the curtain. "Looks like Jenna found a CD player," he said. "Didn't find any clothes, though." He grinned. "I think a swim would be nice."

The sound of voices trailed away, and Darryl slowly opened his eyes. The world was still a fishbowl, but it wasn't a blue fishbowl anymore. White shone from behind gray. Walls? Shadows? Where am I? Suddenly Maryanne loomed over him, in the same white shirt, the beautiful red flower on her chest. He squinted sore eyes, trying to focus. It wasn't a flower after all, it was blood, a ragged hole had blown through her chest.

"Hey, baby," she said. "I missed you."

Weak screams crawled through the motel. Nobody heard them.

July 17: Interstate 80, Nebraska
CHAPTER 37

Darryl knew he was sick. He wondered how long he'd been ill. Had there been a crash? A car crash? The light hurt his eyes as he slid them open, early daylight piercing a split in the curtains. *Where the hell am I? A motel?* He tried to remember something, anything. A mermaid. Had he seen a mermaid? There were no real mermaids, only Disney mermaids. Was it …? Maryanne's face surrounded by blue grew in his memory. No, not a mermaid, Maryanne. Maryanne stood over him as he lay in the back of a red pickup in midday, her blond hair pulled back in a ponytail. He remembered Maryanne smiling at him, then a red flower bloomed on her chest and she sank out of sight. She'd said something to him, but why couldn't he hear her words? Explosions, there'd been explosions, and a boat. Boat? No, it hadn't been a boat; something just as strange. A tank, and the tank blew the shit out of something while Maryanne talked to him. *What was she saying?* he wondered.

"I was trying to tell you I love you," Maryanne said. Darryl turned his eyes to the left; Maryanne stood over his bed. Yes, he lay in a motel, but where? And why was Maryanne here? She was dead, or was she?

"No, you weren't," Darryl said, although he didn't feel his mouth move. *Was that just in my head?* "You were going to kill me."

Maryanne leaned over, smiling, the gaping wound in her tight, white shirt hovered near his face. "Yes, I was going to kill you, baby. You ran out on me. Nobody gets away from me. Nobody."

"Leave me alone."

Her smile, a joyless smile, deepened to a grimace. "I'll always be here, baby. Every time you go to sleep, I'll be right here. And one day, I'll take care of you. I'll take good care of you."

"No," hissed from Darryl's dry mouth. "No."

Something moved in the room and a woman, a dark-haired woman stepped through Maryanne, the vision of the Devil woman faded from Darryl's view as the dark-haired woman took her place. *Do I know you?* Darryl wondered.

"Hey, are you awake?" she asked. *Am I? Am I awake? Have I been asleep? What's happened to me?* Darryl nodded.

"Hey, guys," the woman called through an open door. "Herman Munster's awake."

He didn't like their story. The wreck lingered somewhere in the deep recesses of his memory. He could feel it, but details would be long coming, if it ever did. The infection, the truck ride, Arnold, the tank. No, he didn't like their story at all.

"Maryanne," he whispered. Weakness began to drag him back into sleep, but he wanted his question answered, he had to have it answered.

"Who?" one of the men asked. Somebody had called him Dave, or Doug, or Darren. He couldn't remember. "Maryanne?"

"Devil woman," Darryl whispered. "Blond. Was she at the red truck. Dead?"

The D man's face grew solemn. "Did you know her?"

Darryl nodded.

"Was she important to you?"

Darryl shook his head slowly, once, twice.

"Yeah, she was at the truck. Shot through the chest."

A smile grew across Darryl's face. "Dead? Really dead?"

"Yes," the D man said. "She's dead."

The smile stayed on Darryl's face as exhaustion dragged him into sleep.

"What do you think?" Doug asked Nikki as they sat by the swimming pool drinking beer, Terry back at the room on Herman Munster duty. Jenna sat next to Doug in her bra and panties. Sure, it was nothing more than he'd seen at swimming pools hundreds of times, more modest in some cases, but white and clinging wet, he wondered why she bothered with any clothes at all.

"He might be okay for travel tomorrow," Nikki said. "His leg looks a lot better. The fact that he remembered something makes me feel a lot more comfortable about his head." She took a swig of warm beer. "He still needs a doctor, though." She looked at Doug, squinting through the sharp sunlight. "Omaha, huh?"

Doug turned toward the pool, the once sparkling water dim, settling dust already forming dark, muddy spots on its white concrete floor. "There's supposed to be a survival shelter there. Maybe they've got the power back on by now. Clean water. Restaurants. I don't have any answers. I just know that's where everybody from the survival shelter in Kansas City was headed." He turned back to her. "I'm working on faith here."

A kiss dragged Darryl awake. Maryanne stood over him again, in the same place, same clothes, same deadly chest wound, same wicked smile.

"Go away," Darryl said (aloud? Or in my head?). "You're dead."

"Not dead enough, baby." She stood straight and walked around the perimeter of the bed, running an index finger down his naked leg, across his toes, and up his injured leg. "Remember how we used to rut? Banging away like a couple of high schoolers? You want some of that?" She pulled up her shirt, her firm breasts with round, pink nipples, jiggled like a stripper's. Blood oozed from the gunshot wound between them. "One more romp for old time's sake? It won't hurt much." She'd reached the bandage and jabbed her finger into his healing wound. Pain stabbed through his body. "I just want you to do something for me first." The words dripped from her lips like saliva as she dug her finger deeper.

"What?" his mind screamed. "What the hell do you want?"

She pulled out and the pain grew into numbness. "Kill these people."

"Okay, okay," his mind heaved like it vomited. "Just leave me alone."

Darryl woke the next day with a clear head, the morning sun glared through the window, showing a painting of a sailboat on the wall behind a black-screened TV on a long writing desk. He smelled something. Coffee.

"Is anybody there?" he said weakly.

An auburn-haired woman leaned from the door that joined the rooms into a suite and smiled. She looked into the other motel room.

"Hey, Herman Munster's awake." She turned back toward him and smiled. "Are you hungry?"

Darryl sat with his back against two pillows and ate cold scrambled eggs out of a thick plastic pouch. It was the best tasting food he'd ever had in his life.

"Where were you from?" a man asked, his name started with D, but Darryl couldn't remember it.

"Goodland, Kansas," Darryl said between small bites. "I started out for Kansas City because somebody blew up Denver."

"Blew up Denver?" the other man asked.

Darryl nodded. "I don't know what happened. I just know the last news I heard said to stay away." He paused and took another small bite of eggs. "I got to Kansas City and the signs told me to go to Omaha, so that's where I was going when I guess I wrecked my car."

Terry laughed. "Wrecked is a nice word for it. You're damned lucky you're alive, man."

"Kill that one first," Maryanne whispered into Darryl's ear. He closed his eyes, and almost fell back to sleep. He pulled his eyes open.

"Thank you," he said. "Thank you for taking care of me."

The big man stood and put his arm around Nikki's shoulders. She looked nice, Darryl thought. He didn't want to kill her.

"Do it, you fuck," Maryanne hissed.

"You need to thank her," the big man said. "She took care of you." He paused. Was the big man tearing up? "And Arnold. He's the one who died getting your antibiotics."

Good God. I'm not killing anyone, Maryanne. Fuck you. Fuck you, fuck you, fuck you. "You will, baby," she whispered in his ringing ears. "You will."

Darryl looked up at the four faces staring at him from around the motel bed. "Where are you guys headed?"

"We got the same message in Kansas City," the D man said. "We're headed toward Omaha."

Darryl sat his empty egg package on the vertical-striped, earth-tone comforter that covered the bed. Maryanne with her gaping chest wound stood next to the big man, holding a mock noose around her neck, coughing. Darryl looked around; no one saw her. No one at all.

"Can we go now?"

More abandoned cars dotted Interstate 80 than they'd seen so far. Doug drove the H3, Jenna next to him. Nikki asked to drive the pickup, and Terry said okay; he'd have more time to pick out all the Metallica he wanted to play on their way to Omaha.

"There's plenty of room up here, Herman Munster," Terry said to Darryl before they pulled away from the motel.

Darryl shook his head. "No, but thanks," he said. "I need to sleep." Goddamned Maryanne. Bitch is dead. These are good people, people who've lived through everything. Darryl didn't want to hurt them. He sat in the bed of the pickup on the soiled mattress, soiled he knew because of him, and watched as the greens and golds of Iowa sped by. He didn't correct the big man on his name. Herman Munster was good enough. He felt like a fictional character anyway. Darryl pulled a Budweiser off a six-pack and cracked it open. He wasn't healthy enough for beer, he knew. He just didn't give a damn. But one should do what he wanted.

"You are such a pussy." Darryl turned to find Maryanne sitting next to him on the mattress. She grabbed the beer from his hand and took a drink. Darryl craned his neck to look into the cab, his head reflected in the rear-view mirror. Maryanne wasn't there. He looked back at her flawless face. "The guns are up there," she said. "How can you kill anybody if you're sitting back here?"

Darryl grabbed another beer and opened it. Maryanne wasn't going to give his back, even though she was dead. "Why do you want me to kill them?"

Maryanne chugged the Budweiser and tossed the can onto the highway. Darryl wanted to hear it clink, to have something physical in this insanity, but could only watch as the can bounced twice and faded quickly into the distance.

"Baby, I want everybody dead," Maryanne said. "Now, what are you going to do about it?"

Nothing, nothing, nothing.

"They saved my life," Darryl said. "I'm not going to kill anyone. Now why don't you just fuck off?"

Maryanne laughed, the high cackle pierced his soul. "Don't you get it?" she said. "This world is gone, dead. And some people are just too fucking stupid to play along. That's where you come in, baby. You are my tool. You are going to do what this hole in my chest wouldn't let me do. You're going to kill everybody else, just like God intended."

Darryl looked back at the rear-view mirror in the cab. The big man and the dark-haired girl laughed. They were talking about something, but not this.

"Well," Maryanne whispered, her breath hot in his ear; a lithe, soft hand rubbed his crotch. "Are you going to do it for me, baby?"

"Nooo," Darryl screamed and struggled to his feet, the field-covered scenery dashed by at high speed. He bent his knees, the pain in his injured leg screamed through his mind. The kind, glowing face of Tanya Smithmeyer pushed Maryanne from his vision as he jumped, and his smiling face met the asphalt of Interstate 80 at seventy-six miles per hour.

July 17: Omaha, Nebraska
CHAPTER 38

Doug dropped his beer can and watched it fall fifty feet into the muddy, churning water of the Missouri River. Terry stood next to him, leaning on the bridge railing. They stared across the river, a great, gray steam engine and yellow diesel, the words "Union Pacific" painted in big red block letters across the sides, sat on short rails on a hillside park overlooking Interstate 80, an American flag and yellow Union Pacific flag flapped in a slight breeze overhead. Doug had pulled to a stop halfway across the river. Omaha was there, on the other side of the bridge, and he didn't see anything moving. Nothing at all. That bothered him.

"Did you see Herman go?" he asked.

Terry nodded. "Nikki saw him in the rear-view mirror. He just stood up. She said it looked like he was talking to someone. I looked back in time to see him take a header out the back of the truck. We were going pretty fast; I didn't see any sense going back to look." He finished his beer and dropped the can in the river, too. Where would it go? Kansas City? St. Louis? The Gulf of Mexico? It didn't matter. What did? "What are we doing here, Doug?"

"In Nebraska?" he asked.

Terry pointed at a small green sign about ten yards away, bolted to the railing. It read, "Welcome to Nebraska."

"We're still in Iowa," Terry said. "I mean the bridge. Why did we stop on the bridge?"

A bird cawed overhead. Doug watched as it made its way across the river toward Nebraska. It was a crow, Doug worried it would be a buzzard; that thousands of buzzards would be circling the city, painting the sky black, but it was just a crow. At least a buzzard would have told him something. The silence told him nothing.

"Something's wrong over there," he said. "This was supposed to be a shelter. People were coming here from all over. Don't you think we'd see something moving over there, or hear something? Music, machines, anything?"

Terry started walking back to the pickup. "We're not going to find out standing here."

The first homemade sign, "Survival Shelter Ahead," appeared at the end of the bridge. Another sign followed, and another, and another. A large red, spray painted arrow directed them from the highway up an exit to Thirteenth Street, a billboard advertising the Henry Doorly Zoo rose from the off ramp.

"That's a good zoo," Nikki said, the tension in the cab almost vibrated. There was terror in the cab, down deep, and they didn't want to let it get too cocky. "My dad took me there when I was a kid. It had a great shark tank."

The animals. As Terry drove up the ramp and closer to the zoo, the dome from the desert environment only a few blocks away, he knew he should have smelled animals – especially if they were all dead, rotting in their enclosures.

"I wonder what happened to the animals." Terry asked. How much food would it take to feed elephants? Bears? Gorillas? Nikki's sharks? The homemade signs pointed toward the zoo. When Terry pulled onto Tenth Street, the clean avenues of Omaha changed. Tents, many collapsed, lined the grassy median that circled a parking lot covering city blocks. Larger ones, the kind of tents people used to rent for summer parties, dotted the vast lot surrounded by vehicles sporting license plates from all over. North Dakota, Minnesota, Missouri, Kansas, Illinois, Iowa, Utah, Kentucky. People came from a long way just to get here. So, where were they?

"Looks like this is our shelter," Nikki said.

"Well if this is a survivor shelter, where the hell are the survivors?"

Nikki pointed toward an RV surrounded by military Humvees, some mounted with machine guns. "That looks important. Try over there."

Terry pulled the truck to a stop outside the military perimeter and stepped from the cab, Nikki followed.

"Where is everybody?" he said, pulling his shotgun out with him. Doug hopped from the Hummer and walked toward him, resting his shotgun on his shoulder.

"I don't know. I don't like this at all." He stopped. A black figure perched on the handle of a machine gun mounted on a Humvee. A turkey buzzard. No, nothing was right here. The bird's bald, red head turned toward Doug and stared at him. Terry raised his shotgun, but Doug gently rested his hand on the barrel and shook his head. That's not the kind of noise they needed right now.

"This tent is full of bodies," Jenna said, standing at the flap of the closest big party tent. Great party today, mates. Thanks for inviting all the cadavers. "They're wrapped in garbage bags."

Nikki looked in, the bodies in black bags stacked four high filled the tent, just like at St. Joseph Hospital, just like the stacks where Gene Holleran lay rotting. She turned her back to the open tent, tears threatened to erupt.

"If they're moldy, the bags must be shut really tight." She paused, and gently used the back of her hand to erase the moisture from her eyes. "What now?"

Yeah, what now?

"Hey, bossman," Terry called. He stood beside one of the Humvees and nodded his head to the other side of the RV. "You need to see this."

Brass shell casings littered the ground around a line of Humvees, their massive machine guns all faced the same direction. Doug stepped next to Terry, his boots sent casings jingling across the asphalt. The carnage was unbelievable. Hundreds of bodies lay strewn across the parking lot covered in gray fuzz, the stalks fresh and filled with spores rose from their chests like a crop. Hundreds of swollen bulbs turned to face them.

"Holy fuck," Nikki whispered.

"Shot?" Doug asked.

"That's sure what it looks like," Terry said.

"What happened here?" Jenna asked, stepping beside them.

"The Army killed these people," Terry said, backing away from the nearest soldier, the growing fungus on the body seeming to move because of his presence.

"So the Army just killed everyone and what? Left?" Jenna asked.

"That's sure what it looks like, "Doug said. "But why?"

Nikki came from behind them holding a yellow standard sized piece of paper. "Because of this. It was taped to the door of the RV." She looked around. "You want me to read it?"

Jenna nodded. "Please."

"'Attention' in big bold letters. 'In the event of a biological attack or the introduction of a highly contagious disease affecting the public, the U.S. health system may take measures to prevent those people infected with or exposed to a disease or a disease-causing agent from infecting others. The federal government has jurisdiction over interstate and foreign quarantine, and may use the military in enforcing quarantines.'"

"That's a lot of enforcement," Jenna said, her voice soft. "This for the fungus thing?"

Nikki shook her head. "No. Something else is going on here. The fungus people died themselves; they didn't need any help."

Terry walked around the first row of civilian bodies, they all lay face first in dried spots of blood and gray fuzz spilled from their bodies onto the asphalt, tall gray stalks sprouted everywhere.

"Looks like they had personal hygiene problems," he offered. "I think we need to leave."

"But this doesn't make any sense," Jenna said. "We had a pandemic, an end of the world thing. I get that. But those people died on their own. Why shoot these people?"

Nikki stepped into the center of the group. "Because something else happened," she said. Everyone grew silent. "Everything in nature mutates all the time. That's how diseases get from animals to people. In this case, when people got sick, they died, wandered around for someplace suitable to fall, then grew mold."

"And that creepy corn stalk thing," Jenna said.

"And the creepy corn stalk thing." Nikki brushed her hair from her face. "Then those fucking pods started to burst. They were full of spores. What the hell did those spores do to people?"

The butt of Terry's gun hit the pavement in a sharp snap. "They're making them into zombies," he whispered. "When this shit started, I was worried all the video zombie killing training I'd gone through wouldn't do me any good because these walking dead people aren't real zombies. But now they are."

"They're not zombies," Doug said.

Nikki shook her head. "They're sort of like zombies. The fungus kills people, but still makes them walk to wherever the fungus thinks is best."

"Wherever it can spread to another host," Doug said, and pulled Jenna close to him.

"Yeah," she said. "Except the fungus doesn't spread by a bite."

Terry took another step back, away from the sprawling field of moldy bodies. "It spreads from those pod things."

"No," Jenna screamed, tears ran down her face. "We're fucked then. We're all just fucked," she spat between sobs. "We're going to die no matter what."

"Hey, Doug," Terry said, pointing to another civilian body.

"We might as well just drive into the fucking river all the good this is doing us …"

"Doug."

Jenna leaned into Doug's chest and cried. Doug looked at Terry. "Yeah."

"Whether the Army killed these people or not, something's been eating this guy."

"Yeah," Doug said, caressing Jenna's hair. "There have to be buzzards in and out of here all the time. It's like a buffet."

Terry shook his head. "No. I'm not talking about pecking, I mean eating. Chomping. Crushing. This moldy guy has chunks out of him. Big chunks. Bites. No turkey vulture did this." He scanned the parking lot. A lot of things could be hiding around those tents, and among the cars. "What do you think could have done that? Dogs, maybe?"

Nikki turned around, the yellow warning dropping from her hand. "Oh, shit," she hissed. "The zoo." They all turned toward the Henry Doorly zoo, the front gates hung wide.

"You think some asshole was stupid enough to let the animals out?" Doug asked.

"Yeah, I do," Terry said backing away from the field of bodies. "Nikki went there before. What did you say they had?"

"Big cats, you know, lions and bears. Leopards. Bears. Sharks."

"I'm not too worried about sharks, Nikki." Terry gently took Nikki's arm and started walking back to the Ford. "You had me at lions. I think we need to leave now."

The turkey buzzard on the Army Humvee perched silently; as Terry and Nikki walked by, it slowly spread its six-foot wingspan, greasy black feathers shone in the afternoon sun. Then it took off, the beats of its wings loud this close; seconds later its shadow flew over Doug.

"Right now," Terry said as calmly as he could muster. "We need to leave right now."

Doug was the first to round the perimeter of Humvees, Jenna's hand pressed firmly into his. Terry came next, then Nikki. It was Nikki who saw it.

"Stop," she hissed. Everyone froze, and Nikki pointed toward a line of trees in a median strewn with camping tents. About twenty yards from them, a bear, a grizzly, a Kodiak, or fucking Fozzie Bear for all they knew, lay half out of a small tent like a puppy in a doghouse, its huge head faced them.

"We need to run for the trucks," Doug whispered. "If it looks like we're not going to make it, shoot that thing."

Terry swallowed hard; sweat began to run down his back. "That's just going to piss it off."

Doug nodded. "I know. Run."

The bear lay still for a moment, cocking its head. Maybe it was full of dead guy, Doug thought, or maybe it was just playing with them. Bears are cocksuckers like that. The four had closed to within about ten yards of the trucks when the beast pulled its 600-pound bulk out of the tent, and shot toward them at incredible speed.

"Holy shit." Terry reached the F-150 first, threw open the door and pushed Nikki inside. Jenna scrambled around the far side of the H3 and hopped in. Doug pulled open the door and jumped behind her, the bear's face filled the window as it hammered the side of the truck with its body, slamming the metal door on Doug's ankle. Pain lanced through him as the weight of the beast crushed the bones in his lower leg. He screamed.

"Doug," Jenna yelled. She reached over him, grabbed his leg, and pulled it into the cab as the bear reared back and slammed into the side of the Hummer again, lifting the heavy truck onto two wheels.

"Shoot it," Jenna screamed at Terry who couldn't hear her. The bear stood back, and the H3 dropped uncomfortably back onto all four wheels. "Shoot the goddamned thing."

She pulled Doug out of the driver's seat and crawled over him; he moaned in pain as his ankle bent at a right angle. She plopped into the driver's seat and grabbed for the keys, the beast's slathering jaws pressed against the glass, foam dripped down the window, its bloodshot eyes blazing. She screamed, and a horn honked from somewhere. The monster dropped below the view of the window, then brown filled Jenna's world as the beast sprang and struck the H3 again; the metal groaned under the impact. The horn honked again. Jenna looked; Terry waved her on.

"Go, go, go," Doug shouted through clenched jaws.

Go, yes go, ran through Jenna's head. *There's a bear out there. Go dog, go. Go bear, go. Go, just go.*

"Just fucking go," Jenna screamed aloud and turned the key in the ignition; the engine fired. She slammed the automatic transmission into drive and punched the accelerator; the Hummer screeched to life, hopped the curb and skipped onto Tenth Street. The dented metal door grated and popped as the massive beast slammed into it again. Terry fired his horn again as the F-150 shot past.

"Get to the highway," Doug whispered, his voice choked by tears.

Jenna yelped as something bumped into the Hummer. She looked out the window; the bear ran alongside, its face in a grimace. Is that how they looked on Animal Planet? Shrieking tires from the F-150 next to her snapped Jenna's head back to the road.

"Oh, shit." She slammed on the brakes at the mouth of an intersection; the bear skidded onto Thirteenth Street in front of two military Humvees. A gunner on one aimed the mounted machine gun at the enormous beast and let loose a deafening barrage. The bear's body shook like it was in the mouth of a great, angry beast as government lead ripped it to pieces. Then Fozzie lay still.

When the gunfire waned, Jenna realized she'd been screaming.

July 17: Western Nebraska
CHAPTER 39

Two more Humvees appeared on Thirteenth Street. Soldiers in biohazard gear stepped away from their vehicles, the stocks of M27s pressed against their shoulders, the barrels pointed at the trucks.

"What's happening?" Doug asked, all strength gone from his voice. He lay low in the seat, his eyes closed; sweat ran down his tightly clenched face.

"The Army," Jenna said. "What do we do?" No answer. "Doug?" She turned toward him; he had lost consciousness. A tap on the window brought her head around. A soldier stood there, his young face tense with fear from behind a protective hood. He motioned for Jenna to get out of the truck. She raised her hands and nodded. Another soldier carrying a clipboard pulled at the latch but the bent door wouldn't move. He pointed to the rear door, then pulled it open. Jenna crawled over the seat and stepped outside. Terry and Nikki stood next to the F-150, their hands atop their heads. Jenna slowly raised her hands over her head and rested them there, too.

"He's hurt," she said, nodding back inside the Hummer.

"Are you infected?" the soldier asked.

"What?"

"Are you infected?" he shouted. "Have you ever taken Ophiocordon?"

Jenna shook her head. "No. We're fine, except our friend. He needs medical attention. His leg is broken."

The soldier must have heard her, but she couldn't tell. "Where did you come from?"

From? When? My mom's uterus? St. Joe? Barton? Allenville? The Hampton Inn? "Kansas City. We just came up from Kansas City. There was supposed to be a shelter here."

The soldier didn't relax at the news. "Have you had any interaction with anyone you don't know?"

Yes, a crazy bastard who likes to jump out of the back of a moving pickup onto the interstate. She shook her head. "No. I haven't accepted any packages at the airport, and I've never been to West Africa."

"Do you have any of the following: headache, fever, delusions, dizziness, body aches, excessive hunger?"

She shook her head again. "No. We're fine. But our friend needs …"

He pulled out a penlight. Jenna started to take a step back toward the truck, but the second soldier, the one with the gun firmly pointed at her face, forced her to steady her legs. The soldier with the light shined it into one eye, then the other.

"She checks out," he shouted back to the Humvees.

"These check out, too," another soldier next to Terry and Nikki shouted as well.

Another soldier in a biohazard suit opened the passenger side door of the H3 and examined Doug. After a few moments, he raised a thumbs up. Two men in bio-gear ran from one of the trucks with a stretcher, and they loaded Doug onto it.

"Okay," the first soldier said, stepping back from the H3, his weapon now pointed toward the sky; he waved everyone toward him. "I'm sorry, but you'll have to leave your personal belongings. You may be allowed to return for them at a later time. You will be traveling with the United States Army to a secured facility where you will be placed under quarantine until it is determined you are not infected with the human form of Ophiocordyceps unilateralis."

"Ophiocordyceps unilater …" Jenna started.

"If it is determined you are infected with Ophiocordyceps unilateralis, you will then be placed under isolation where you will have no contact with another human being until either the fungus has run its course, or you accept Option Two, which will be discussed in full at that time."

Bodies. The bodies of all those people lay strewn in rows in the zoo parking lot. Jenna wondered if they chose Option Two.

"Any questions you have," the soldier continued, "will be answered after you receive a thorough medical evaluation."

Jenna watched as Nikki's mouth opened to say something, then closed, her eyes dropped to the pavement. *Yeah, babe. From here on out we gotta pick our battles.*

The Army made the Nebraska Medical Centre ready for an invasion. A twelve-foot-tall chain-link perimeter fence lined with razor wire surrounded the complex in a two-block radius. Soldiers patrolled the fence, machine gun nests sat atop the three-story parking garage, and other tall buildings around the hospital. That's just what Jenna could see. She knew there had to be more, a lot more. A soldier in olive drab on guard duty, no biohazard suit here, baby, pulled open the gate and the line of Humvees rolled through.

"When…" Jenna started, but a soldier's black-gloved palm stopped her. She didn't try again.

People in biohazard suits – doctors Jenna thought; they didn't walk like military men – escorted them to different rooms. Two chairs, one a rolling stool, sat next to the wall, a countertop with a sink held glass jars with tongue depressors and Band-Aids; the center of the room dominated by an examination table where she sat in a paper gown. Jenna's doctor smiled at her through his biohazard hood.

"What's your name?"

"Jenna. Jenna Elaine Mullins."

The man scratched her name onto a form on a clipboard. "How old are you, Jenna?"

"Twenty-three."

"Do you smoke?"

The doctor ran through a long list of medical questions, and no, she'd never had unprotected sex with a man from Algeria before 1985. She wanted to cry, needed to cry. As she lay on the examination table atop a long strip of sterile paper, she knew she couldn't. Everything she had was gone, taken by something they now called Ophiocordyceps unilateralis. Now this whateverthefuck threatened to take the rest, too. The only thing she still had was somewhere in this building, his leg broken. He was in pain; she wanted to stay strong for him.

"Now I'm going to take some blood," the doctor said, wrapping a rubber hose across her arm just above her elbow. "This will let us know if you have Ophiocordyceps unilateralis. Make a fist. Keep making it. Now … oh, that's a good vein. You're just going to feel a little pinch."

Jenna didn't see anyone other than a series of male nurses with side arms for three days. On Day Four, her doctor returned, without his biohazard suit; however, a mask covered his nose and mouth, safety glasses covered his eyes.

"Hello, Ms. Mullins," he said. She thought he smiled under that mask. Jenna wondered if it were a real smile, or just good bedside manner. Sorry, Mrs. Smith, your husband is dying of syphilis, but doesn't my smile make you feel better? "Every test checked out fine."

She sat up in bed. "What were you checking for?"

He leaned back into the counter, holding her clipboard to his chest. "HG-17, a mutation of the fungal infection brought on by the antidepressant Ophiocordon, which is made from the fungus Ophiocordyceps unilateralis. This mutation is delivered by the fungus itself, after it has consumed a body. From the …"

"Spores," Jenna said. "Yeah, I saw it. Those stem things explode."

The doctor nodded. "It comes on like influenza. Aches, pains, slight fever, but after a couple of days HG-17 shuts down the higher functions of the central nervous system, meaning the thought process, and leaves everything else to take care of the fungus' only function. To reproduce. It's highly contagious."

"And I don't have it?"

"That's right," he said. "You're perfectly healthy."

"Great. Can I go?"

His smile faded. "It's not going to be that simple. HG-17 has wiped out a massive part of the world's population. It's surprising how many people are on antidepressants, even for me. And I'm a doctor."

Jenna looked at the doctor's kind, clean-shaven face closely. "Are these things zombies?" she asked.

The doctor smiled again, then shook his head. "No, of course not, although at the onset of the infection, people do look like something from a George Romero movie. They're brain dead, and if one bites you..."

"You turn into one, too," she whispered.

The doctor laughed out loud, the smile behind his mask grew bigger. "No, but you might get a nasty infection if you don't clean the wound. Human saliva is swimming with bacteria. However, the spores are another story. The government is conducting a massive operation so this fungus doesn't kill the human race. We're taking precautions."

"What does that mean?"

The doctor's voice smile disappeared. "I think it best you get that from Col. Corson. Now, come on, let's go see your friends."

A nurse, the military belt that held a .9mm handgun out of place around purple scrubs, took the doctor's place in Jenna's room and stood quietly, his back to her as she got dressed in a pair of hospital scrubs (just until your clothes are washed, the doctor told her), then escorted her to the elevator. When the doors slid shut, he pushed the button marked "B". Jenna's stomach lurched as the car dropped. She'd always hated elevators.

"Where are we going?"

"Ma'am," the nurse said, not taking his eyes off the elevator door. "I'm not authorized to answer that question."

"You can't even tell me where you're taking me?"

He stole a glance at her. "Sorry. Cafeteria. The doctor thought you could use a meal not brought to your room on a tray by a man with a gun."

"What's going to happen to me after that?"

"I'm not authorized to answer that question."

The door slid open after a four-floor drop and they got out, a green line on the floor took them to the cafeteria. The nurse opened the door and held it open. "Ma'am," he said, nodding at Jenna. She stepped in and he shut the door behind her, a slight click told Jenna he'd locked her in.

Nikki, Terry, and Doug sat at a table lined with steaming bowls of food set up family reunion style; Doug at the end in a wheelchair, his left leg in a cast up to his knee. Jenna ran to him, pounced in his lap and kissed him deeply, his clean-shaven face smooth against her skin. When she finally broke off, he smiled.

"I missed you, too."

They talked during the meal, the same doctor telling them the same story. They were all healthy and, at least weren't some kind of fungus monster. Terry drained three beers during the meal; he grabbed a fourth and pushed his plate away.

"They said I could have as many as I want." He grinned like a kid. "They don't know me very well, do they?"

A half-hour later the same armed nurse in purple scrubs opened the door; an officer walked in. Terry and Nikki started to stand, but the man shook his head and motioned them to sit.

"No need for that," he said, his voice firm, but calm, his big face friendly around his breathing filter. He grabbed a chair turned it backward and sat, resting his arms on the chair back. "I'm Col. Corson. I was briefed about your collection." The word 'collection' hung in the air like a heavy cloud. A grin broke across his face. "A bear, huh? If it makes you feel any better, the moron who opened all the cages didn't make it past the bear. You're lucky to be here."

"Was that bear a, a ..." Jenna asked.

"Zombie bear?" Corson said. His grin disappeared, his face pure military. "I would say I'm not authorized to say that, but I am. I hate throwing that damned word around, but yes, the bear had become infected with the HG-17 fungus, and if he'd bitten you ..."

"I'd be a zombie?" Terry asked.

The colonel smirked at Terry. "No, you idiot. You'd be in his fucking stomach. It was a goddamned bear. Besides, there ain't no such things as zombies." Then he pointed at Nikki, then Jenna, and Doug. "You three, however, might have become infected if you'd waited around for the fungus to kill the bear and send one of those stalks shooting up through its chest."

"What's going to happen to us, Colonel?" Doug asked.

"You'll be relocated," he said. "To ensure the survival of not only our country, but our species, the United States government has established a number of secure communities in areas of Nebraska, Montana, and Wyoming. There are thousands of survivors like yourself living in these safe, comfortable communities until we get this mess cleaned up."

"How long do you think that will be?" Nikki asked.

"Not sure, ma'am," Corson said. "There's a bus leaving tomorrow morning to take the survivors we've collected to this compound. You've been assigned to Community Number Six in western Nebraska."

"Do we have a choice in this?" Doug asked.

The colonel shook his head. "Not any, I'm afraid. Consider this your duty, not just as an American, but as a human. Our race depends on this."

They couldn't see their driver. The cab section of the olive drab bus was cut off from the passengers by a sheet of reflective, two-way glass, probably bulletproof. Ten other people sat in the bus that was designed to hold five times that many. A number of the people slept, some cried; in the back, someone coughed.

"How long we been on here?" Terry asked.

Doug shook his head. "I don't know, four hours, maybe more."

"I don't like this," Nikki said. "Something doesn't feel right."

"They're going to kill us," a gravelly voice said from behind them. A man, too young to sound so rough, leaned over the back of Nikki's seat.

"How do you know?" Nikki asked.

He scratched his stubbly chin and frowned. "You got that 'good for the human race' speech, right?"

She nodded.

"I got the feeling Mr. Military Man thinks I ain't good for the human race. So, that means you ain't good for the human race either." The man leaned back and threw an arm over his face and coughed.

"I think you're wrong," Doug said. "They wouldn't have bothered to fix my leg if they were just going to kill us. Doesn't make any sense."

The man finished coughing and snorted snot back into his sinuses. "Whatever. I just ain't gonna gloat when I'm right."

July 17: The Community, Western Nebraska

CHAPTER 40

The "Community" didn't look anything like any community Doug had ever seen, and he didn't like it. A soldier in a biohazard suit stepped from the cab of the bus, unlocked and slid open a gate in a fence that stretched as far as Doug could see. Barbed wire lined the top of the fence on metal poles, which pointed inward.

Terry leaned over his seat and whispered to Doug. "That's not for keeping things out," he said. "That's for keeping things in."

The bus pulled into the Community, tents and Quonset huts labelled by letter and number, A-4, B-5, dotted the ground. The bus door slid open.

"We have now reached your Community," an emotionless voice spoke over a loudspeaker. "Please disembark and report to the Community Hall for assignment to living quarters, and food distribution policies."

"I'm not going anywhere," Gravelyman said from behind Nikki. "You can kiss my flag-waving American ass."

Doug pushed himself to one foot, Jenna helped him with crutches and they left the bus in a line with the other ten people who accompanied them on the nearly five-hour bus ride. With so few people, Doug couldn't help but think the Army was about finished rounding up survivors. What's next? Jenna wrapped an arm around him as they walked along a path between the tents and temporary buildings, people, most covered in filth, stared at them with blank, empty eyes.

"Hey, I'm an American citizen, you can't do this to me, goddamn it," Gravelyman screamed behind them. A soldier in a biohazard suit dragged the kicking man off the bus and threw him into the dirt. "I'm an American citizen."

The bus drove back the way it came, and the gate slammed shut. They were prisoners.

"How many people you suppose are here?" Terry asked as they walked slowly toward something they didn't know. "Hundreds?"

"Thousands," Doug said.

Nikki shook her head. "I'd say a lot more than that. A lot more."

"All these people look sick." Jenna kept close to Doug. "The doctor told me I was fine."

"Me, too." Nikki walked next to Terry, the dirty, silent faces that stared at her from open tent flaps and doorways were unnerving.

"Yeah, he told me that. So why are we here?" Terry asked.

"I don't know, Terry," Doug said. "Let's find out."

Signs led to a large green tent, the sign "Community Hall" hung on a pole high overhead. They walked to the door flap, followed by the stragglers from the bus, the Gravelyman nowhere to be seen. A blank-faced fat man in a *Big Bang Theory* T-shirt and dirty cargo shorts wobbled past them as Terry held the flap open and they hurried in. Water spigots lined one wall, nearly empty baskets marked "clothes" lined another. A speaker and large red button sat in the center of the tent.

"Push it?" Jenna asked.

Doug and Terry nodded; she wrapped her hand in her shirttail and punched the button.

"Welcome to Community Six," a computerized voice said. "Water and toilet services are located at various points throughout the compound. Food drops are twice per week. Please take only what you need. Avoid anyone with a cough. Avoid anyone with white eyes. Avoid anyone who won't respond when you address them. Unclaimed living quarters can be found." The computer paused. "Between X through Z, twenty-two through fifty-nine. Frequent this Community Hall for updates. Enjoy your stay in the Community."

"Automated," Nikki said. "There's nobody in charge here but us, whoever we are now."

"What do we do?" a crying woman from the bus asked, bright crimson blood leaked from her nostrils.

Doug grabbed Jenna's shoulders and pulled her away from the woman. "Let's find our new home," he whispered.

As they made their way deeper into the Community, Doug swinging between two crutches, the butt of the metal poles digging into his armpits despite the padding, he knew Nikki was right. There weren't just thousands of people here. There were tens of thousands, probably a hundred thousand or more.

"That crazy bastard on the bus was right, wasn't he?" Terry said. "They're going to kill us."

Doug gritted his teeth, and stared straight ahead. "I'm starting to think so."

The tents that lined sections X through Z, twenty-two through fifty-nine, each held two sleeping bags, eating utensils, empty water bottles, two chairs and a chamber pot. Doug and Jenna took one tent, Terry and Nikki another, a bit too close. As the days passed, Doug almost grew comfortable listening to their rutting. A food drop hit the next morning. The roar of military planes pulled Doug from sleep, sunlight slipped through the tent flaps. Pain ached through his leg, the itching under the cast quickly becoming unbearable.

"Hey, Jenna," he whispered. "There's a plane. I think we're getting food."

She rolled over and opened her eyes; Doug couldn't believe someone could look so beautiful in the morning, in a tent, in what he knew now was an internment camp. She smiled. "Let's go." Dust encrusted people appeared from their tents along with Terry and Nikki, as the airplane flew overhead, a black spot appeared in the sky underneath, and the plane kept flying. A big, white parachute opened above the black spot and the crowd slowly moved to where it fell. The mob might have turned violent, but it seemed like no one was in a hurry. Most people around them, pulling open boxes, didn't seem to have the energy to fight over the food. Many of them didn't look like they could figure out how to open the boxes.

Jenna, Nikki, and Terry each carried a box of canned food back to their tents; Doug limped on crutches behind them.

"What are we going to do, Doug?" Terry asked as they sat on chairs outside Doug's tent eating cold SpaghettiOs out of cans with plastic spoons. "Just wait?"

"What can we do?" he said, holding up the spoon. "Dig under the fence? I don't think there's anything we can do but wait and see what they're going to do with us."

Terry almost dropped his breakfast as he broke into a coughing fit. Nikki put a soft hand on his shoulder.

"You okay, bud?" Doug asked, his voice as calm as he could muster, waiting for the blood to shoot from his face, waiting for Terry's death knell.

Terry wiped tears from his eyes and swallowed hard. "Yeah, I'm fine." He held up a half-empty water bottle. "Just went down the wrong hole."

Doug and Jenna woke the next morning to Nikki shaking them. "Jenna, Doug," she whispered hurriedly. "Wake up. Something's happening."

Doug winced as he pulled himself up on the sleeping bag, stiff pain shot through his rebuilt leg.

"What is it?" Jenna asked, following Nikki outside into the warm light of the dawn, the eastern horizon smeared with watercolor. Doug heaved himself into one of the folding metal chairs, "Scotts Bluff UMC" stenciled on the bottom, before he pushed himself onto the crutches and lumbered out through the flap. Nikki stood with Terry and Jenna; she was right, something was happening. A steady hum of far off airplanes played under a long series of distant pops, the ground vibrated slightly like driving over a stretch of rural road.

"What's going on, boss?" Terry stood in dusty jeans and T-shirt, holding Nikki gently in his arms.

Doug wished he knew.

"I told you." A man, his filth smeared clothes hung loosely on his shoulders, stood outside a tent about ten yards down the row. The Gravelyman. Had he been there the whole time? The Gravelyman coughed from deep down, and used the back of his sleeve to wipe blood from his nose and mouth. "I fucking told you. Our great government has caged us all, now they're going to kill us." He took a step toward them, but Doug pulled up his right crutch, and pointed it at the Gravelyman.

"Don't come closer," Doug shouted, leaning his weight on his other crutch. "We're not infected, and don't intend to be."

The Gravelyman laughed, a spasm of coughs threw him forward, hands on knees, blood shot from every point of his face, and pooled by his feet. "We're not infected. We're not infected," the Gravelyman mocked, then laughed through the coughs. "It doesn't matter. We're all going to die."

"Shit," Doug hissed. "He's got the fungus thing they tested us for. They must have known he had it."

"They knew," Nikki screamed through tears. "Those fuckers knew, and they sent us all out on that bus together anyway."

Jenna buried her face into Doug's chest. "If he has it, we all probably have it."

Doug held her tight. "We don't, at least not yet." He paused. "But most people in here have it. This place, these Communities aren't to protect us. They're to protect everybody from us."

"Corson said we were in here 'until we get this mess cleaned up,'" Nikki said softly, wiping tears from her face. "We're the mess. What do you think they're going to do with us?"

The Gravelyman laughed again. He was down on his knees now, hovering over a pool of blood. "I told you. They're going to kill us. Sweep us under the rug. They don't want to cure us; they're the cure *for* us. You hear that noise?" The Gravelyman coughed and collapsed into his own blood.

Terry grabbed Doug's shoulder. "That hum? Yeah. Those are jet engines."

Doug stood silent for a moment, resting on his crutches. Yes, jet engines, but just one. "Maybe …" Doug started, then stopped himself. The distant pops suddenly stopped and the roar of military jet came softly, then gradually grew louder. "He's right. They're going to kill us all."

Jenna was the first to react to the scream behind them. She pushed Doug to the ground as a man, a line of spittle running from his blood-encrusted face, ran over Doug and stumbled onto the dirt of the Community street. *My God,* she thought, *his eyes.* His eyes were crying blood.

"Son of a bitch," Terry yelled, and grabbed Doug, and pulled him to his good foot, draping Doug's arm over his shoulder, one crutch clutched in Doug's hand. "Run. Run." Nikki and Jenna snapped to action, running next to Terry and Doug, Jenna threw Doug's other arm over her shoulder. "Head toward Z-14."

They ran toward the Z-14 spray-painted in green stencil over the metal door of the nearest Quonset hut. Terry's hand reached the door first; he pulled it open and they limped inside. Terry hammered the door home as the Blood Crying Man slammed into it, his drooling face pressed against the door's window, red, angry eyes ablaze, his mouth moved like it had a mouthful of gum.

"Now," Terry said. "That's a zombie. I've trained for this shit since the first 'Resident Evil' game, and I don't even have a fucking shotgun."

Nikki locked the door and turned toward the interior of the arched, tin building. The jet sound grew closer, shaking the ground under her feet. She turned, and screamed. Mold-covered bodies on Army cots lined both sides of the hut, tall, solid stalks, their bulbs stretched like a ball with too much air, rose from their chests like this was a gardening nursery. The closest ones leaned toward them.

"Guys," she whispered. "You need to see this."

"Fuck," Doug spat as he turned and saw the fungal horror. "We have to get out of here. Now. *Now.*"

The bleeding man rammed the door again; blood from his face streaked the window next to Terry's face. "What about Night of the Living out there, boss?"

Doug pushed his metal crutch into Terry's hand and forced a smile. "It's your destiny, man."

Terry grabbed the crutch and shifted Doug's weight onto Jenna's shoulder. He smiled, but his was real. "Right, boss." He turned to Nikki, tears ran from her dark eyes. "I think I love you, Nikki," he said, and turned her chin upward with gentle fingers. She smiled as he pushed his lips onto hers.

"I think I love you, too. You big idiot," she said.

Terry nodded and pulled the door open, the fungus man fell into the Quonset hut, arms and legs flying around it like it was running the 100-meter dash. Maybe in its limited mind, it was. Terry raised the crutch like a club and brought it down on the fungus man's head. Blood shot into the air in a thin ribbon. Terry bashed its head again, and again, until the body stopped moving. Nikki grabbed Terry's head and kissed his rough cheek.

"Now I know I love you."

Terry winked at her. "Me, too."

The ground shook like an earthquake as they spilled from the Quonset hut, Terry and Jenna held Doug between them as well as they could. Black Batman planes appeared on the horizon. The B-2. The B-2 wasn't there to drop more food, Doug knew. The B-2 was built for one thing – dropping bombs. Corson said there were Communities across Nebraska, Montana, and Wyoming. They were Communities of the infected. Communities of the dead. And the government was destroying them all, today.

"This is a saturation bombing," Terry said.

"A what?" Jenna looked at him, her face drained of what little color it had, her mouth pinched tight.

"A saturation bombing." Terry said again. "Thousands of Mk 82 dumb bombs. No nukes, just lots and lots of explosions. The military can wipe this place clean in minutes and leave it ready to farm again. No radiation, no poison, no damage to anything."

"Except us," she whispered.

Terry nodded. "Yeah, except us, and they don't even have to see our faces."

"How'd you know that?" Doug asked.

Terry forced a grin. "If you play as many video games as me, you learn a few things about military procedure."

Explosions pounded closer, Terry and Nikki squeezed Doug close before the vibrations brought him to the ground. More black dots began to appear in the morning sky.

"What are we going to do, Doug?" Jenna asked.

Doug looked into her frightened, freckled face and smiled. "I don't know, baby," he said.

The first airplane flew overhead. Doug thought he'd heard somewhere they flew out of Whiteman Air Force Base in Missouri, that they could fly all over the world without having to land. He didn't know why that came into his head. Jenna, he should be thinking about Jenna. He reached for her hand, and found someone's. Doug's eyes followed the bomber as it traveled over the Community, black spots fell toward them at incredible speed and the B-2 banked to the left and kept moving. This time there was no parachute; the black spots grew larger as they fell to earth.

"Oh, shit," came from his lips.

An Mk 82 crashed out of sight, but the explosion moved the ground under their feet. Jenna wrapped her arm around Doug's waist to keep him from spilling onto the dirt. Bomb after bomb rattled the ground. The B-2 looped for another run, joined by a number of other bombers. Weak screams pierced the morning before explosion after explosion drowned them out. Dust and rocks filled the air, and rained down upon them. Wave after wave of Mk 82 dropped from overhead, consuming the Community like a brushfire. The falling bombs grew closer. A shattered board slammed into Gravelyman's bloody, mindless body, crushing his skull. Doug turned to run, to limp out of the way on his ruined foot, but didn't know where to go. Jenna looked at him and bit her bottom lip, the pensive flirtatiousness out of place in the destruction. More planes appeared in a formation on the horizon and grew closer, and more bombs lit Community Six on fire. An explosion launched the old metal Quonset hut into the air, the one full of fungus-riddled bodies ready to turn everyone into fungus monsters; it crashed into a nearby section of fence, and penned it to the ground.

"Fuck this," Terry tried to scream between the explosions that filled the air, and pulled Nikki toward the tear in the fence.

Jenna grabbed Doug's arm and tugged him into motion, her face suddenly flush with color. "Come on," she yelled, but Doug couldn't hear her. He didn't know if he'd ever hear anything again. He moved as fast as he could as he held onto Jenna, the ground shifting beneath him. They neared the fence, a place Doug had avoided during his short stay at the Community. He looked out over the vast plain that was Western Nebraska; another Community (Community 5?) lay about a half-mile north, the ground between them painted gray with Ophiocordon mold that grew over the hundreds of thousands of human bodies that lie in the dust. *To ensure the survival of not only our country, but our species, my ass.*

A bomb struck three rows over and knocked Doug to the ground. He spat dirt as he tried to stand, but arms suddenly wrapped around him. Terry dropped Doug across his shoulder and moved toward the break in the fence. Nikki hopped onto the crushed roof of the Quonset hut and held her hand out to Jenna as a bomb exploded at their feet, and everything went black.

SEVEREDPRESS

 facebook.com/severedpress
 twitter.com/severedpress

CHECK OUT OTHER GREAT ZOMBIE NOVELS

VACCINATION
by Phillip Tomasso

What if the H7N9 vaccination wasn't just a preventative measure against swine flu?

It seemed like the flu came out of nowhere and yet, in no time at all the government manufactured a vaccination. Were lab workers diligent, or could the virus itself have been man-made? Chase McKinney works as a dispatcher at 9-1-1. Taking emergency calls, it becomes immediately obvious that the entire city is infected with the walking dead. His first goal is to reach and save his two children.

Could the walls built by the U.S.A. to keep out illegal aliens, and the fact the Mexican government could not afford to vaccinate their citizens against the flu, make the southern border the only plausible destination for safety?

ZOMBIE, INC
by Chris Dougherty

"WELCOME! To Zombie, Inc. The United Five State Republic's leading manufacturer of zombie defense systems! In business since 2027, Zombie, Inc. puts YOU first. YOUR safety is our MAIN GOAL! Our many home defense options - from Ze Fence® to Ze Popper® to Ze Shed® - fit every need and every budget. Use Scan Code "TELL ME MORE!" for your FREE, in-home*, no obligation consultation! *Schedule your appointment with the confidence that you will NEVER HAVE TO LEAVE YOUR HOME! It isn't safe out there and we know it better than most! Our sales staff is FULLY TRAINED to handle any and all adversarial encounters with the living and the undead". Twenty-five years after the deadly plague, the United Five State Republic's most successful company, Zombie, Inc., is in trouble. Will a simple case of dwindling supply and lessening demand be the end of them or will Zombie, Inc. find a way, however unpalatable, to survive?

SEVEREDPRESS

f facebook.com/severedpress

y twitter.com/severedpress

CHECK OUT OTHER GREAT ZOMBIE NOVELS

900 MILES
by S. Johnathan Davis

John is a killer, but that wasn't his day job before the Apocalypse.

In a harrowing 900 mile race against time to get to his wife just as the dead begin to rise, John, a business man trapped in New York, soon learns that the zombies are the least of his worries, as he sees first-hand the horror of what man is capable of with no rules, no consequences and death at every turn.

Teaming up with an ex-army pilot named Kyle, they escape New York only to stumble across a man who says that he has the key to a rumored underground stronghold called Avalon..... Will they find safety? Will they make it to Johns wife before it's too late?

Get ready to follow John and Kyle in this fast paced thriller that mixes zombie horror with gladiator style arena action!

WHITE FLAG OF THE DEAD
by Joseph Talluto

Millions died when the Enillo Virus swept the earth. Millions more were lost when the victims of the plague refused to stay dead, instead rising to slaughter and feed on those left alive. For survivors like John Talon and his son Jake, they are faced with a choice: Do they submit to the dead, raising the white flag of surrender? Or do they find the will to fight, to try and hang on to the last shreds or humanity?

SEVERED**PRESS**

 facebook.com/severedpress
 twitter.com/severedpress

CHECK OUT OTHER GREAT ZOMBIE NOVELS

Z BURBIA
by Jake Bible

Whispering Pines is a classic, quiet, private American subdivision on the edge of Asheville, NC, set in the pristine Blue Ridge Mountains. Which is good since the zombie apocalypse has come to Western North Carolina and really put suburban living to the test!

Surrounded by a sea of the undead, the residents of Whispering Pines have adapted their bucolic life of block parties to scavenging parties, common area groundskeeping to immediate area warfare, neighborhood beautification to neighborhood fortification.

But, even in the best of times, suburban living has its ups and downs what with nosy neighbors, a strict Home Owners' Association, and a property management company that believes the words "strict interpretation" are holy words when applied to the HOA covenants. Now with the zombie apocalypse upon them even those innocuous, daily irritations quickly become dramatic struggles for personal identity, family security, and straight up survival.

ZOMBIE RULES
by David Achord

Zach Gunderson's life sucked and then the zombie apocalypse began.

Rick, an aging Vietnam veteran, alcoholic, and prepper, convinces Zach that the apocalypse is on the horizon. The two of them take refuge at a remote farm. As the zombie plague rages, they face a terrifying fight for survival.

They soon learn however that the walking dead are not the only monsters.

www.ingramcontent.com/pod-product-compliance
Lightning Source LLC
Chambersburg PA
CBHW031950170626
46807CB00006B/2430